Until blood burns...

DAUGHTER OF DESTINY

REBECCA PARCHA

A UNTISH SERIES NOVEL

 Formatted with Vellum

To anyone who has felt lost, this story is for you. May you find solace in the greyness, joy in the light, and strength to tell your own story.
You matter. Your story matters.

THE EMBASSY
NORTHERN OUPOST
BLUSH CASTLE
CABIN
WESTERN OUPOST
HUMAN REALM
HQ
WASSENVINE
BROOKSIDE
SINDERWELL
BEXLEY
EASTERN OUPOST
SOUTHERN OLPOST
OAKSHIRE
WATAEDGE
THE SEA
YATES
THE GLENN
THE FERN

GLOSSARY

Untish (You-n-tish): A group of people who are made up of three species: vampire, human, and Fae.

Seven Chairs: The leaders of the Untish Tribe at the Embassy, one representative of each house: Blush, Night, Iron, Beacon, Livish, Luna, and Frost.

Embassy: The city of the Untish Tribe on the planet Shappa.

Shappa: A planet divided by the Four Vamps, the Embassy, and a veil that splits the vampire realm from the human realm.

Mydant (My-dant): Home of the Fae and the origin of the Untishee, their kingdom.

Royal: A member belonging to the House of Blush, the Royal House—one of the seven Houses on Mydant—and the Blush Tribe, one of seven tribes on Shappa.

Darkling: A member belonging to the House of Shadows, one of the seven Houses on Mydant, and the Shadow Tribe, one of seven tribes on Shappa.

Ironhead: A member belonging to the House of Iron, one of the seven Houses on Mydant, and the Iron Tribe, one of seven tribes on Shappa.

Beacon: A member belonging to the House of Beacon, one of the seven Houses on Mydant, and the Beacon Tribe, one of seven tribes on Shappa.

Liver: A member belonging to the House of Livish, one of the seven Houses on Mydant, and the Livish Tribe, one of seven tribes on Shappa.

Luner: A member belonging to the House of Luna, one of the seven Houses on Mydant, and the Luna Tribe, one of seven tribes on Shappa.

Blight: A member belonging to the House of Frost, one of the seven Houses on Mydant, and the Frost Tribe, one of seven tribes on Shappa.

Member: A Untishee who has passed their assessment and is an active member, assigned to a tribe at the Embassy or House in Mydant.

Ghoul: Milky-white scaled beast crafted of dark magic that wields red flames.

Tarragon (Tare-a-gone): Mini dragons, warped by dark and raw magic, to create a new race like that of gargoyles.

Anax (An-ax): The highest-ranking leader in the military outside of the president and the council.

Dux (doox): The equivalent of a colonel in the military; directly underneath the Anax rank.

Du-Arche (Doo-Are-key): A step down from dux, but a step above arche.

Arche (Are-key): The equivalent of a private in the miliary.

Dokimos (doe-ki-moes): A trainee in the military.

High Lordship: The enforcer of the council's decisions and the Glenn's laws.

Vamp: A vampire country ruled by its own government.

The Glenn: One of the four Vamps.

The Fern: One of the four Vamps.

Wataedge: One of the four Vamps.

Yates: One of the four Vamps.

Veil: The wall between realms.

Seething (Seethe-ing): A creature crafted of dark magic.

CHAPTER 1
TATE

The air was cool, crisp even. We'd been traveling for blood knew how long with Aether clutching me tenderly in his talons. He was silent—had been since we left. Not much to say anyway, I supposed. The ground below me moved, flowing in wisps of white that slowly drifted down to coat the ground—snow. The air felt blissful given my extreme temperature shifts. Currently, I was still very hot...but cooler after having transferred my energy to Aether. Sweat pooled under my arms and threatened to cool in the night air. Perhaps it would freeze without Aether's body's proximity to mine.

Dragons were warm beasts.

Vala and Jared flew beside us. Vala, a much smaller white dragon, had Jared carefully held in her clutches. Somehow, the positioning simultaneously surprised me and was yet expected. Vala was clearly the alpha. But why wasn't Jared flying?

Aether banked, his talons tightening ever so slightly, before circling down toward a cliff with a cave carved into the mountainside. He landed and a plume of snow filled the air...so similar to the scene we'd just left.

Ash. Blood. Smoke.

The entire base had exploded, leaving charred ground marred by violence and death. Those things, those seethings, were the embodiment of evil and I didn't regret my actions. I didn't regret setting the charges, didn't regret slaughtering them. And yet...I'd fled. I'd left Shae, the only family I have left, when I allowed Aether to scoop me up and flee. I—

No, I shook my head. *Too* soon. I would think about all that had happened, about the ones I'd *abandoned*, later. Much later. Once this splitting headache left me.

Hold on.

It was the first thing I'd heard from Aether since we'd left. A command. Perhaps he was reverting back to old ways, returning to his 'Mardi'-like state. Blinding darkness enveloped me, bright somehow, and full of energy as the air sizzled.

He was shifting.

A moment later, I was clutched in the capable arms of Aether's bare body, his feet rested on wet stone—the snow had melted, as if shrinking back from his mere presence. He looked down at me with dark eyes that were surrounded by blood and ash. In fact, his entire body testified to the recent battle we'd all been a part of—I no doubt looked worse.

"We need to get her cleaned up," Aether said over his shoulder as a bright flash of white occurred—Vala shifted.

Her dark, nude form looked glorious against the sparkling snow. She pulled at the air and her breasts and nudity became covered in a hazy light—a blurry silhouette.

"Aether, don't we need to um, I don't know, get her back to the Changing grounds asap?" Vala challenged. She looked exhausted and worn, but not at all uncomfortable with his displayed nudity. Her eyes never left his face, not even to sneak a peek as I'd been tempted to do, perhaps would have, if exhaustion hadn't wrecked me so thoroughly.

I nestled my head further into Aether's chest, savoring its heat and the steady thump of his heart. Allowing myself to absorb the comfort of his bare skin touching the parts of my exposed flesh.

"We will. But first, we need to do a little housekeeping."

"Aether, that's not how—"

"I will handle this, Vala. Just take care of Jared." He nodded to the ruddy male who was on his knees in the snow. Dried blood was on his shirt and pants. Maroon icicles clung to his form.

Without waiting for a response, Aether turned—with me under his arm—and walked into the cave. His bare feet melted the snow with every step he took, as the dried blood coating his body began to melt or crack, and then disappeared into the air, leaving his skin unmarred. The cavern was large, but not large enough to fit Aether in his dragon form. The deeper we went, the darker it got. Until at last, a firelight from above formed and highlighted a large door just up ahead. It was made of iron and had large, golden handles—a foot wide each— gracing each of the double doors. He didn't hesitate as he pulled them open.

The room inside lit up instantly, small lights like that of stars filled the stone ceiling. The entire space was carved of manicured stone. It was...elegant, almost. Lush rugs graced the floor and overstuffed cushions were sprawled throughout the room. Bookshelves lined one side of the room with books, albeit dusty, covering every shelf.

Aether removed his hands from my shoulders and walked further into the now glowing room. His glorious glutes were on full display as sweat dripped over his exposed skin—his proud expanse of muscles— and danced with his movement.

"Mage lights," he explained, pointing to the ceiling.

I had, yet again, no idea what he was talking about, but instead of saying so, I simply nodded. I was done being the ignorant fool, at least out loud.

I shivered as the sweat from my body turned to a sudden rush of *cold*. I was as out of control of my temperature as I was my mind, apparently. Sniffling, I wrapped my arms around myself.

Aether flicked his wrist and a once empty hearth roared to life with fire, black flames that were somehow bright—instantly warming the space to a comfortable temperature.

"There's a bath in the back." He inclined his head.

I stood there staring numbly at the dark flames that licked at the logs but never incinerated them. It made no *logical* sense. But then again, so much of my life was now defined by what I once believed to be impossibilities.

I looked down to my legs. Small patches of my leathers remained, connected like a spider-web—the rest had burnt off. My top was in no better condition. It was practically an elaborate pattern of patches connected to pasties. A night ago, I would have laughed at this. Now? I felt nothing.

I began walking in the direction he had indicated. The room in the back was small, and through it, I could see the entrance to the bathroom—or at least, I assumed it was given the tub in the center.

Compared to the rest of the home, this room was rather empty. A tub, a stand, buckets, and a pot—one I didn't want to think about—made up the bare furnishings. I shook my head; the tub was vacant.

"I'll be right back," Aether spoke as he shouldered large buckets. I was vaguely aware of the pants he now wore but couldn't bring myself to care that I could no longer ogle him. He left without another word.

I stared at the empty copper tub. The symbols cut into it were rough to the touch. So much had changed. I had changed. Images of Shae held by the giant seething flashed through my mind. *Horror.* Such undiluted horror still raced through my veins as I recalled the way she sounded when she hit the ground, the unnatural angle of her leg. And I'd left her. Abandoned. Fled. Like a fucking coward.

I would make it right; I'd find a way.

Aether returned several times with basins full of snow. Each time, he'd dump them in the tub and then extend his dark flames to melt and heat it until, at last, it was full.

"I'll just be outside."

I turned, but he was already gone, closing the door behind him. A bar of soap and a towel graced the edge of the tub. I could do this. I had to. I pulled at the material sticking to my skin and pried it off. Dried blood flaked to the ground as the sound of leather being peeled from flesh filled the space. Slowly, so slowly, I picked each piece off and unstrapped my ruined boots before stepping into the gloriously hot water. Steam rose from the tub, and I allowed it to purify my body. Willed it to clean my soul, to spare me from the memories assaulting me, from the smell of ash and the sound of screams that still claimed my senses, even now.

A knock sounded at the door. "You okay?"

"Fine," I spoke, not caring if he knew it was a lie. I grabbed the bar of soap and began to scrub at my skin, washing away the past as the once-clear water turned blood-red.

CHAPTER 2

AETHER

She looked frail, wounded, and broken. I hated it. Hated that I was in part to blame. Hated that I couldn't have spared her from making those choices, from the feeling of abandonment and shame. I could sense her turmoil, hear the guilt coursing through her very soul.

At least I could offer her some comfort. I hadn't missed the little sigh that escaped her lips when she'd lowered herself into the tub. The small moans slipping from her would be my undoing—I'd had to remove myself from the adjoining room and now stood in the study, idly staring at the flames, and pointedly ignoring the daggers in Vala's eyes. She could be pissed all she wanted. I'd be damned if I delivered Tate in her current form. Not to mention, we needed to *handle* a few things before seeing Arithi and the other chairs.

She would be safe; I would not fail her—this I swore to myself. A black tidal wave of protection rose within, prepared to devour any threat to Tate.

"Aether, we need to talk," Vala said as she stood and squared off with me. Jared laid on the couch, unconscious, but cleaned after the sponge bath Vala had given him. His wounds would heal—he would survive.

I nodded. Condensed, dark energy gathered behind Vala, my power barely restrained. The need to guard, to claim, to defend Tate from all was nearly suffocating. But she'd never forgive me if I eliminated one of her only friends—someone she's come to view as a comrade.

The dark flames coiled in on themselves, the tension lessening, but nonetheless threatening.

I cleared my throat. "Do you know why I selected you and Jared for this mission?"

She just stared at me.

"I picked you because of your spirit. It's untamed and untainted. I asked for Jared to come because you two have been matched, even though you're not yet bonded. Do you know why they send bonded pairs into battle?"

"Bonded?" she spoke slowly.

"Yes," I responded. She remained silent and simply nodded. "Not only does sharing a bond mean sharing magic, thus making you stronger, but you share a certain emotional and mental connection that gives you an edge, as well as loyalty."

"Okay." She threw her hand on her hip. "What does that have to do with Tate?"

I sucked on my fang before exhaling. "Did you know I was once bonded?"

Her eyes were weary even as she nodded in confirmation. Odd for her to be the silent one.

"Her name was Cher. She was a magnificent female and far greater than me in many ways. She had combat experience and skills. Skills I'd only hoped to one day possess. She died because of those skills…gave her life for Mydant," the words barely rolled off my tongue. I hated to talk about this, but what I was about to ask of Vala would be treason… it would be a betrayal of her country. I needed her to understand *why* I was asking it and why, if it came to it, I would act against her if she could not *bend* accordingly.

"She died in battle?" Vala began, finding her tongue. "I'm so sorry, Aether. I mean I'd heard rumors, but no one would confirm them, and —" she splayed her hands wide, "—you're usually not the talkative one, so I'd never ask, and—" Her eyes snapped to mine. "Wait. What about Tate?"

And here we were. "I can't explain it, Vala, but Tate is my...equal. She fills so many missing pieces and my magic recognizes hers on an intrinsic level."

Silence reigned.

"What you're saying is incredibly rare, Aether."

"I know. I never thought I'd have another match, let alone one like this." I looked at her, allowing my emotions to surface. Willing the *force* I actively restrained to diminish further.

She gritted her teeth as she glanced back to where Tate was bathing. "What would you have me do?"

"Protect my bonded." The words felt foreign on my tongue. I knew them, my soul's magic acknowledged their truth, but until I'd spoken them aloud, I could ignore it. No more.

"How?" she challenged, magic gathering at her fingertips. Mine responded in kind, circling her for the first time—she took a step back as she saw the wall of raw power building.

"Conceal our bond. Train Tate, take her on as your pupil, ensure her safety," I asked the impossible. Voiced treason.

"Why should I?" She lifted her chin, the shimmer at her fingers increasing. My magic too swelled, begging to be unleashed, but I pushed it back. Vala would first be given a chance to help.

"Because I'd do it for you and Jared," I whispered.

She swallowed. Her eyes locked on mine—she was searching. Silently evaluating, as most Luners would. I could sense her magic prying at my mind, asking to *see*.

I allowed her a glimpse. A show of the bond I felt with Tate, a peek at the magic coursing through me that was somehow linked to Tate.

Vala gasped but didn't relent as her magic pried.

She wanted more, to dissect me further, but I shut her out. Instead,

I showed her what I'd done to my enemies...of what I would do to *anyone* who threatened Tate. My power thrust her out of my mind and circled her in a wave of dark energy.

I could hear the blood coursing through her, the sound of her pulse increasing as she recognized me as a threat. She swiped at her nose and dropped her gaze to Jared, who was currently snoring on the couch.

"What you ask is treason," she stated, the sparking at her fingers vanishing. "If I help you, I'd be turning on my fellow Luna Tribal members, along with all of Mydant. Do you realize what you're asking? I mean..." She swallowed. "It's no small thing. Like, this is a *huge* ask. And...I'm not even sure I could help if I wanted...and I don't know what I'll be able to do besides conceal and even then, I'm not the best and—"

Jared grunted as he rolled over, ripping her attention from me. I held up a wall of power, swirling visibly around him, beginning to smoke and slowly constrict.

"Aether!" Vala snapped. But I continued to allow the energy to build, to shrink in closer around Jared.

"I need you to understand that *Tate* is my priority—the only person that matters. I will protect her, always, no matter the cost."

Vala's jaw ticked as she nodded. "Stop. I understand. I'll...I'll help you."

The beast within wanted to eliminate any potential threat. I closed my eyes. I didn't need to see to know black flames now swirled around Jared. "If you betray me—betray Tate—I'll seek retribution and even then, Tate and I will be fine. We will win. We will survive. I can't say the same for you and yours."

Fear, pure and undiluted, shown in her eyes. "I understand. I said I'd help, and I will, so don't you dare hurt him."

I released the power in an outward blast. The books shook and fell from the shelves, the tables toppled over, and Vala lost her footing tumbling to the ground as Jared rolled from the couch and landed on the rug with a dull *thump*.

"I'll need some reassurance you won't betray me."

She looked up incredulously at me. "You mean beyond threatening those I love?"

"Yes." I hated myself even as I responded, but it didn't matter. There was no level too low, no pit too dark, that I wouldn't succumb to if it meant keeping *her* safe. Whole. Protected. It was my holy duty, even if *she* hasn't acknowledged or accepted that truth.

"Okay..." Her jaw clenched. "A blood oath?"

I nodded.

"As you wish, jackass..." I didn't miss the way her voice whispered the last word. Her spunk and clear defiance were part of why I trusted her with this. She stood and swiped at the dust now covering her pants before pulling out a blade.

In one motion, she slit her hand before extending the knife to me. I too slit my palm, then clasped her hand in mine.

"I swear to you, Aether, that I will not betray, harm, or deceive you. I swear the same for Tate. I will do everything in my power to protect your bonded."

"I accept your oath. Should you break it, may you never know happiness, may your magic turn sour in your veins, and may nature take from you what you will have taken from me."

We released our hands as my black and gold aura sealed with her cloudy, white one. Done. A promise sealed in magic—she could not betray me without costing herself something very, very dear.

"Now what?" she asked, brow raised.

I closed my eyes and the charge gathering, concealed in the corners of the room, dissipated.

No need for violence...at least not where *Vala* was concerned. I looked at the unconscious male lying in an unnatural heap on the floor. He was Vala's match, her bonded-to-be, and thus, their magic was linked. If Vala lost hers, his magic would be impacted—and given that his power stores were minimal compared to most Untishee, he'd likely lose his magic altogether—but would that be enough to ensure his cooperation? I clenched my jaw, I doubted he'd even have enough magic to seal a blood oath.

"What of Jared?" I asked. Perhaps killing him here would be best, it certainly was the safest option, and yet mahogany eyes flared to life in my mind—would Tate forgive me if I struck him dead here?

"He won't like it," she said nodding to Jared.

"Can you convince him?"

"What do you think?" She smirked, her old swagger returning.

"If you can't, you know I'll have to—"

"I said I'd convince him. I'll tell him of my oath. He'd die before allowing my magic to be stripped from me, not to mention his."

I nodded. It was, as I hoped, a true bonded connection between them, even if it has yet to be officialized by the chairs.

"But Aether, her hair..."

"I know. I've got a plan."

CHAPTER 3
TATE

The bathwater had cooled. I sat in the now red-black water, my knees pulled close to my chest. The pink slashes across my skin had indeed scarred. Marks reminding me of the father figure I'd lost...the very one I'd failed. Fletch.

A knock sounded at the door. I said nothing. I barely breathed.

A gentle sensation reached out, caressing my back. Aether. I resisted it at first, blocked it with my own, but with its gentle prodding came the reminder that I wasn't alone—even if I deserved to be. I met its caress with one of my own and the door clicked open.

"Okay if I come in?"

I was in my most vulnerable form. Months ago, hell weeks ago, I would have demanded he leave. But now? Now I couldn't care less. My life, my being, was not what I'd once thought.

"Fine," the words narrowly left my chapped lips.

"How are you feeling?" he asked, his tone tentative and gentle. I hated it. Loathed that he treated me like I was broken, even if I was.

"Never better," I snarled.

"Ah," he said, and I found his simple response irritating.

"What do you want, Aether?" I sighed, resting my head atop my knees—not caring that my bare back was to him, that he could see the marks across my body representing *who* I was, the monster within.

You're not a monster.

There it was again. His voice in my head, in my heart, somehow speaking to me.

Stop doing that, I shot back.

Why?

I grunted. If he wanted to speak that way, fine. I wouldn't engage. I didn't have to like or accept *what* I was.

His footsteps were heavy as he approached. "May I?"

The question was jarring—almost as unnerving as the sound of him kneeling beside the tub. His question hung in the air.

"Your back still has...unwashed bits."

Neither of us spoke for a moment as we both remained completely still.

"Fine," I spoke through tight lips.

He wasted no time as he reached for the bar of soap, along with a rag, and then dipped it into the tub. I squeezed my legs tighter, prepared for the sting of soap on my back's wounds. He pressed the cloth gently to my back, and the pain was instant. I had cut myself more than I'd realized, as evidenced by the fresh blood now swirling in the water.

"Sorry," he whispered. The water began to glow with a black haze and got gloriously hot again. The heating stopped, but the dark fog remained, offering me privacy. A kind act, one that only annoyed me further.

He continued to wash, in slow circles, and the stinging faded to nothing as the hot water massaged my aching muscles—that or Aether was manipulating the force around me, again.

I closed my eyes.

A dragon. He was Untishee. He was working with Fletch. Fletch was a member of the Untish Tribe. So many random facts that seemed impossible.

"Could Fletch shift?" The question had been nagging at me.

"No," Aether responded, his breath hot on my neck. "Not all Untishee can shift."

Interesting. I had nothing more to say. Nothing more to give or ask. I simply remained silent, even as he stopped washing my back and cleared his throat.

"We, uh, need to talk. There are certain delicate things that need to be discussed." He started moving around to face me for the first time—the water still clouded and dark, hiding my nakedness.

"Not interested." I sounded pathetic. I knew that, but I was drained physically and emotionally.

I'd left Shae behind. Fletch was dead. I was a monster.

"You're not a monster, Tate. You are a glorious creature. One that many wish they could be. It may not seem like it now, but you have a gift. A power—"

"I don't fucking care. I didn't ask for this. Any of it!" I threw my hands out, splashing some of the dirty water on Aether and the surrounding floor.

He slipped into silence. I was such a child. What is wrong with me?

"We can talk later. This is a lot..." he pulled out a bowl I hadn't previously seen. "But one thing that can't wait is changing your hair."

"My hair?" Was he serious?

"Yes. The pink ends have to go. The color indicates something and with it you won't be safe—not from Arithi or the powerful chairs. You'll be viewed as a threat by them *and* our enemies."

I didn't understand. He wanted to hide me from Arithi?

"Why?" The question was simple, but the look on Aether's face told me the answer would not be.

"There are many reasons, but I don't think you're ready to address them...yet. For now, let's just say your bloodline has pink hair, and with it comes inherent power and certain rights. Rights that threaten any existing leadership."

"So, I would be a threat to your precious Arithi?" I bit out. "Why don't you just end me now?"

The look in his eyes deepened.

Concern. Understanding. Care.

No. I did not want to *feel* his emotions; I had no interest in them. I threw up a wall and his eyebrows lifted. Evidently, I was capable of more than I knew.

Much more. But you'll need practice.

He spoke even through my walls. Bastard. I locked eyes with his black ones. The chocolate flecked with gold. So unlike any I'd ever seen, so full of promise and immensely deep with an emotion I didn't want to recognize.

He released a sigh, even as his eyes remained focused on mine. "I promise this will make sense. You will be given choices. But for now, I need you to trust me. We have to dye your hair. Just the tips."

He lifted a bowl holding a charcoal looking color in a squeeze bottle.

"You want to make me a brunette?" I couldn't believe it. I liked my blonde, even if the last third of it was now rosy-pink.

"No, I wouldn't wish to change a thing about you. But...the tips have to go...at least, for now."

I stared at the bowl he extended to me. I didn't want to do it and frankly, I didn't have the energy. He nodded in understanding as I turned around and offered him the back of my head. The water in the tub began to bubble and swirl, gloriously massaging, as he reached for the first section of hair and squeezed the color on. Methodically, he moved from one section to the next until no pink remained. He rinsed it out and then stood.

"I'll leave you to get dressed." He nodded to a pile of clothes on a chair beside a cup of blood. "Dress, eat, rest. You'll feel better soon. When you're ready, we'll leave."

I was once again alone in the room. The black mist concealing me faded and revealed muddy-like water: dirty, foul, impure. I was disgusted with myself. I stood, bracing my hands on each side of the basin, before stepping out onto a furry rug and wrapping myself in a thin towel. The effort of it nearly sent me falling to my ass. I was so weak. I swayed a bit but made it to the large glass of blood, practically a pitcher. I lifted it to my lips and sniffed—rich, powerful hints of cherry and ash—not human. I studied the blood, noting how the gold ribboned through the red, how the golden swirls formed the same disturbing symbol I'd seen only days ago: a dragon. I knew whose blood it was, but I refused to acknowledge it. Instead, I sipped it and savored the way my nerves fired in recognition. I embraced the tingling in my toes, my fingers, my lips. My strength was returning, but even still, sleep tugged at me.

I downed the rest of the liquid and then grabbed the clothing. A pair of black linen pants and a matching tunic sat there—undergarments that appeared to be purely practical were folded next to it. *Not what I would've expected.*

I put the crude granny panties on followed by the sports bra before I slipped into the pants—they fit more like leggings—and then pulled the tunic on. It flowed loosely from my shoulders until it was cinched with a golden clasp at my waist before dropping down to my knees. The slits on each leg allowed for practical movement, even as golden embroidery etched the hem, suggesting luxury. It was simple but elegant. Most of all, it was comfortable.

Padding on uneven legs from the bathroom to the bedroom, I noted my silhouette briefly in the mirror—I had brown hair. More than that, the guara tattoo, a brand on my shoulder, screamed at me. A reminder of those I'd failed.

I threw myself onto the furry comforter that looked like it had once belonged to a bear, or perhaps a buffalo. Either way, I didn't care. At this moment, its cozy embrace cradled my body as my aching limbs finally accepted rest.

The weight from yesterday's events were crushing me and becoming unmanageable. I needed a break—just a small one.

I AWOKE WITH A START. I wasn't alone, I could sense *him.*

Sorry, just checking on you.

Stop talking to me like this, it's weird.

Aether grunted as he pushed off the wall nearby. "We still need to talk."

No, I wasn't ready. None of this was something I'd ever imagined for myself. Was I throwing myself a pity party? Absolutely. But at the moment, I couldn't bring myself to care.

"No," I said simply, rolling over and tucking the fur comforter around my body. The air tightened slightly, and I swore it was laughing at me.

"I wish that were an option..." He ran his hand through his loose hair as he spoke. "But...we must do something before we leave. Something, that you may not like."

I sat upright at that and gave him a pointed look.

"Come with me," he spoke as he walked to the door. He didn't wait to see if I'd follow, just strode through and allowed the force around me to spur me on—encourage me forward.

Prick.

If you'd like.

I threw my mental wall back up—no matter that he could slash through it with no apparent effort. The mere presence of it there was enough to send a message. I wished to be left alone.

Still...

I sauntered out of the room, hobbling on uneven feet and hating that, yet again, I appeared weak. I was weak. And now they knew.

"Girllll...you look like a *spicy* brunette," Vala spoke, wagging her brows.

I snorted in response. Vala stood next to Aether near the hearth, a hearth that was lit with black flames. Yet another reminder of how little I knew. I swallowed back the bitter bile.

"So, what is this thing that, *allegedly*, I must do?" I asked.

"Vala will cloak our...connection." At Aether's last word, Vala raised her brows but remained uncharacteristically quiet.

"OK..." I let the question hang.

"It's a simple ceremony, but it will block any detection from the chairs. It will add a certain level of protection," Aether answered.

I should push further. Ask why it needed cloaking, what connection he spoke of...and yet, I knew. Or at least had an idea and I wasn't ready to pull back the curtain fully.

"Vala." Aether gestured for her to begin.

She nodded and stepped forward. "Join hands, please," she spoke softly.

I stepped forward, limping as I did, and extended my hands. I swallowed back the uncertainty even as I felt it crossing my face. Aether matched my steps, closing the distance much quicker. He enveloped my hands in his large rough ones, at least twice as big. His hands had known work. I focused on the heat I felt, the friction.

Vala reached out and tied a string around our hands, forming an infinity symbol before looping around it several more times, closing it off. She then closed her eyes and spoke in a language I didn't recognize. The string lit to a white color and began to buzz before vanishing in midair, the magic settling down, blanketing our hands, and strengthening the connection I'd already felt with Aether.

"Done," Vala said.

"Thank you. I expect you to uphold your oath," Aether said, challenge and threats lacing every syllable. What the hell?

Glancing between them, I sensed a new tension but noted that neither seemed likely to discuss it. Fine, I wasn't sure I wanted to get in the middle of *that* anyway.

"What do those words mean?" I asked, more from habit than actually wanting to know. Knowing meant acknowledging something I wasn't ready for.

"It means: conceal thy bond to the extent to which it is strong. That none may see or know until the connection is assured," Vala answered.

Her answer only gave me more questions, but instead of voicing them I asked, "When do we leave?"

CHAPTER 4
CHANCE

The machine was sounding in reassuring measures. Her blue hair was lifeless against the pillow. The blood and dirt had been washed away, and now her hair wasn't matted against her head. More than that, she was alive.

Beep. Beep. Beep.

Shae lay there, unconscious. Her leg was wrapped in a cast. Even with the healing tonics they'd administered, she'd be in pain when she awoke. *If* she awoke. She'd passed out just as we'd made it to the forest. That was two days ago. She hadn't stirred since. A coma, that's what the medics called it. I wondered if it was in part to her exposure to the dark magic...the explosions, that beast, and Tate...

Tate.

I fisted my hands as anger fueled my belly. She betrayed the Glenn. Somehow, worse than that, she betrayed Shae...she betrayed me. She possessed undocumented magic, unnatural from what I could see. She was working with those monsters, the enemy. The dragon—

His roar echoed in my ears. Disbelief still radiated through me. How could that have been real?

A knock at the door drew my attention and a guard entered. "Dux Dale, the president is requesting an audience with you, now."

I stood and ran my hands over my tired, sweaty face. I had asked to see him hours ago but, naturally, he was too busy. I followed the guard through the door and down a series of hallways to a meeting room—the command center at the heart of the base.

There he sat. Cool, calm, collected. Staring at a disk's display, not a care in the world.

"You wanted to see me," I spoke, mentally reminding myself of my rank. He was my father, but more importantly, he was my president—my leader.

"Yes, sit," the command icily flowed from his lips.

I sat, biting back the retort begging to be freed.

"I imagine you have some...questions," he said, sitting across from me in his pristine suit, a pink rose pinned to his lapel. "First, let me ask. What did you see?" He leaned forward, hands bridged together, eyes focused on me, lit with curiosity.

"I saw the enemy."

"No, Dux Dale. What did you *see*?" he pressed.

I thought back to the monsters, those beasts swarming the yard on all fours. The ones walking upright, the ones who attacked me. I saw that giant seething who held Shae in its claws—the one who called Tate its *maker*—and then threw Shae, breaking her.

"Evil," I responded. "I saw evil."

"Son," he tsked. "What you saw was *power*. Pure undiluted power." He pulled out another disk and tossed it across the table. "You've been asking the *wrong* questions. You've made stupid assumptions—your research didn't yield anything useful and that was a...disappointment. However," he drawled, "you did find the base. And your performance was admirable. For that, I'll give you some acknowledgment. You are, after all, my son." There was that word again. Son. Something he hadn't called me in years, not since I first made Dux.

"I don't understand. Those *things* were made with dark magic. I was right, all along. I was right." Anger rose in my chest, red beginning to fill my vision. I began shaking and my fingers sparked with a red light before zapping the disk in my hand, completely frying it.

"Marvelous," my father spoke, a serpent smile pulling at his lips. "I've always known you had more power than you realized."

I stared at my hands numbly. How had I done that? "I've been infected."

"No son, you've been awoken."

My eyes snapped to my father.

"Don't look so surprised, Chance." His use of my first name threw me. "You have power in your veins, it just took exposure to awaken it. With your discipline, you could be the best controller yet. You could rule, for me of course, but you could *create*. You could be more powerful than—"

"What are you talking about?" I demanded.

He sighed, releasing a heavy breath in annoyance. "Play the tape, arche."

The projection lit up in front of me. I saw humans, like the comatose ones we'd encountered at Brookside, in neat lines on gurneys, IVs connected to each of them. A scientist, no, not just a scientist, but Doctor Worshah's predecessor, Dr. Mews—who died about a year prior—came into view. "We are beginning initiation trials, part four," he began, clearing his whiny voice. "Thus far, no signs of acceptance."

I watched as he walked to a mutated human and commanded it to stand. It didn't move. "As you can see," he started, "we've received zero response to the blood administered. We believe the energy stores in the donor blood are not proper enough, not rich enough, and that these humans lack the marker we need. We will dispose of and move on to the next batch."

The video cut before Dr. Mews filled the screen once again, eyes darker this time—sickly, even. "Trials, part ten. We've isolated the necessary human gene in the last pool, and we've moved the comatose humans to a transition phase. However, only some are responsive, and none are evolved enough to be a threat. We need more power siphoned." He sighed before stepping back and allowing the camera to scan over the humans, the creatures. They were moving, limping, and crawling with black drool falling from their mouths. Their skin was grey, almost black, and in some cases, scales sprouted.

A command was given to them, but they didn't respond. They were commanded to stand, two attempted, and then fell, seizing as they did. "Failure," the scientist spoke, pulling at his thinning hair.

The video skipped again to trial twenty. Not much change. These creatures were moving more fluidly on all fours, but still unresponsive to commands.

Finally, the clip glitched and then Dr. Mews appeared again, only this time his skin was purple with black veins sprouting from his eyes. Trial fifty-eight. Dated a little over a year ago. "We've done it. We've seen movement. The key is a *controller*." There was that word again: controller. "Watch and learn," he said as he stepped toward the beasts in a cage. About ten of them stalked on all fours. My stomach dropped. They looked just as I'd recalled—grey and black scales over sleek, muscled bodies that threatened violence. "Stand!" the scientist commanded. As one they stood. "March!" Again, they obeyed.

Remarkable. "No wings or powers, but immense progress." The scientist stepped into the cage. "Halt!" He held up a hand. The beasts stopped and stood still, until one began to move. Ever so slowly he stepped forward. "I said halt!" but the beast didn't listen, instead it smiled and then charged. Dr. Mews ran for the door, but he wasn't fast enough. The beast lunged at him and within moments, Dr. Mews lay in a bloody pool on the floor, dead.

"Enough," my father commanded. "There's much more, but you get the gist. We have been studying the creation of a creature so fierce that we can stand, uncontested. War is coming, son, and with these seethings, we can save lives."

I stared, numbly. Not a week ago, I'd thought that any studying of dark magic had been within the past year—based on the report Holland had shown me—but it appeared it went further back than that. Much further. And he knew. The son of a bitch knew. Not only that, but I now understood he was unequivocally responsible for the creation of those beasts...those things that killed our own. Those... seethings. They had a name, and *he* created them. Seethings.

"They killed our men! By the dozens!" I slammed my hands on the table, red bolts jolting from them, dancing across the monitors in streaks of lightning. I jumped back. What had I become?

"Those were unfortunate. Unintended. The controllers weren't strong enough. But someone who has power in their veins, the right markers, someone who can influence their will as their own, they *would* be strong enough. We have a few like that, but not enough. We need a leader; we need a dux with power." His voice trailed off as his eyes lit with delight at the red sparks still flying from my hands.

"No. I refuse to be a part of this." I turned to leave and tripped over a chair, bolts streaked from my hands and steadied me before I hit the ground.

"Truly remarkable," my father awed.

I couldn't breathe, couldn't be this...this *thing*. I ran from the room, red lightning trailing behind me.

CHAPTER 5
AETHER

Tate stood there, shaking. But she wasn't cold. No, I knew this type of shaking. She was still adjusting, and from what I sensed, she wasn't ready to mentally bear the burden of a bond—of comprehending *all* that it implied. I could wait; I would wait.

I was a patient male.

Vala had already moved outside, with Jared in her arms. She'd carry him, again, to the Embassy—the headquarters in this realm for the Untish Tribe.

"We should get going," I spoke slowly.

Tate nodded, not speaking. I sent a gentle caress out, savoring the way I could feel her body relax and respond to my influence even from here.

I fucking loved my gifts.

When I was young, I wanted the power of invisibility, but now? Now I loved being able to control through energy, force, and manipulation. I loved that she welcomed my energy's closeness, even if she held me at arm's length in every other way. Loved that I could manipulate energy to where it was a dark wave or appeared like that of black shadows.

I led her outside, giving her space to walk at her own pace. While she had slept, I'd repaired her ruined boots as best as I could with the measly supplies we had here. They weren't great but they were better. I knew she was self-conscious about her uneven footing. When I'd handed her the boots, her eyes widened but she said nothing. It didn't matter, I'd *felt* it. The awe, the thankfulness, the wonder. At least I'd done something right.

She didn't look half bad as a brunette. The ends of her hair, the last four to six inches, were dyed black. Her delicate warm blonde now was black tipped—like mine. She'd be placed in the House of Shadows, Shadow Tribe. Under my protection.

Outside the wind whipped at our faces, our hair, our bodies—ice in every gust. This place was nothing if not frost-covered, forgotten terrain. How anyone preferred this northern icy land was beyond me. Vala was already in her dragon form, Jared in her clutches, wrapped in a plaid blanket.

I turned to Tate to see her gazing at Vala with wonder. I suppose for someone who didn't grow up seeing dragons, the sight was mesmerizing. From here, Vala's beastly form was partially concealed by the snow and wind. She was, after all, a white dragon. She belonged to the Luner tribe and was a magic wielder who specializes in potions, wards, and protective shields. Another reason I'd initially chosen her to accompany me on the mission.

"Ready?" I asked. Tate eyed me, squinting at the brightness of the snow-covered stones. I didn't wait for a response, and instead, shifted. After decades of training, I could do it quickly. In a burst of black light, the air thickened, sparked, and at last I huffed. Transformed into my beastly state.

The pure power from this form never faded.

This way, I was closer to my instincts. The need to claim and protect what was *mine* was nearly all-consuming. Instead, I acted as civil as I could. I gently reached out for Tate—so tiny, so fragile, in her humanoid form—and extended my paw, willing her to climb in.

Trust me.

Her eyes lit with fire.

I can't speak verbally in this form, dear. Humor me, will you?

She didn't respond but began to climb into my extended talon-tipped paws. I gently closed my talons around her, and then willed the space to hold her secure—she would not be jostled.

I hoisted us into the air with a few massive pumps of my wings. For better or worse, we were headed to the Embassy.

CHAPTER 6
TATE

We had been flying for hours. The wind whipped at Aether's body, but it barely brushed past me. No doubt, Aether had taken action to shield me from the worst of it— even if I couldn't see more than the faintest shimmer, I could sense it surrounding me, encasing me, protecting me.

I shook my head. So much of this I didn't understand. I trusted Aether, and that confused me more than I'd like to admit. Strands of hair blew gently across my face—the black tips of it foreign to me. Why did I need to hide who I was? Especially if *I* didn't even know that answer, at least not fully.

Still, that was a rabbit hole I wasn't sure I was ready for—not yet. I didn't want to mess with *another* government's politics, and didn't want to consider the implications of what Aether had said about my natural color. But, given the situation, I had a feeling the time for avoidance would be cut short.

Vala flew next to us, the most marvelous-looking white dragon I'd ever seen—the only one I'd ever seen. I huffed. I was so ignorant it stung. Perhaps it was time to end my willful ignorance, to start with something easy.

"Why can't all Untishee shift?" I voiced the question, softer than intended. I doubt he heard—

Not all Untish blood contains the specific marker to shift. That's what makes us actual shifters so unique, so valuable.

I gritted my teeth, the sound of his voice in my head still shook me. Weird and unnatural—or at the very least, unusual.

It is. Not many can telepathically communicate. In dragon forms, most of us can extend certain feelings or general commands, but it's not easy—it requires a substantial amount of energy.

He was far more forthcoming with information than I expected. Would he finally be open with me?

Just ask.

It reminded me far too much of a game we'd played while hiking just days ago. Then he didn't answer everything. Then, it still felt like half-shielded truths. How could I know that he'd answer me honestly?

Test me.

I looked out at Vala. "Can she hear us?"

No. She's not strong enough to communicate this way. Plus, she's missing a certain...connection we share.

He left it hanging there, again. I could ask, but did I really want to know? My heart suspected the truth, but my mind wasn't ready to accept it. It wasn't possible. I laughed dryly. When would I stop thinking so many things couldn't be?

"Why is she white? Is that common?" There, another easy question.

I could feel the air surrounding me warming, gently swirling across my skin to keep my circulation flowing. It was, to my chagrin, delightful.

Yes and no. She's part of the Luna Tribe, a Luner. If they can shift, then they are all white dragons with gifts at wards and wielding magic—shields and potions, usually.

"So, there are different tribes?" The question left my lips before I could stop it—I was getting into dangerous territory.

Yes. Seven to be exact. I belong to the Shadow Tribe, I'm a Darkling. As are you, or so they will think, thanks to your new tips.

It dawned on me then. Vala's new pixie cut with the white tips, Aether's darker ends. They were symbols of their dragon forms. But what was Jared? His hair was one solid wall of auburn.

"Can Jared shift?"

No.

Ah. Perhaps that was in part why he hated me so much. I didn't understand much about myself, I've never shifted into a dragon. But now, after the Changing, I supposedly could...

"What is the Changing?"

The Changing is a time in which the Untish magical genes awaken and express themselves fully for the first time. The Embassy will help with this transition.

The place where, yet again, I couldn't be fully myself. "How?"

The Embassy is strategically located at the axis of the planet, near the strongest magical stores innate in the soil itself. When you're going through the Changing, you need large amounts of energy to fuel you and refill the expression of the newly matured genes. The mere presence there will refresh you continuously and you'll be able to subconsciously pull, or rather your magic will, and take what you need to complete the Changing.

So much of this was hard to conceive. Magical stores? "Magical dirt? That's why we're in a rush to arrive at a place where I may be in danger?"

He chuckled in my head, sending chills down my spine.

You have essentially completed the Changing, but I can still...sense your great need for more magic. More power. You've had blood, and the refreshing runes on the tub gave you what energy they stored, but you still require much more. You need to refuel and stockpile large quantities of energy to strengthen these newly emerged genes and allow them to become permanent.

I had nothing to say to that. Not as black hair tickled my arms, not as my mind felt numb and my soul flared at the truth of his words.

"The blood I had earlier," I cleared my throat, willing courage to find me. "It had gold in it. Why is that?"

My heart pounded for a moment, then two, then three…

Some bloodlines have golden-red blood, some are pure red, some are golden maroon, and still, some are red-black. It just depends on your blood-line and the way magic expresses itself. Many who are pure Fae or mostly Fae have golden maroon blood, like James, while others, such as myself, have it passed down through the bloodline.

A new ache filled my heart at the thought of my bloodline—at the loss of Irene and Fletch and the revelation from the secrets they'd held. I was Untish.

"What tribe do I actually belong to?" I stilled my nerves as my heart rate increased while I waited for the answer.

Silence.

"Hello? Oh, Darkling, wielder of shadow flames, I'm testing you… just like you requested."

I could sense turmoil filling the space around me, but still, silence reigned. The wind bellowed, and the dragons huffed—steam filling the frost-chilled air.

And still, he remained silent.

I could feel my insides roiling, rage—possibly undeserved—beginning to pour over at the male who was currently carrying me like a piece of luggage. Perhaps that's all I was to him, something to discard. A task. Not worth the trouble, not—

What you ask…you're not yet ready for. I am not even fully certain of the answer.

"What the hell does that mean?" I demanded.

As if the line fell dead, Aether's words stilled. The air tightened as he banked left, the breeze gently tossing my hair, and then he straightened.

It seemed he was done being forthcoming. Test me, my ass.

This was getting old.

I threw up my mental shield again, feeble as it was, and instead focused on the way my nerves were firing. I felt everything. The gentle breeze that tickled my skin, the moisture in the air increasing, the rough yet smooth feel of Aether's scales and talons. It was as if I could feel every molecule.

I reveled in my newfound awareness.

The landscape below slowly turned from ice to brown dirt, from dirt to lush and green. It was beautiful. Ahead, I could see a brief shimmer—almost like magic itself was pouring down from the sky.

Flowers covered the hills in various colors and the air held a certain sweetness to it. In the distance, I could hear waves crashing. I adjusted in Aether's grip and saw it then: the sea. Glorious and free. The salt richer, and more promising than I was used to. And the air held something else, something ancient that I couldn't place...it almost smelt like sulfur. Oddly sweet if it were.

The shimmering wall came closer, and Aether didn't hesitate as he flew right through it. Immediately, my skin began to glow, my insides began to sing as my internal pool brightened and then became wholly lit with fire.

Welcome home.

Home. This was where I was from?

Drink.

I ignored his command, even as my very being began to hum and feel satisfied for the first time in days. The ache coating my nerves and gut, along with something deeper, began to lessen, it began to fill. Without any effort, I could sense new energy pulsing through me.

Like I said, the refueling is innate. While you're here, you'll automatically have access to refuel at any time, at least during the Changing days when your genes are solidifying. After that, it will have to be intentional

I marveled at my heightened senses and noted how some of the sickness stabbing my gut eased along with the tension coiled in my shoulders. Perhaps this auto-fill thing wasn't so scary after all. The fragrance in the air increased tenfold and the colors were more vibrant than any I'd ever seen before. I could hear *everything* with heightened clarity. The beat of Aether's wings, the whooshing of his tail slicing through the air. The heavy huffs of both his and Vala's pants. The sway of the grass, the frothing of the sea.

Everything was heightened.

Everything was glorious.

Everything felt right.

The ground below became a moving tapestry, full of life as the neon flowers bloomed.

Home. I was home.

CHAPTER 7
TATE

After another thirty minutes, Aether landed near the sea on a flat expanse. The stones below us were dry, warmed by the sun. The internal satisfaction I'd initially felt had slowed and now my inner pool burned brightly with pink flames. Contentment coursed through me with my renewed vigor.

The air sparked, a black cloud surrounded us, and within moments, I stood in Aether's arms. Held close, enveloped by his body. His very *naked* body.

He smiled crookedly as his eyes deepened—eyes that were not black with gold flecks, but chocolate with golden whorls actively *moving* as he stared at me, into my very soul. I could feel *her* awakening, surveying this land, surveying *this* male—the magic within sparking to life.

Aether tightened his hands on my hips, steadying me. In this place, I felt new. The waves crashed against the sea with gusto, and I could have sworn the residual mist was pink. *His* salty ash scent was all I could smell—even smothering the floral scent that blanketed the air.

Aether caressed my chin with his hand.

Marvelous.

"Vala, cloak her," he commanded, stepping behind me, just out of view.

I flinched. Not what I was expecting.

Vala turned, her nude body barely covered with a shawl, and nodded before lifting her hands and drawing various shapes in the air with...nothing? But it wasn't nothing. After a moment the air pulsed and the symbols lit up in white flames, swirling above my head—encasing me. Slowly, they began to settle into my skin. Pain seized me for a moment, and then, my skin singed briefly at my shoulder as the guara tattoo dissolved...gone or simply hidden?

The magic continued to work and the freshly awakened pink fire in my internal lake became opaque—hidden in murkiness.

Panic clawed at my heart—I'd been cut off from my power.

"What the hell?" I snapped.

"Vala," Aether spoke, ignoring me. "I trust you and Jared have spoken?"

Jared stood, arms crossed as he glared at Aether before nodding once and storming off toward several homes and buildings nestled into the side of the cliffs—a city I hadn't noticed before. All the structures were built in various sizes, and they dotted the stone's face.

"Yup." Vala cringed before turning to follow Jared. Their forms became specks as they crossed the hill and descended into the white city below.

Aether cleared his throat. "You are special, Tate." He stepped into my view, towering over me. "And not just to me." Aether's voice was soft as he spoke, sincere. "You're so incredibly special to everyone here, especially leadership—" his lips were full and wet from his tongue, "—so we concealed our connection and now Vala has concealed the flavor of your magic, just for now." Each syllable poured slowly, so slowly from his full lips.

I found myself staring at them, focusing on the way his tongue swept over them, wondering what else it could do...

He smirked at me and raised a brow.

Distracted?

The heating in my core vanished as I shook my head, recalling my anger. He'd had Vala cloak me, whatever that meant. So much of this was unknown and he'd deliberately blocked me from my magic, the one thing that *could* help me in all of this was gone.

He sighed, running a hand through his unbound locks—still gloriously naked with nothing but the sea behind him. The perfect accent for muscled, sun-kissed skin.

I promise, next time I'll communicate first. But this is...a lot. There's much about this place and the Untish culture that you don't know, and that puts you at a great disability.

"Use your voice!" I shouted, like an irrational child. "I should have a say in *my* future—in what I can and can't access. You had no right to choose that for me."

"I'm sorry." His simple words threw me. "You're right, I should've discussed this with you first, it's just—"

I silenced him with my hand before massaging my now-aching temples.

His jaw clenched and unclenched as he took a deep breath. "You asked a question earlier and I owe you that answer." He appeared to be visibly holding himself in check.

I forced my eyes to stay locked on his face, willing them to not venture below his chest to inspect his... endowment. Instead, I noted his strong jawline with visible stubble beginning to form. My fingers itched to trace the scar cutting through his right eyebrow. What was wrong with me? One minute I loathed him and the next I burned with desire for him?

"The Changing can heighten certain emotions," he said as if reading my thoughts.

"The *Changing* or you?" I challenged, recalling how he'd manipulated me just days before.

He froze. Even the breath in his lungs stilled as he visibly swallowed. "Never. What occurred before...I promised I wouldn't influence them again, and I meant it."

"How can I trust you?"

"Tate," he sighed. "I promised you I wouldn't, and I meant it. But you should also know, my giftings at emotional manipulation are essentially *void* on Untishee once their magic is fully awakened—it repels any emotional magical tampering from our own *kind*, so there is no way to warp what you feel. And it's the same for *any* other emotional manipulators here at the Embassy—we're rare, given that emotional manipulation is strongly a Fae gift, and even then, most Fae are not strong enough to break through the intrinsic Untish defenses that awaken at the completion of the Changing."

I clenched my jaw.

"You're safe here. No one can touch your emotions. I promise—"

"So, what, you only prey on the helpless?" I couldn't keep the bite from my voice or the sting from my heart.

"Never. With you...it was complicated. We were on a mission to stop the seethings and save as many—"

"It was wrong. It's always wrong to warp what someone *feels*."

He looked as if I'd struck him.

"I'm sorry, you're right." His eyes became distant, and I swore I saw shame there.

I ignored my inner voice that reasoned he was trying to gather life-saving intel from me in a frazzled, tight-lipped, shocked state after witnessing Fletch's death.

My heart throbbed at the thought of Fletch.

I didn't want to think about any of that, it was too painful. Instead, I glared at him, noting once again the strength of his masculinity. His villainous eyes and seductive lips...

He smiled crookedly, eyes going smug.

My anger renewed with a lustful edge that both confused and excited me.

"Well, you said you had some truths to offer me?"

He placed a gentle hand on my shoulder, mercifully following my lead. "Tate, your natural color is one of a dragon tribe that hasn't existed here at the Embassy in quite some time. They've had no new members in the past ninety years, and no one from your tribe has walked here since. At least, none that have been announced. It would upset the delicate balance here."

"So, you want me to hide?" Just like Fletch and my mother had, both claiming it as protection. I shook his hand from my shoulder, his jaw flexing with the action.

"Not forever, just until I can verify a few things, and you're more adjusted from the *Changing*."

How could I protest or present an argument if I didn't understand anything about my magic, this place? Hell, my very origin was a mystery to me. And how could I learn about my magic if I was shielded from it? I still didn't understand what all the *Changing* stage entailed, or why my hair's pink tint meant anything special, only that it did.

I sucked on my fang as my stomach growled.

"Arithi will want to see us, but first I can arrange for some refreshments."

I smiled at him, cool and distant. So many secrets.

"Fine." I gestured for him to move. His eyes bored into mine as I felt his mental presence gently knocking against the wall I still held erect.

I averted my gaze. The sea below continued to crash, beckoning me forward.

"This way." Aether turned and began walking toward the city, his glutes dancing with his movement and highlighting the most perfectly formed ass I'd ever seen. His back was broad with scrawling tattoos climbing up over his shoulders and peaking at his neck before disappearing. His arms were well-sculpted. It was as if someone had taken a block of stone and simply chiseled every part of him. Suddenly, I wished I'd allowed myself the dalliance of drinking in the *hard* front of him.

Careful, darling, or I might comply and give you what you wish.

My face flushed and I was suddenly glad his back was to me. The air around me swirled, but I swatted at it—it didn't need coddling or prodding. I may be ignorant and completely unable to control my thoughts, or his apparent ability to hear them—jackass—but I wasn't a damsel to be toyed with. I shoved against the air with my fury, willing it to slip down the insufferable male's throat in front of me—

If we're slipping things down one another's throats now, I have some ideas...

I lost my footing and was caught by what appeared to be *nothing*—only it wasn't nothing, it was Aether intervening—again.

Prick.

I mean, if you want the full show, I can certainly oblige.

I opened my mouth to respond but...nothing. What could I say to that? No one had ever shaken me like this male in front of me. The way he spoke, the way he teased, his quick wit, it was all vastly different from the mindless males I was used to. Yes, he was unlike any male I'd ever encountered before. Well-practiced, restrained, powerful. But still...

I smiled.

Pulling a mental image of a knife slicing the balls right off a male, I sent it flying out toward Aether who, to my delight, stopped abruptly.

What the hell?

I smirked.

Violent one, are we?

Perhaps. Scared?

He resumed his footsteps. Shoulders squared and then *he* willed my feet forward with the gentlest pressure at my calves, my thighs, my upper thighs, and higher...

Not in the least. Who's to say I wouldn't enjoy that...kink.

The blood rushed to my face again. Bastard.

His chuckle, both in my head and aloud, was unnerving.

I just needed to regroup and my old swagger would return. He'd be on the receiving end, and I'd hold the power once again.

Mmm...you in charge? Tell me, what do you do to those who need punish—

A dragon roared in the near distance, drawing my attention. Just ahead, I could see beasts circling a large field and landing. Fire filled the air in colored bursts of black, green, and red. Dragons. I was at the home of dragons. These magnificent beasts were the perfect distraction from my disorienting opponent. This insufferable male, striding nude just in front of me with his absolutely gorgeous tan skin on the most beautiful—

Most people would remain fixated on the fire-breathing beasts, especially if they'd never really seen dragons before. But you? You're fixated on me. I'm flattered.

He began to massage my back with manipulated air molecules as he sent me the most unnerving image of him on his knees before me, looking at me with reverence, his mouth wet and lips ready... My bodice was that of tight black lace and leather, I held a small whip in my hand as I stood in stilettoes just above him, lips screaming his name—

"Micro Dick, huh?" I said the one sure thing that could break the male euphoria and change the power dynamic.

He froze. The look in his eyes as he gawked at me from behind his shoulder was nothing short of incredulous.

Sometimes it was the small victories that tasted the sweetest.

With elegant steps full of renewed confidence, albeit clanky in these boots, I focused on the white stone city ahead. I increased my pace so I walked beside the male, not behind where I was more likely to get...distracted. Slowly, the entire stretch of buildings became clear. It was glorious, cut from white stones with blue roof tiles.

Gorgeous.

Mesmerizing.

Home.

There were several large flat spaces, fields cut into the stone, the same size as most small towns—they went on for hundreds of yards with dragons using the space to land on or take off from. In the distant sky, I could see the outline of *dozens* of dragons flying.

Amazing.

We dragons are indeed something to behold. You will be the fiercest of us all, I can sense it in you.

I rolled my eyes at the tone Aether used as we continued down the trodden path and made our way past one of the landing fields. In the distance, I could see a large dome, easily big enough to house a dozen dragons with colosseum seating around it. Odd.

"What's that?" I nodded toward the arena.

"That is the grand coliseum. Wars have been resolved there. Fights to the death. Meetings, training, you know, the normal," he said as he winked at me.

None of this was normal.

This odd exchange? Not normal. Verbal sparring with a male who infuriated and simultaneously captivated me? Definitely unusual. Being bested in quick wit? A first.

Back in the Glenn, I could handle Aether—the commanding male with a mission. But now? Now I was lost. So completely disoriented in myself, my future, and the glorious expanse of tan skin covered in tattoos. I was lost in the male that continually confused me while eliciting the strongest reactions, igniting passion and desire, and still somehow managed to overstep and irritate me while providing protection and comfort. I was adrift, and yet, somehow, I was found. This was my home. He was my home, even if in this moment, I didn't understand how. Didn't understand this...connection we shared and the odd abilities that came with it. How could I have such a sexual appetite with a male I barely knew? Trust him, even with his infuriating half-truths?

I could sense desire coursing through me, but it wasn't my own. It felt as if it were his. How was any of this possible? Even this majestic city was so magical it felt fake. Perhaps if I'd grown up here, it would all seem normal. Casual. Not like a dream that, if I weren't careful, I'd wake up from at any moment to meet the steel-cold reality of a cruel world.

We walked in silence for several minutes, and for that I was grateful. We passed statues, several looked ancient. At least hundreds of years old if not thousands.

This is where your ancestors lived.

My breath caught and I bit my tongue. My ancestors. The pain from my fang piercing my tongue was immediate, just what I needed to pull myself out of my mental fog as I was walking into a new, unknown territory—a place where, seemingly, my heritage could place me in danger.

I snorted at the thought. I didn't even know *what* my heritage was. I shot a glare at Aether. He knew more than he told me. Everyone in my life was handling me with fucking kid gloves.

And I was so done with it—fucking done.

I could sense the inner beast attempting to rise and then immediately vanishing into a now hazy pool within. *He* did that to me. Blocked my power without so much as asking. Cut me off from myself.

Didn't block, just cloaked. You can still access it, but with the upcoming interrogation with the chairs for the post-mission debrief and your interview, we need to be careful. This will make it hard for them to sense what type of magic you have.

Ah. So, he did offer some specific answers—when he wanted. I made a mental note to remember this next time my thighs started heating up and my eyes wandered.

You still should have asked. I shot the response back and immediately shook my head.

It was *strange* to communicate like this with him.

The air around me tightened, Aether's reassuring force. His power reached out and massaged my shoulders. This time, though, instead of rebuffing it, I sank into it even as I walked. The tightness in my chest lessened slightly.

I was nothing if not a mess.

A beautiful—

I shoved out my hand, silencing the thought. His mouth hung ajar as his voice vanished mid-sentence. My eyes widened and I relished the way Aether cocked his head at me. I didn't know *how* I'd done that, but I certainly wasn't about to admit it even if he already knew it too.

We passed a pub, or what I assumed was a pub, with several Untishee drinking deeply from red-filled glasses. Some sloshed out of them as they clanged together in celebration—cheers sounded in unison.

As we continued, we approached another clearing. A few dragons were occupying it. They huffed and their breaths steamed the air. Two of them were green with yellow eyes. Smaller than Aether in his dragon form, but bigger than Vala. They kneeled to Aether as he walked by, but it did nothing to stop the inquisitive looks I received. One dragon, a white one, further in the plain, was drinking from a trough. Its body was nothing if not pure muscle and each gulp shook its entire being. It raised its head and red dripped from its snout, down its neck, and onto the ground in thick drops. Even from a field away I could smell the iron. Blood.

I surveyed the massive expanse: dragons, blood, fire, skin...I did a double-take. Sure enough, here and there across the field were *nude* figures, shifters in their humanoid forms. Something warm heated my chest at the realization that I truly was not alone. I'd never known another shifter before, let alone been surrounded by dozens of them. My eyes snagged on a male closer to the path. His blond hair cascaded down his back and he stood near a beast, cup of blood in hand. His manhood was fully erect and on display, even as he casually crossed his arms and leaned against the large trough. His yellow eyes locked on mine, and he smirked as my jaw dropped and my cheeks flushed. He was completely comfortable watching me observe him in his barest form.

See something of interest?

I startled and nearly lost my footing at Aether's voice in my head, noting the slight edge to it.

If I did?

I tried to release the breath I was holding, to savor the intense tension I could feel radiating off Aether—even if I didn't fully under-stand why.

But the male's yellow eyes never left me, not even as two nude females strode toward him, and one threw herself into the trough of blood, laughing as she bobbed back up, black hair soaked in red.

I looked away.

The beating of wings filled the air as several large beasts took flight. Dust was kicked up and began clouding—it would have gotten in my eyes, but it was gently rebuffed by a slightly hazy, but mostly invisible, shield.

Aether, protecting me.

It irked me, even if it shouldn't have.

A large red dragon was intently watching me. It was just ahead of Aether and to the right. The large beast smiled as it squinted its maroon eyes. With two powerful beats of its wings, it was airborne. A moment later, it lifted its head and roared, shaking the very ground I stood on.

I found myself scared. Unnerved. And I hated that I felt timid.

I shouldn't feel this way. Shouldn't be so curious. Shouldn't demand to understand the world and simultaneously reject it. This was *my* home. These were *my* people. And yet, the feeling of comradery and that of a trespasser warred within.

Even the sound of wings beating set my nerves on edge. I needed *her* in her full glory to rise within, to quash the tide of panic. But she was silenced. Blocked. All because of an order from the ever-maddening male beside me.

I bit my lip to prevent choice words from spilling forth. I knew I was acting insecure...scared. And I hated it.

After several minutes of walking on the smooth stone, the field ended, and we passed through a dome into another district. At the outskirts, Aether opened a door to a large room, revealing racks filled with spare clothes.

"Shifting and all. We try to limit nudity in the residential portion of the city." He donned a pair of black loose trousers and then shut the door behind him before carrying on.

I found myself simultaneously grateful and dismayed by his modesty.

This path appeared to be full of houses. Homes cut into the stone. A small child darted out of one alcove with another one hot on her heels.

They laughed as they ran around, playing. A foreign concept to me. I stood there, staring like an idiot. Back home—no, back at the Glenn—children rarely showed unrestrained joy.

"You're back!" the boy chasing the girl screamed as he spotted Aether.

"I am," Aether chuckled. The boy ran up to him and threw his tiny arms around Aether's legs.

Aether's laugh deepened as he tussled the boy's hair. A paternal move and yet the boy looked nothing like Aether with his red curls and green eyes.

Not mine.

I could feel my face turning several shades of red. I really needed to learn how to block him out of my mind and from my more embarrassing musings.

"Show us again! Please, you promised!" the boy begged.

Aether smiled and outstretched his hand as a black dragon of pure flames flew through the sky, dancing and soaring, before raising its head and roaring. The image hovered above the boy's head before flying down the cobblestone street. Laughing, the boy chased the shadowed dragon before tripping on his feet and falling—well, nearly falling—as Aether caught him mid-fall. He was suspended a foot off the ground, eyes widening as he howled into the sky. Slowly, Aether lowered him to the street, the dark shimmer disappearing when the boy's feet hit the stone.

"Again!" the boy pleaded.

"Not today, Clarence. Later, okay?"

"But your magic is what I want to have! Just one more time, please Uncle Aeth! Then I can catchy up-p to Ruby!" Clarence rubbed at his runny nose, marking his face with bits of dirt as he pleaded.

"No! It's my turn!" a little girl shouted. She was taller than the boy and had similar red curls. But her eyes were very different—they were dark, chocolate almost, and they had distinct golden flakes.

My eyes darted to Aether as he knelt before the small girl.

"Ruby." He pulled her into a hug. "You've grown!"

"Mama says a whole two inches since you were here last!" Ruby beamed.

"Sprouting like a weed!?" Aether exclaimed, still holding her.

"It won't be long until I can be out there with you!" Ruby pushed back against Aether. "I'll be shifting in no time!"

"You're going to put me out of a job before I know it." Aether smiled sadly, before releasing the small girl as Clarence jumped on his back.

My heart ached within. This whole place, this idea of a family with children who were loved and happy was so foreign. What could have been...

I gritted my teeth. My mother did her best. She loved me the best way she knew, and she protected me in the ways she could. Fletch did too.

"Who's that?" Ruby asked, squinting her dark eyes at me.

"This," Aether said as he stood, Clarence still clinging to his back, "is Tate." I didn't miss the sparkle in his eyes or the simultaneous narrowing of Ruby's.

"Nice to meet you, Ruby and Clarence." I offered what I hoped was a gentle smile.

"Hmm." Ruby lifted her nose in the air. "Nothing special." With that, she turned and stalked off with a straight back to the home she'd run out of only moments before.

"Please, just one more time!" Clarence begged.

A gong sounded.

Saved by the bell.

"Looks like you've got to get back to your lessons and learn so I can one day count on you to be my second in command," Aether said, setting the boy down.

Clarence smiled, highlighting his missing front teeth, and squealed before darting back toward the home he'd left. Clearly, Aether was cherished here. It shook me to see *this* side of him.

Aether tilted his head, a fond smile still playing on his lips.

"Just through here," he said as he began moving and led us through an arch, into a small home just across the street.

Close, very close to where those children lived.

"So, Clarence called you Uncle?" I pried—I knew I was entering dangerous territory.

"Yup," he simply responded as he painted symbols in the air in dark fire before the large iron door swung open. "Come on in."

It was elegant inside, beautiful even. The floors were made of white stone, as were the walls, and the home was lit from the skylights above; windows without glass dotted the external wall, toward the sea, and lamps throughout made the place cozy and, somehow, regal. The counters were made of marble and the furniture was a brown leather with black pillowed accents. Fur rugs lined the floors, and the hearth, like in the cave, was lit with a black fire. Bookcases lined the walls on either side of the deep, ebony mantle and contrasted the brightness of everything else. Simple, if not masculine.

Taking a step further in, the scents assaulted me. Ash, spice, salt. This was *Aether's* home. I didn't detect any other aromas which brought me an odd sense of relief.

I blinked. I'd have to examine *that* emotion later. Much, much later.

Aether walked into the kitchen and grabbed a couple of glasses from the doorless cabinet on the wall. A cabinet that held two glasses, two plates, and two bowls.

Two.

I gritted my teeth as envy rose within. I had no right to feel however it was that I was feeling. Fuck it, if this whole place wasn't messing with my head.

"Clarence is James's boy," Aether said as he pressed against the stone wall. To my surprise, it clicked open revealing a fridge. Clever.

"Here, drink," he spoke as he filled both glasses with blood.

I stood momentarily frozen. I'd been expecting to live feed. Come to think of it, since we entered the city, I hadn't seen *anyone* partaking in live feeding. Relieving, but also odd.

"This place is different." He winked, reading my mind—again.

"Stop doing that," I demanded as I grabbed the glass—the blood was cold.

"Doing what?"

"Reading my mind," I spoke the obvious before sipping from the purely red glass. Disappointment flooded my senses. It was human blood. Of course, it wasn't the *good* stuff, it wasn't like he'd drink his own blood. The image of him feeding from himself, sinking his own fangs into his arm, or slitting his wrist to fill a pitcher, made me smile, even as Aether choked—clearly, it wasn't *always* pleasant to read someone's mind. A satisfied smile pulled at my lips.

"I'm not a mind reader, dear. I just can hear you because you're *screaming* your thoughts at me." He took another sip. "And no, I don't drink my own blood."

My face blotched red as embarrassment had me downing my cup. It was one thing to suspect, but another to have it confirmed. I shivered at what else he may have 'heard'.

"Mmm, and is Ruby your niece?" I pried, trying to drive the conversation elsewhere. From the shifting of his feet, I could tell he was uncomfortable with the new topic.

"Here, eat this." He set out a plate holding a large wedge of cheese with a small knife beside it.

I simply looked at him. Eat?

He smirked as he broke off a large chunk with his hands before shoving it in his mouth, his tongue licking off every crumb from his large, now wet, fingers.

I swallowed as his eyes darkened. Coming to my senses, I grabbed a small chunk of cheese and was pleasantly surprised by the intensity of flavor that sparked in my mouth. It was more than just cheese, it had to be.

"It's endowed with Luner magic and produced here in the heart of the Embassy. Both the dairy cows and the herbs originate from large stores of magic," he said, answering my unspoken question.

I took another bite and moaned slightly at the pure pleasure from its aged flavor...why had I never had this before?

Desire.

I looked up from the cheese and was met with Aether's heated gaze. My hand tightened on the cheese as blood rushed to my face. Bits crumbled from my fingers to the counter, but his eyes never left mine.

"Arithi wants to see you...pretty much immediately. I'll be presenting you to the chairs for Judgment," he spoke as he refilled our cups.

A sigh escaped me as I shoved the remaining cheese in my mouth, savoring its blissful flavor. "What happens then?"

"Then they confirm you as a Untishee and assign you to a Tribe, my Tribe," he finished smugly.

"Yours?" I said, both a statement and a question.

"Yep, mine." His eyes intensified, as did the temperature in the room. This was different from our verbal sparring, this was deeper...

My toes began to curl in my boots as I looked at the male in front of me. He was complex, more so than I'd originally thought. His face was one of violence, but it was also tender and when he smiled, it made him appear gentle—beautiful, even.

He cleared his throat. Dammit, I looked away before he could see how truly mortified I was.

"One thing, Tate, do not let them know you can hear my thoughts, and I yours. It's not common and could place you in greater danger," he said.

"Why bring me here if it's nothing but danger? Why'd Arithi want me if I'm nothing but a threat?"

"She doesn't know *who* you are." His statement confused me. Didn't she know my mother?

"Will you be there, at the meeting?" I asked. I wanted him near, although I wasn't really sure exactly *why*.

"Yes and no. I'll present you and then you'll continue the questioning without me, but I'll still be in contact...if you know what I mean." He placed his empty cup in the white stone sink before turning on the tap.

I gave him a questioning look.

Like this. No one can hear us, only a few have ever been able to communicate this distinctively. It's very, very rare.

"If it's rare, then how can we communicate this way?" I still wasn't ready to speak into his mind.

You really want to know?

No. No, I wasn't sure I did.

Disappointment flashed across his face and then it was gone, replaced by his mask of indifference. "Just don't tell them you hear my voice or can communicate that way, and if you talk to me while you're in there and I'm not, don't do so verbally."

No shit. I wasn't an idiot.

His lips tilted up in a half-smile.

"When do we leave?"

As if in answer, a small female appeared outside the still-open front door. She was dressed in all-black linen covered in scales. Her brown hair was braided in twin braids from the top of her head down to just past her shoulders—the ends were black. She was a dragon, a Darkling if memory served me. Perhaps I'd be a quick learner.

"Anna, is it time?" Aether asked.

"It is, sir." She saluted him and stood back, still not entering the home, and allowed Aether to pass through.

"Ms. Aaralyn, after you." His formality threw me.

Darling, he cooed in my head.

I stumbled as I crossed the threshold.

CHAPTER 8

CHANCE

I couldn't get enough air down. I couldn't breathe, couldn't calm myself, or think clearly. All I saw were red streaks, they filled my vision and dominated my senses. Power. I had power, and I had no idea what to do with it.

The air in the lower courtyard was cool—the place was empty. All dokimoses and arches were in their barracks, well, all except for the patrol squads. And leadership has been scrambling since their covert ops base was blown up.

But none of that mattered. Nothing did, nothing but the power coursing through my veins and redefining my very being.

Was I a monster?

This was a direct result of the exposure to dark magic, it had to be. I didn't have it before and now I did. I was evolving. Or was I? My father claimed it had merely awakened what had been there all along. I'd rather believe that...but that would mean agreeing with the very male who betrayed his country and the laws he helped enact.

Perhaps I'd both been awakened and was mutating.

A cold laugh slipped through my tight lips at the thought.

"I thought I'd find you out here," Holland said as she approached.

I glanced up to meet worried honey-brown eyes. She'd been exposed too. Did she also have powers?

I grunted in response, another lash of red fleeing from my body and attacking the nearest security camera. It sizzled and popped as it burst apart. Nothing remained but a smoking, broken stub.

"Wow, that's uh, something, Dale. You sure you haven't been hiding that—"

"Never. I was always honest with you. I don't know...don't understand...it's just..."

Words failed me. How could I express this if I didn't understand it? Anger once again became my companion. A bolt shot out from me and hit the nearby arch.

"Stay away! I could hurt you!" I shouted. I nearly hit her. I would not hurt her, never willingly and I'd be damned if I did it accidentally.

"Dale, your fear is not helping. You need to master this, you need help," Holland said as she stepped closer, her brown boots crunching the loose gravel on the courtyard floor. This place was a mess.

"Holland, I don't even know what *this* is. I could be becoming one of *them* for all I know. I should be locked up!" I threw my arms wide and instantly knew it was a mistake. Red bolts shot out of my fingertips hitting the walls and then webbing out from there.

"Dale, it's going to be all right. Let's just get you—"

"No!" I shouted and the red vines pouring from me got brighter. I didn't know how to release them. Shae would know. I chuckled a dry laugh. Shae, who was now in a coma, was someone I thought could help. We didn't even know *why* she was in a coma...only that she had a bad reaction to the magic, or that's what the medics said. At least she survived, unlike Arche Damaris.

We'd lost him the day of the explosion, he didn't survive the exposure to the dark magic—we carried him back, half alive, only to arrive at the Southern Outpost with a corpse.

We've had enough death; I would not cause more.

"Holland, just go away," I said, and the bolts vanished. I had control, if only for a moment.

"She's right, you know," came the voice from hell. A voice I never wanted to hear again. "You must face this and master it." My father's cane clipped on the floor as he entered the courtyard.

A red bolt flew out, striking his heart—a bolt that killed. My father crumpled to the ground.

I shook my head, and the vision cleared. My father stood there, disappointment once again gracing his features—features that were more purple than I'd noticed before.

"If you're not willing to learn control for yourself, then do it for Shae. Do it for Holland," my father spoke, smiling while he did so.

"What the fuck are you talking about?" I demanded.

"They too were exposed. Not just to the dark magic being used by the creatures, or from the stores that blew up, but from the rebels. From the enemy. They've been exposed on a level we haven't seen before. The creatures we've recovered are evolving quickly and changing. It was a catalyst. Shae is unconscious and Dux Holland seems unaffected, but we don't know. You, however, have a gift that has awakened. If you can control it, we may be able to help Shae and Holland before it's too late for them..." He let the unsaid hang in the air. It was just like him to hold their well-being over my head.

I hated him. But I also hated myself. Fuck, he was right. "Holland, this asshole created those things. We were behind it, the Glenn; the higher moral ground is much lower than I thought. You were right, Holland, all along," my voice broke, and I dropped to my knees.

"Pathetic," my father quipped. "Pick yourself up and get down to research. You need to be tested and begin working. This is *all* that matters." He moved closer, cane still tapping the floor. "You were always *too* idealistic. Have you ever stopped to ask yourself why? Be realistic boy. These *things*, as you call them, will save lives and if you cooperate, you too could save Shea and possibly, Holland."

When I looked up, he was gone. Walking down the hallway, cane in hand. Hate welled within me, and another red bolt shot out and hit the arch above the hallway he'd disappeared down. Stone crumbled to the ground with mortar as black marked the place where I'd struck.

I was pathetic.

Holland looked to me, pleading in her eyes. "Dale, they may be able to help...you don't have to suffer. This isn't on you."

But I didn't believe her, I couldn't. I could go submit myself to tests, allow them to train me or whatever, but did I want to help *them*? The creators of this problem? This pure evil that now lurked and hunted within our borders?

I locked my jaw, and I swore I could feel red lightning shooting around my heart, stabbing haphazardly. I was broken.

"Dale, I—"

Holland dropped to her knees, clutching her chest as her body began to shake and tremble. She was seizing. I ran to her side and reached for her, but I felt nothing but air. Where her warm body should have been, only cool air was to be found; red danced across my vision. "Holland!" I shook my head and reached again to where I knew she was, and I felt her warm body shaking violently. The red cleared from my sight as I tried to stabilize her.

She continued to shake, and I held her head. "Help! Someone, help!" But no one came. The cameras were fried. I cradled her head until she stopped shaking. "Holland," I called again, turning her face toward me.

My breath caught.

There across her forehead were tiny black lines, webbing out from a purple diamond etched in her skin.

Trembling, I picked her up and cradled her small body in my arms. I moved as quickly as I dared and reentered the base. She needed medical attention and I needed to submit to testing.

My pride wasn't worth her life.

CHAPTER 9
TATE

The perky brunette led us down a series of streets, passing several homes, another landing field—one that opened to the most breathtaking view of the turquoise sea below—and past several businesses. She moved quickly, but quietly. I didn't hear a single one of her steps, unlike my own clumsy ones. Especially in *these* boots that weren't quite right. The heel to the left shoe had been altered, but it was far from perfectly smooth or flat. Even so, Aether's gesture had surprised and warmed me.

He walked beside me, his shoulders tight. The usual comforting presence on my shoulders was missing—I didn't realize how much I'd come to rely and count on *him* to calm me. In only a few days, had I already become dependent on a male?

I shook my head.

"In the High Council room." Anna stopped just outside and nodded. I didn't miss the gleam in her eyes, or the way they slightly tightened in dislike when looking at me, or the flush in her cheeks when Aether thanked her.

I didn't like this Anna.

We entered the main chamber. It was empty save for the individuals who sat perched in their seats. Seats that were on the floor—not a stage as I had expected. They sat in chairs sculpted from stone and carved into the room itself. White chalk dusted the ground and clouded the air with every step I took. This place felt oddly *holy*.

Do as I do.

Aether approached the seats and knelt, his huge body curling in on itself, flexing the glorious, scaled material he wore. I stood there, staring and mute, like a complete idiot.

Darling?

Jolting forward, I knelt beside him—sparing him a quick glare—before focusing ahead on the people in front of us. Seven chairs—six were filled and one sat empty, chalk thickly dusted the lone seat.

"My chairs," Aether spoke, bowing even lower. "I present to you, Tatealia Aaralyn, Untishee by blood, member of the Shadow Tribe."

"Thank you, Aether," a male spoke, waving a gnarled hand toward us. His eyes landed on me and widened before slipping back into a neutral mask. "Welcome, Tatealia Aaralyn, to the Embassy, home of the Untish, here on Shappa."

Aether stood and I nodded to the male. Unsure what to do next, I cast a questioning look to Aether.

Stand.

I found my feet and squared my shoulders. "Thank you."

"It is good to see you again, Daughter of Night," Arithi spoke. She sat in the middle, next to the empty chair. She seemed the youngest of them all, even with wrinkles creasing her eyes. Her hair was tipped in bright red.

Arithi is the chair of the Iron Tribe; she's an Ironhead.

I clenched my jaw and smiled wider. How had I not noticed her hair before?

The tips of the hair identify which tribe they belong to. A testament of magic's calling.

"Thank you," I replied to Arithi. I sounded like a damned idiot. Apparently, I knew only one phrase. I mentally kicked myself.

Breathe, you're doing great, darling.

Stop calling me that.

As you wish.

Aether smiled.

I refocused on Arithi who now was looking at me intently. She wore a red tunic and pants, both covered in red scales. Her golden boots were laced up her calves and tied at the knees, and her tunic had matching golden embroidery etching the hem. A golden and red twig rested upon her head, almost like a crown.

I glanced to all the individuals, noting they too held some form of adornment upon their heads.

"What of her…giftings?" Arithi asked, arching a brow.

"Minor, given her lack of training." Aether paused, and I flinched inside at his description of my abilities. "But," he continued, "we witnessed her move rocks in a fit of emotion as she began the *Changing*, heat temperature spiking, and I believe her gifts are that of the House of Shadows. She is a Darkling." I didn't miss the note of pride in his voice.

"As evidenced by her hair," a tired male voiced.

I looked at him, he sat on the other side of Arithi and had white hair on his head that ended in black. The leader of the Shadow Tribe.

Enzo, he's the Shadow Tribe's chair, a Darkling.

"She is one of us," he confirmed.

"But her mother was a Beacon," a female replied. She sat at the end, her pale white-blonde hair ending in a brilliant yellow. "She could be a Beacon, when they're in *Changing*, it's hard to *tell* which tribe they belong to."

That's Chiara, a Beacon, chair of the Beacon Tribe.

My heart raced. I didn't know this female; Aether had never mentioned them before. In fact, he hadn't mentioned much of anything of real importance.

"Yes, but her hair tells all," Enzo spoke. "Really, Chiara, I know your tribe is shrinking, but to poach one of my—" A cough interrupted the male's admonishing. I didn't miss the way the cloth reddened or the way Arithi eyed it. He wasn't well.

"Enzo is right, I confirm that she appears to be a Darkling. It is, as Chiara pointed out, unexpected. Irene was indeed a Beacon. However, her father's bloodline is somewhat...unknown." I didn't like the look Arithi gave me or the tightening of her eyes.

Aether tensed beside me. "She has demonstrated giftings that are undeniably in line with the Shadow Tribe," he spoke.

"This we shall see for ourselves. Depart," Arithi commanded.

Aether's jaw ticked, but he bowed and didn't look at me as he left.

It will be okay.

The comfort of his words was at odds with the tension in the room. Was I to perform?

Just a small demonstration, nothing for you. But make sure it's almost nothing.

I didn't like the sound of that. The door clicked behind me; I was alone with these rulers—these tribal heads.

"Well, what did you have in mind, Arithi?" Enzo voiced, his words wet. I cringed as I noted more blood on the cloth he clutched tightly.

"Just a minor show of these gifts your nephew claims he's seen."

Nephew? I looked closer at Enzo. He was small, much smaller than Aether, but his facial symmetry did remind me of Aether...a little.

"Very well. Tatealia, please show this court an example of your giftings," Enzo spoke.

I looked at them, wide-eyed. "I don't know what you mean."

"Her candor is markedly a gift from the House of Beacon. She is one of us," Chiara spoke, earning a glare from Enzo.

"Tatealia, please. Just show us what you showed Aether," Arithi commanded. Her smile, while gentle, hid a violence evident in her eyes. This female, the one I once thought of as elderly, had a lethal edge. I shivered at the thought.

Aether, I...

Words escaped me. How could I ask for help? Until this moment, I wasn't sure *how* I felt about this kind of communication, but now I fully embraced it and was overwhelmed with gratitude.

Just picture the air around one of their heads, perhaps Chiara, and then make it dance. The Beacon Tribe cannot manipulate air.

I did just that. I focused on her hair, the crown of sunflowers gracing her white head, and felt for the energy around it. I could see it, almost, and I willed it to stir. Nothing.

You're trying too hard. Just follow your instincts, darling.

I said…

Use your rage.

That bastard, I inwardly snarled. But he was right, I'd forgotten about my effort as the crown of sunflowers now lifted from Chiara's head and was swirling about. She gasped as she felt my power brush her skin. I smiled; I liked this—the power.

Now, lose control.

What? Why?

Now.

I did as he commanded and the crown went crashing to the floor, smacking Chiara's face on its way down.

"Well, well," Enzo stood, shaking as he did, "she is one of us."

Chiara grimaced as she bent to collect the sunflowers and Arithi just stared at me, a cat assessing its prey.

"Very well, Tatealia Aaralyn, it appears you have the giftings in accordance with the Shadow Tribe. However, you are unskilled, untrained, and your loyalty—while vouched for by High General Brychan—is not enough to ensure your place as an active member in the Shadow Tribe." Arithi smiled.

"Now, see here, Arithi! She is one of my own and as such she—" Enzo bent over, coughing heavily once again into his handkerchief.

"Enzo, she is yours. But as leader of the Tribal chairs, I decree she should be entered as a cadet into Trials and Training. It is the same protocol we use for all transfers," Arithi challenged.

"I would have to concur," Chiara spoke. Clearly, she was miffed that I wasn't a Beacon.

Enzo shook his head. "I am the Shadow chair and I say—" more coughing "—that she is ready if Aether says—" he inhaled deeply, pausing.

"Enzo." Arithi stood setting her hand on his shoulder. "Miss Aaralyn was my selection, the one I tasked your tribe with her recovery. I need her to be at her full force, and to do so she needs training. More than High General Brychan can provide while seeing to his other duties. Surely, you see this. Unless, perhaps, it is time for you to step down..."

"How dare you!" Enzo threw out his hands and a wall of black flames engulfed Arithi. Or so I thought. I gasped as she stepped out of those flames in both a shield and a wall of red fire projected from her fingertips.

What's going on?

I couldn't respond to Aether, not as Arithi stalked toward Enzo who was now on his knees grunting to hold his own against the female who undoubtedly would win.

"Yield," Arithi demanded.

Enzo heaved a sigh and then his flames died. He spat blood at her feet—deep red with hints of gold.

"Miss Aaralyn, your training begins tomorrow. You will need to be evaluated by the proper channels to determine your schooling prior to any further action." Arithi cleansed the bloodied spit from her boots with a wave of red flames and then returned to her seat. Enzo remained on his knees, chest heaving.

He looked to me and nodded in confirmation. "My nephew will take you for your evalu—" he broke out into a new round of coughs.

A male with green ends to his hair and oddly yellow eyes stood and helped Enzo out of the room. I made a mental note of the colors I'd seen as well as the sheer force of power Arithi possessed.

My pulse was still hammering through me as I rose and began walking toward the door, chalk coating the air as I moved. Instead of the panic filling my veins, I focused on the facts. I was new, young, and ignorant, but I wasn't stupid.

"Knowledge is power." Fletch's voice filled my head.

My heart ached. Perhaps, he had prepared me for this, after all. I could do this; I could do more than simply survive.

Chiara, yellow.

Enzo, black.

Arithi, red.

I also noted the male with the green hair, the female with the white ends to her locks—like Vala—and one other male with hair tipped in blue. Six filled chairs. Six colors. Six tribes. One empty chair.

There she is.

I tuned out the pride in Aether's voice as his footsteps sounded. He nodded to Enzo, still standing with the green-haired male, before gently grabbing my elbow and leading me from the room.

"Where are we—"

"Evaluation," he interrupted me. I glared at him, a little stunned by his rudeness. I hadn't heard *that* tone since he was pretending to be Mardi.

Trust me.

I rolled my eyes but didn't say anything more. He led me to a chamber at the end of a series of hallways and doors. Inside was a couch, leather from the appearance, with a chair next to it. A female sat there, her hair in a neat bun, and her dark skin beautifully contrasted the white of her uniform. The tips of her coiled hair were frosted, white. She smiled at me, and I didn't miss the way her nose kicked up a bit, just like Vala's...

This is Vala's mother, Pegansha. She is a Luner, general of Science and Research in the Luna Tribe. She is kind but fierce. Fair. You will be fine with her as your evaluator.

I smiled. I could handle an interrogation from Vala's mom.

What is she evaluating?

"Please, have a seat, Tatealia," Pegansha spoke.

Aether nodded and left the room.

She will be looking for knowledge and magical holds. Do NOT reveal your inner dragon. Leave her hidden.

I sat as Pegansha motioned for me to do.

"Let's begin."

CHAPTER 10
CHANCE

The straps to the table were tight, uncomfortably so. I had been down here for blood knew how long. They'd taken vial after vial. Finally, Doctor Worshah entered the room.

"Dux Dale, thank you for your patience. We've seen some, uh, abnormalities in your blood. New markers," he spoke as he pulled up a stool and sat on it—the wheels squeaking as it moved.

"Abnormalities?" I asked.

"Yes, we will need to test things further, in a new way. It may be uncomfortable, but first, we want to rate your power's strength." He looked at me, dark eyes piercing.

"Okay," I sighed.

He nodded. "This may be a bit painful."

I remembered what it was like to be tested when I first turned. I was down in a lab like this for days, my father demanding they hadn't pushed me enough. Claimed they didn't break me hard enough, didn't test correctly. That my magical stores had to be higher, that my genes should be stronger. Finally, after two weeks of endless tests, my father accepted me for a failure, and I went home—bruised on the inside and out. And now, now I would *willingly* submit to it all over again.

The image of Holland shaking still hadn't left me. The strange marking on her brow had to be from her exposure to the dark magic. She needed help and like it or not, I was her best shot.

"I know, just get on with it," I said with a rough voice.

"Very well." He stood and unfastened the manacles at my wrists. "Follow me."

I followed him out of the clinic, massaging my now-marked wrists as we walked down the corridor to a room like the one I'd spent many painful days inside. It was made entirely of stone, but this one also had a metal wall with a mirror and several spouts in the ceiling. Doctor Worshah opened the thick glass door and stepped aside, allowing me to go in, alone.

I swallowed back the nerves as I walked in, head high. The door clicked behind me, and I stood facing a one-way mirror, of that I was sure. It was built into the center of the metal wall.

"Hello, daddy dearest," I spoke as I combed through my tangled curls with my fingers. He was there. I knew it in my bones. No way he'd miss this upcoming test.

My father on his knees, gasping for air as red electricity covered his body, tightening and contracting...

I shook my head as I focused on my reflection in the mirror. A shadow of a beard was forming on my chin, light brown contrasting my dirty, tousled blond curls. The blue eyes in the mirror looked cold, far too cold for the magic roiling within.

"The test will begin in one moment, be prepared," a robotic voice drifted through the room.

I gritted my teeth. Waiting was the worst part. I didn't have to wait long though, a moment later the room hummed, and I could feel the frequencies coursing through the air changing. They weren't going to make this easy. Fine. I could handle it.

It went from tingling to instant pain. I dropped to my knees and clutched my chest as the waves in the room poked at me, trying to find my power. Red streaked across my vision, threatening to burst forth. I held it back for a moment, I needed to learn control.

The pain intensified as a new frequency was hit—this one much closer to my newfound power—and it raked over my body, boring its way in—demanding I accept it, allow it. I bit down on my tongue, ignoring the blood now pouring from my lips, the iron swelling in my mouth.

The charge increased and I screamed as my hands clutched at the ground and red sparks flew from them, embedding in the tile. Agony tore through me from the room's charge, and the red dancing across my body combatted it, sizzling but not harming me.

The voltage in the room increased again and the beast within took over.

I threw back my head as my soul screamed, red bolts flew from my hands and feet, impacting the stone and shaking the room. The walls were covered in red, electric webs of my power. It worked its way over to the cameras that instantly popped, fried.

More, I needed more.

I released more of the anger, the power thumping through my being, and the walls no longer danced with my lightning, but became devoured by it. The stone went from marred to gouged, chunks falling into the room from all around. The mirror fractured and the room shook.

I loosened a cry from the very core of my being and the entire room was swallowed in a cloud of red. The mirror burst and shards of glass danced through the air; screams sounded from beyond, but still, I didn't relent. I enjoyed the power. I savored the fear I could hear from scared doctors thrived on it.

"Enough," a familiar voice commanded. Father?

No, this wasn't nearly enough.

I drew from the storm within and pushed out further with red vines of pure energy. The room beyond the mirror sizzled as the control panel combusted from within. More pained screams came, but all I could see was red power—light, fire, energy. It was me and yet, it wasn't.

My euphoria was growing.

I was madly powerful.

Pain erupted from my back along with the sound of a shot. My eyes darted to the room in front of me, through waves of red I could see my father. He stood stoic with a dart gun aimed at me. Had he shot me? For what, being *too* powerful? Damn him.

I stood, ready to face off when my internal power spurted, the room blurred, and I found my wells empty—disembodied.

Drugged.

CHAPTER 11
TATE

"Can you tell me the origin of Untish magic?" Pegansha asked yet another question I didn't know the answer to.

I stared at her dumbly.

"I see. Can you tell me the origin of any magic?"

"I...uh, I mean we were taught magic is rare. That it is a blessing or curse from Mother Blood," I said lamely. "But aside from giftings, like agility or increased speed and endurance, magic wasn't really something we had in the Glenn. At least not commonly."

Pegansha just noted it and then flipped to the next page in her book.

"And do you know of anything regarding the Seven Untish Tribes?"

My silence was answer enough. I was a fool.

Any help would be nice. I sent the message, but it was met with no response.

Aether had been silent for the entirety of this lengthy interrogation.

"All right, and have you ever shifted into a dragon?" she asked, not looking up.

"No." The admission hurt more than it should have.

"Did you know you could shift into a dragon?"

"No."

"Have you ever shifted at all?" She raised her eyes and began searching mine.

"Yes, into a raven," I answered, glad to say something other than 'no' or 'I don't know'.

"A raven?" Her eyebrows shot up. "As in, the *bird*?"

"Yes," I hedged. Why was she acting so strange?

"How long have you been able to shift for?" Her brown eyes still hadn't left mine.

"Since I was, I don't know, seventeen? Not too long after I transitioned."

She nodded.

"And your mother, did she ever shift?"

"No." My heart ached at the admission. According to Arithi and Chiara, my mother *could* shift. She was a Beacon. And yet she'd left me in the dark.

"All right, we'll move on to a more intrinsic line of questioning now. Just relax and it should be over quickly." She set down her notebook and with a motion of her hand, the lights in the room dimmed.

I could feel it then, the gentle prodding. It circled me and then caressed my skin—not in a comforting way like Aether's, but in a predatorial way. It was curious. It sent out tendrils, poking at my poor defenses. I tensed. Readying my wall, as pathetic as it was, to protect what I could.

"It's all right, Tatealia. Relax," Pegansha commanded.

I tried, but the wall I resurrected would not be dropped. It didn't matter though, with a force of her will, it crumbled, and I felt her poking within me. Searching. Even with her eyes closed, it felt like she saw too much.

Far *too* much.

She began digging, pulling at my magic until she found my string —the one I located when I wanted to shift. The one that led to a now murky pool, thanks to Vala.

Understanding dawned on me.

She continued to dive toward the pool, and I willed her away, but it didn't deter her, she followed the path getting precariously close to my internal power—my beast.

I threw walls up, but nothing worked. Nothing stopped her. Pathetic, I was pathetic, and I was angry.

"Use your rage," Aether had said.

I smiled as I used my anger to deter her, to draw her attention to another outlet of power, the one I'd been able to tap into when manipulating things and expressing energy. It worked, like a predator smelling blood, her inquiry turned and followed my new scent. It tugged at the wall I'd partially erected until she saw my power of manipulation. Her exploration stilled and sat there for a while, examining it like a rare jewel.

Then she began to explore again, this time in my head. No, I was done with that. My eyes snapped open, and I snarled. No one would prod through my memories.

I threw my energy against her and her prodding in my mind was ejected; she visibly rocked in her chair, eyes wide.

I heaved, breathing heavily. "It's impolite to go digging in people's minds."

My own words shocked even me.

"We're done here," she spoke as she stood and then exited the room without another word. Somehow, I knew I'd screwed up.

Later that day, I sat on Aether's deck. It overlooked the sea and was completely comforting. We were awaiting my assigned training class. Aether had been furious when he'd confirmed I'd have to go through the testing any new recruit or transfer would, regardless of age or experience—it seemed common sense to me, but the way Aether acted...

I wanted nothing more than to run back to Shae, to save her and kill President Collin Dale. But I had no idea how to control my power—

actually shifting into a dragon was foreign to me. How was I supposed to end an evil regime and defeat the embodiment of dark magic if I didn't even know who I was? Or if I couldn't access my magic effectively?

I shivered as the images of seethings raced through my mind.

I would end them, this I vowed to myself. I would save Shae. I just needed to get stronger and smarter first. I needed a team, perhaps Aether's team and a few more would be enough to challenge the Glenn, to tactically behead Collin Dale and destroy his research labs full of vile creatures.

I snarled inside even as the crashing waves calmed the rising tide of ire. So much needed to be done, and yet I sat here waiting. Best case, according to Aether, was that I'd get basic in training and magic source, while still allowed to go on tactical intel missions with him. Whatever that meant.

A seagull flew overhead and cawed. Children danced on the cliff's edge, playing tag, their laughter surrounding me. This was a place marked by peace. How odd was it that here, fierce warriors resided, and yet—children knew no harm. Joy abounded.

Aether stepped out onto the deck with two large pints of what I hoped was bloodwine, and handed me one.

I sipped it.

"The good stuff," I teased.

His eyes assessed me. Looking deep to my core. I could tell there was more he wanted to say, some things I still needed to accept, but right now I just wanted some light conversation. So instead, I asked, "Have children always been happy here?"

He looked surprised by the question. Eyes widening and then something like understanding settled in. I looked away; I was not going to be pitied openly.

"For nearly a century, this place has known laughter."

I smiled sadly. At least someplace in this realm was happy. "Why?" I couldn't stop myself from asking. "Why does any of this exist? Why hide?"

"I once asked myself the same thing. After the Great War, the Untishee were sought after, the Vamps wanted us as their warriors, mercenaries. But we are sworn to be impartial. To not fight for any side other than Mother Blood's and Mydant's. To uphold justice," he paused and looked out across the expanse of the sea. "The Vamps didn't understand and wouldn't accept this. It made us dangerous to them. If we weren't on their side, we were against them—or so they thought. Since we didn't align with them, we were hunted."

Like so much of life—power fears power. "How? Dragons are the fiercest warriors—vampires cannot withstand fire."

"Not all Untishee are dragons." His words sunk in along with a certain sadness. "They hunted the weak members, our camps used to be spread out throughout the lands, one in each kingdom. But they raided our villages and murdered the vulnerable. It didn't matter how old they were, they slaughtered those who couldn't shift and even managed to kill a few who could."

I sat there quietly as he explained the race's decline—the injustice that had occurred.

"In the end, most Untishee returned to Mydant."

There was that name again: Mydant, the elusive place of Fae. Perhaps not so mysterious.

"The few that remained are sworn to uphold Mother Blood's laws as impartially as we can," Aether continued. "And we've taken a foothold here in the cliffs. The chairs rule us now with oversight from Mydant. This place," he gestured to the city below, "this is the true Embassy. This is our secret, the home of the Untishee on Shappa."

This was all that remained of the Untish Tribe here on our planet? "So, the rest just left you here? Why didn't you all flee?"

"Some suggested we should, the royal line left to ensure the safety of Mydant from rumored attacks of the other Houses. And...also, because residing here made them even easier targets to enemies both at home and afar. But the rest of us stayed to protect our monarchs, our children, our origins. The Untish here are but a fraction of our members, most are home in Mydant."

"Mydant." There was so much I didn't know. So much I didn't understand.

"Our homeland."

Ours.

I took another sip and marveled at the way my body responded. For the first time since the Changing, I felt whole. I didn't feel out of control or overheating, I felt stable. Even my mood had seemed to finally find steady ground.

"What's in this bloodwine?" It tasted different, powerful somehow.

"Are you asking if it's my own blood?" He gave me a mischievous look as he sipped from his glass.

I rolled my eyes at the male with a good memory and a penchant for teasing.

"There's an herb in it. It heightens magical properties and the Luna Tribe endues it with additional magic so that any blood source is as fulfilling as that of Untish blood. Our lands here—" again, he gestured to the sea and the village, the rolling green hills beyond, "—are rich with magic. But even so, we are part vampire and so, you know, we need blood." He winked at me.

Part vampire? My jaw dropped and Aether smirked as he stood staring, hands bracing the railing.

Smart-ass.

His grip tightened on the rail, but still, I felt no connection to him, no tightening of the air around me, nothing intimate beyond his mere presence.

"I don't understand this idea of mixed origins. Fae and vampire?" The words just tumbled out of my confused being.

"Some who have never left Mydant don't understand it either. Some hold to the idea of a *pure* bloodline, of being superior for holding only *one* blood type. The royal line is one of the most heavily manipulated and so it's frequently contested, especially by those with prejudice." He paused, eyes becoming distant. "Untishee weren't always in power, we are a mixed breed. We originated from *solely* Fae. But then, that was back before my time, long before the Great War. I've only ever known the Untish Tribe as it is now, composed of shifters: part vampire, part Fae, and part human."

My head was spinning. But one thought was jarring. "Wait, how old are you?"

His eyebrows shot up and his mouth opened to answer, "I—"

A knock sounded from the exterior door. Aether waved at the air and a shimmer pulsed before a figure emerged: Anna.

"I have a missive from his lordship, Night Chair Enzo." She extended a sealed scroll.

Aether thanked her and took it. She, to my chagrin, stayed by the door—eyes drinking in Aether. His dark hair, tied at the nape of his neck with a light leather strap. His black tunic, tapered at his waist, accentuating how wide his shoulders were. His strong jaw, now slightly shadowed with stubble. Every ounce of him was purely male, and from the look in Anna's eyes, she thought so too. I didn't miss the way they darkened as they followed his shapes, his cut forearms, and every appealing ounce of him. The scar that cut through his right eyebrow and jutted down his cheekbone before ending in a jagged cut only increased his *it* factor. His formed legs sprouting from sturdy hips supported the swelling of his well-endowed...

Don't stop yourself, darling. Finish the thought. Better yet, perhaps I should show you how well-endowed I am.

Pink spread across my face.

I was going to say feet.

He snorted and Anna shifted uncomfortably, even if she couldn't *hear* what we were saying, she was visibly uncomfortable. Perhaps she thought Aether's snort was directed at her.

"This is unacceptable. Tell my uncle I want an audience," he spoke to Anna before jotting a response on the back of the scroll and sealing it with a dark band of energy. He extended it to her, a clear order.

She nodded and then left, perturbed nervousness written on her features. Aether watched her go and then stalked inside and strapped his sword across his back before adding several sheathed daggers to his body.

"What's wrong?"

"Nothing I can't fix."

That wasn't going to work. I stopped his hand from grabbing the next dagger, his eyes snapped to mine. Heat sparked between us from the contact.

"Aether, what's wrong?"

CHAPTER 12
AETHER

Her touch would be my undoing.

Well-endowed feet? She would never stop surprising me. Everything about her was engulfing me, swallowing me whole. Fuck, her mere presence dominated all of my senses. I should've spent these past few hours preparing her. Explaining things, explaining us...

I shook my head as her grip on my hand, tender yet firm, remained. She was *willingly* touching me. Suddenly the stakes were too high. What if she rejected the bond? Or didn't feel it? She seemed to dislike our internal communication, what if that wasn't just posturing?

The possibilities loomed in front of me. I wanted to force them from my mind. She would want me, in fact, I think part of her already did. The signals she'd given me were proof enough, and that time in the room...

"Aether?" Her mahogany eyes latched on mine, pleading.

Fuck. If she didn't want me, I would respect it, but it would kill me. I would be dead without her. In a matter of days, she'd become my undoing. There wasn't anything I wouldn't do for those eyes.

"I have to go see my uncle, there's been a misunderstanding." A hell of one. Like hell I'd leave her here and go on a mission—tonight. Not happening. Especially when his message made it clear that the evaluation was not a good one. Tate's *allegiance* was being questioned. It didn't make any sense.

"Aether, I'm not some fragile girl to be tossed to the side. Tell me the truth. What. Is. Wrong?"

Her will was iron-strong. One of the things I loved about her. But this? How could I tell her that after dragging her across the world, after all her sacrifices and losing the people closest to her, that our chairs doubted her priorities—her loyalty? And worse, they didn't trust me. They wanted me back in the field, away from her and the power they possessed. I thought I'd hidden our bond well enough, but I hadn't. They detected it somehow. If not the bond, then something else. It was not normal to be sent out this quickly.

"Hell is going to be raised; I'll explain when I get back. Just stay here, answer to no one. Not even Vala and Jared. Tate—" I ran my thumb across her cheek, "—trust no one."

Concern laced her eyes as she wrapped her arms around herself.

"It's warded, I'll just activate it when I leave. You'll be safe."

I moved toward the door, but her hand snagged my bicep. "Safe from what?"

"Shitheads."

I stormed out, leaving my bonded, my world, in the room, steaming. It wasn't lost on me that her eyes flared, hands on hips, while her nose began to lift in a snarl. She was a force to be reckoned with. A force I would gladly fight for.

FIFTEEN MINUTES later I stormed into Enzo's office, door splintering from the force I exerted.

"Now, Aether hold—"

But his old voice died out as the air around him choked his words, lifted him up, and held him suspended a foot above the ground. Members stormed in, my men, comrades looking at me like I'd lost my mind. I was attacking our leader—the one we were sworn to serve and obey. They paused only a moment before raising their guns.

"Release him," Juda commanded. She was equal to me in rank, a high general, but usually the level-headed one. Even with black-tipped blonde hair braided and coiled around her head in precision, even with her assault rifle pointed at my heart and eyes full of promised violence, I ignored her.

"He has some answering to do," I bit out as my uncle gasped, hands clawing at the air and blood seeping from his lips.

"Aether, drop him. Now," Juda lowered her voice. There would be no further warnings, it didn't matter.

I threw out my hand and the guns followed, aiming mid-air. I pushed and they were ripped from their grasp, clattering to the floor. They tried to advance, but with one thought, they were suspended, frozen mid-step.

"Why the fuck is Tate under *review*?" I growled. "You are sworn to protect yours. You claimed her with the chairs. How the fuck are you now questioning her?" I released the air and he crumpled to the desk, spurting blood out of his mouth and spitting it on a handkerchief.

"Leave us," he commanded the members. They gaped at him. "Now!" he shouted.

Rare for him given that he was normally composed.

I released them and they filed out, collecting their weapons on their way. Juda eyed me and glared in warning before departing.

"What the actual—"

"Please, allow me to explain." His power silenced my words. There was a reason he was still our leader. My power rivaled, hell it even surpassed his, but he was seasoned. When he wasn't suffering from one of his bouts, he was a fierce warrior. I inhaled, willing the thumping in my veins to quiet, the pounding in my ears to still.

"Tatealia Aaralyn isn't really a member of the Shadow Tribe, is she?" His question was what I had thought—they didn't believe us. He didn't believe me. "Don't bother lying, I had my suspicions when I first saw her. And now...now I sense it in you. One of the perks of being the head of this shit-show." He reached into his desk and pulled out a bottle—aged blood scotch. It stopped being made just after the Great War. For him to be enjoying that now...

"She's my bonded," I said the most dangerous sentence I could utter here. But, if he accepted it, he would be duty-bound to protect her—to accept her. Furthermore, if he confirmed what I suspected of her heritage, he'd be sworn to her.

He stopped mid-pour, his gaze slowly lifted to meet mine. "How? After Cher..." his voice trailed off. Cher's loss, while seventy-five years ago, still stung. They were...close.

"I don't know, but she is everything I am and more. She is my missing half. My magic knows hers. Search me." I knelt before him and withdrew a dagger, slicing my hand. While Luna members could easily search magic, the Shadow Tribe needed a blood connection.

I extended the blade to him and waited.

His black eyes deepened. One moment, two, three.

"Very well." He grabbed the blade and slit his own palm.

Our hands met in the middle, and he pulled. It felt like my magic was being pried from my very being, dissected, and investigated. It was the most violating thing a Untishee could experience, and I openly surrendered myself to it. Crude were the ways of the Shadow Tribe, but once he saw the truth, he would be bound to act honorably.

That or I would kill him, grab Tate, and run.

I hissed as he increased the pull. I could feel the bits of Tate's magic, the shards that were already intertwined with my own, being inspected. He pulled at those further and the slight displacement was agony—like she was being taken from me. I gasped as he turned those pieces of Tate over, around, and then looked deeper.

A moment later the pain ended. He withdrew his hand, his tan weathered face now pale. "Mother Blood." He moved from behind his desk and knelt in front of me. "Does she know?"

I stood, looking down at him. "No."

His eyes widened. "You mustn't tell Arithi. In fact, we need to get

Tatealia to Mydant. If anyone learns of her bloodline *and* her bond...the prophecy."

"The prophecy?" I laughed. "I know you're old, uncle, but senile?"

"Aether, you cannot pretend that it doesn't exist. This all lines up exactly as it's been foretold."

"This is nothing like that. Even *if* the prophecy wasn't absurd hocus-pocus designed to support the simple-minded—"

"*Survived from annihilation. From the blood of forgotten royalty, bonded with that of darkness. Concealed until ready, exposed by the highest death—*"

"STOP!" I commanded. "That gibberish means nothing. *Nothing.* Even if it did, Tate's bloodline is faint and not nearly strong enough for her to be the foretold *heir*."

Enzo just looked at me, appraising. "What then is your plan?"

"As you said, we need to get her to Mydant. She's not secure here, not if her actual tribe is discovered by the self-serving and disloyal— the ones who crave power—the ones hiding among us who likely had a hand in what happened to the *last* royals here." I exhaled. I'd been holding my breath for several moments. "Could we receive the Six Blessed to cross over?"

That was the problem I'd been mulling over in my head. In order to secure Mydant's borders, no one was allowed to cross over except for once a year during the new moon celebration or by containing a drop of power from all six chairs, the Six Blessed's power. Arithi would never allow it—not without looking closely at Tate and examining her blood. That was a risk we couldn't take.

But...this year was different. The king of Mydant was ill, nearly dead. This meant we would be welcome to return for the funeral and coronation of the new Crown.

"We will wait. Tell no one, my boy. When the time is right, when his majesty passes, we will sneak her in with us for the upcoming coronation. You will need to prepare her; she may need to challenge," Enzo spoke, reverence in his words.

I wanted to deny his claim about the challenge, that wouldn't be happening, but first things first.

"Thank blood you see it this way, uncle. But I will need your oath. Swear your fealty to Tate, to protect her and her inheritance." My dagger was inches from my hand, a flick of my wrist and he would be dead. I would surpass him, most likely duel Juda, but I would win. I was the most powerful and next in line for the chair.

My uncle gripped my extended palm once more and placed it in his. "I swear upon my blood, my magic, and my life that I will serve Tatealia Aaralyn and her interests. To protect and serve."

"To protect and serve or your head *will* roll."

Our hands separated. The oath sinking its claws into Enzo as a black haze of power, fire, and energy blanketed his being.

I breathed. I'd done it, secured a chair's loyalty. This was good. Better than I'd hoped.

"I need you to get Tate assigned to Vala for magic manifestation, the best classes for advanced learners regardless of her evaluation— just the bare bones so she can pass the entrance exam—and I need her to be given leave or sent on harmless maneuvers so I can train her away from prying eyes."

He nodded, still ashen and speechless, still on his knees.

"She will reside with me, in my home. She has no family here—no home of her own."

"Yes, yes. That would be wisest. I'll issue the order," Enzo spoke, voice growing wearier with each word.

"And...I need you to revoke my most recent assignment."

"The housing issue is easy enough, transfer cadets with no local family often reside with generals until they've become active members, safer for the entire Embassy that way. But revoking *your* assignments? That will be hard and—"

"Delay it then," I snapped.

"As you wish." He bowed and then stood.

I turned and left the office, bumping Juda on the way out. "You have a lot of nerve, I should—"

But her words were cut off as I sliced the air from her lungs for a moment. She dropped to her knees, face turning red and purple. I passed through the hall and then released her; she crumpled to the floor, greedily inhaling air.

Only one thought drove me: Tate.

She needed to know we didn't have long, and yet, could I just dump *all* this on her? If she needed more time, I would find it. Somehow, I would find it. Fuck, I hoped Mother Blood smiled on me and that Tate was ready for the truth.

CHAPTER 13

CHANCE

Shae was still unconscious. Her leg had been removed from the cast and was now wrapped in several strips of gauze. The last time the medic came in and changed her bandages I caught a glimpse of her leg—it was purple and grey. Unnatural.

Bruised, I told myself.

"How long have you been in here?" Holland voiced from the doorway.

"Not long. I woke up in a bed like this an hour ago." The words felt dry coming from my mouth. I was still shocked I wasn't locked up somewhere. It was as if my father wanted to test fate or Mother Blood herself. "I'm glad to see you're doing okay, Holland." I wouldn't look at her. I didn't want to see the mark.

"Dale, things are..."

There were no words for how fucked things were.

"My father was behind it. You were right, all along." The admission hurt the first time, and repeating it only further agitated the wound. We'd fought about this so much last week and yet, she'd been right. My father was a monster and a traitor to his country.

"I know." She placed her delicate hands on my shoulders.

I shook from her touch, a touch that was almost lost. "I'm sorry. So sorry, Holland, it's my...I should have..."

Nothing I said would make a difference.

"Dale." She lifted my chin to meet her honey-brown eyes. "The doctor said it was a minor seizure, I'll be fine."

Minor seizure? I looked above her head and stared. The mark was gone. The diamond and black lines weren't there. Had I imagined it?

I traced the place where the diamond had been with my thumb, soft unharmed skin met my touch. Her eyes sharpened and then filled with concern. She reached up and cupped my hand in hers before bringing it down to her cheek. "Feel this?"

I did. I felt the warmth of her flesh, saw the pink tint to her otherwise tan skin. She moved my hand further down, so it rested on her chest. "And this?"

I swallowed. Beneath the lush swell of her breast, I could feel her heart. Pounding. Alive. Gloriously reassuring, beating against all odds. Holland. My Holland.

"I'm so sorry—"

My voice broke as tears, of all things, began to run down my face. I crumpled into her lap, not caring that I was weak. She stroked my back in reassuring circles.

"This isn't your fault," she said softly.

Wasn't it though? I was the spawn of the devil—of the male who *created* those things, who made *me* an abomination. Our leader violated his own laws and the result cost men, my guaramen, their lives. It cost Shae far too much and Holland...

Weeping overtook my body. What the fuck was wrong with me? I huffed mid-wail. The answer to my question was easy: there was so, so much inherently wrong with me.

"Dale." Holland shook my shoulder gently at first, then firmer. "This isn't on you, you know this. We will find a way to stop this, to make it right."

Her words barely registered. I should be clinging to them, declaring them myself, vowing vengeance. Instead? Instead, I cried. Pathetic.

She lifted my chin and met my eyes. I swiped at my nose and cleared some of the tears running down my cheeks. Her eyes shimmered, shined, and held back their own tears. Dammit, now I made her cry.

"Holland, I—"

Her lips silenced me. She kissed me, full of promise and life. She was alive. I rocked back into my chair, and she climbed on my lap, not letting go of my face with her soft hands, my lips with her moist ones.

I savored the flavor of her. Desired more. More life, deeper kisses, things of the living. I wrapped my hands around her hips and squeezed. She moaned in my mouth before deepening the kiss, sweeping in with her tongue, and gliding over my teeth; my very essence became coated with her own.

I was a fool to not want her before. A coward for fearing commitment. Insatiability fueled me—I reached up and tilted her head back before kissing my way down her chin, her neck, until I found her clavicle. There I hovered in silent question. It was forbidden, but what the fuck did that mean anymore?

"Dale," she whispered before nodding and digging her hands into my shoulders.

Permission granted.

I sank my fangs into her delicate flesh, piercing and claiming her in a way that was far more than just sex.

The moment her blood hit my tongue I lost control. We were standing, she was pressed against the wall, legs wrapped around my waist. I pulled again and her blood became a symphony that captured every sense. There was only her.

Cherry, honey, passion, promise...

The music of my soul met hers, note for note.

We were on the ground, my shirt off, along with hers. All of our clothes lay on the floor, and her golden-brown hair was loosened from its tiny pony, falling across her shoulders. She leaned forward reaching for my neck.

Hell yeah.

I adjusted for her, and she pierced my flesh with her fangs. Pain, hot and sharp, jolted through me before she pulled, and her venom took over. I was swept away in every flavor that was purely Holland. My world was Holland. My breath, my blood, my very life belonged to her.

No one else.

I was aware but...not. I looked down and saw our bodies intertwined, simultaneously pulling, connecting, draining, sharing. It was the most intimate act and it felt wholly right. Holy.

I felt her soul in mine, flowing through me; I could see her eyes, the pure joy, the lust, the longing. More. We needed more.

I removed my fangs from her and surrendered myself to her entirely. I was on my back, she was straddling me, then I was in her. Thrusting. I was completely hers.

I heard her breaths, pants, and moans. I saw only her—her eyes, her hair, her gorgeous nude skin. I could taste her on my lips, my tongue, and my mind.

I knew her.

Her body writhed atop mine as her fangs held their purchase at my neck.

Her core tensed around mine as she moved up and down. The friction was everything, too much and still not enough. I thrusted again, moving with her, giving her all of me.

She tilted my head back and I complied. She wanted more and fuck me if I didn't give it to her. I drove harder, flexing as I did so, filling her fully. She tensed, and power shot through me as I seized, allowing myself the glory of my climax.

Red danced across my vision, I was vaguely aware of it, but my senses were solely on Holland.

She pulled her fangs out and savagely claimed my lips. Our bodies were entangled, breaths heavy, until she pulled back and rested her head atop my chest.

I saw it then.

The purple diamond, the black streaks...but still more concerning, both our bodies were covered in red static, bolts of power, and yet neither of us was harmed.

Her golden eyes locked on mine, and pure wonder shown. We were one.

CHAPTER 14
TATE

I'd been sitting alone, for hours. Aether left me here—without an explanation, he just stormed off ready to kill. The look on his face as he gathered his blades promised violence and...he just, left.

I'd helped myself to more of the *good* stuff while he was gone and there was quite the possibility that I was a bit...inebriated. I swayed as I walked back to the large room at the end of the hall—Aether's bedroom. Before, I had hesitated. I didn't want to intrude. Now it didn't seem like such a violation.

I pressed open the heavy oak door and stepped into what was indeed the grandest bedroom I'd ever seen. While his estate was minimalistic, humble even, this room boasted success and wealth. The large four-poster bed was made of a dark wood that complimented the black, silk comforter. Cream fur pillows decorated the bed and were thrown about the room as lush, soft red blankets were folded on a deeply cushioned chaise that was positioned so it could perfectly see the patio beyond and the fireplace. A fireplace that was alive with dark flames.

I strolled through the massive room to its private patio, nearly tripping on a step I didn't see, and winced as wine sloshed across the white stone floor. Oops.

I continued to saunter forward, using the frame as a handrail, until I was out on the glorious balcony. It was even more impressive—if that were possible. While the other deck opened out to the city and the sea, this faced *only* the sea. It wasn't lost on me that this balcony was the largest one I'd ever witnessed. It was at least a hundred yards out, overhanging the sea. I hadn't realized his home was built on a cliff. The shape and emptiness of the balcony could only be for one thing... shifting.

A shiver, not my own, danced across my back.

"Look what the cat dragged i-n-n-n," I teased, clearly intoxicated.

Amusement.

"What? You find this funny?" I said, only to be met with silence. Had I imagined his presence?

I turned around and there he stood, the dark angel, leaning against the doorpost, drinking me in with his hooded eyes. I raised a brow.

Are you suddenly too shy to speak to me? I questioned.

He remained unnervingly silent. I took a step, albeit wavering, toward him. "Care to tell me why you stormed out of here?"

He smirked. *Care to tell me how much you've had?*

None of your business, I shot back.

"Tate, things are...complicated. And there is much we need to discuss, but first, let's sober you up." He disappeared inside the house only to reappear with twin pints of what suspiciously looked like *only* blood.

"Darling," he said as he extended one to me.

I raised a brow. I still wasn't sure what to think of his new pet name for me. Even so, I dropped the empty bottle, not blinking when it clanged against the stone and shattered before I grabbed the mug he extended.

It was warm.

"I heated it for you. We don't live feed here at the Embassy, but we still like it served as if fresh." He smiled crookedly, the left side of his lips lifted, and the sight of it sent shivers down my spine as pure need heated within.

"What things do we need to discuss?" I asked, perhaps the lapse in sobriety brought out the courage that had been hiding. I could feel the pool within begin to glow, slowly breaking free of the haze, begging me to look at it and recognize what I was. Still...

I wasn't ready. I focused instead on what was in front of me: a handsomely built, magnificent male.

"We do, but first let's have a brief history lesson while you eat." He gave a pointed look at the mug.

Fine. I took another sip, unable to hide the delight as my senses sparked alive. This blood *was* good.

Well, it's either good or you're just very easy to please at the moment.

We could find out.

Trust me, I'd love to but not this way.

What's that supposed to mean?

I swallowed the blood with a sudden lack of interest as a renewed annoyance claimed me.

He cleared his throat. "How do marriages work in the Glenn?"

I choked on the blood.

"What?"

"I mean, are they arranged by the council or is it a free-for-all?"

I wasn't sure I understood what he was asking.

"We marry who we like," I said trying to hide the tone that insinuated his question was stupid, or at the very least, odd.

"Right, okay. That's what I thought. Things here are...different," he supplied, averting his gaze. "Here we marry those we match *well* with."

My irritation was suddenly far less interesting and the blood was very sobering. I could feel my senses beginning to hammer back into my skull. "A match?"

"Yes, our strengths and gifts can complement one another. They can, in fact, heighten existing powers. It's the mixing of magic, of souls."

I shook my head, the pounding increasing. The mixing of souls? I tipped the mug all the way back and finished the blood, suddenly acutely aware of my previous behavior...of *where* I was.

"The blood was doused with a hangover cure. It clears any inebriation from alcohol and will fix the headache in just a moment," he said, still obviously reading my mind.

"How do you do it? Know what I'm thinking?" The question had been burning on my tongue since he'd first answered one of my internal questions.

"I told you. You practically scream your thoughts at me." He set his empty cup next to mine.

"I do not," I challenged. The pounding subsided as a tightening at my shoulders and waist helped ease the tension that was building in my head. "And how do you do that? Comfort me as if you are touching me but...not?"

"There's much to explain, and I will with time, I promise. But for now, the short answer is that it's one of my giftings, my magic. My power is to manipulate and control matter within my magic's grasp if not my physical. Magic, in many ways, is its own entity, Tate."

My name on his lips elicited things from me I'd never admit. I cut him a glare before he responded to that thought. He bit back a smile.

"So, you were talking about marriage customs. Things are barbaric here and you can't pick your own spouse?" The thought was upsetting. I didn't like the idea of anyone being forced to—

Never forced. I'd never allow that to happen to you.

I looked at him then, truly looked. His hand was bandaged, the blood seeping through was in a straight line indicating a recent cut. The rest of him looked just as he had when he'd left. Well, except for the small smear of blood on his forehead near the scar that jutted across the right side of his face. A scar that didn't diminish his looks but enhanced them. The black scaled vest he wore covered his tunic and matched his black linen pants. Combat boots graced his feet. He was fit, unnervingly so, and undoubtedly lethal as hell. I'd seen him in battle, but I'd yet to see what *else* he was capable of...

He groaned in my head and I could see him adjusting to cover his enlarging cock.

"Teach me to shield my thoughts," I interrupted him. This mind-reading needed to end, it made me feel vulnerable.

"Of course, you just have to picture a mental wall—bricks or stone, that's my preference, and then you *will* the magic to enforce it." He made it sound so simple.

I tried, but how do you will magic? "I can't."

"With time you'll be able to. It just takes practice, and we can work on it. As you understand more about your nature, you'll master things like shields." He took a step toward the railing and then leaned on it with his arms, releasing a long sigh.

Patience.

I felt the word he sent out, knowingly or not, and noted the tightness in his chest, the way he seemed to be physically restraining himself. "What is it you were getting at? The marriage customs created by alpha-males intended to control wee damsels?"

He looked to me then, eyes full of emotion—my attempt at humor had failed. Was that fear swallowing his irises?

You can trust me, Aether.

The need to comfort him was nearly too much. With a mere thought, the air around him tightened and his eyes widened. I smiled. I could do it too!

Delight swelled in my chest.

"It's just that...I need you to understand I don't expect anything from you, Tate, and I won't enforce it unless it is also your wish."

I could sense the energy in the air shift, nervously moving. A breeze blew some strands into his face as a wrinkle appeared between his brows.

This male who had protected me, with power so unlike anything I'd ever witnessed or seen, was scared? This high general who seemed to know things I didn't even know about myself, was anxious?

Aether who had come out here talking about marriage—

I locked eyes with him. For a moment, I wanted to run—move

backward, flee. But then I breathed, and the air was sweet. Full of his ash and salty musk. I felt a spark within and then my arms began to glow along with a pink halo that filled my vision—the internal pool burned brightly with a rosy fire and that beast, my beast, reached out and roared.

I could feel it then. The energy connecting us.

I sensed Aether's dragon roaring in response and felt his black flames intertwining with my rose gold ones, even inside me. Dark flames danced across his arms and surrounded him. We were in a cloud of his making, a cloud of dark energy—like that of shadows—and it concealed us, surrounded us, protected us.

Without thinking, I released my own power, and a pink aura enveloped us.

A gentle caress at my mind moved slowly, asking and waiting. Aether's eyes deepened as he gulped. I could see the golden swirls in his dark eyes, feel his power in the very air I breathed, but also within my soul. It was as if my magic was connected to his, but more than that, it was like we *shared* the same source of power.

My eyes widened.

"It's the mixing of magic, of souls," Aether's words played through my mind.

This was what he'd been wanting to discuss. This is why I'd felt so in tune with him, drawn to him.

"We're matched," I whispered the words.

The wind whipped around us, power in every gust.

"More than that," he said. "We're bonded."

CHAPTER 15

AETHER

I stood there. Enveloped in our enmeshed power, blending and dancing with one another, my inner dragon begging to be freed. The desire to claim nearly became unbearable, but I contained it. I didn't move. I stood stoic as I watched her.

She knew.

I always suspected on some level she understood, but now she undoubtedly knew. There was still much to explain to her and understandably, the concept of bonding was foreign to her, but still, she didn't run. I sensed the emotion, the fear, and prepared to throw myself off the cliff if she ran—if only to stop myself from chasing after her.

But she stayed. She *looked.* And now, she stood.

She was a goddess of pink and gold in a cloud of my black flames. She didn't look afraid, if anything she looked curious.

I shoved the thought back. I wouldn't force this on her. "I meant what I said before: you have a choice." Even if that meant her saying no. Even if that meant I'd live every day with an unquenchable thirst and desire for her. "Always a choice."

"How? If our magic is…shared, there is no choice," her words were quiet, and each one stung.

She felt trapped. Fuck.

I commanded the cloud to drop, the energy to dissipate. The sherbet, pink-orange sun poured down on us, and the balcony became a pink wash once again. Tate's own power sputtered out and she stood there, skin returning to its normal nude hue.

"There's always a choice. Even if our magic recognizes one another, even if we share it, you are free. I promise you this, Tate, you don't have to accept this bond. Just say the word, and I'll leave you and still ensure your protection." My hands shook with the energy of self-control. I wanted to dominate, to claim, to follow my natural instincts that had heightened since she recognized the bond—it was now awake, and alive. The pull tripling in force.

"Can I think about it?" she asked.

I closed my eyes, just for a moment. I could do this. Fuck, I would do this. She was all that mattered, if she needed time, I'd give it to her. "Of course."

"I am painfully aware that I lack knowledge about pretty much every damn thing concerning magic…" She bit her lip. "Can you teach me?"

I sensed it then, the uncertainty in her eyes. She reached out for me and then dropped her hand, visibly shaking for a moment.

"Yes," the word was husky. I needed to expend some energy in a safe space, to cool down before I broke my promise to her. "But we need to talk about a few things, beginning with what life looks like in the upcoming weeks."

I could do this. I could be professional. The gentle sway of her hips as she turned to sit down made the swell of her ass too enticing.

"I'll be right back." I threw myself off the balcony and shifted. My beast free, I threw back my wings and pumped.

Air and space surrounded me.

I flew higher up into the clouds, ignoring the other fire-breathing serpents occupying the space, and roared, freeing the liquid flames that demanded to be released.

A**FTER A SWIFT FLIGHT** that lasted mere minutes, I landed back on the balcony and shifted. My head was now clear enough to have a serious conversation with the female who had so thoroughly wrecked me.

The patio was unoccupied, but even from outside, I could sense her. Even if she rejected the bond, it would still exist. Some things would always remain. I swallowed the isolating thought and began stalking for the door when I felt the triggering of my wards. I paused mid-step as I mentally reached out to feel the essence. James. He was here, requesting entry. In a way, his presence could be helpful. I allowed him through.

A moment later he appeared out of thin air, transported right to my balcony.

"So, what has you all hot and bothered?" he asked. His hair was, as always, annoyingly perfect—too perfect. I often thought it made him look pompous, but it was a point we never agreed on.

"Go swimming?" I teased, pointedly nodding to his sleeked-back hair, thick with gel.

"Have a good release?" he retorted, touching his locks—it was so crisp that it didn't even move when he tried combing his fingers through it.

"What do you want, James?"

I crossed my arms, not caring that even after releasing as much power as I did, my cock was still rock hard. And a pointed look from James confirmed he was all too aware. I snarled at him.

"Well, Jared filled me in on your trip," he paused taking a step forward. "And he seemed pretty tight-lipped about it. I'm assuming Tate ended up being more trouble?"

Maybe allowing him entry wasn't a good idea. I gritted my teeth and his eyes lit as he noticed the tension coiling at my shoulders. I let him in, I could just as easily force him out. "It was an eventful mission. Full of classified information."

"Where is she?" He began walking toward the door. I didn't hesitate before stopping him. He was suspended mid-stride, eyes flaring. He attempted to extend his blue magic to break through the bonds I'd placed on him, but I was stronger—thanks in part to the bond—but also the better warrior.

"She's inside. What do you want?"

"I was sent to assess the situation. I saw her classes and they want her tomorrow morning. It would appear that she's more advanced than either of us initially assessed..." He gave me a pointed look.

I just smiled, all teeth. Tate was a fast learner, she'd be fine. Like fuck I'd let her spend a year in a stuffy classroom where her every move would be evaluated. She may be at a disadvantage compared to the other Untishee here, but she was smart. She'd be fine. I'd make sure of it.

James cleared his throat. "I just wanted to check on you, brother."

We may be brothers in many ways, by trauma and war—and we may have fought alongside each other for decades—but Tate was my everything. One wrong word from him to the wrong person and Tate's life could hang in the balance.

"I'm fine. So is she." I stepped past him looking inside. No sign of her.

I sent out a feeler through the home, I could sense her presence— prickly and a little shaken, but there.

Nervous. Anticipation. Fear.

All normal emotions, but I didn't hate them any less. I wanted her to *desire* the bond. To want me. But I promised her a choice and I would uphold that oath.

"Aether, something is up, and if I didn't know better, I'd say she got under your skin." He stopped fighting my hold and just looked at me.

"Maybe she did. But it doesn't matter, she belongs to my tribe."

"I heard that she may not be placed in the Shadow Tribe..."

"From who?" I snapped. The air instantly sparking and the

restraints on James began tightening. Brother or not, I'd snap him in two if he came here to threaten or eliminate Tate.

"Arithi," he said.

My blood cooled.

"Why are you here, James?" My voice dropped a decimal.

"Because you backed out of a mission and Arithi wanted me to check on you, to observe Tate, and make sure *you* weren't being manipulated."

I paused. They thought Tate was a threat to me? A smile played at my lips. "I assure you, I'm well within my depths. I declined the mission; I need a break and my uncle needs me here. He's not well."

James nodded, deep in thought. "If something were off, you know you could trust me? 'Brothers 'til death,' remember?"

I remembered. The blood, the cries, the slaughter. He was my right-hand man; we fought together seamlessly. He was ruthless and capable. I didn't want him anywhere near Tate.

"Got it, but I need you to—"

"Aether?" Tate stood at the door, wide-eyed, taking in the sight. She had a blanket draped around her shoulders.

I smiled as her eyes dipped to my exposed cock and her cheeks flushed. A primal pride took over and I simply squared to face her fully, taking immense pleasure in the way her eyes still were locked on my lower sergeant.

"Tate, James was just leaving." I released some of the restraints on him so he could move, but not much.

"Was he?" She raised a brow, lifting her eyes to meet mine. I could see the inner war, the lust, embarrassment, and pride all dueling it out.

"Unfortunately, yes," James said, adjusting his collar. I released the hold on him completely, but we both knew I could restrain him again with half a thought. "I just wanted to welcome you here, Tate, and check on this one."

I didn't miss the way he drank her in, the way he seemed to be assessing her and noting her dark ends, the fire hiding in her unlit eyes.

"Thank you, James. I'll be in touch," I dismissed him. He understood and with a bow, he turned and then vanished. I reinforced the wards, adding a bit more strength than necessary.

Tate just stood there, suddenly shy. Was she more comfortable when we weren't alone? The thought was disconcerting. Perhaps it was due to my nudeness, the Glenn did seem more reserved when it came to bare skin.

"So..." she hedged, taking a step forward and unwrapping the blanket before holding it out, eyes turning toward the sea beyond.

"So." I took a step forward and retrieved the blanket, forcing my legs to remain still as I wrapped the cloth around my waist.

A tendril reached out to me, curious, and then retracted.

Time, she simply needed time.

CHAPTER 16

CHANCE

"This way," my father spoke, cane tapping as he strode through the hallway.

I bit my cheek. I loathed every moment I wasn't with Holland. Still, I had reluctantly agreed to *more* testing. I'd maintained control since my last outburst—kept whatever new power I now possessed caged.

Shae still hadn't woken up. Holland sat with her every moment that we weren't together—always there to reassure me that Shae was doing better. Bullshit. Shae's color had only worsened, and her vitals were far too cool to be normal. Nothing about this was fucking normal.

President Dale opened a door and led me into an observation room —open to a cage below, a pit. In it, I could see several beasts, turning, pacing, waiting. They were the very definition of restless.

"What do you see, son?" President Dale asked.

"Evil."

"Still stubborn as ever." He snorted. "Watch and learn." He pressed a button on the control board in front of us and a door to the side of the pit opened. Blackness.

It was hard to see if he was letting them out or something in—everything was dark and laced in an unnatural fog. Until, in the darkness, I saw the figure that haunted my nightmares—the humanoid shape made of nothing but muscled layers. The controller from the field.

"Stop," I commanded. I wanted nothing to do with that unnatural beast—the purple man who suddenly scared me for entirely new reasons.

"No." Instead, my father pressed a button on the control panel, and a green light lit up the pit.

The figure looked up, sneering or smiling, I wasn't sure, and then stepped into the giant hole. The seethings froze the moment he approached. I expected them to charge or at least make a sound. But they were completely still.

The figure raised his hand and roared. The creatures, in turn, threw their heads back and roared before lining up in single file, on two feet. These were more evolved then. As one, they stopped and once again remained motionless.

"Let's make things interesting," President Dale said as he pushed yet another key on the pad. A new door opened and this time, a couple of figures stumbled out. They weren't creatures and they had no sign of dark magic. Instead, rags clung to their too-thin bodies as they fell into the pit, landing with sickening thuds and cracks—the sure snapping of bones.

The larger of the two bodies rose and growled at the seethings. His fangs were showing from his peeled-back lip. He was a vampire.

"Stop!" I commanded. "He's one of ours. He's a vampire, this must end now."

President Dale merely shrugged and then pressed another button. Green.

The monstrous thing inside pointed his hand at the vampires, one still holding his broken leg on the ground, and the other searching for a weapon, only to discover there was none.

I could feel it even from inside the control room—the pull from the controller. He was pulling at the energy around the two vampires, they screamed and I could *see* their energy being siphoned. The seethings stopped just short of the two vampires, who were now clutching their heads and bent over.

"Stop this, now!" I shouted, reaching for a button.

My father snagged my hand, stopping me from touching the control board. "No, you need to understand." His cool eyes hollowed out even as the silver in them neared a translucent hue.

"This is wrong," I bit out, yanking against his grip.

"It's science."

The screams from below stopped any further conversation. The vampires' bodies were now crumpling in on themselves, turning into... husks. Images of Lucas assaulted my memory. I looked to the male who sired me, the monster still gripping my hand, in shock and understanding. "You siphoned Lucas Metch's energy from him. His life force. That's what an enthrawment is."

"At last, you show promise," my father smiled as he spoke. "Enthrawment is a fancy word for harvesting one's magic, their energy."

"It's illegal unless authorized by the council, and even then, it shouldn't exist," I bit out.

My father laughed and threw my hand back so it collided with my gut. "Where do you think dark energy comes from? It's the stealing of another's energy." He tsked. "Really boy, after all you've seen, I'm disappointed you didn't decipher that on your own. Why do you think we forbade energy siphoning?"

I stood there speechless. Suddenly I understood the dark circles around my father's eyes—the purple veins starting to grow. Rusty's pallor and his darkened veins webbed across purplish skin. Both had been siphoning. Both were actively using dark magic. My stomach roiled.

"I told you, you *need* to learn," the male in front of me spat out before smiling a cruel, cold, and unnatural smile.

A sickening smack sounded, and I didn't need to look to know the controller had released the seethings; they were now feasting on leathered remains.

CHAPTER 17
TATE

The room was stuffy. I'd been sent here with the other Untishee trainees, cadets who were ready to test out and become active member Untishee. Here, I would earn my independence and hopefully grow strong enough to avenge my mother and Fletch. These lectures were supposed to educate me, sharpen my mind so I could do more than just pass a damned test. I needed to rapidly grow intellectually if I had any hope of outmaneuvering President Dale.

I shivered at the thought.

A student coughed next to me, cursing her parents for forcing her to test out this year. Clearly, I wasn't the only one unnerved by the upcoming exam. The test I'd have to pass was simple, at least it was according to Aether. It mostly consisted of history, a topic I sorely lacked knowledge of, magic manifestation, something foreign to me, and tactical maneuvers, something I'd still badly needed to practice. Piece of cake, *not*. I gritted my teeth.

I looked around the room, most were younger, around eighteen years old. Even with the almost three-year age difference, I was still young enough that I didn't stand out. There were several Untishee cadets in here who had rounded ears like mine, while others were slightly pointed, and a few were very pointed. Somehow, the variety felt like a beautiful mix.

I was grateful my physical appearance blended in, especially given that, compared to these *prepared* cadets, my knowledge made me an outsider. I knew nothing of magic or the Untish history. This was the third period of the day, and all the information was overwhelming. I didn't have a single answer. I shouldn't be surprised, I *was* new. All of this was. And yet, for some reason, Aether insisted I start here rather than the easier courses—a point I was both grateful for and simultaneously annoyed by.

Still…I needed to get back to the Glenn, I needed to save Shae. The faster I grew in my strength and magic, the sooner I'd be able to actually stop Collin Dale.

I bit my lower lip as old frustration returned. Why hadn't my mother prepared me better? Taught me the truth?

Professor Darsew adjusted his glasses before extending his laser pointer once again to the projection. "Next, we'll move on to review the recent biography I assigned last week pertaining to Perry and her part in the magic manifestation," he droned on. An article that, of course, I hadn't read. "Can anyone explain to me why she is considered the mother of the Untishee?"

Several hands shot up. An Ironhead male with red-tipped blond hair was called on to answer. "Because she was pure Fae and mated with a lowling." He smirked.

A what?

"Ut-uh, no racial slurs, Perseus," Professor Darsew corrected. "But yes, she was fully Fae and mated with a half-vampire and half-human. Can anyone tell me his name?"

Again, more hands shot up, almost everyone—well, except mine, naturally. A young female, a Darkling, with broad shoulders and solid black spiked hair responded, "Matias."

"Very good, Anitae. And can you tell me *why* this is important?"

"Because when the three bloods united, the unique Untishee gene was born," Anitae answered, beaming and sending a quick smirk at Perseus.

"Yes, and how is this so?"

"They fucked," Perseus spoke again, earning a glare from Professor Darsew.

"Perseus, I'll see you after class. But the correct answer is that they were bonded, had a daughter, and started our race. They became royalty, the rulers of the Untish. Can anyone tell me how this is, what expression of the Untishee that was born with the union of Perry and Matias?"

At this the whole class had hands raised, I was the only exclusion.

"Carly," Professor Darsew called.

"Shifters." She smiled. "We are dragons. Perry and Matias's daughter was the first-born natural shifter who could not only withstand fire but wield it...breathe it."

Carly sat right next to me. She was a Liver, member of the Livish Tribe. Her brown hair ended in green and was braided in twin braids. Freckles splattered across her small, heart-shaped face, and her pale skin looked practically translucent. Delicate and dainty if it weren't for her too big clothes, sloppy collar, and glasses that were thick-framed. The way she leaned in when Professor Darsew spoke and seemed genuinely interested, suggested she was highly intelligent.

"Yes, very good," Professor Darsew interrupted my thoughts. "And tell me, what was so unique about their bonding? What manifested for Perry herself?"

"She could also shift. This is why we consider her the mother of dragons." Carly beamed, her eyes sparkling at the thought.

"Indeed. Magic is sentient." Professor Darsew pulled off his glasses and swiped at the sweat beads forming on his balding forehead.

If magic was sentient, did that mean there was another force dictating my future, controlling me from the inside?

I swallowed back the annoying internal questions and instead fidgeted with my unmanicured nails, noting a few places where bright blue paint still remained.

Blood, fire, evil...

"All right class, please read the following articles I just sent to your individual disks for the next twenty minutes and then we shall be done for the day. I believe Coach Camella has a particularly grueling exercise outlined for you," he said. I didn't miss the way he seemed *pleased* by this.

My disk buzzed and I pulled it out of my pocket. Sure enough, three articles were there. The *History of Perry*, the *Three Camps of Untishee*, and *Gene Manipulation*. All of which were foreign to me. However, Perry's story caught my attention, so I figured I'd start there.

I pulled up the article and nearly dropped my jaw at how *long* it was. Two-hundred pages. Some of it had pictures, of course it had an index, but it was essentially a book. Not an article. If this was how all classes were here, I was *far* more ignorant than I'd suspected.

I flexed my hands before selecting the second chapter that focused on the love story between Perry and Matias. Perry was pretty—more than that, she was gorgeous. I could feel myself squirming just from looking at her. No one should be *that* beautiful. Her dark, red-tipped hair framed her face perfectly in loose, long curls. She was small—she didn't look more than a few inches over five feet. Her skin was sun-kissed and her large, dark eyes gleamed, even from the photo. But more than that, her eyes...they were mesmerizing. Were they dark brown? Or maybe they held a red hue? Mahogany?

Matias was next to her, while good looking, he lacked the pure allure Perry had. In fact, he was oddly plain. His white-blond hair was accented by golden eyes and a strong jaw. He was *attractive*. But standing next to Perry, he looked so very ordinary.

The father and mother of dragons?

I shook my head and found the text on the next page. Perry was twenty-one when she met Matias. They had, reputedly, fallen in love *after* she'd been bonded with another at a Matching Event in old Mydant. I didn't understand the terms 'old Mydant' or 'Matching Event', but what the text made clear was that they *loved one another*.

And it was forbidden. She was mated with another *full* Fae, not a half-breed. I shivered as I read the word: *Half-breed.*

It reminded me far too much of the Glenn's views of Fae, our races seemed to always categorize things in order to become superior. A bunch of pricks.

The story continued with Perry and Matias sneaking off and *bonding*, a word that greatly interested me, but it didn't explain *how* they bonded. I made a mental note to research that.

Black, gold-flecked eyes came to mind.

I pushed Aether's image back. Not now, I still wasn't ready to confront what he'd said about us being bonded.

Instead, I distracted myself with the text.

Perry bore a child, a girl, who had light brown hair and red eyes. Her hair, to my shock, was tipped in the brightest pink I'd ever seen. Under her photo read: *the mark of royalty. A crown of blush.*

I swallowed back the uneasiness I felt in my gut, even as my internal beast roared, full of life. I shoved her back as I glanced around the room.

The male to my left had bright yellow ends to his hair, pale at the top—a Beacon, member of the Beacon Tribe. The female just below me had green tips to her hair—a Liver, member of the Livish Tribe. The female next to her had blue endings to her white hair—a Blight, member of the Frost Tribe. She was one of the few blue-tipped heads I could spot in a sea vastly composed of red, black, and green—with the other tribal colors sprinkled throughout. But still, there were some with blue hair. Unlike my natural color. I kept searching but couldn't find *any* pink hair. None like the photo and none like mine before it was dyed.

I pulled at my hair, even in its loose pony at the back of my head, it reached around the front and cascaded down my chest. The bottom portion was solid black. I grabbed at a few strands and ran them between my fingers, the color on them *felt* wrong.

I was a fraud. If what Professor Darsew said was true, I was at least in part from the line of Perry—royalty.

I shook my head at the thought. Still too soon, still too much.

My gut turned as I began to connect the dots. I could feel *her* writhing inside, ready to claim. I shook my head, no not yet.

I focused instead on the story—I was, after all, a master avoider.

Perry's offspring grew and she became the ruler of the House of Blush, the Royal House of the Untish. Her child, Aimee, was the first 'natural born' dragon shifter recorded and together with Perry, they forced the other tribes into submission. None could face a dragon, let alone two. They didn't die of fire and had the lifespan of a pure Fae. Not to mention the *magic* of a pure Fae. And Aimee was the strongest of them all.

But how did they ensure the other Houses didn't just breed like Perry and Matias had and then challenge the throne?

I skimmed the pages, no answer. Instead, geological records went on for *dozens* of pages. I reopened the index and looked through the chapters. Chapter twenty-two was titled, 'Securing Power from the Other Houses'. Perhaps that would hold something.

I clicked on it and began reading.

A hundred years after Perry and Matias took control, they had rivals from other homes—namely the House of Iron, Perry's origin home. Odd that in Mydant, they were *House* of Iron, whereas here it was called the Iron *Tribe*. I filed that away to examine later.

The House of Iron challenged the throne in a duel, but purportedly, their dragon died quickly and under circumstances that were unclear. Scholars supposed it was the work of Mother Blood, but still others suspected a weapon had been crafted that impacted the Iron Dragon. And that was it.

No more wars? Peace for the past three thousand years?

I found that hard to believe, but the chapter ended and offered no more insight.

A gong sounded and the students all snapped their disks shut before stashing them in their pockets and filing out. We had thirty minutes until training, whatever the fuck that was.

According to Aether, I just needed a grasp of the basics to test out and join the active forces. That couldn't come soon enough. I'd much rather research this on my own than be the class idiot.

The sun was beating down and I could already feel myself sweating as I strolled outside. Even so, the heat was still nothing like before... when I went through the *Changing*.

"You coming?" a female asked. I looked up to see Carly standing at the entrance waiting for me. A smile curved her soft pink lips.

"Yes." I smiled in return and followed her out. Maybe I'd make a friend yet.

WE SAT under a tree and enjoyed the meal given us, a gallon of blood each, and a wedge of the *delicious* cheese in a paper bag. Not the most appetizing way of serving it, but it satisfied the hunger, especially the cheese. I still couldn't believe I hadn't ever tasted anything like it before. Carly had finished her blood, smears of it across her face as she rested her back against a tree.

"So...you're from a Vamp?"

Ah, so maybe she just wanted the details. I'd be curious too I supposed.

"Yes, the Glenn," I responded. I could feel the slightest tightening around me as my heart rate increased. Even from afar, Aether's presence was still comforting me. I allowed some of the tension to ease as the force surrounding me massaged certain aches and pressure points. I looked to my arm where I felt pressure. I couldn't see anything. Yet, I knew it was Aether—his magic somehow connected to my own.

"What was it like there?" Carly asked.

"Sad, little laughter, and lots of power-crazed people."

She frowned. "So, it's true then, the Vamps have abandoned the teachings of the Untish," Carly paused. "Some of the other...transfers," she said the word carefully, "have eluded to this, but they mostly avoid me, so I've never had the Vamp's disregard for our teachings confirmed."

"If you mean they don't give a shit about humans and think Fae are freaks and mostly extinct, then yes, they've abandoned the Untish ways." I was still trying to understand *what* the Untish ways were exactly. As far as I gathered, Fletch and my mother's teachings on morality were, in fact, very Untish. Which at least made understanding their ethics and way of life easier.

"You're pretty frank, you know that?" She wiped at her mouth, smearing the blood further.

"How so?"

"Most people here are playing a game, concealing and shit, but you just say it how it is. It's refreshing." Her nose wrinkled as she blinked through the sunshine.

"Thanks," I said, snorting at the thought. "So, the other transfers... they don't talk much?" I hadn't seen any, but then again, it's not like they'd have a 'I'm new here' sign on them. In fact, almost everyone in the lecture seemed keyed-in and highly educated, not a foreigner like me.

"Nope. Well, not to me. We've only had twelve other transfers this year and the most recent three were declared Ironheads. The one before was declared a Beacon."

She didn't say more, expecting me to understand what that meant. "They won't talk to you because you're in a different tribe?"

"I'm no one, and transfers..." She shrugged, searching for the right words. "You guys come in with both an advantage and disadvantage, but no matter how you slice it, transfers usually test out within a year, which means being intentional with who you spend time with. Every day here counts, connections count. And since most transfers reside with tribal generals, or at least start that way, they have no reason to speak to me." She smiled sadly, her blood-streaked skin wrinkled with the movement. "Which is why you're so refreshing."

I laughed quietly and dipped my head for a moment. She had a point; I needed every moment to count. Releasing my lip from my teeth I asked, "I'm new to a lot of this, can you explain *bonding* to me?"

Her eyes widened. "What's there to explain, don't you have that where you come from?"

I sighed. "No."

Her cheeks stained. "Sorry, this is er, a conversation that's *usually* had at a much younger age, in puberty, and it's not something I really talk about, but..." She paused and looked around; we were fairly secluded from the other lunching cadets. "What do you want to know?"

"How does the bonding work and what does it entail?" There. I'd asked it.

"Okay, well the bonding is our version of marriage, except it's bound in magic."

Right, magic here was the governing force. That wasn't so hard to understand.

"How?" At my question, her pink cheeks became even more flushed.

"Well...you know, you uh, *do it,* and your magic blends, fuses, and becomes one," her voice dropped to a whisper.

Ah, so that's why she was so squeamish. The intimacy. I looked at her and remembered she was several years younger, perhaps she'd never been with anyone before.

"Is there a structure to determining the bonds?" I diverged a bit from the physical, her complexion paling again implying she was more than happy to not go into the sexual explications.

"Usually, it's confirmed by the Tribe chairs during a Matching Ceremony. Historically, they would have a Matching Event and see what the magic did, and then, based on strengths and needs, they'd match and the two would, uh, bond," Carly finished, standing and brushing grass off her baggy green pants.

"Historically? So is that not how it's done anymore?"

"No, I mean it is. It's just usually we already *know* who we'll end up with. Like when we're born, our magic sparks, and the chairs will pair us, though not officially. When we turn sixteen, we have the Matching Event where our strengths are tested, and our magic freely flows. They see who it blends with and what the magic wants, and then you're matched." She pulled out a blood-apple from her bag and took several bites. The juices dripped down her cheek.

"So, that's all there is to the bond? At sixteen you're forced into it?" Sourness filled my mouth.

"No, you're matched not bonded," she said around the apple in her mouth. "But even at the event, not everyone is matched. Especially for the non-shifters."

"Okay," I hedged. "So matching is different than bonding?"

"Yup." She swallowed the apple chunk. "Then when we turn twenty-one, we go to a Matching Ceremony." She smiled sadly.

"A ceremony? And then you're bonded?"

"Well, sort of." Her cheeks once again brightened but she took another bite of the apple. "You are recognized as bonded by the Tribes and have a ceremony where your magic blends, but it doesn't become binding until the two uh, well, you know," she finished lamely, chomping on the fruit in her mouth.

It was all so official. If this was the case, then how were Aether and I bonded? Or were we just matched?

"Can bonding ever happen without a Matching Event or Ceremony?" I asked.

She opened her mouth to answer and then paused. "Not usually, but it *has* happened, like with Perry and Matias, there was no ceremony or event. In fact, Perry bonded to Matias *while* she was still with Egon." She huffed before tossing the apple core behind her shoulder, its red flesh bouncing against the vibrant green of the hill.

"So, she bonded without an event, but what do you mean about her being with Egon?"

"She was bonded to Egon, but it was arranged at a Matching Event," Carly said.

I blinked. I thought the bond was unbreakable. "How is that possible?"

"Don't really know. My mom said love is a stronger component than magic at times, that it is its own form of magic, and that it surpassed the bond she had with Egon. But really, except for them, I don't know of any couples that have bonded without going through the steps…but then again, I don't exactly research your specific questions. They're, uh, not things I commonly think about," she said winking at me. Her green eyes sparkled, she may be young, but I highly doubted she was ignorant.

I wanted to press further about the bond, but I didn't know what to say, so instead I asked, "Are you matched?"

She looked down and fidgeted with her hands. "Yes, at the event my magic found its equal."

She didn't seem too pleased about it. What type of culture promotes acceptance of all life forms and then forces arranged marriages?

"With whom?"

"Perseus."

CHAPTER 18

CHANCE

The medic removed the syringe from my flesh and then, after checking that all twenty of her vials were full, she moved to the IV poking in my forearm.

"Great, just one more additive, and then you're done," she spoke as she inserted some clear fluid into the IV line.

"And this will help him, yes?" Holland asked. She sat on the chair next to me, holding my left hand in hers. The steady beeping of Shae's machine became a constant, soothing sound. I insisted on having the draw and feeding occur in Shae's room. I wanted to be here when I wasn't required to be elsewhere...learning. I shook at the thought of dark magic and the evil my father had not only allowed but participated in.

"Time will tell. Doctor Worshah will have to see the results and will go from there," the medic responded. "There, I'll take the IV out now." She removed it and then left the room, carrying a tray full of blood samples that slid as she moved.

"Holland, if things progress further and I can't control it, I want you to kill me."

Her eyes snapped to mine. "Excuse me?"

"I won't be like him."

"Dale, you could never be like him. You have good in you and this new power *could* be a good thing. We know what we're up against. I saw that dragon too." It was the first time she mentioned that beast since the compound blew up.

"I won't become a monster."

She squeezed my hand. "I'm not afraid of you, Dale. You shouldn't be either."

She hadn't seen it. Didn't witness the dark magic being formed, the energy siphoning, the evil my father tested. Evil he wanted me to embody. It was clear he was attempting to groom me to become a controller. Not going to happen. Ever.

"Hey, look here," Holland said as she lifted my chin. "I see *you*."

I leaned over and gently pressed my lips against hers. Their softness was my home. She welcomed me and returned the kiss while wrapping her arms around my neck. I could feel my blood sparking, the power surfacing but not in a way that lacked control—in a way that was pure excitement.

"Fuck," I murmured against her lips.

"Oh, you think?" She nipped at me with her fangs and then adjusted so my back was pressed against the edge of Shae's bed. I could feel the sheets behind me pulling tight as Holland climbed on my lap and began stroking my neck while she kissed me.

Home. She was my home.

"I wouldn't object," I spoke into her mouth and then moved to kiss the lover's mark I'd given her. She moaned as my fangs grazed the now-healed puncture marks.

"Metamorphosis," Shae said, voice broken.

I jolted against Holland and stood upright, nearly dropping her. She ran a hand through her now tousled hair and blushed.

"Shae!" I dropped to my knees beside her. Her grey eyes were wide and, aside from a sickly pallor, she looked like herself. Her roots had grown out and you could see the dark brown fighting against the now faded blue.

"I knew you two would work it out." Shae smiled as she looked behind me. "But, uh, not in *here,* eh?" She winked at Holland who I could *feel* blushing further.

"How are you feeling?" I asked, grabbing her hand. It was cold, far too cold.

"Alive. Chance." Shae swallowed and took a moment before she spoke again. "Where's Tate?"

Hours had passed. Shae had fully awoken, the medics took samples and administered several medications, along with blood. Shae didn't flinch when they pricked her skin. Didn't think twice when they took more blood. Instead, she glared at me the entire time. We were in a fucking stalemate.

"She's one of us," Shae insisted for what must've been the hundredth time.

"She's the enemy. She flew off with that dragon." I strained to control my temper. Holland sat next to me, silent.

"She flew off in the *clutches* of a dragon. We don't know anything!" Shae shouted. "Bring me my disk, now!"

"No. You need to rest."

"No, I need to work. I was deciphering data before shit hit the fan, we hacked the base and had some footage and files I haven't even started to decrypt. I need my fucking disk! I could find Tate, you giant blockhead." Shae pounded the sheets with her fists. Even in her anger, her fatigue was clear.

"You need to rest. I'll check back later. They need to run more tests on me." I couldn't keep the snap out of my voice.

"You're better than this. Are you really going to betray Tate, again?"

"That *thing,* you know the one who threw you in the air, called Tate his maker. She left with a dragon. She has stores of magic stronger than I've ever seen. She isn't the person we knew."

"Get out of here," Shae snapped and looked away, intentionally ignoring me.

"Shae—"

"Go!" she shouted, her voice full of hurt.

"Dale, maybe we should just—"

"Shae, dammit. How can you be so blind? It's been under our noses all along. Evil. Pure evil growing, right beside us, closer than we ever knew, and we didn't see it. Didn't notice it. Never saw the signs and if we did, we never acknowledged them. She made us fools!" I stood and threw my hands behind my head. "She played us. Everything we believed was a lie. We've enmeshed ourselves with evil, slept with the enemy!" Red static shot out of my hand and hit the wall opposite me. It laced up and down before pooling on the worn, dirty floor.

Tate looked up at me from the ground, eyes full of terror. Blood poured from her mouth and nose. She whimpered as my bolts claimed her and bored into her, under her skin eating away at her flesh. She screamed—

Holland's hand on my shoulder brought me back. I was standing, bolts still pouring from my hands and hitting the wall opposite me. I closed my eyes and called the power back in.

"Who are you to talk?" Shae bit out.

I looked her in the eyes and immediately regretted it—all I saw was hate and fear.

I turned and stormed from the room, red bolts of power dancing across my forearm. I could hear Holland's quick steps from behind me, keeping up. Space, I needed space.

Anger began to bloom in my chest. I could feel the power swelling, commanding to be freed. I increased my pace and headed for—

Fuck, where could I go?

"Dale!" Holland called from behind, but I didn't slow. Not even through her panting, her footsteps now running trying to keep stride with my larger ones, did I adjust my pace. No, I wouldn't slow. Not as I felt the tidal wave of rage building.

I let my feet blindly lead the way until I ended up in the control room overlooking a pit of dozens of creatures. All on two feet. All prowling aimlessly around the large pit. The personnel in the room looked at me, shocked. Their clipboards in front of them were full of notes, they were cataloging data.

On the pit floor I could see the remains of several corpses...the tiny hand in the corner, disembodied and pale, drew horror from me. I didn't think then, I simply gave into the rage.

My body danced with power, electricity ripped from me and devoured the scientists in an instant—they were nothing but charred remains, twitching as my red lightning still webbed over the corpses. I threw several bolts at the glass window in front of me and it shattered. But I didn't stop there.

I jumped into the pit, and the beasts turned toward me, snapping —ready to fight. They didn't stand a chance.

"Dale!" Holland's voice was but a distant cry.

The power ate me—became me. I was nothing but pure energy. Nothing but anger.

Betrayed.

I ripped into the seethings nearest me with my lightning and savored the way they cried.

Evil.

Human or vampire. They were once holy, now they were a monstrosity.

I called my ire, a pure fire, to pour out of my core, and released it in waves of red lightning that streamed out from me, swallowing every remaining beast whole. I could feel it then. Their power. Their energy.

The magic within me acted on its own accord. It pulled and began siphoning. I could feel the essence of the seethings—they were no longer beasts, they were people. Humans, mostly, with a few vampires. Their magic, while tainted, was special—their flavor unique.

"Dale! This isn't who you are!" Holland's voice reached my ears.

Holland. My Holland.

I opened my eyes and saw the creatures all lying dead, my lightning still surrounded them and illuminated the entire room. But what was more disconcerting was the light, the aura drifting from them and funneling into me. My hands were outstretched, clawing at it and commanding it.

More.

No. I pulled the lightning back and shoved the magic down into my core. I was in control. The room became dark. Nothing moved.

"Dale," Holland whispered.

My chest was heaving. Even with the magic stuffed down, I could feel it—the dark magic now mingling with my own, growing. I was corrupt.

Clapping sounded from the control room above. "Excellent." My father stood there, a smile on his face. "This is excellent. You'll be the greatest controller yet."

Before I could think, I threw a bolt at him.

He was responsible for this madness.

My father blocked it with a shield I didn't even see until it was too late. The bastard directed it toward Holland. She shrieked as it was hurled at her.

Immediately, I pulled back, and willed it to dance over her and not touch her. But it didn't respond to my will. The power enveloped her, hiding her for a moment, before revealing Holland seizing on the floor.

Monster.

I ignored the voice in my head as I jumped up to the platform before clawing my way into the room. I dropped to her side and cradled her head as she shook.

"Medic!" I called out, my voice raspy.

Several stormed into the room and they placed her on a gurney before strapping her down and rushing her out. I turned to follow them, but my father's voice stopped me.

"I wouldn't," he said. "You did that son, you are dangerous. You need to learn control. I can help you; let me help."

Hate.

I lunged at him, red lacing up and down my arms. I impacted his shield and was thrown backwards. Before I could act, I felt it—the needle plunging into my neck. A small medic stood behind me, fear in his eyes. I stilled my reaction, and called back my internal power.

I still had good in me.

That thought comforted me as the drugs made my head swim and my limbs became paralyzed.

"Move him to Exam Room E," my father commanded. "We have work to do."

CHAPTER 19
TATE

I tried to quiet my anger.

Perseus. That's who Carly was matched with? Sweet and small Carly, who was so thin her clothes were baggy, was committed to that egotistical jackass? Him, out of all the trainees? Trainees, because as I learned from Perseus's sneers, while inside the classroom we were classified as 'cadets', but outside of it, we were classified as 'trainees'.

Any hope I'd had that perhaps I'd misjudged him fled over the course of this past hour. The assistant coach, Ellen, had us out here running for the past thirty minutes. Not only had Perseus lapped us all several times, but he taunted Carly and I when we stopped due to one of my side stitches. Carly glared at him, and he only managed to laugh harder before taking off again, lapping us once more. Cardio was *not* my thing.

Human-side of the veil, I could outrun most humans and barely break a sweat. But here? Amongst these warriors, I could hardly keep up.

We'd just made it back to the training dome when the head coach entered. She was small—much smaller than Ellen who was tall and lean, red hair gleaming in the sun. Coach Camella was short but well-built. She wore tight black shorts and a sports bra with nothing else. Her legs were huge and made of nothing but muscles, her arms the same. Tattoos of dragons scrolled down her left arm from her shoulder to her wrist with different symbols on her right arm. Seven of them. Her head was shaved on the sides and the remaining solid black hair was pulled up into a bun at the back of her head.

"What tribe is she in?" I asked Carly. I suspected the answer, but I wanted it confirmed.

"Shadow," she replied windily. We both were still bent over, attempting to catch our breaths. At least, in this, I wasn't alone.

"All right, now that you're warmed up, we're going to focus on fitness today and then maneuvers. Everyone, find your station," Camella commanded.

Without hesitation, all the trainees found an empty mat that had dumbbells and some sort of stick beside it. Other equipment also was placed in front of each mat. Perseus, naturally, chose the front. I found my spot next to Carly in the back...as far from Camella as possible. Even from so far back, I swore her blue eyes found me.

"I'll demonstrate the first set and then you will all copy," Camella spoke. She climbed up on a stage and strode over to her own setup. Within a moment she was doing several pushups before standing and doing a series of squats and then ending with burpees. This was going to hurt. "Now, your turn. And if I'm less than satisfied with your effort, I'll make it harder." She smiled, showing a tongue piercing that matched the one at her brow. "Begin."

Everyone dropped to do their pushups. I managed one and then collapsed. Carly made it to three before she too bellied out. I could sense Camella's focus. I forced myself up and tried again, I made it almost all the way up when my arms gave out and my belly caved.

"Pathetic." Camella was standing over me. "Again."

I tried, but the moment I was up she pushed me down with her foot. "Your form is wrong, watch and learn." She dropped into a pushup, directing my attention to how her butt was level with her back and her stomach wasn't dipping. "Do it again," she commanded.

I got in position.

"Lower your butt," she ordered. I complied. "Pull in your stomach, weakling." I tried and held it for a moment. "Good. Now dip." I dipped and...didn't come back up. Camella exhaled through her teeth. "You will meet me here every morning before lessons until you can properly do a pushup."

A snarky remark formed on my lips, but before I could respond she had already moved on, and was yelling at another trainee.

I lifted myself to begin my squats, noting that I was already behind. After the first ten, my legs were throbbing. She did thirty-five. I had twenty-five more to go.

I gritted my teeth and lowered myself into a seated squat and then rose again. Sweat dripped in my eyes and pooled in my chest. Carly was already onto her burpees and was surprisingly in shape—after our cardio, I hadn't counted on that.

Another five minutes of agonizing squats left my legs on fire. But I wasn't done. I bit my lip as I growled before I began my burpees. My muscles screamed at me with each one I completed—the jumps were nearly impossible to land on tired limbs, especially given my bone discrepancy. The boots I wore had been altered by Aether at the cave, but they still were less than ideal. The makeshift heel on the left was wobbly at times and not fully supportive. I'd need new shoes, and soon, if I wanted to make it through training without injuring myself, or worse, embarrassing myself.

I may be ignorant to Untish history and their way of life, but I had no excuse for my lack of fitness.

I felt an increase in the energy around me. I didn't need to investigate the stands to know Aether was nearby. Instead, I focused solely on my panting breath, the sweat stinging my eyes, and the burning in my muscles.

"Good. Now let's move on. Watch and learn," Camella spoke as she was once again on the stage. Her gaze drifted behind me, and she smiled, almost looking feminine, before she dropped and picked up her weights, demonstrating a shoulder press followed by curls and then, naturally, weighted squats. "This is your new super-set, begin now."

The trainees just complied, not a single one complaining. But my body was screaming for a break. I was exhausted and not used to this amount of training. I started with the press, awkward as ever. Camella walked by, I didn't miss her grimace before she strode past and headed for the stands. Good, maybe I'd make it through this set. I adjusted the weights and did the curls, not too bad. But when it came time for the squats, my legs were done. I did two and then stood, willing my shaking muscles to stop spasming.

"Is there a problem, Aaralyn?" Camella barked from beside me.

"Just need a moment," I panted.

"You go until you drop."

I clamped down on my tongue, I would not be humiliated in front of Aether. I wasn't sure why I cared so much, but dammit I did.

I dropped and squatted, then rose, legs shaking as I did so. And I dropped again, and again, and again. Each ascension was harder, burned more, and was slower. But finally, I did it. I completed the twenty-five squats and let go of the weights, bending over.

Nice view.

Surprise filled me as I realized I actually *liked* his voice in my head. I smiled in spite of my pain.

Camella is the best Coach. She's tough, but her trainees are strong and do well in battle. I chose this specific class for you.

Okay, maybe I didn't want him here. I sent him a mental picture of me giving him the bird and in return, I felt...amusement?

If it's too much, I can have her lighten up a bit.

I am doing just fine, thank you.

My chest heaved as I tried to gulp down another breath. I would be fine once I got some water.

"All right, let's move on to hand-to-hand combat. Today, we have a special guest so pay attention to his maneuvers," Camella spoke as she stepped into a circle drawn in the center of the stage. A sparring ring.

The figure that entered next was all too familiar. His frame I'd recognize anywhere, even after such a short time. Aether. His dark hair was pulled back and he wore a tight black tank and black pants. He unsheathed his weapons before he entered, completely unarmed.

"Pay attention. Per the norm, there will be no weapons and no magic. This is purely hand-to-hand. Many of you leave here focused on the power of magic, but often it is the hand-to-hand combat that can save your life," Camella said as she hopped from foot to foot—on *bare* feet.

I swallowed.

I glanced at Aether's feet and noticed the same thing. No shoes. I closed my eyes and willed my heart to calm—I could do this, I had to.

Camella laughed as Aether stretched and got into his fighting stance. She was a good foot shorter than Aether, but she didn't seem scared. Instead, from here I could see her eyes gleaming like they knew each other well, and that bothered me more than I'd like to admit.

She ran her tongue over her bottom lip as she wagged her brows. She was anticipating this fight.

Ellen whistled and the fight began. For a moment, no one moved, but then Camella struck. She threw a series of punches, all of which Aether deflected easily, but then she jumped, rolled, and sprung up, managing to get behind Aether, tripping him with her feet. He lunged forward but pivoted and was instantly upright again, just in time to intercept Camella's kick, deflecting it with his hands.

He threw a series of punches, all of which she avoided. She was fast, very fast. Aether managed to get a strike to her stomach before gripping her shoulder and arm with his hands, strong-arming her. But she twisted out of his grip, grabbed his arm, and then *jumped* over his shoulder—sending him rolling with her.

Incredible.

Even in the Glenn, I'd never seen a fight like this. They continued sparring for several minutes until, at last, Aether fired a series of kicks and punches, landing several that pushed Camella to her back on the mat. Before she could move, he had her in a choke hold with her arm locked and extended—he could easily break it. A moment later, she tapped out. Match over, Aether had won.

I smiled.

I thought she would kick your ass.

Aether's eyes whipped to mine.

Really now, dear?

The heat from his gaze made me want to squirm, but instead, I lifted my chin, my grin spreading wider. His returned smile did things to my heart, such terrible, wonderful things.

Aether stood and offered his hand to Camella who accepted it, and together they walked to the edge of the stage, hand in hand—internally I growled. Scratch the wonderful things, no, everything he inflicted on my heart was purely evil.

"You all saw High General Brychan get the better of me, but that happens. The best thing we can do is learn to fight better, be tougher, faster, and stronger. Everyone, pair up with your partner from last week. It's time for drills," Camella spoke, finally releasing Aether's hand.

At the sight of it, the tension in my shoulders lessened and I tore my eyes from Aether's now empty hand to roam over his majestic face, strong jaw, and piercing eyes. Eyes that were still locked on me. I swore as I realized he could sense my jealousy. I shoved the green-eyed monster back down and instead recalled the way she had sucker-punched him, sending that image down the bond. His eyes flared as his lips pulled into a half-smile, making him look young, boyish almost.

I'm offended, greatly.

Good, I shot back.

His laughter echoed in my mind and sent every sliver of my being dancing. My core heated and I could feel desire turning. It instantly froze when I saw the smug look of satisfaction plastered across his face.

Oh no, I don't think so.

I smirked as I sent him one more mental image:

Skin-on-skin, gloriously bare and glistening. His lips parted in a moan as his hands grazed the lush swells of my hips. My lips uttered his name, as I held a delicate whip in one hand with him on his knees before me, willing to serve. Begging to serve. To please me with his fingers, his mouth, his cock...

Desire flooded our bond as Aether visibly swallowed, and his crotch enlarged. His eyes shown with pure lust and desire and need—such power, such heat. It was primal.

Bingo, the score was even.

Tate...

I winked at him before turning to find Carly, willing my mind to focus on far less sensual things. But as I looked around, I noted with dread that everyone was now barefoot, shoes littered the ground. Worse yet, Carly was already gone, paired with Perseus who was laughing as he jumped from foot to foot. Carly glared at him as she flexed her hands.

Next to them stood another couple, and to them, another. Everyone was paired. Well, everyone except me. The padding of feet on stone told me I had a partner, and one glance confirmed my fears, Camella.

"It's you and me," she spoke. "Remove your shoes, we fight in the traditional Untish manner."

I leveled a look at her but made no move to untie my laces. My heart pounded and sweat slicked my palms. All my gusto from my exchange with Aether had fled. Ellen blew the whistle, and the trainees began to attack one another in a series of practiced steps.

"Miss Aaralyn, take off your shoes. It's disrespectful to those you fight with and to the ground on which you spar," Camella commanded.

I can intervene.

Don't you dare, I shot back.

I had stood on my own two feet my whole life, endured the taunting and whispers, the looks of pity...I could do so once more.

Gritting my teeth, I bent over and untied one boot before tossing it aside. I reached for my left boot, pausing for only a moment, before yanking at the laces and removing it as well. I chucked it outside the ring Camella had drawn in chalk and then hobbled closer to the center where she waited.

Her face had no sign of surprise or pity, which was oddly refreshing and simultaneously disconcerting. "Good, now we begin." She nodded to me.

I expected criticism and jabs, perhaps even an easier spar, but she gave me none of that. It was as if my shorter limb were perfectly normal, not a difficulty in this already insane pairing.

"I won't take it easy on you," she warned like she was reading my mind, as she waited for Ellen to sound the whistle once more.

If you're not screaming your thoughts at me, it's written all over your face, dear.

I flipped him off, earning a quizzical look from Camella, before sending an image of my mouth on a savory part of him, enjoying the way I could sense the bond's tension building.

Just to fuck with you, I quipped.

That can be arranged.

I snorted.

You wish.

"Miss Aaralyn?" Camella blinked at me, annoyance on her features.

"It's fine. I wouldn't want you to go easy," I replied—both to her and Aether—as I flexed the muscles in my hands, willing the nerves to vanish.

Aether moaned in my head as I could sense an image loading down the bond, one of him reciprocating my earlier suggestion—and with *much* enthusiasm.

I shoved him out of my mind—I didn't need the distraction, even if it *did* ease my nerves and awaken a deep chasm inside of me. He wasn't the one standing in a ring with a badass. He wasn't the one on uneven footing, as I was in so many ways.

The whistle sounded. "Show me what you've got," Camella said.

Before I could respond she swiped at me. I jumped to the right and barely missed. My left foot throbbed from the pivot and even as I tried to regain my balance, she turned and kicked out her left foot, catching me in the gut. I doubled over and dropped to my knees.

"Pathetic," she said as she raised her hand getting ready to deliver a blow.

Block!

I rolled as she swung and then climbed back to my feet, nearly falling in the process. I was up and ready when she came at me again, this time I missed her kick and her punch, but when she jumped and landed behind me, I was thrown to my knees and found myself with her atop me, her forearm at my throat with my airway slowly constricting. I smacked the stone.

She removed her pressure from my windpipe but leaned in closer to my face, so our noses were almost touching. From here, I could see the brilliant blue of her eyes, brighter than I'd ever seen before. "Every morning, before lecture, *you* will meet me here," she whispered and then righted herself.

She stepped back and looked at me, again. "No one graduates if they can't stand in a fight for three minutes. No one. No exceptions." Her words slowly resonated.

I looked up to see Aether, arms crossed and expression unreadable.

"Again," Camella commanded. And so, we fought. And over and over, I ended up tapping out after mere seconds of fighting.

CHAPTER 20
AETHER

She was an incredible female. The lust roiling in my veins still hadn't subsided. I wanted it, everything she suggested—even if only to tease—was now forever scarred in my mind. The images of her atop me, writhing as she screamed my name, commanding...her mouth on my cock and the sly look in her eyes at the power she held.

Fuck, it took all my restraint not to whisk her away and claim her in every possible way.

Every. Single. Way.

I rolled my shoulders and slowly exhaled, pulling back the image I longed to send to Tate, and the need to elicit more of her desire. Desire that I knew was there, I'd felt it.

Instead, I tried to mute my lust and prevent it from flooding the bond. She needed to focus.

Watching Tate out there was the hardest thing I'd ever had to do. She was in pain and time after time, Camella sent her crumbling to the ground. I couldn't hide my grimace or anxiety from slipping down the bond—and her responding looks were purely indignant. Wild thing.

Delicious thing...

I hadn't missed the fear and embarrassment she felt when she first removed her boots. Nor did I miss the looks the other trainees gave her when they noted the bone discrepancy. Some jeered, others whispered, and some outright laughed when she faltered on her feet and fell. I made a mental note of those I'd pay a visit to later. Thank blood Camella didn't treat her differently—one of the many reasons I wanted Tate in this class.

The ground was covered in blood, Tate's lip was busted and bleeding, her knees scuffed. The desire to end this was nearly suffocating. She was in so much pain.

Finally, after hours of grueling duels, the training ended, and Tate limped out of the arena. I walked behind, tailing her. I wanted to give her privacy, sensing her need for it, but my very being cried for me to run to her, to offer what comfort I could. She did well today. Better than I'd thought she would have. But she was undisciplined when it came to combat—I already knew this. Magically, she was gifted. She was athletic and I knew she had potential. But she lacked control and it appeared she hadn't had any prior practice with hand-to-hand combat.

Tate walked past children playing, and I couldn't help but notice the way her eyes lit up or the longing I swore I saw there. I could picture it then, our children. A little girl with Tate's eyes, a little boy with mine, looking up at us, trusting us—

I shook my head. Too much, I'd chosen long ago not to have the responsibility of children. The sweet redheaded girl with my eyes was better off. Much better.

No, that chapter in my life had been shut, and it was better this way.

A child nearby cried as they fell and their mother rushed over to pick them up, and then pulled them into a hug. Tate smiled at them as she walked past, limping slightly as she did so. Even with her boots back on, her limp was bad. She was injured worse than I'd thought.

Anger rose in my chest, urging me to exact vengeance—irrational, I assured myself. If anyone was to pay, it was me for bringing her to the Embassy. And I'd asked Camella to train her. This was all on me.

She rounded the corner and then disappeared into my home—our home. I followed her inside and cleared my throat. She was in the kitchen pouring a glass of water...not what I expected or would have personally chosen.

"You did well today," I spoke, trying to control the wild emotions coursing through me as my primal side awakened, turned wild by her mere presence.

"Me? You're joking. I was the weakest and the worst," she said before lifting the full glass of cool water to her lips. Dried blood, chalk, and dirt covered her arms and streaked across her face. Even still, she was breathtaking.

"Far from the weakest, Tate. You just need practice, tactically." I took another step toward her but stopped myself and planted my hands on the stone counter; I would control myself. I had to...even as her imagined moans echoed in my mind. "How were the lectures today?"

"Good, we learned about the history of the Iron Tribe." She bit her lip. "And...I learned about *bonding*." She didn't say anymore, just looked at me.

Both those things were extremely important, and both needed to be addressed. But...my instincts took over.

"And?" The question came out a whisper.

"And, while it seems barbaric to be forced to be with someone against your will, like that of an arranged marriage, our bond feels... different," she said softly. I felt her reaching out, curiously exploring. This time I reached back. Her eyes widened, but she didn't retreat.

"I meant what I said, it is fully your choice," I forced the words out and gripped the stone harder. I would not be an animal. I would never break my vow to her.

Aside from how the bond is formed, what does it mean? For us?

My breath caught.

It was just the two of us, and she was speaking to me in the most intimate way. Suddenly I was so unworthy. I swallowed back my inadequacy; she asked a question and the least I could do was answer.

It will strengthen our gifts and power stores. We would share magic and be bound to each other. An example is this form of communication, it is incredibly rare for even the strongest of bonded to be able to speak telepathically. But we can and we haven't fully bonded yet, there's just so much potential...

She nodded and looked at the floor for a moment before walking to the other side of the counter and leaning on it, toward me, meeting me with her enchanting mahogany eyes.

What does that entail, sharing power?

Fuck, her scent from this close was nearly enough to send me crawling over the counter.

A pet to its master.

Instead, I bit my tongue.

You would have access to my magic wells and I yours. We would feel each other's pain and emotions much more than we do now, though there's ways to shield that, and...depending on the depth of the bond, our souls would blend to almost a cellular level. We would be intertwined.

I held my breath. Waiting.

I see. And does the bond last forever? Like, are there divorces?

Usually, it's until death.

She stared at me, considering. Her emotions flooded my senses, with one stronger than the rest: *acceptance.* It washed over me like a tidal wave, calming and pure, absolute.

"Are you sure?" I asked, voice hoarse.

"Yes." The word barely left her lips before I launched myself across the counter. I picked her up and sat her on the marbled stone, staring into her eyes, barely keeping my hands to *only* her waist.

Images of her pleasuring herself at the outpost flooded my mind, the kiss we shared in the river had continuously haunted me.

"If we do this, there's no going back," I confirmed, each breath heavier than the last. I was more than ready, my enlarging cock a physical sign of my eagerness. But still, I waited. I locked my eyes on hers, boring into her soul.

Uncertainty crossed her face and I flinched. She wasn't ready, not yet. "We can wait." I swallowed.

"Maybe, just for a little bit, just so I can fully wrap my mind around it…" She lowered her gaze to my lips. "If I kissed you, would that complete the bond?"

"No, it would strengthen it, but it's not complete until—" I exhaled, willing my hands to *not* dig into her lush hips "—until you and I are one, physically and magically. Bound together, forever."

She smiled and her scent increased. She wanted me, of that I was sure. I closed my eyes. I could wait, if she asked for more time, I *would* give it to her.

But the soft brush of her lips on mine was my undoing. I kissed her back, greedily, devouring her. She moaned as she pulled me closer with her legs, trapping me against her. I welcomed it, welcomed it all. Everything she'd give me, I'd take. Even if, in the end, she didn't want me. Even—

She deepened the kiss as her hands found their way across my back, my neck, and into my hair—so like the image she'd sent me earlier, only this was real, and clothes separated our bodies. She pulled at the leather strap binding my hair and then sunk her fingers into my scalp. I moaned as I swept my hands over the lush swell of her hips, her trim waist, and I found the nape of her neck with one hand.

More.

It was a quiet plea from her, and I didn't hesitate before complying. I lowered her fully onto the counter and climbed atop, savoring the way her chest raised to meet mine with every breath, the energy that began to swarm us.

The air heated and I knew our magic was dancing. Knew that if I took my attention from the glorious female in front of me and instead looked at the room, I'd see fire dancing and sparks flying.

But I didn't care. Nothing mattered but Tate. Nothing.

She clawed her fingers deeper into my scalp and slid her foot down my ass and legs, hovering at my calf.

I swept my tongue into her mouth further, savoring the flavor that was entirely her. Sweet and floral...just like her scent that had kept me awake at night and was always on my mind. I inhaled it, drank it, and kissed her deeply. With my free hand, I reached down her neck and found the swell of her breast, peeking out from under her shirt.

Her hand at my shoulder stiffened as waves of new emotions crashed into me.

Uncertainty. Panic.

I began to shake with restraint. She wasn't ready. I forced my hands to the stone counter and braced myself before prying my lips from hers. I hovered just above her and noted the way she breathed deeply, the way her lips were swollen, her cheeks flushed...

Her eyes bored into mine, wonder shown there.

The tension building in my veins was flooding my system. I ground my hands into the counter and forced the energy to pour there, my eyes steadfast on Tate.

A boom sounded and shook the home, the solid stone counter cracked, separating on either side of Tate from where my hands were braced. Her eyes widened and I sensed her excitement.

She was worth the wait.

I stood and then without a word, walked to the balcony seeking its air and space from the one female who had me senseless. Space. *I* needed space before I did something well and truly stupid.

See you later. Her words caressed my mind along with a smirk I felt lacing them.

I launched into the sky and shifted a moment later, letting my inner beast fly.

CHAPTER 21
CHANCE

"Y ou did this to her. You struck her. You lack control," a cool voice said. It was the voice of nightmares—my nightmares.

"I didn't mean to!" My throat burned even as the words were ripped from me.

"You lack control, you're a failure. You hurt the ones you love. Without my help you'll become the very thing you fear," the stern voice continued to speak, cane tapping on the hard floor.

"Never—I'll never be—"

A scream ripped from my throat as the searing pain once again took over. Magic. It was testing my own. I could feel its unholy quest, the way it probed me and searched. Worse, I could sense this new magic in me responding in kind—longing for control, power, more...

"Stop!" I screamed the word.

"My son." President Dale's face loomed overhead. "I cannot. I won't. This is for the greater good."

Without warning, the pain returned tenfold. I threw back my head into the seat's cold metal, yanking against the arm restraints as I did so. Time had no meaning. Nothing did.

Images of Holland unconscious, videos of her convulsing, crying, and fainting played on repeat. The white walls all had become a screen —overwhelming me.

"You will not fail me again. We will fix you." President Dale touched the side of my sweaty face, cupping it gently. "I promise."

More pain exploded in my core as I was being sifted internally. Needles poking, blood being taken and administered. I sat there, strapped to a chair and bound not only by the iron cuffs but by magical bonds I could feel tethering me to the seat.

Power. Release.

I could feel the magic begging to be used, for me to unleash the new force of energy within. A force that was stolen and corrupt. I shut the mental pathway down, even as the pain intensified.

"You will become my controller, the best of the best. It's in your blood, son. You are stronger than you know," my father said. No, not my father, the gargantuan atrocity that merely donated his semen to the female who died birthing me.

I was an abomination from birth.

"Good. I can see the fight in you!" He reached for my head and this time I snapped my fangs toward his hand, grazing the side of it and drawing blood.

"Sir!" voices came from the side of the room.

"Ut-uh," the vile male beside me said, holding his hand up to the light, smiling. "This is good. There's hope for you yet, Chance. Doctor Worshah, take things to level two. Do not disappoint me." His cane followed his footsteps until the room once again fell silent.

For a moment, I could breathe. For a moment, it was over. But then the video sounded, Holland's cries—my lightning bouncing from my father's shield and engulfing her. Shae's body filled the screen next.

She was on a gurney and completely unconscious until she was writhing in pain and screaming. Her skin was all grey and purple and muscles began to sprout over muscles. She screamed again.

"Stop!" I pulled against the cuffs restraining me, fought with my core to free myself from the seat. But it was useless. Failure, I had failed so many.

The power within thumped, I could stop this—I just needed to release it, to allow it to take hold of me. I could rip at the magic changing Shae, eat it myself...

Shae's screams heightened along with the pounding in my chest.

My breaths came in shallow pants as I fought against the restraints, and still maintained a tether of control over the borrowed magic.

Shae's arms had tripled in size. The female crumpled on the floor near the gurney looked nothing like the friend I once had. Her head was bald, and her eyes were black with red and purple veins sprouting from them, covering her body that was now larger than my own. Her cries ended. She turned her head and looked at the camera.

"You did this to me, Chance."

"No! I didn't—"

"You could have stopped this," Shae's voice withered.

The pain intensified inside my skull, I could feel magical talons scraping against my mind, pulling, prodding, and rearranging. The IV in my arm was being tampered with and I had the vague sense of fluid being administered.

The video changed and Holland was staring at the camera.

Black lines sprouted from eyes that were no more—they were hollowed out, missing, and empty. Her flesh steamed and was charred—burnt, electrocuted, and destroyed.

"Chance, you promised to protect me, why did you hurt me?" Words came out of a fleshless mouth, but it was not her speaking, it was the voice of death.

I screamed and pulled against the restraints, snapping the physical ones on my wrists and ankles. I forced the power building up within me to fight the bonds holding me at bay.

"Help me, Chance, save me," Holland voiced.

"Please Chance, fix this. Save me," Shae cried, her tears dripping to the floor and pooling in red.

I swallowed back the blood in my own mouth as undiluted horror gripped my soul.

Holland was burning alive, dancing in red flames; Shae stood in front of her, pulling energy from Holland in a wave of black energy.

I shouted as I opened the door to the power within and let it free. Chance Dale was no more.

CHAPTER 22

TATE

My body throbbed, ached from the night before and after this morning's training with Camella, I was even more sore. Worse still, my feet were bloody, and my blisters had broken, they oozed. Even now, hours later as I waited in the landing plane, every single step hurt. The new boots I'd found from Aether this morning were a pleasant surprise—they fit like a dream with the extra cushions, and the sole of the left boot had been meticulously, beautifully crafted with precision. I swayed from foot to foot, but even with the new boots, the throbbing in my left leg intensified, and the stabbing pain from the exposed sores stole my attention. If there was a silver lining, that was it.

Aether fled the house last night, and while I knew I was the cause of it, I still mourned his absence. The look on his eyes as he hovered there, inches from my face, the intensity in his gaze...

I shivered as my core pulsed with longing.

He made me feel powerful—safe, desired, and worthy. In his presence, I felt so many things.

I wasn't entirely ready to call it *love*, but I knew I was attracted to him, and not just on a physical level. Some deeper part of me craved him, his flavor still fresh in my mind.

I was beginning to see the upside to this whole bonding thing.

A stupid smile played at my lips as I waited in the corner of the field for my tutor. I fiddled with my hands as I stood, tired and hot in the sun—warmer still inside from the memory of the kiss from the night before. His skin had been soft, warm, but his grip was strong, commanding. The way my heart raced, and my breaths shallowed from just a kiss was unlike anything I'd ever experienced before. It wasn't only lust or love, it was a powerful mix of both, and it was so unknown and so foreign, that it was terrifying. And yet...

And yet, he'd left. He'd honored my wishes.

I hadn't been scared, not of him. No, I'd been frightened by how much *I* wanted him. How much I desired this all-consuming, unbreakable bond with a male I'd only known for a short while. Had he not left, the primal need would have led me to fully give all of myself to him, in every possible way—blood knew I had *many* ideas—and loving every single moment of it. No, this was very new water for me. Uncharted. The purest form of desire. Was that what bonding was?

Fire filled the air just above my head and had me flinching back to the present.

An Ironhead student stood nearby, smirking as he wielded more fire in the sky above, aimed at me. I cut him a glare before moving another twenty feet away as his tutor reprimanded him and advised control. As if that prick contained any.

Carly's tutor had come and got her a few minutes ago, and they were now a few hundred yards away while she tried to wield a shield. I could see sparks of magic. From class this afternoon, I gathered the Livish Tribe were gifted with shifters, some shields, and wielding light in their humanoid forms—not flames. It seemed their tribe was important to battle, both defensive and offensively, but they lacked the brute force and power the Shadow Tribe had. Pride swelled in my chest as I thought of *my* tribe and the male who made it so.

A burst of light shown, and Carly cheered as she harnessed her power. Anticipation filled me and for the first time, I was *excited* to train. Magic wielding was at the top of my list of priorities.

"Tate! Girlll, look at you!" Vala's warm voice tickled my ears.

"Vala!" I turned around to see her only a few paces away. I threw myself into her arms, and she chuckled as she embraced me.

"I missed you too, it hasn't been the same without you, and like, my days and drills are all so repetitive and boring...but then I knew I'd get to see you again, and here you are!" She squealed. The same Vala.

"So, you're my tutor?" I asked.

"As blood, or a big lumbering jackass, would have it, yes! We get to spend hours together wielding. It's going to be the absolute best!" She raised her voice with the last note.

"I'm glad, this place has felt a bit lonely."

Her eyes shown with sympathy. "Yeah, Aether can be something else. But let's get started." She winked and then pulled out a device and threw it a couple of yards away. It opened a hole, tearing through the air just a foot above the ground, swirling and pulsing with power.

"Follow me," she said as she stepped into the void. I hesitated. The moment she was completely through, she vanished. But this was Vala, and I trusted the male who arranged for her to tutor me.

Taking a step, before I changed my mind, I entered the portal.

My feet hit lush, green grass and the smell of honeyed flowers filled my nostrils. My skin jumped and danced, the comforting presence that had become a second skin to me was much lighter like the distance diminished my connection to Aether. My heart jolted, what if I needed him and he couldn't sense—

Right here, love. Portals can only transfer you short distances, and besides, a mere portal can't break our...connection.

I breathed deeply, assured that I wasn't alone, but also very aware of his choice of wording. He didn't say 'bond'.

"Okay, so first things first." Vala flexed her hands and *pulled* energy from the ground. I could see waves of it flowing through the air and into her palms. Then she reached out and pushed it, it flew through the air and formed a dome above us, a hundred yards in diameter. "There. Now we have privacy."

"For what?"

"Training. I've cloaked you inside the city's borders of the Embassy, but you Tate, are no normal Untishee. I've seen your power, it needs containing and hiding, for now, per Aether's orders." She took a step toward the center and then dropped to the ground, sitting cross-legged. She gestured for me to follow, and I did.

The ground was cool, soft, and rich to my touch.

"I've been meaning to ask. When we first arrived and you cloaked me, the tattoo, it's gone?" I gestured to my still bare shoulder.

"Concealed. It would be much harder to remove. But for now, it's hidden."

Like so much of myself, my life.

"Tate, I can sense it in you, but can you sense your own magic firing?"

"What?"

"Even with the cloaking I did, you're stronger now. Your Untish genes are fully established. Any cloak will not impact your ability to shift or access any of your magic, it merely makes it harder for those on the outside to see it, and if they do, it will appear different—like that of a Darkling." She winked at me. "I'm pretty damn good with wielding and cloaking."

"I'm lucky to have you."

"You have no idea, girl." Vala smiled at me, chest buffed a bit. "So, just tuck that kernel away for later and look inside to feel your magic."

I did. I could see my inner pool, sparking with pink flames.

"Good, now close your eyes and reach into the dirt with your fingers. What do you feel?"

I raised a brow. Vala had closed her eyes and looked like she was one with the elements as her brows smoothed in relaxation, fully at peace.

"Tate, close your eyes," Vala said, eyes still shut.

A sigh escaped my lips. I could do this, I just needed to shift gears.

I complied and dug my hands through the grass, into the dirt. My fingers felt the small grains brushing past my bare skin.

"What do you feel?" she asked.

"Dirt. It's cool and soft," I answered.

"Of course, you feel dirt, silly, I mean what *magic* can you sense?" Vala asked.

I paused and tried to see if I could feel it. I felt...energy? Perhaps a pulsing, even, but it was hard to tell. I was too untrained. "I don't know."

"Ah, okay that's totally normal, especially for a beginner—you should have seen me when I first started, you would be laughing so hard—but I can help you—in a way I wish my tutor had, the ol' jackass." Her words tumbled out. "I'm going to reach out with a strand of my magic to yours and just follow it, all right?"

What the hell was she talking about? But before I could even ask, I felt it. It was soft, like that of snow, and beckoned me forward. I followed it as it went down, past the thumping and into the heart of power.

I gasped and threw open my eyes. Vala was smiling.

"Good! You feel it! That is why we chose this place for the Embassy, it's the axis of the planet and rich with magical stores. What you tasted was but a glimpse of the reserves we can access here." She splayed out her hands to the ground and then lifted them, shimmering bridges arched from the ground to her hands. She threw her hands into the air, releasing the energy, and fireworks went off above us.

"Amazing," I whispered.

"It is, but we need to stay on track. You know very little about magic for someone your age, so we need to start at the beginning."

Ouch, I knew my own deficiencies and didn't particularly like having them thrown at me. I gave her the side eye, but simply nodded.

"We have magic in us. You have magic in you. However, you can only hold so much at a time. Everyone is different, but you have stores that you draw from, and once expended, you must restore them."

"I'm guessing it's not innate anymore like when I first got here?" I asked.

"I wish but no. After the initial fill, once you've gone through the Changing and filled your stores for the first time, you have to be intentional about it." She paused looking at me. "Think of a cup that runs dry, it's still a cup but it needs to be refilled. So, when you expend magic, your stores are lower, and you will need to replenish. Since we are Untishee, there are different ways we can refill." She pulled magic from the ground, and it began to rise in a steady stream. "We can transfer energy to one another," the wave of magic pulsed between her hands, "but this requires a deep magical connection between the two sources, and so it's very uncommon. We can draw from the land—my personal favorite as it's *sooo* rich." She pulled the stream of magic from the ground and lifted it higher, so it was chest level. "Like have you noticed the lushness of these volcanic mountains?" She released the magic streams, allowing them to dissipate as she splayed her hands wide to the towering hills richly adorned with every shade of green. "We can drink blood rich with magic, either real or manufactured. And..."

Wait. Drink blood? Like Aether? I opened my mouth to ask—

"And lastly, when our lineage passes or we take a life, we can inhale *their* magic to refill our stores," she continued. "But this is actually not allowed because it can warp the wielder and can turn dark if not freely given, like those things, the seethings, they were created with stolen magic that became warped. And so, it's actually taboo... which means there really are only two recommended ways." She winked at me. "Got it?"

Did I get it? "So...I need to refill, and I can do so with blood or by pulling from the planet?"

"Yes!" She smiled encouragingly.

"Aether said something similar. So, when he gave me blood during the Changing, he was refilling my newfound magical stores?"

Her eyes widened making her large facial features even bigger, more mesmerizing. "Well, yes, but it's not allowed during the

Changing, not without the chair's approval, so really he shouldn't have, but the amount of energy you were expressing is nearly unheard of and could have been fatal without a sufficient filler immediately and—"

"Wait, Vala, what do you mean *not* allowed? You just said we need it to refill our stores." Impatience was pulling at me.

"We do, but during the Changing, your Untish blood is awakening, the genes are realigning and preparing themselves to express the full potential of your magic for the first time, and you're susceptible to bonding more than ever. Which is why, once you turn sixteen and begin the Changing, you start attending Matching Events so the chairs can watch, but they don't allow blood sharing cause it can warp the bond."

"Vala, what—"

"But in your case, you went through the Changing far *later* than most. Like, here, if your genes don't awaken by seventeen, we go through the *burning* to help expedite the process. However, you didn't start the Changing until recently, and I'm still not sure how that's possible, but since you couldn't draw from the planet's core because it was darkened there, Aether had to—"

"What do you mean—"

"—you know, give you his blood, and I understand that—"

"Vala, stop." I threw out my hands and was a bit shocked the air around Vala responded, tightening. Her jaw hung open, mid-sentence. "What do you mean, 'warp the bond'?" My heart was pounding. Fear began to take over and claim my fragile heart, my newfound kernel that could be *love*.

"Well, maybe not 'warp' but—" She abruptly stopped, realizing her misstep. "It's not like that, Tate. What I mean is that when you share blood, it can strengthen any potential for a bond. It's been outlawed since the beginning of Perry and Matias—you know they were *not* approved to be bonded, in fact, Perry was bonded to another —but she and Matias *did* bond, shortly after blood sharing, and well, the whole race was born. It's like magic just took over and, well, it doesn't really matter. No one knows. I think it's magical and romantic."

I massaged my temples as her words sunk in.

Warped. Manipulated. Not real.

The words repeated through my mind, a gong sounding my internal alarm. I couldn't shake the nausea rising within or the shame that I'd believed him, trusted him when he said I had a choice. Believed he'd let me actually determine my future, accept or reject the bond. A bond that I now knew had been tampered with.

"I talk too much, Tate. Just know, it's allowed if you're already bonded." She clamped her hand over her mouth as if that would stop her from spilling more secrets.

I could feel myself firing within, my inner beast roaring. I needed to think.

"It's fine, Vala. I already know about the bond." But I didn't know he gave me his blood *knowing* it would strengthen our connection. He'd promised he wouldn't force me, and yet, he had done that very thing. "Does blood feeding make a bond happen?"

"Oh no! It just makes it easier for magic to mix, heightens the connection. The possibility has to be there in the first place, but if it's there, it like, you know, it gives the bond a boost."

"So, what you're saying is that Aether giving me his blood actually *boosted* a bond that was already there? Isn't that manufacturing it?" My ears began to pound with the pressure of my blood rising. Just when I'd trusted him. Just when I thought I was okay with this bond, I find out he *made* it happen.

My choice, my ass.

I could feel a tendril of him reaching out, even from the distance, trying to calm me.

Stop it, I commanded. Before shoving against it with my own force. I needed to be clear-minded.

"No! I mean, sort of, but no! The bond had to exist to begin with for it to be strengthened. If there was no bonding possibility, then there would be nothing to be strengthened." She smiled weakly. "Shit, Tate, you can't be mad at him. He felt the bond and you *were* going through the Changing. You could've died without a refuel, even a small one from his blood might not have been enough. He would have felt compelled to take care of you, to claim—"

"To claim me like I'm property?" My voice rose with every word, as did the fire in my veins.

"No, not exactly. I meant to claim you as his. But really his magic would have been driving the—"

"Teach me to shield." My command had her eyes widening. "You said you're to tutor me in magic. Teach me to protect my mind."

Vala gaped a moment and then silently nodded.

Aether didn't own me. If I chose our bond, then I would do so and he fucking wasn't going to manipulate that. I hated the sting in my heart as I felt, once again, betrayed.

CHAPTER 23
CHANCE

Red covered the ground in veins of static, pure undiluted power. Red danced across my vision. Red consumed the walls, and swallowed the corpses on the floor.

Red walls, red bodies, red blood.

Red and red and red.

More.

There was nothing but red...

CHAPTER 24
AETHER

I felt it the moment our connection was blocked. Tate was shielding, hiding herself from me. At first, panic laced my system as all the possibilities hit. I pressed against her shield and easily broke through, but the moment I did, I felt the full force of her fury. I backed off and allowed her to rebuild her walls. They were weak but better than before. Vala was teaching her well.

I locked my jaw. Even with Tate's shield in place, I could sense her anger. Something had happened. It took all my restraint not to rip into the void and join them. Vala must have done or said something.

I cursed under my breath.

I threw a few more punches at James. Since she left this morning, we'd been sparring this entire day. I needed to find *other* outlets while Tate marinated on what she wanted.

James threw a punch, and I deflected before throwing a series of hits myself. If he suspected what had me bothered, he was gentle enough not to state it, even if his eyes were full of mirth.

I kicked his feet out from under him and was on him in a second. Pinned, he tapped out.

"Fuck, Aether. You haven't fought like that in years," James said standing up, sweat pulling at his chest and pits.

"Yeah, well, never too late to return to the basics." I grabbed a jug of water and tossed him one too. While we needed blood to live, the human in us appreciated the water. We were beautiful blends, or mixed-breeds and halflings as some called us.

"So, is Tate adjusting well?" James hedged.

"Fine." I wasn't going to get into it with him.

"Does she know you're leaving soon?" James drained his water and tossed the empty jug to the sweat-splattered stone balcony.

"No, I'm not sure I'm even going." I snarled at the thought. I'd tried to get out of it, could have, but that would entail explaining *why* to Arithi and the other chairs. I wasn't chair of the Shadow Tribe, yet, and so I was subject to them. I never thought I'd see the day when *I* wanted power, dominion.

She truly had turned my world upside down.

I raked a hand through my damp hair. I couldn't leave her here with these snakes, I needed her to come with me. And yet, she wasn't ready. It would be a quick ops mission, just to gather intel, a flyover basically...but to leave her here in Arithi's clutches was dangerous. Especially if they discovered *who* Tate was, even if I didn't fully know that answer myself. I pulled out my disk and checked my messages. Nothing from research.

"She'll be fine, she's got Vala. Aether, you know there are reasons we have training. Sending her into the field unprepared can get her killed, I mean even Cher was the best and—"

I threw a punch before he could finish. He barely evaded and I threw another. Rage fueled my movements.

"Fuck, Aether!" James exclaimed as he blocked a series of punches and kicks.

"Fight me!" I commanded.

Tate was still shielding against me.

She was stuck here in this viper's nest.

They wanted me gone.

The thoughts pounded through my mind as each punch was thrown. I would not lose her too. I couldn't.

"You want to get into it?" James challenged as he went on the offensive. "Have you spoken to Uley lately? I heard you saw Ruby."

The mention of her name sent another wave of fury through me. I lanced out with my power, but James was prepared, and he vanished before reappearing behind me a moment later. No matter, I flared my power again in a whip of dark energy.

"She said Ruby met Tate. Tell me, does Tate know *who* Ruby is?" James spoke, evading me again. He hadn't materialized yet, or he had but he vanished just as quickly.

A growl escaped my lips.

"I guess Ruby felt a bit threatened. Uley believes she's figured it out, at least in part, not surprising since Cher was also—"

I sensed him a moment before he appeared and wrapped him in a tight embrace of energy, slicing his words from his very throat.

"Mind your own business and look out for *your* daughter. Ruby deserves to be protected, *brother*."

I released him and he vanished, teleported away. Good. I reinforced my shields as I lumbered into the kitchen in search of a strong drink. I didn't bother with a cup, instead I pulled straight from the bottle.

Ruby. With her deep red hair and dark gold-flecked eyes, she was the definition of innocence.

I was dark. Where I walked, death followed.

I pulled again from the bottle, savoring the way the thick iron coated my throat. I preferred my bloodwine aged, and if it could be augmented by the Luna Tribe, even better. This was the best of both. I continued to drink, not caring that I was now in the living room sitting on a leather chaise, blood dripping down both sides of my mouth, in nothing but black, sweat-drenched pants. I didn't care that my stench was filling the room.

Nothing fucking mattered. Cher would be ashamed. And yet...I'd done the best I could. Ruby was better off.

I would not become my father.

I stood and stalked to the cellar where I retrieved yet another ancient bottle and proceeded to down most of it as well.

Guilt was ever the drinking companion.

I stalked back into the living room, the dark fire roaring, matching my mood, when I felt the air's charge increase. Her scent followed, intoxicating as ever, but this time it held a lethal edge.

My equal in every way, I laughed dryly.

I leaned against the hearth, aware of my current appearance, but somehow it didn't matter. I could sense the fight rising in her.

Tate's frame filled the door, and from my peripheral, I could see her aura glowing around her. She cleared her throat.

"It's my choice, huh?" Her voice dripped venom as she spoke. My eyes snapped to hers, rings of pink fire swirled there. Her hair began to lift and instantly I knew she didn't just want a fight, she needed it.

Fuck, we both did.

I pulled a disk from my boot and threw it toward the fireplace, a portal opening to the woods just outside city limits.

If we fight, let's do it where the neighbors can't hear, darling.

Why? Afraid to have witnesses see me kick your brooding ass?

I didn't respond, and instead stepped through the portal, still holding the half-empty bottle of bloodwine, and allowed the magic to sting my skin before spitting me out into the forest floor. I stumbled but caught myself.

Ruby, Cher, my mother. So many females I'd let down.

I waited.

The portal hovered there, opaque and spinning. Perhaps I misjudged her. Maybe she wasn't ready for a challenge, maybe she didn't need the same release I sought...

Her molded leg stepped through the portal, tentative at first and then she lunged. Her force sent me careening backwards, nearly falling. I righted myself, calling my magic to surround me, as I tossed her the bottle of wine.

She caught it midair and arched a brow, standing there, stoic, ever the warrior. Even with her walls in place, her emotions were smothering:

Betrayal. Anger. Indignance.

I stood there, ready to take a beating. I said nothing, allowing her to speak first. She circled me, a predator sizing up its prey; the air around her stirred, and with every step, leaves fluttered about, displaced.

"How could you?" The accusation in her eyes was damning. Her lips quivered a moment before pulling back in a snarl that revealed her fangs. She dropped the bottle, allowing the precious liquid to seep into the forest floor.

Before I could respond, she launched herself at me. I could have easily evaded, instead, I allowed her to strike, to catch me in the gut, to send me to my ass. She hovered above me, hand raised—I could tell that even after just mere days, her skills were improving.

"Don't fucking smile at me," she hissed before throwing her hands forward and swallowing me whole in pink flames. They danced over my skin and stung. Still, I sat there. "Fight me, coward," she bit out.

She wanted a fight? Needed a real fight? Fine. With a fluid motion, I was on my feet, meeting her rosy flames with black ones of my own. They collided in the middle, forming a wall, half black and half pink. They fought each other, but neither one inched one way or the other. I forced more power into it and sent her flames back a foot, then another, and still, another. She threw back her head and screamed, forcing more power into her fire—my flames flew back at me, and I sidestepped to miss the blast of her power.

I readied a shield and then threw a strike of fire at her, but she was prepared. Her flames swallowed it whole and held it at bay.

Even untrained, she was magnificent.

"You said I had a choice." She threw a bolt of fire at me, barely missing. "You said you wouldn't force it." Another wave of fire, blocked by my shield. "And yet—" She released a stream of liquid fire, I ducked and rolled. "—You lied."

I could end this fight now, but I deserved this beating.

"All along—" she threw another blast, "—you manufactured the bond. You forced it on me from the beginning."

I dropped my shield and allowed the volley of fire to hit me, to throw me back. This was what she's upset about? I looked through the haze and saw it—her inner dragon dancing in her eyes, barely restrained. My pulse quickened. Even my sexual appetite disgusted me.

She was right. I had strengthened the bond. I was a liar. I had failed so many and lied to the rest. I deserved my punishment.

With sure steps, she stalked toward me and withdrew a dagger, its blade glinting in the light of her aura. "You betrayed me."

My beast clawed at me, begging to compete—to be freed. But I silenced it. Even in my foggy state of mind, I held it on a tight leash. A few bottles of bloodwine were nothing compared to decades of training and practiced restraint.

I had told myself all along I'd accept her decision, if she didn't want me, I wouldn't force it. Even if the only way to prove that was to die. We hadn't bonded yet; if I died, her magic would be fairly unscathed.

"You're right," I spoke slowly, remaining on the ground. "Exact whatever justice feels right." The flames at my fingers died out. I was wholly at her mercy.

She stood over me and paused. Anger filled her eyes.

I trusted you. Was it ever actually up to me?

The pain in her voice broke something inside me. I was a beast. Just like my father, I saw what I wanted and made it happen.

I clenched my jaw. No words could justify this or make it right. I had strengthened a bond that existed. I had tricked her, even if it was done to save her life—to protect her. Wasn't that the motto that so many smothering jackasses used to justify their means? No, Tate was better off not tied to me. Just as Ruby was.

Her eyes flashed with hurt. Had she heard my inner dialog? My chest was rising rapidly as she stood there, the executioner and bearer of my fate, blade in hand.

She sniffed and I felt it then, the examination of my mind. She was a fast learner—and a clear royal. A pure Shadow Tribe member would need a blood connection to read the other's mind. But not Tate. Her stores of power and abilities were truly amazing.

Even so, she was untrained. I could block her, but I wouldn't. Instead, I allowed her to search, to see.

Pain exploded behind my eyes as she pulled a memory...but I released it, the discomfort easing a bit as I focused instead on the slight buzzing in my mind, one good thing about intoxication.

Water from the river flowed passed us, Tate stood before me in gloriously nothing but her bra and thong. The water barely covered the swell of her breasts, breasts that were partially hidden by her wet blonde hair, translucent in the stream.

"You need me. I need you," she said, voice husky.

I pulled back, just enough so I could see her whole face. "Tate, you hate me remember?" I swallowed; my eyes lowered to her heaving chest then back to her lips. Lush, full, promising... "Trust me, you'll hate me for this."

Then our bodies were interlocked, her lips on mine, the air around us swirling in a cyclone of our making.

The memory faded and the pain in my head became acute as I could feel her shoving it back. She pulled at another and then another, briefly viewing them, before shoving them back.

The knife dropped from her hand.

I looked up, the aura around her faded as the red-brown shade of her eyes returned, the dragon assuaged and re-caged. "See you at home, *dear*," she bit out before retreating into the portal.

I noticed the blade on the ground, mere inches from my hip—she could have emasculated me. Killed or maimed. But she left, almost like it had been dealt with. She'd passed her judgment. But I wasn't fool enough to think this was over. No, something told me the damage done wouldn't be so easily remedied.

I stood up, noting the broken branches scattering the forest floor—the piles of leaves and bare spots of dirt from where her power gathered. She was, in every sense of the word, remarkable.

CHAPTER 25

CHANCE

"Dale! Stop, this isn't who you are," a distant voice called.

I knew that voice. They wanted me to stop. But could I? The rage I'd freed consumed me. Power became everything. Nothing else mattered. I could only see the atrocities that were Holland and Shae. What I had *done* and *become* that allowed this to happen.

Sparks shot from my hand and engulfed the hallway, eating at the ceiling.

"Dale!" a female voice cried. I could feel the gentle pull, her magic heightening my inner emotions. A wave of blanketing calm took over, smothered the flames, and began to quiet everything else.

I threw bolts of lightning at the gentle caress. I didn't wish to be soothed. I wanted revenge. Fuck, I needed revenge.

"Dale," her whisper was jarring.

Through the red, I could see a small-framed female approaching me. Her hair was short and her swagger...

"Holland?" How could that be? She was dead.

I felt the wave crash over me, and I dropped my shields of pure lightning. I allowed her power to calm my ire, to still the storm within.

Love, pure and undiluted, swelled where my internal hate thrived. "Dale."

Holland was alive. She stood in front of me, honeyed eyes full of compassion. The red faded from my vision and the hallway went dark. It would have been pitch black had it not been for the broken window letting in light.

"How?" I asked as she stepped closer and placed her hand on my chest.

Her honeysuckle scent brought me to my knees. I pulled her into my chest and held her, looked up at her, worshiped the female who wasn't lost.

"It's okay. I'm all right," she spoke even as I could feel her quieting my internal thoughts. "Everything's all right." She held me for several moments and stroked my back.

"I thought you were dead." The admission hollowed out my gut. "I thought I'd killed you, I—"

"Shhhh, I'm right here."

I looked at her. Really looked at Holland who had somehow come to mean so much to me. There was no mark on her forehead. No purple or black veins, no charred skin, nothing like the horror that I had witnessed.

Her short, light brown hair just dusted her shoulders and her pale skin was flushed. Whole and alive.

"What about Shae?" the words tumbled out.

"Shae is fine, I was just with her. She's recovering well, asking for you, and being very philosophical, but she's fine. She's with Dux Carran as we speak."

Shae was whole too.

"I don't understand. I saw you both, you were…" I couldn't finish the sentence.

"Dale, I don't know what you witnessed, but we're alive. Look at me." She gripped my chin, and I adjusted my gaze to meet hers. "We are fine."

She lowered her lips to mine and kissed me. It was gentle and soft, a healing balm to my soul. I kissed her back even as my grip around her tightened.

I stood and picked her up, pressing her against a wall. I hadn't failed. Her tongue swept in and deepened the kiss. My soul quaked, and I could feel a tingle against my skin, the tell-tale of the red static dancing across my flesh.

Clapping sounded, along with the clipping of a cane. "Very well done."

I broke my kiss with Holland to look straight into the eyes of my father, President Dale.

"You have a lot of fucking explaining to do!" I threw bolts at my father, but he easily shielded, and then *inhaled* my power. I side-stepped Holland and blocked her from him.

That bastard wasn't getting an inch closer to her.

"What you saw was a gift."

What the actual fuck? "A gift?" I couldn't believe my own ears.

"Yes, you were given the rare gift of sight. Of what would be, could be, if things don't change. I don't know what you witnessed, but I hope it was enough to convince you that we need your cooperation. We need your power, Chance."

I snarled and threw more power at the shield my father still had erect. "Fuck you."

In a fluid motion, he pulled the power into himself. I'd just fed him —again.

"My boy, tell me, what horror has you so upset? If you want to stop it, I'm offering an alternative path." He extended his hand. A hand that *didn't* brandish the mark of my fangs—a hand I had only moments ago ripped open, or had I?

I stood there, unable to move. Had it all been a vision? Or had it been real and time lost all meaning?

Was there any way my father actually meant well and was offering to help? I wouldn't fool myself into believing in his nature, he was evil. I was sure of that. But perhaps, he did intend to save the Glenn. Perhaps, he meant to help...

"No." I turned and shouldered Holland before stalking down the now crumbling hallway.

"Son! If you don't allow me to help, then whatever you saw will come to fruition!" His voice trailed me as I walked.

I shook my head even as my steps increased. Like hell, that would happen. Holland allowed me to drag her through several hallways until we were, at last, outside in the cool night air.

"Dale, what's going on?"

"How did you know where to find me?" I hated the bite in my voice.

"I...your father told me you were in trouble," her voice dropped to a whisper.

"My father." I gulped and shook my head. He was the master of fucking mind games. "He can't be trusted, Holland."

"I only wanted to help you."

"I could have killed you!" I shouted, gripping her shoulders. "I could have killed you, Holland. I—"

"You didn't. And you won't."

"You don't know that! You don't know what I saw. What I *lived* through. You have no idea what I'm capable of. Dammit, I don't even know!" I threw out my hands, red sizzling at the surface, and took several steps back. "You need to leave me, I'm not safe until I figure this out."

"I'm not going anywhere." Holland took a step toward me.

"Holland, go!"

"You don't get to tell me what to do! I get to decide. Me—" She poked her chest. "—not you. *We* are in this together, Dale." She continued walking toward me.

Holland's missing eyes, black veins on purple, charred flesh that was still smoking...

"I don't need your help. I don't want your help," I snapped before launching myself into the night, the blades of grass ate at my feet as I ran. I needed to remove myself, to create enough space where I wouldn't be a threat to her.

I needed to be far, far away.

CHAPTER 26
TATE

Days passed, as did the weeks. I still hadn't spoken a word to Aether. He'd nearly vanished. I could sense him close, always nearby, but I never saw him. Vala and I worked on my shield building. My mental shields were getting better—still not good enough to block Aether completely, but...part of me savored the way I felt *his* emotions and vulnerability. His pain.

The other part of me loathed that I could feel anything from him at all. And still, guilt gnawed at me for causing his discomfort.

I was a complete mess.

And...I still hadn't managed to shift. *She* hadn't manifested. It didn't matter how much Vala tried to coax her forward, showed me how she shifted, and explained the strands of magic, my inner beast refused to surface.

It was infuriating.

"Maybe I can't shift." I threw my hands up in surrender.

"Tate." She gave me a pointed look. "Trust me, you can. You said you've shifted before, into a bird, yes?"

I nodded.

"Well, then you can shift. Have you tried to shift into a raven since you've been here?" Vala waited, giving me another look.

I hadn't. In fact, I'd been so enraptured in becoming one of them, in stepping into my Untish origins, that I hadn't given it a thought. Shifting into a raven when there were fire-breathing beasts flying around felt pitiful.

Vala cleared her throat.

Fine. I closed my eyes and found the shifting thread, willing it to reveal my raven but...nothing. It was as I'd suspected, but had never voiced, the raven was gone. Replaced by this dragon, this inner beast, who refused to awaken.

"No. I can't, I think the beast killed her."

Vala began laughing.

"What?"

"Tate—" Her chest shook from giggling as she spoke. "—your raven was likely a different manifestation of your beast—prior to the *Changing*. It's likely that since you've completed the *Changing*, your shifting expression has also changed. So, I'd say your raven has merely *evolved*. Maybe she wants you to talk to her like before!?"

"That's absolutely ridiculous." Even as I said it, I inwardly assessed and looked for my old friend. I sent a wave down the string calling for her, but only the eyes of a dragon responded, squinting, before huffing and curling around herself further. "Definitely not the problem. Is it common for shifters to have alternate forms like I did, besides dragons?"

"Not for the Untish. I mean, in some rare cases, *uber*-powerful shifters can shift into other creatures prior to the Changing, but they almost always lose that connection once their Untish genes fully express themselves, they become all beast." She raised her hands and scrunched her fingers like claws. "Rawr!"

I snorted and shook my head. "Well, *I've* heard there are shifters who can become *cats* and *birds*," I challenged, if only to prove I knew *some* things. "I mean, we even had some shifters in the Glenn who were killed because of their ability."

She grimaced. "I know. It's horrible."

"So why are they able to shift into something else, but the Untish can't?"

"I mean, *Fae* can sometimes shift into other creatures, and sometimes if you're part Fae, you may be able to shift, but of the few Fae we have here at the Embassy, none can shift—*especially* not into a dragon." She tilted her head and shrugged. "Some would like us to believe they're superior because of their *pure* Fae blood, but really, we can kick their ass in an instant. But, uh, don't tell James I said that."

I laughed at that. James would undoubtedly be offended by the insinuation. But still, some Fae could shift into other creatures—at least the shifters in my mother's stories were real.

Were the shifters who dwelled in the Glenn part Fae or full Fae who could shift? My mother had told me stories about the Fern Vamp's leniency toward their citizens who could shift—I'd often thought we'd end up there one day, not that I'd end up here at the Embassy by myself.

I thought back to the Shifting Vamp she'd mentioned, the hope she'd given me of an alternate path, the one I'd long ago suspected she was trying to locate.

"Vala, are the Untish considered a Shifting Vamp? Like a rogue group?"

My heart pounded as all the pieces came together. As the half-truths and deceptions finally untangled from their intricately woven web.

"Oh, yes. I mean, before the Great War, that's what we were *heavily* considered. But obviously we're not just vampires." She rolled her eyes. "In fact, *any* vampire who can shift would have to have some expression of Fae blood in their veins, but to your question, yes. Long ago, we were referred to as that. And since, we've become a mythical group to all who are unaware of the Untish Embassy."

I released an aggravated breath.

I knew Irene and Fletch were working with Arithi—that realization had stung. But to now realize she'd merely alluded to the Embassy while lying to me about it when I was desperate for shifters and people like myself? It hurt.

"Why didn't my mother bring me here?" I whispered.

Vala's sympathetic look had me instantly regretting the question, I moved to get some space, to return to our training, but she grabbed my wrist, stopping me.

"Tate, they *were* working for us. I mean, from what I gathered, Irene and Fletch were Untish operatives placed in the Glenn not long after the Great War." Her eyes held an appreciative hue. "Their work was invaluable. Because of them, we learned of the seethings, and they were helping gather as much information on their creation as possible. That's...that's how we found the compound that we destroyed. It was because of Fletch continuing your mother's work. His last transmission contained the coordinates for the base and a promise to find more...and well, when he went silent, Aether gathered a retrieval team, including yours truly—my first real mission—to go get you and bring you here."

My chest felt impossibly tight.

I recalled Fletch's laugh and Irene's green eyes.

Their lives had meaning, purpose.

Angry tears seeped through my eyes, and I swatted at them wildly. They did what they believed was right, they sacrificed themselves to save innocents.

"I'm so sorry," Vala whispered as she pulled me into a hug.

I crumbled into her embrace, leaned into her warmth. I stayed like that for several minutes as my mind pulled at the different strings, deciphering my reality.

Aether reached out through the bond, testing, but I shoved him away. I had enough to deal with at the moment without recalling my anger toward him.

She *roared* within, stirring my energy.

I was powerful. I would continue their work and stop the seethings. I would master this magic, and avenge my mother's death, Fletch's death, and the hundreds of others who were cruelly slain. I didn't understand Irene's secrecy, her lies, but I did understand she believed in the good of all, in protecting the innocent, and in justice.

I would avenge her.

And so, we practiced, and I went to work with renewed vigor.

THE REST of the afternoon we worked on growing my skills. I still couldn't shift—a fact I'd tried not to focus on too much, it was... depressing.

We'd moved on to other expressions of magic, namely shields. I focused on the ground in front of me. I'd been able to manifest one, small, but powerful. I just needed to learn to build domes like Vala had. It wasn't lost on me that the Luna Tribe gifts were in magic manipulation, shields, and potions. I may never get as good at shielding as Vala simply due to my *genetics*.

I huffed. Even our training field was shielded by a visual dome Vala had erected.

It was as if I was given the ability to manifest each tribe's gifts, but perhaps never as powerfully as they could. Quantity over quality, just my luck.

I still had yet to research and willingly understand my genes. I was ever the embracer of ignorance—a bird burying my head in the sand. And for right now, I was more than okay with that.

I tried again to form a dome, a strong shield. It blinked and then vanished.

Thus far, I was supposedly gifted but couldn't shift, could barely shield, and I still sucked at hand-to-hand combat. Apparently, for the Untish, vampires from the Glenn were like fighting children. They didn't compare to the skill the Untish fought with.

I may never get as good as Camella in sparring. Something she didn't understand since I was, to her knowledge, a member of the Shadow Tribe. Brute force and power were *supposed* to be my gifts. Her frustration with me was becoming evident.

The shield formed in front of me, and I held it for a moment, smiling as I did so. Perhaps I would master this, and then I'd go and kick Camella's butt and—

The shield blinked out.

I hissed through gritted teeth as I focused on the strands of magic, pulling and webbing them together once again. The air shimmered around me, forming a dome, and I pushed more energy into it.

"Good! Trust your instincts," Vala commanded.

I did, I felt the pull and followed it until the shield fluttered above me and pulsed. Solidified. It was small, barely encompassed my body, but I'd done it.

"Amazing! Girl, that's soo impressive. I'm not sure I've seen anyone outside of the Luna Tribe do what you just did." Vala jumped to her feet. "Let's test its strength." She physically pressed on it; it didn't budge.

Vala's smile was radiant.

She withdrew a dagger and tried stabbing the shield near my feet, still it held. Lastly, she threw her magic at it, trying to disassemble and commandeer it.

No, this shield would not fail.

I forced more of my anger and power into the wavering dome.

She continued to press with her magic, willing my shield to fail me. At first, it wavered, but then it pulsed and Vala was blasted backwards, landing on her ass.

"Shit, Tate. That's as good as *my* shields! We just need to work on physical awareness now and then we can work on *projecting* shields. You're a quick learner," she said as she brushed herself off and stood up —pride shining in her eyes.

"You're a good teacher." Fletch would have liked her. The thought sent pain through me.

I shook my head as I silenced my thoughts. I didn't want to think about the male I'd failed. The one I ignored, disregarded, and then was in part to blame for his death.

"So, uh, how are things with his royal jackass?" Vala pried.

One sobering thought to another. I let the shield drop, the energy from holding it was exhausting.

"The same," I bit out. I inhaled the air and energy from the land, rich and ready like Vala had said, and refilled my stores.

"You can't stay mad at him forever. I mean, you *could* have killed him, and you didn't soo...you must not hate him. And I know he is all about you," Vala said.

I shrugged. "He lied. He manipulated our bond, and with it, the cause of my emotions. It's going to take time, Vala."

"I know, but time is something that we have lots of until we don't, you know?" She adjusted her stance. Odd for her to be short when she normally rambles.

"What does that mean?" I pried. "What do you know, Vala?"

She bit her lip. "Let's start working on your manipulation of fire. We'll do some basic tactics, although honestly, Aether will be better at this than me..."

"Stop evading. What do you mean about time?"

She sighed as she tilted her head to the side. "Just that when we lose those we love and can't get them back, we reevaluate the use of our time when they were here." She sniffed. "I lost my sister a few years ago, we were twins."

I didn't move. "I'm so sorry, I didn't know."

"Nothing for you to know about. I just miss her. But it has me thinking about what she'd be doing if she were here. What she'd think of Jared, who she'd be matched with?" She sighed. "Tate, if Aether did *die*, how would you feel?" She raised her brows in emphasis.

I sucked on my fang. Point taken. "Let's work on fire."

"Right. But you need to get out of your mind. You can do this."

I simply shook my head and squared my shoulders. I'd been able to summon flames briefly, but never control the fire. It appeared that since my dragon was AWOL, my fire was temperamental...at least for the most part.

"Okay, will the flames forward, just like you did with the shield.

Feel the strands within, and force it to materialize while fueling it with energy from your stores or, if you can, the stores from the planet."

"Is that all?" I asked; this task seemed impossible.

"Nope, summon the flames and then hit that tree over there, but don't burn it."

I looked at her like she lost her mind.

"There's power in restraint, Tate."

The wisdom in her statement gave me pause. It reminded me of Shae; they would get along great. The thought echoed with a pang in my chest. I was doing this in part for her, to set things right. I was sharpening my arsenal of weapons to get back to Shae.

"All right." I aimed my hands and felt the power pulsing through my veins. I could sense the pink strand growing, building with energy. I hadn't been able to successfully access it since I fought with Aether, and then I was so enraged I didn't pay attention to *how* I'd used my magic.

I felt the flames building, and could see them in my vision a second before I tried to release them. They flickered and then died.

"Tate, you said when you fought Aether, you used fire, yes?" Vala asked.

"Yes," I replied through gritted teeth.

"Why do you think you were able to do that then and not now?"

"I don't know." Anger rose in my belly at the admission.

"You want to know what I think? I think you've got an emotional blockage. Free it, Tate. Don't be afraid of it. Use the anger," Vala coached as she challenged me with her eyes.

My anger rallied and flames materialized before flying, a stream of pink fire, engulfing the tree. I stood there, shocked for a moment. I'd done it, summoned fire—but only through emotion. I tried to pull the flames back, but they devoured the elm in seconds. Moments later, it was completely burnt.

"Well, I'd say we have our next thing to work on," Vala chirped. "Try again, this time attempt to *control* it."

CHAPTER 27

TATE

It was quiet when I entered Aether's home. I walked past the kitchen and went to the balcony, the waves crashed against the cliffs, providing the only sound. Everything else was quiet—Aether wasn't here.

Disappointment flooded me, along with the irony of that emotion. I drove him from his home and then had the nerve to miss him.

Worse, I was angry that he wasn't here. I couldn't show him my anger and process it out loud when he wasn't here to listen. Vala's words filled my mind. If Aether died and I didn't explore the bond with him, how would I feel?

Like shit.

I wanted the bond. Missed and craved him, but I loathed that it was, in part, because he manipulated the initial bond. I lowered myself into a stuffed patio chair and pulled out my disk.

The list of unread documents was vast. I needed to study...not think about the male who was, as Vala commonly stated, a royal jackass

I'd been too focused on training with Vala—hoping to finally shift like all the other shifters in my class—and busy with Camella, getting

181

my ass handed to me in training, to read. Or at least, that's the excuse I was willing to recognize.

It had nothing to do with me *not* wanting to learn about bonds and avoiding my potential heritage.

I hovered over the library's research tab, pausing only a moment before I double-tapped, opening up a new display. I wanted to know more about Perry and Matias's bond—they blood shared and supposedly that's how they bonded. But I wanted the details. Aside from the fact that she was already bonded to Egon and then re-bonded Matias, I didn't know much.

The facts I did know were unnerving.

Too similar to my story, and from what I gathered over the past few weeks of lectures, being bonded *outside* of a Matching Ceremony was incredibly rare.

Practically undocumented.

I searched the database for the origin of Untish bonding and several articles appeared. I tapped on the top result, but a box popped up blocking it.

Restricted.

I bit my lip.

I needed an access code. I tapped on the next and got the same message. So...I could either read the articles and books with data assigned to me, or I could get a general's passcode to read what I really wanted to know.

Do you have a passcode for the database? I asked the void between Aether and I.

A moment went by and no response. I lowered my walls, and I could *feel* him again, relief flooded me. His mere presence, even from afar, had a comforting effect. It felt oddly natural.

Yes. 083400323.

I punched in the code and then threw my walls back up. His presence diminished and my stomach knotted.

I locked my jaw.

He did this to me—made me a conflicted internal mess.

The article opened and I began reading. Perry was bonded to Egon, but they had only been together for a couple of years. She was young and her magic was wild, impractical. He, too, was pure Fae. He was a high lord from the House of Iron; before they had chairs, they had rulers—much like modern governors in the human realm, I surmised. Egon was responsible for an entire Iron clan territory.

By all accounts, Matias was a servant in his house—a *half-breed*, part vampire and part human. I wrinkled my nose at the slur; even then, people were assholes.

I continued skimming. So much of this seemed like speculation. Where was the actual testimony? Did Perry have an autobiography? It irked me for some inexplicable reason that this female, the mother of dragons and the Untish clan, was being surmised about. That her romantic life was being exposed and commented on by males from centuries ago.

Even still, I kept reading. Allegedly, Perry spent time with Matias while Egon was afar, traveling or—according to this article—entertaining one of his mistresses. Suddenly, I understood Perry a little better. While the content mentioned Egon's many dalliances, it focused primarily on Perry and Matias's friendship before it finally discussed their bond.

It is believed that Perry and Matias ran away together to the Cave of Unity, where their magic bonded and, according to Perry's recovered journals, so did they.

I paused, making a mental note to find the original journals before reading the copied entry:

"His golden eyes beckoned me. I should have been more afraid, he was a vampire, after all—well, in part." Perry's recorded entry began. *"But it wasn't because he was mine, and I was his. Our magic knew one another, bound us before we'd even agreed. It's as if our love was an afterthought, second nature to the entity that is magic itself. We were helplessly bound in its echoes of love, and in that cave, it became unrestrained. Like a kaleido- scope, our magics blended and became one. The force was one that could never be undone. Could not be rejected. There were no choices. We were*

bound, even before our joining. Our love merely intensified the bond that had formed, and, after our joining, Matias and I were more connected than Egon and I ever could have hoped to be."

The journal entry cut out for a moment with more surmising what this meant, before allowing Perry to speak for herself once more.

"The bond I had with Egon snapped. It was nothing compared to the force of true love—of a pure bond, chosen by Mother Blood and magic herself."

Perry didn't seem too distraught over not having a choice. Magic as its own entity? Hadn't Vala said something to that sort? Or was it Professor Darsew?

I reread that line: *"The force was one that could not be undone. Could not be rejected. There were no choices. We were bound, even before our joining."*

Could there be some twist of fate that had joined Aether and I prior to our agreement, to our knowledge? I bit my lip.

"The pure bond that I have with Matias is nothing short of blissful. I've never known true joy before and never will again. I am convinced that when he dies, so shall my heart. Extending his life force is of the utmost importance, but first I must ensure our survival. There's nothing I won't do for him," Perry wrote.

The text went on to explain the war that ensued. Houses stood up against them, led by Egon and the House of Iron, but they all fell as they witnessed what Perry had become. None could face a dragon. I may be new to the Untish history, but I understood enough about research to understand that the author of this biography selected which excerpts of Perry's journal to include. I couldn't help but wonder what was excluded. Was this idea of magic being an entity really one Perry shared? Or had her words been chipped at to provide that narrative?

"With our magic mixed, I changed. I altered on a cellular level and had access to magic I'd only dreamt of. It was not pure, like the force of my own blood magic. It was wild, it was beastly, it was vengeful. It was the breath of

a dragon that Matias had awoken inside me, gifted me. He too rose up, but not like me—he couldn't bear fire, he was still susceptible to it."

Interesting. So, Perry transformed into the first dragon recorded *because* of the 'lowly' blood of humans and vampires, just as Professor Darsew taught. I recalled the lesson from weeks before, Perry and Matias were the parents of the Untish Clan—a breed of shifters that were mixed by all three races: human, vampire, and Fae.

I closed out of the article, making a note to visit it later, and searched for *Perry's Journal* as cited in the content I'd just read. The database displayed several secondary sources, and other articles about Perry, but not the actual journal.

I had suspected this would be the case, but it still stung.

The Untish, like the Glenn, hid certain truths from its citizens. I tried an alternative search, and it yielded the same results. I'd need to ask Aether about it later.

Even still, the information I'd just gained was helpful.

As the truth slowly sunk in, it demanded I recognize my bond for what it was: a repeat of history.

My ancestor experienced something so similar to what I had with Aether. She too was bent by magic's will.

That is, assuming Perry's account was authentic. I shoved the disk in my bag and began a series of squats, allowing the burn of stretching muscles to silence my thoughts.

CHAPTER 28

CHANCE

I leaned over the plump female and savored the way her body trembled from my presence. A whimper escaped her lips as I retracted my fangs from the base of her neck and slowly righted myself, but not before allowing a brief caress of the exposed swell of her breasts. They were, after all, on display for all to see. It was partly why I picked the plump ginger as my vessel. She looked nothing like Holland.

I stood, dropping a few coins into her pouch, and then began briskly pacing through the room toward the exit. Fresh blood usually elicited the most sensual impulses, but now? Now all I wanted was Holland, and I could be *nowhere* near her. It wasn't safe.

Breathy moans peaked as the couple ahead on the chaise climaxed, the vampirical female taking great pleasure in fucking the vessel. He too seemed lost in euphoria as he grunted with his orgasm.

I tuned out the noises of the sex-addled and instead increased my pace as I passed several more vampires feeding, most of which were actively fucking—including a threesome in the corner.

Even with the amount of sexual stimulation, all I craved was the honeysuckle scent of Holland. All I wanted was her blood. But my magic wanted more, it wanted to taste hers. That wouldn't happen.

Three females dressed in nothing but pasties and thongs looked at me, eyes alluring.

"We could all take turns," one said.

Another wiggled her finger. "We don't bite, that's your job."

I shook my head as I moved quickly past them, thinking again of Holland.

I was too fucking sober for this mental battle. I pushed the heavy door open, slunk through the piano lounge, and then into the adjoining unkept pub. The gloriously window-free, forget your worries, dux or higher pub.

I took an available seat and ordered several pitchers of bloodwine, and a few of plain wine. I wanted to become lost and unfindable by my worrisome thoughts. Even after downing the contents of three pitchers, I was still sober. Sober enough to note how the table beneath my elbows was rough, splintered. To pick out several bits of wood from my arms and be irritated that I was concerned about these tiny wooden flakes when I should be sinking into sweet oblivion, if not the arms of the female I loved.

And so, I drank.

And drank.

And still, I continued to wash away all traces of my troubled thoughts and confusing desires.

My consciousness came and went in waves. Duxes came and left; the barmaids changed several times until the small female now tending the tables was the one I'd first met when I'd entered. In this decrepit little pub, a place for the 'elite', I'd wasted away. Allowed myself to throw a fucking pity party. But it felt...quiet. Not numb, no, the magic refused to be silenced, but it was more of a whisper now.

The pitcher of bloodwine in front of me was nearly empty. I clutched it and tipped it back, allowing the iron to coat my throat until it was well and truly void.

A roar of laughter erupted from several vampires who exited the pub together, leaving the place emptier, but still much too loud. There were maybe only twenty other vampires in here. Most were in groups; the rest, like me, were loners. I'd look up from time to time, checking to see if I knew anyone, part of me longing for Holland to stride through the doors, and the other part dreading it. I didn't recognize most of the individuals in here. I snorted. Why would I? It had been a while since I'd spent any time at Southern Outpost in revelry.

"Another!" I commanded. The small human approached with a pitcher in her wobbly hand. Her eyes widened as she looked at me. "What's wrong, never seen a drunk-k before?" I snapped at her, not caring that I was spitting as I spoke.

She dropped the pitcher to the table and then stepped back. "No, I mean yes, it's—" she gulped "—just that—" She abruptly stopped speaking and then turned and bolted from the room, nearly knocking over a large male in her hurry.

I shook my head and reached for the pitcher. I saw it then. The consuming hue of red.

Red.

Red dancing across my arms. Red lightning, red static, red death...

I clenched and unclenched my fist before adjusting my coat to cover my wrists, minimizing its exposure. Sure enough, or perhaps, *drunk* enough, the coat blocked the static and I appeared normal. But I was anything *but* normal.

A monster. That's what she saw.

I grabbed the pitcher, along with the cup near it, and then poured myself another large pint. I couldn't change what I was, but I could drink to forget. A male wobbled as he exited the bar, inebriated beyond normal limits. Perhaps this is what became of outcasts. We isolated and drank ourselves into senselessness.

The power inside was growing, it wanted to be freed. To show the world how magnificent *it* was. I could feel the magic and energy pouring from each vampire in the pub. Funny since we were taught at a young age that vampires *didn't* possess much magic and were required to disclose any we *did have* upon transitioning. All gifts were to be used for the benefit of the Glenn. Even still, strong magic was rare. Gifts like agility and speed, like my pre-monster powers, were common. Holland's emo-tasting gift was rare, but well-known and understood. But the magic I was sensing in this room from these individuals alone?

It was clear we'd been lied to about what magical stores we *all* possessed.

Most in here probably didn't even know how to wield what they had, or perhaps it hadn't awakened yet. It was hard to imagine not knowing you have magic, especially if it was strong and wild. Like the couple across from me, their magic was potent—I couldn't identify what their gifts were, but it felt mysterious. I bet they'd be useful spies.

The group to my left had magic that reminded me of brute force. Others had mediocre scores of power, indicating any possible gift. I laughed dryly before taking another swig of the rich iron. Our very DNA had been hidden from us, our very giftings undisclosed. How different would the world be if every citizen could harness their giftings?

I itched my new scruff, a 'beard' as I'd once proudly called it, and cracked my neck. This was all too much. Too much thinking, especially with the amount of liquor I'd downed. I needed more. Something stronger.

The male in the corner ordered another pitcher while he stared at the other patrons, much as I did. His power felt strange and smelt sour somehow. I tried to focus on him clearly, but in my buzzed state, his features were blurry. Sniffing again, his odd scent met my senses, but I still couldn't recognize its flavor.

Even a few of the human servers had an alluring pull to them, their magic smelling different—unpredictable even.

I had become a fucking bloodhound.

I emptied the cup and filled it again. The door opened and several males strode in, laughing as they took seats at a large round table not far from the corner I was in.

"Ach! You should've seen 'em! He was all twisted around her

finger!" a large ginger nearly shouted as his belly jiggled from his roar. His unkempt beard had several bits of spit dotting its frayed bed.

"You mean her ancient finger!" a blond male responded, slapping the ginger on his back.

"Ach, yes! Could you imagin'?" the ginger roared again before pounding the table, signally he wanted service.

The small human girl approached with three pitchers and cups. She placed them on the table before stepping back.

"Now you're a wee thing, what has you workin' a place like this?" the brunette asked. He appeared to be the fiercest of them, jagged scars covered his arms and neck. His magic was strong. It smelt like that of a protector—a shielder, perhaps. If that were even a thing. Then again, that bitch who was with Mardi formed a dome, so shielding was unquestionably a gift.

"I uh, l-live near here and n-need the, th-the money," she whispered before curtseying and scurrying away.

A round of laughter ensued as the males mocked her and took turns imitating her stutter and insecurities. Brutes. Powerful ones.

I could feel the pull of their magic, it tasted different. Wild.

I grabbed the pitcher and began drinking straight from it. I needed to numb everything.

"So, when did that lumbering giant say we were leaving for HQ?" the ginger asked, speaking as bloodwine dripped down his beard and onto the table.

"Ach! A matter of days. I guess there's been some trouble near the city, and we have to fortify troops there, build up some sign of force or some bullshit," the blond responded. "You really think another Vamp would be stupid enough to go to war with us?"

I sure as hell did. More wine, I was still far too coherent. I needed *much* more wine.

"You know what they say, we got the brains, and they got the booty!" the ginger roared, before bending over in laughter.

I cringed as I bit on my lip to keep my retort inside.

"The whole outpost is on alert. Several leaders are being moved like bloody chess pieces. So yes, I believe we are truly going to be battling some foreign ass," the male with dark hair responded. "We *won't* let Dux Carran down."

The men nodded. "To Dux Carran!" They raised their cups and clinked in the middle, wine sloshing, before they drank.

So, troops were being relocated. Odd considering the S.O. was on the border. Unless...unless there was concern about an attack on HQ. The thought had my stomach souring.

Perhaps, it was merely optics. Or better yet, the idiots currently drowning themselves in bloodwine were fools and had no idea what they spoke of.

Yes, I liked that option. The alternative of an open attack on a civilian-filled city was jarring, as was my sobriety.

I drank deeply, even as several patrons began to clear out. The large male in the corner strode for the door, his red pompadour as obnoxious as his scent.

I wished I'd never wanted power.

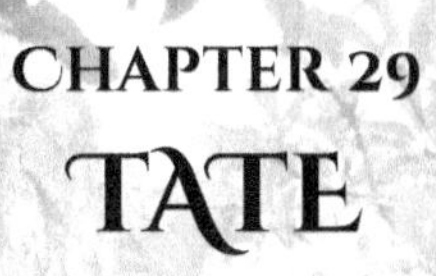

CHAPTER 29
TATE

"Again," Vala commanded.

I grunted in response and once more tried to reach for the internal thread that led to my shifting pool. I felt *her* laughing at me, refusing to surface.

I growled as I yanked on the string and...nothing happened.

"Yes!" a nearby Liver shouted to his pupil who had managed to shift into the ugliest green dragon I'd ever seen—the shade of vomit. But even with his unfortunate appearance, I'd take that over *not* being able to shift.

"Remind me *why* we are practicing here today instead of in the valley?" I muttered, pulling the loose grey tunic closer to my body—feeling exposed.

"Because a change of environment is good. You were having zero breakthroughs in the valley. And—you know, you're my first pupil, well you and one other, but this is new to me—and so I thought seeing several others shift could be helpful. So again, look for that thread and just...shift?" She cringed at the last word while smoothing her white tunic.

Naked males and females strode about on the flat expanse of the field—the shifting platform as it was known. Two females giggled as a male, a black-haired mountain of a Darkling, strode past and winked. His butt cheeks were chiseled, and he obviously had no shame in showing his arousal—fully on display.

My cheeks flushed. "This is stupid, Vala. You said I need to be careful not to show anyone my magic, and yet here I am out in the open." I lowered my voice as I spoke, "I don't want them to you know, see…"

"Don't worry about that. I'm actively reinforcing the cloak on you *and* I've got a shield in place that will alter what they see. It's incredibly draining, but worth it if you can find a breakthrough."

I looked closely at her then. For the first time, I noticed the sweat pooling at her hairline, around her eyes, and wetting the white fabric loosely covering her chest.

I'd been self-obsessed. A bitch, in many ways, a borderline—

"Let go! Release some energy, fly!" the Liver nearby was screaming, legs splayed wide through the thigh-high slits of his green tunic, at a beast who was beginning to violently shake.

It threw back its head and roared.

"Breathe fire!" the tutor screamed as his shield began to dome around the two of them. Even from a hundred yards out, I could feel the violent tremor coming from the dragon.

His cries filled the air, quickly followed by screams and whines as the vomit-colored dragon transitioned back to his humanoid form and shrieked. In a flash, he was curled up on the ground. Not only was he *naked*, but he was bloodied—no, he was blistered and burned—and he just kept screaming.

He. Would. Not. Stop.

I cupped my hands over my ears as Vala formed a second shield, silencing the noise. A noise dome.

"Thank you," I muttered.

She simply nodded, another tell-tale sign of her exhaustion. She couldn't keep this up forever, and from her appearance, this training session wouldn't last much longer.

"Why is he in pain?" All the other shifting I'd witnessed seemed... harmless. Victorious, even.

"If it's not done correctly, it can hurt. But, like, he probably was trying to hold the power and manipulate it further against its will, and...magic does *not* like that. When you are in your beast form, everything is heightened. Everything you feel and everything you see will be intensified tenfold. But with this comes an increased connection to your magic, to the inner and external pools of power all around you. In this case, it would appear he didn't harness it correctly and didn't express any of it, so he burned from within and that forced an immature transition back." She blew a stray, white-tipped curl from her face.

"Expressed how? How does one let go of energy while remaining a beast?"

"It can be done in many, many ways." She shrugged and gulped. "Breathing fire, flying, manipulating air, or using other giftings, if you're capable—not all dragon shifters are. Sometimes, the beast form is the fullest expression of magic, but that doesn't negate the need to express some of the energy from time to time. His tutor should have prepared him better."

I gave her a pointed look. She'd just now chosen to tell me this... and I'd been trying to shift for hours. Days. Weeks.

She waved me off.

The male finally ceased screaming as several Luners carried him off the field, a blanket of magic surrounded him, easing his pain.

Vala released the noise dome and panted. "All right, I say we give it one more good try, and then...then we change tactics."

One more try? I could do this. I nodded in response and then closed my eyes. Where was she?

Come out...come out...

Inner fire erupted down the string, singeing my internal pull. Clearly, she didn't like to be taunted. Well, neither did I.

Not. One. Bit.

I pulled aggressively this time, willing *her* to awaken, to finally get off her ass and do something. Instead of shifting, she nipped at me and growled before curling into a tight ball. All the internal fire I'd felt vanished.

I was cold. I was empty. I didn't shift.

"Well, that's okay...we'll just keep trying," Vala said encouragingly.

"Sure," I huffed. "Maybe *someday* I'll be able to shift...when I'm dead."

"Tate." She rolled her eyes at my dramatics. "You'll get there. In fact—" Vala's eyes got wide. "Follow me."

She began striding off the field, her long legs elegantly slipping through the hip-high slits on either side of her tunic—a tunic that was only pinned at her shoulders and hips, the rest was loose and flowing so as to allow optimal comfort when shifting. I snorted at the thought.

Vala continued stalking across the field and only glanced over her shoulder once. After a moment of hesitation, I jogged after her.

My muscles ached from the work I'd been putting in, the hundreds of squats and pushups and sparring and—

An Ironhead female winked at me, striding by with long blonde hair that turned red at the ends. Her painted lips were blood red and her eyes...bright red. Her breasts bounced as she walked, and she swayed her hips emphasizing every ounce of exposed flesh. Confidence. She didn't just have it, she possessed it.

A Blight stepped up to her and, almost as if driven by an invisible force, they jumped at each other. A clusterfuck of limbs and bodies, hovering in midair, before shifting into massive beasts that pumped strong wings higher and higher into the sunlit sky—their bodies were perfectly entangled. I shivered as their dragon *moans* echoed across the extensive field. They were doing it? In dragon form? My eyes bulged as I studied the scene above, fully transfixed.

"Tate?" Vala called from ahead.

I shook my head, kept my damn eyes down, and rushed after her. I'd had enough nudity for the day.

．　．　．

VALA HAD TAKEN me to a small overlook, partially jutting out over the turquoise sea below, with an infinity pool that poured over the cliff's edge...just vanishing. There was a Untishee school below, just in the distance, but close enough to observe each small figure running around. Small children. Some practiced their magic as they ran about, and others were simply playing. Laughter rose to meet the sound of the crashing waves and the slow drizzle of the water pouring over the edge.

The breath I'd been holding was finally loosening. Tension drained from my shoulders as a smile played across my lips at the pure joy in the children below.

"I thought this might help," Vala said.

"Hmm?" I reluctantly pulled my eyes from the happy scene to meet Vala's chocolate ones. She had stripped out of her tunic and boots and stood before me completely nude.

My cheeks heated, and I looked away, swallowing my nervous laughter.

"Well?"

I blinked. "Well, what?"

"Tate," she laughed. "We don't have suits...and this *is* a holy pool." She pointedly nodded to the infinity pool that overlooked the sea.

"Oh." Confidence, I could possess it—or at least try. I reminded myself that I was a dragon shifter, and that nudity was a part of my way of life. I removed my boots and then yanked off my grey tunic and let it fall to the ground in a crumpled mess before striding, head high even with my uneven steps, into the heated pool. Sulfur filled the air along with steam.

A presence coated over me. Calming. Transfixing. Mesmerizing.

Vala stepped in and the water moved and splashed, only adding more steam to the air. I sank further into the glorious pool until everything but my head was submerged.

Hello, daughter...

Peace, unbeknownst to me, blanketed every nerve ending. Any

remaining tension vanished. I was a puddle, a pile of goo and putty, completely moldable in this pool of tranquility.

"I thought you'd like this," Vala said, but even her voice sounded different. Less pitchy. Less energetic. Nearly distant. "This place is holy to the Untishee, some say it's hogwash, but I believe in its restorative powers and given that you seem to be facing an emotional blockage, I thought this could help."

Her words just washed over me and didn't stick. Not as I threw back my head and allowed the water to fill my ear canals, savoring the way I simply just...felt.

"Mmmm."

In the distance, I could feel Aether's power riling...begging to connect, but then it snuffed out. Respectfully. He hadn't pressed things since I'd made it clear I needed space.

Space.

Time.

More space.

Would I ever heal?

I wasn't so sure. But in this moment, the beckoning of the water massaged my aching muscles. It emptied my well of pain, cleansing me from all the shit I'd been through recently. Images of my mother in this very pool flooded my mind. I bet she loved it here.

Even Fletch probably enjoyed a rejuvenating soak from time to time.

Silent tears began to pour down my face, absorbed by the pool. Absolved.

The guilt I'd been clinging to was flaking from me, being pried from my soul and coaxed out bit by bit.

It wasn't your fault. Fletch's voice sounded.

Alarmed, I jerked up, searching. He wasn't here. In fact, no one was...not even Vala. I turned and searched more. But I was alone in the pool.

The panic faded as laughter from below sounded. I swam to the pool's edge and propped my head on my arms as I gazed down at the children playing.

A little girl was being chased, her deep blonde pigtails were bouncing wildly in the wind. A mother ran after her, somehow familiar...her mahogany eyes, blonde hair that faded to...pink. She caught the girl and swung her around.

"Mother, you caught me!" she squealed.

"Always, Tatealia," the female said. She looked up, and her eyes locked with my own. A sad smile graced her lips before she looked to the child in her arms once more and spun around in circles, laughter coating the air. The little girl wiggled her feet, suddenly shoeless, highlighting her bone discrepancy. The mother jerked violently and then tripped, stumbled, and fell to her knees as black veins crept up her cheeks. The child flew through the air, headed for certain pain and death at the impending cobblestone railing.

I jerked in the water, willing her to stop but nothing happened. She flipped over herself, once, twice, three times...

She was nearly at the cliff's edge.

A cry clawed up my throat but before I could release it, two able-bodied arms caught the child midair. Another female.

"Mama!" the girl squealed.

Except, this wasn't the same female as before. No, this female was wholly known to me. Her green eyes and dirty blonde hair. Her smile and splatter of freckles. Irene.

"I got you, Tate." She nuzzled the little girl while squeezing tightly.

By the fountain in the courtyard beyond, the first female lay crumpled. Her flesh grey, her life drained. Gone. Dead.

I shook my head as inexplicable sobs overcame me. I'd witnessed death before. I'd seen the impact of sickness, and yet...this was opening a deep chasm of pain within my soul.

Irene looked up at me, she waved and smiled. "I'm proud of you, my girl."

I threw out my hands, reaching for her, but she and the child in her arms vanished. A plume of mist and smoke filled the air and she was no more. The corpse, too, was gone. The courtyard was empty.

I swiveled in the water, searching for anyone.

But I was alone.

Alone.

The crack in my heart further fractured as tears welled and began to pour, an unstoppable torrent of pain. Pain I hadn't known I'd held. Truths I had long ago buried. Truths I still didn't want to fully face.

But in the midst of turmoil, came a certain reassurance. A certain calm. I had made it. I was *home*.

Ash and salt flooded my senses along with the dark, brooding presence of Aether in my mind.

In a plume of smoke just hovering over the water, I could see Aether. Staring at me, but not. This wasn't real. I *knew* this, and yet...it felt real. Just like the vision from the courtyard. Just like Fletch's voice...

The vision in the smoke changed and now it was Aether, defending me from Jared and protecting me in my vulnerability at the settlement after I'd witnessed seethings for the first time. Even in that circle, when my powers were manifesting, Aether stood by me. Protected me. Even from *his own* men.

With a swirl, the image changed again to show that gruesome valley with the seethings pouring in over the trees, Aether standing alone—the avenging angel—ready to fight and kill and protect. Except, now the emotions I'd felt from him were clear. They were *his* emotions. The terror, the rage, the awe...they had been from *him*. I'd felt the connection then, but seeing it written all over his face now...it was too much.

Tears gushed from me as the image blinked out and only smoke swirled silently over the pool. I crumbled as the overwhelming feeling of *love* washed over me.

Our bond *hadn't* been manufactured.

All of that had occurred *before* he'd given me his blood. Before our connection was strengthened.

Our bond was pure.

Right.

Whole.

And most of all, it *was* organic.

A sad smile played across my face as I recalled all the insults I'd hurled at him and the way he'd just taken it. At how he took the brunt of my pain after Fletch's death and let me take it out on him, blame him, beat him.

He was willing to bear my agony if it made me whole.

I began laughing deliriously as joy filled the dry caverns in my soul, in my heart. Its healing warmth began to web across the void within and cover, connect, and bind my fractured being.

Yes, Aether had previously manipulated my emotions. But that was before I'd completed the Changing, and only twice, if he was to be believed: once when he interrogated me about what happened to Fletch, and again when we were on an ops mission and I was panicking, placing us in danger.

I chose to believe him, to allow myself to trust him.

"I choose you!" I shouted before spinning, gloriously free in the healing waters. Even my normally pain-filled left leg was silent, healthy, and strong.

Welcome home, daughter of destiny.

I embraced the voice, swallowed it deep in my belly before surrendering to it completely, floating on my back.

The sky above was beautiful. Dragons soared. Fire erupted from the throat of many, victorious. A smile tugged at my lips as hope blossomed.

My soul was lighter.

My heart was fuller.

My spirit freer.

Healed.

My very being was being slowly mended, slowly restored, slowly made right. Stitch by stitch, until the wounds of the past were closed.

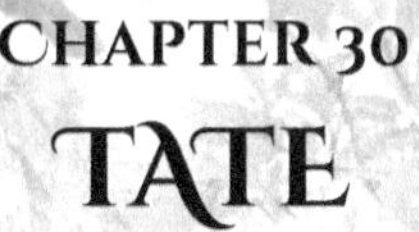

CHAPTER 30
TATE

Will you be home tonight?

I sent the message and dropped my walls, savoring the way ash and salt flooded my mind. The dark parts now lit with *his* fire, if only for a moment before vanishing.

If you wish.

Did I wish? After my senses came back and Vala dragged me from the pool, I'd told her—briefly—what I'd experienced. She was awestruck and told me that kind of breakthrough in the pool was *rare*... to say the least.

Yes, we need to talk.

I gripped my hands, willing my nerves to calm. I understood so much now. It was time for a reckoning with this male.

My male.

I left my walls partially down so I could still feel his presence, but not be consumed by it. Instead, I shook out my limbs before dropping and doing a hundred squats. Weeks ago, I wouldn't have been able to finish. Now? Now, I did nothing but train in one way or another. Aether had pushed me into these classes to prepare me faster. Every single day I spent here, was one more day that the Glenn suffered under President

Dale's leadership. One more day those seethings continued unchecked, spreading like a virus and destroying the land—a cancer, destroying the good left in the Glenn.

Urgency fueled me and so, I squatted, stood, and then squatted again.

Be back soon.

I shivered at his sultry voice, coating my mind. I had come to terms with our bond and my past...but we still needed to talk. I still had questions. Many, many fucking questions.

After my squats, I practiced my shields, erecting one in front of me, to my side, all around me.

I smiled, proud of my progress.

I attempted calling forth a small flame. Nothing. I tried again, mere sparks at my fingertips followed by small bursts of fire, but nothing compared to what I'd previously commanded. My nerves were jumbled up, that's all it was, right? Was it emotional blockage as Vala had suggested? Hadn't I just experienced a life-altering encounter with bits of myself and my past?

I laughed at the thought. My rational mind reminded me that healing takes time. Even with breakthroughs, I needed to be patient. Not my strong suit, but nevertheless, it was required.

I would master this magic. I would get stronger. I would avenge my family.

Huffing, I turned my inspection inward, feeling the different threads within me, identifying which led where and powered what type of magical expression.

It was a maze, but I enjoyed exploring it.

I hopped from foot to foot, smiling as I realized sparks were forming from where my feet connected with the stone terrace. Perhaps, I wasn't hopeless after all. Perhaps the work that began in that pool was still growing, blooming, and mending.

Maybe, just maybe, I'd be whole again one day soon.

The sun dipped and the moon appeared over the sea, sparkling and lighting the water. This place was beautiful, peaceful even.

Hours passed. My body was slicked in sweat and my concentration was on my burning muscles, the pain claiming my immediate attention—a distraction I welcomed.

And yet...still, Aether wasn't back.

Would he not come? Had I ruined our relationship?

Panic laced through me, but I swallowed it. Dammit. I was a grown-ass female, and I could handle myself, I would. But even my internal dialogue did nothing to quell the rising tide of fury at the thought that maybe he didn't mean what he'd said, maybe he wouldn't wait, maybe he'd moved on...

Assessing his presence, I felt a strain, but he was still there. I would wait. He would come, he said he would. If he didn't, well...then I had my answer.

I felt a pull, out toward the sea. Following its lead, I stepped closer to the railing. The air shimmered and I saw him then, flying over the waves in a black shadow of pure wild strength. His scales glinted in the moonlight and even from afar, I could hear the beat of his wings. He approached and was a hundred yards out. My breath left my lungs at his sheer size. I'd forgotten how magnificent he was in this form.

I sensed his smirk and immediately shut it down with a flash of my teeth.

He approached the balcony, and in a shadowed flash, he shifted and launched the final ten feet to the terrace. He dropped, rolled, and then stood from a crouch. Naked.

His eyes hooded, ever the lethal male.

If I wasn't careful, he'd win my entire heart *before* I'd get all my answers.

CHAPTER 31
AETHER

She stood there, hands on her hips, a delicious sweat dripping down her brow. Her scent, fuck if it didn't nearly bring me to my knees, begging. But I stood, waiting. She'd asked me to be here, the hope swelling in my chest could be crushed with a brush of her hands or a few uttered words.

I carefully remained motionless, acutely aware of her scent increasing at the sight of my *length*.

This was a delicate situation. I would be patient. I had been patient, even forcing myself to go on brief recon missions for a few hours at a time. I hated being further than an hour away, but she had been very open with her need for space.

"I have a question, and I need you to be honest," she began.

"Of course, I—"

She silenced me with her hand. "Please, first cover yourself."

I chuckled before striding into my room and grabbing a pair of loose trousers and then reappearing on the terrace. Slowly, I approached her, cautiously, until I was only a few feet away.

Her scent was different. Even down the bond, I'd felt it. Earlier that day, I'd nearly gone into a panicked frenzy at the quieting of our bond, but then it sprung to life, and it felt new somehow. I sensed something had changed, and then she asked me to come here...

I swallowed, trying to keep my emotions in check.

Hope, if crushed, could kill.

She pinned me with a loaded look before sighing heavily. "Please, be completely truthful and hide nothing, no omissions." She arched a brow. "Did our bond exist before the blood sharing, or did you do that first in an attempt to awaken it?"

I breathed, willing the intensity in my gaze to calm. "It was there. I'd felt it long before I gave you my blood. From the moment we met, our bond was forming. And when you started the Changing, it heightened the bond on my end. I'd *felt* the bond that day on the field when you first saw the seethings and came to fight with me. My magic recognized it," I said. There was so much more I wanted to explain, to discuss, but I chose to keep it simple.

My truth lay bare.

"Magic is its own entity," she murmured, eyes averted. "Swear this to me, swear that you speak the truth, and that *magic* chose before you interfered."

I dropped to my knees before her, pulled out my knife and I slit my hand without hesitation. As my blood, deep maroon and gold, pooled and then dripped, I locked eyes with hers. "I swear to you, Tate Aaralyn, on my life and magic, I did not conjure up this bond. It existed before I gave you my blood. It is *because* of this bond that I gave you my blood. And should you choose to reject it, I will honor this, even if it kills me. Let magic be the judge. Search me."

She looked at my hand and paused.

"Now, you," I cleared my throat, "need to mix your blood with mine to seal the oath, and then magic will guide you through my mind to see the truth for yourself," I explained, extending the knife to her.

She grabbed it, and instead of slicing her tan flesh, she tossed it to the side. "I think magic has had more than enough influence on us. Will you willingly let me see?" she asked before nibbling on her lip, her perfect fucking lip.

I nodded, completely awestruck. She was giving me a chance. She was choosing to trust me after what I did. I was undeserving. "Whatever you want."

She reached out and grabbed my wounded hand and then closed her eyes. I could feel her presence knocking on the door to my mind and, without hesitation, I allowed her in.

She jolted in my hand briefly as my essence surrounded her before she began assessing the many, many files that defined me. I was old, over a hundred, but still young by Fae and Untish standards.

I could feel her running her fingers over my memories and when she hit a sensitive one, I reflectively flinched. She paused. But I allowed her in, opened the folder for her, and showed her the shit I wished I could erase.

Cher's body lay before me, cold and lifeless. I could feel the magic, her magic that was bound within me, wither until her breaths were no more. Even with her gone, a portion of her bonded magic remained alive within me —she was the more gifted one. Cher had given more of herself to the bond than I had—she was older, stronger, braver. Everything I wasn't. I'd failed her, didn't see the magic-laced death bullet before it hit her right in the chest. I wasn't fast enough. I was unprepared...and she'd left me with a monumental responsibility.

Tate pulled out of the memory and slammed the folder shut, shivering physically as she did so. I thought she might step back, reject me then and there after seeing me for the failure I was, but instead, she went to the next folder. Also classified. My breath caught and sweat began to pebble my forehead. I didn't want her to see this, to know this, I wanted to guide her away. But I unlocked it anyways and allowed her in, gritting my teeth through the pain.

My mother sat in a chair overlooking the sea. Her right eye was swollen and her left arm was in a sling. He'd beaten her again.

"I'll kill him," I vowed.

"Aether, that is not what I want. Your father didn't mean it. It was just a misunderstanding," she spoke through a barely healed split lip.

"This," I gestured to her broken arm, "was a misunderstanding? How

many does that make this year?" I demanded, face turning red from rage. I ran my hand through my short black hair.

"The mender will return soon with the potion, and I'll recover quickly. I failed him. I'm the halfling, I'm supposed to produce him heirs, and I..." Tears fell down her pale skin.

"Mother, this isn't your fault. You've already given him me. You owe him nothing, you never did." I grabbed her hand and knelt in front of her.

Laughter flitted from the courtyard below. There my father staggered to the fountain, drink in hand with a female on each side. My mother's grip tightened.

He dared to take his dalliances and parade them in front of my mother?

Hate swelled within me. I threw myself from the balcony and landed with primal grace. My father's eyes widened and then hate laced them.

"Ah, ladies meet my greatest failure. He was supposed to win the battle of the Waters, but he lost and his bonded died. Pathetic, that's what he is." He spat at my feet before glancing up to my mother and smiled. "Just like his mother, he's useless—"

I threw a punch before he finished speaking, blood sprayed, and he staggered back. He threw up a wall of power, shadows at his command. The females screamed and fled while I sent my black flames flying at the male who sired me. He met them with his own shadowed flames and the trees around us burned, withered, and smoked. I released lashes of my power and knocked him off-balance before I pinned him with my will, manipulating the air around him.

I stalked toward him, rage my only focus. His face was turning purple, blue even. Still, I squeezed. I was vaguely aware of my mother's screams, her cries to relent, of the garden burning. I could hear the guards quickly approaching, trying to end this...

But instead of restraint, I ended the guards with half a thought. They'd allowed my mother's abuse. They chose to turn a blind eye.

My focus was locked on the vile man before me, burning in flames. I didn't stop. I poured my liquid flames down his throat and his body writhed. The chair of the Shadow Tribe was on his knees before me, dying. Cher was *gone, but some of her magic remained—an extra force of power my father couldn't match, especially when drunk.*

The ground shook as I threw blows of power that would have sent him tumbling if not for the force I insisted keep him at bay. His flesh burned from his face and was blown away by a gust of my energy, revealing bones and muscles. Even still, I continued beating him with my will, burning him from the inside out, until he sat there suspended by my power, nothing but a skeleton.

I was shaking, sweat pooling at my back. Tate's chest was heaving as she pulled herself out of the memory and let go of my hand, staggering back with eyes full of pain.

This was it. The moment she realized how broken I was. The moment she would reject me, and rightly so. I didn't deserve her.

But instead of running, she pulled me into a hug and caressed my back with her hands. Her presence returning to my mind, a healing balm.

You are a good male, Aether.

And with her words of kindness, with her absolution and actions, I crumbled. Silent tears fell from my eyes, my shoulders shook from the force of emotion.

How can you say that? You saw my failures, who I really am.

"Shhh," she murmured into my shoulder. "I get to decide what I saw, and it isn't your failures that define you, but it's the courage to *feel*; the desire to protect the innocent. And that makes you good." She said the words my soul had never thought I'd hear.

Even so, I didn't believe her. She may think I was good, but I knew, deep down, I was only darkness.

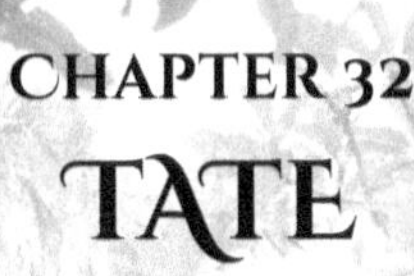

CHAPTER 32
TATE

I held him there for a moment. This male thought he was unworthy? Thought he was evil? How could I show him he wasn't? I knew guilt too well and understood the power of shame.

The feeling of his fury still crawled over my skin. I had felt what *he experienced* in those moments all those years ago; his pain when he lost his previous bonded, and his rage when he took his father's life. It was darkness, loss, and despair. But it was also fueled by indignance at the destruction of innocence and life. I understood that too well.

Images of Roy's body flooded my mind. His severed head, mouth agape—an abuser no more.

I wasn't anyone to pass judgment.

Instead, I rubbed his back and ignored the wetness on my hair. I knew he was crying, even if silently. Had no one ever absolved him of his guilt?

He stiffened and then embraced me tighter before pulling back. "I'd understand if you want nothing to do with me. I can ensure your safety from a distance, if you wish."

"No," I spoke with resolve. "No, I think not. I have had enough distance and time to sort through things. I understand why you gave me your blood when you did, and I could see myself doing the same thing," I admitted to him what had kept me awake the past several nights.

He looked into my eyes, the gold spinning. I became aware of our power mixing and his hiding my pink aura with his black flames, spinning around us, shielding me from any prying eyes.

What do you want?

I knew he was asking about the bond. He'd left his mental shields down and I could sense his emotions: pain, regret, adoration, commitment, shame...

I didn't answer for a moment, sorting his emotions from my own. I missed him even when I was angry; I found his presence comforting on a soulful level and felt naked without him. I couldn't stop thinking about him and the sexual pull I felt toward him was unparalleled. The breakthrough I'd had in the pool was still fresh on my mind and his words, his memories, only confirmed what I'd already accepted: our bond was real.

Authentic.

We were mated. Mates. Fully bonded in the purest way.

I wanted this male.

I wanted the bond.

Not my magic, though that certainly was drawing me to him—along with my inner dragon, *she* wanted him badly. But me, Tate Aaralyn, *I* wanted Aether—the male, not the dragon, though I wanted that part of him too.

I placed my hand on his cheek and smiled. "I want you."

I want the bond, Aether. I accept it. I spoke into his mind, confirming my physical words.

His eyes widened as his emotions of love and amazement crashed into me. He stood there, speechless, as I pulled his face down to claim his mouth with my own. To declare him as my own.

His lips didn't hesitate as he savagely returned the kiss. His hands found the base of my head, and his fingers dug in, attempting to become one with my body. He moaned in my mouth before possessing it again with his tongue, his hands roaming my body at the same moment.

My hand dropped from his cheek, trailed down his neck, and then lingered over his pec—every part was perfection, every ounce of this male was *mine*.

His kiss became feral, wild, and his hands tightened on me. More, I wanted more.

Needed more.

As you wish, my dear.

He picked me up and carried me to the bedroom, before dropping me to the bed and crawling atop me, lips once again finding mine.

Home, he felt like home.

The lingering remnants of anger inside dissipated as I allowed myself to accept this bond, to forgive his actions, to *acquit* this male.

Trust was earned, yes. But it was also a choice. Nothing in life was safe and without risk.

Nothing.

I met his tongue stroke for stroke as my hands searched his back, clawing at his bare skin with primal need. The need, the desire, continued to build until it felt like a tidal wave that would wipe me from existence if I didn't give in, didn't accept it.

I dug my nails deeper into his flesh. Accepting. Allowing myself to trust even after the betrayal I'd felt. I was going to move on, and fuck it if it didn't feel good to finally let go.

To forgive.

His aura pulsed and danced with mine. It pulsed again, but this time it was full of agitation.

He roared into my mouth as he released a wave of dark power, shaking the walls. My very body shuttered along with the bed beneath the mammoth-sized male. Another pulse. And then, another…

He tore his lips from mine and growled. "You've got to be fucking kidding me."

I looked at him puzzled.

He sighed. "It's your quest time."

"What?" I studied him, the need within me still throbbing. Begging. Demanding...

But as he stood, I realized *I* would have to wait.

Impatient little thing, aren't we?

I smirked through lust-hazed eyes.

He ran his hand through his hair before throwing on a wrinkled shirt. "This couldn't have come at a worse time."

"Hmm?" My mind was still hazy, eyes solely on the *large* expanse currently tenting in his pants.

"They're here. It's customary for a surprise quest to occur right before the test-outs, it's an evaluation of sorts, but also serves as a training exercise. If I don't let them in and, fuck I *really* don't want to— especially when you're looking at me like that." He paused a moment, devouring me through hooded eyes pure of carnal promise.

"What? They'll what?" I challenged, spreading my legs apart a bit further. Inviting.

Testing.

Teasing.

Savoring the way he swallowed, the way his hands flexed with restraint. "Aether?" I let my left leg drop completely to the side.

He cleared his throat. "Then..." He forced his eyes to the door beyond. "They'll report this, and it will draw unwanted attention." He sighed. "I have to let them in."

"Suspicion?" I tsked. "We can't have that now, can we?"

His body visibly shook in response. I smirked before standing, slowly allowing my hair to drape across my body, and then stepped toward him placing a delicate hand on his chest. I savored the way I could feel his heart pounding.

"Best let them in," I said coolly before reaching with my free hand to cup him roughly.

He bucked at my touch as his eyes flared.

He opened his mouth. "Tate—"

Pounding sounded at the front door. Then it crashed open, even as Aether pried himself away from me to give us an appropriate distance.

This isn't finished. He promised.

I smirked. *Of that, we are in agreement.*

Members poured in, suited in the purest black—the Shadow Tribe. Their leader, a lean female with blonde hair tipped in black, stormed into Aether's room as if it were nothing. Unphased by the snarl on Aether's face, or the black flames rising at his back, threatening to devour.

"Tate Aaralyn, it's judgement time."

CHAPTER 33
TATE

Juda, as I'd gathered after she and Aether exchanged *many* choice words, had just stepped through the portal before it sealed off. I was in a dark space, the floor smooth. I could see numerous figures across the room. If it even *was* a room. The air was fresh, like that of outside, but it was wholly dark, with the exception of mage lights dotting the ceiling like stars.

"Remove your shoes," Juda commanded.

"Excuse me?" I tensed.

"This is a holy place for the Untish. This quest is for holy battles. You will spar, no shoes or weapons." Juda extended her hand with long slender fingers and waited for me to hand over my knife. I removed the sheath from my upper thigh and handed it to her before bending over to remove my boots.

I tossed them to the side and then hobbled forward.

"Good. Go check in with Camella, she is responsible for all those in the Shadow Tribe."

I glanced ahead and did indeed spot a group of individuals I recognized: the Shadow Tribe trainees. That meant Carly wouldn't be there. I swallowed back the disappointment.

Biting my lip, I limped forward toward the group. Even in the dimness of the room, I didn't miss the whispers or the sneers. After all this time, I was still worthy of gossip. In the juiciest and cruelest forms, looks of pity and despise; words of hate and verbal jeers.

Heat began to rise within my chest. I was not a charity case. They were just a bunch of stuck-up—

"All right, we're all here. This is how it's going to work. I will not repeat this, so listen carefully," Camella began. "Each of you will duel members of your own tribe and then one member of a competing tribe. Lose the first duel, and your second one will be matched with someone deemed more challenging. Win your first, get an easy second. This is not *just* practice. You will be judged, ranked, and this *will* impact your final test-out positioning as well as the general's opinions of you, which if you know anything, they fucking matter. They determine if you stay here for more training or get to become an active member in your tribe." She gestured to the void beyond, to the dark. "*They* select your missions, if you manage to get any as a first-year—" she leveled her gaze at each of us, my palms became sweaty when her eyes landed on me "—so you do not want to fail."

Her glare flattened us all.

"Don't fucking make me look bad either. For that, *I* will make you pay. If you tap out, you will be disqualified. There will be no reassignments. The matches will be selected at random."

I swallowed. *Aether?*

Silence.

Aether? Can you hear me?

Here, but best to minimize this contact. I can see you.

I whipped my eyes up; I didn't see anything but a black ceiling and mage lights that reflected dimly off the polished stone floor.

You can't see us, but all generals, high generals, and chairs are allowed to witness this. We're just shielded from your sight.

I nodded. Enough said, I was a spectacle. All of us were.

"I'm going to read off the first matches, they will all occur in waves." Camella began reading names. Several grumbled or moaned when their name was called and their match announced, others laughed and sounded borderline psychotic when their paring was selected.

So far, mine hadn't been read.

"Luensky vs Salie in ring six, Jordan vs Brid in ring seven," Camella finished reading the last two pairings for the first wave of matches.

"Shit! I don't want to face off against Brid," Jordan whined. "Why couldn't I get lucky and get the cripple?"

Heat stained my face. They couldn't see it, I was sure, and yet I felt all eyes focus on me.

"Get to your ring," Camella commanded.

"Jordan, just keep your hands up," another trainee, Sheila I think, said trying to calm the nervous female. "It's going to be fine."

"Easy for you to say, you'll probably get the newbie with unsure footing. One kick and she's down," Jordan spat.

My heart began beating erratically. I'd heard passing comments, seen their looks, but I hadn't really spoken much to any of the other trainees aside from Carly. Evidently, they all had been watching me and were acutely aware of my shortcomings.

Some things were universal truths: the strong preyed on the weak.

I'll kill them.

I sent a silencing wave to Aether as I tried to erect a wall. I hated that I knew he not only heard what they said but also sensed the way it made me feel—ashamed.

I didn't need that on my mind, not now.

Not as I considered who was yet to be called: Gene, Kyree, and Nova. They were the big threats left. If I could swing not getting one of them, I'd be all right. The sucky part about being in the Shadow Tribe was that I was supposed to be tough like the rest. My gifts were *supposed* to be that of strength and brute force. We were the 'warrior' tribe by many standards.

The biggest dragons. The strongest fighters. The most talented in combat.

The whistle sounded and the matches began. I stood between two rings. One held Luensky and Salie, and they began fighting, an even match by many standards and a boring duel. Instead, I focused to my right where Jordan and Brid sparred. Brid allowed Jordan the offensive. He was much larger than her, easily six and a half feet, and made of solid muscle. Back in the human realm, he would be deemed a gym rat, or a meathead. Here, too, I supposed. Jordan landed a series of kicks, most of which Brid deflected, before he took his first swing. He was slow. Much slower than her, but the force behind his punches would be hard to recover from. Jordan danced around the mat, throwing a kick or a punch as Brid closed in on her.

"Kick his feet out!" Sheila cried.

"Get her, Brid! Make these females realize why we're better!" Trever shouted from across the ring, sneering at Sheila who flipped him off.

I tuned the rest of their slurs out. Jordan, too, ignored the crowd's shouts and instead focused on Brid. She twisted and landed behind him readying to punch and kick but he was prepared, he turned— faster than I would have guessed—and threw a punch that caught Jordan in the lip. She slammed backward into the stone floor and didn't move.

The crowd silenced.

Camella strode into the ring, stepped over Jordan's silent body, and lifted Brid's arm in victory. The match was over. Sheila rushed to Jordan's side, concern lacing her face.

"Is she—" I began asking.

Sheila glared up at me. "Fine, no thanks to you. But if she took this beating, just imagine how much worse you'll be, *freak*."

I bit my lip. It was deferred anger; the logical part of my brain knew this. But it didn't hurt any less. A minute later, a second whistle sounded.

The first wave of duels was over.

"Well done. Those who lost, lick your wounds and get ready for your second duel. Those of you who won, get ready to do so again. Here's the next lineup for the second wave." Camella began, not waiting for those who were bloodied to even leave their rings before reading off the next matches.

I listened silently, waiting for my name. Gene and Nova were paired. Thank blood I didn't have to fight either of them.

"Kylee and Raina ring five," Camella said, and I loosened a breath when my name wasn't called. It would be okay. "Tate and Sheila, ring six."

The blood drained from my face.

I could see Sheila's eyes sparkle. This would be personal. Regardless of the fact I hadn't hurt her friend, Sheila clearly was looking to dole out a beating.

You got this. Sheila is arrogant and fast, but just wait for the right moment.

I blocked Aether again. I didn't need his voice distracting me. It was bad enough that I may get my ass kicked, but now I may have to endure a beating while my bonded watched it...my stomach roiled.

"Get to your rings," Camella ordered, and everyone obliged, heading for their positions.

I limped over to my ring and stepped inside. I didn't expect to feel the spark as I entered the ring. I should've guessed magic would be used to control the fighters. I could sense all my magic being tampered, cloaked...as if I couldn't access it, even if I needed to. I bit my lip as Sheila entered.

"I'll make it quick, freak." She smiled, all teeth.

"Not fair! I told you, Sheila, you'd get the cripple," Jordan mumbled. I glanced at her and noted that she was being supported by other trainees, nursing her busted lip.

I just needed to block them out. Pricks will be pricks.

I recited the things I'd told myself all throughout high school.

The whistle sounded and before it ended, Sheila charged me. She threw several punches that I evaded but stumbled in the process of doing so. I wasn't prepared for her speed. She threw out a kick and I dodged it, barely, before throwing a punch of my own. She easily evaded and was behind me before I could even blink. I pivoted on my feet, left leg throbbing from the swift movement, and was prepared for her upcoming attack.

Camella had been training me. Camella was better than Sheila. If I could survive Camella, I *would* survive Sheila.

"You're nothing. You don't belong here. We don't even know why the chairs let you in. You're pathetic." Sheila spewed her words at me, a blade to the heart. It shouldn't have sliced and stung, and yet...it did.

I felt off-balance and she capitalized on that by sweeping her foot behind me, knocking me on my ass. The room cheered as Sheila jumped on me and began punching my face. I threw up my arms in defense but was too slow. She landed a punch to my right eye, and before I could blink, she threw yet another punch.

Panic.

I could sense Aether's emotions, even as he remained silent.

"Stupid bitch, you don't belong here." Sheila battered me with her words and fists.

One punch.

Another blow.

With a third, my skull slammed into the concrete beneath me.

Again, and again, and again.

I couldn't withstand this for long. Already my head was splitting with pain, my vision was blurry, and everything seemed to be dancing...even the mage lights from above. Pretty, sweet little lights. I bet they were soft to the touch and—

Get out of there!

Aether's words jarred me back, I blinked as she paused her assault and raised bloodied fists in the air, a smile plastered across her face. I needed to change positions. I pivoted and tried to dislodge her, but she wouldn't budge. I bucked and she lost her balance. Before she could recover, I threw a punch of my own, it connected with her jaw. In that moment, I threw my hips up and sent her toward me while I twisted my body out from under her. She hit the stone floor.

"Sheila!" Jordan cried.

I ignored them all. I ignored the pain stabbing in my limbs and the buzzing in my head. I ignored my blurred vision that spotted and multiplied what I saw. Instead, I stumbled to my feet and then launched myself at the middle version of Sheila lying crumpled on the floor. My fist came in contact with her mid-section, and I readied another blow. Confidence flooded my system and clouded my judgment. I didn't see Sheila move, didn't notice the curve of her lips until it was too late. One moment she was beneath me, and the next, my face was being slammed into the stone, arm extended behind me, and with a thrust of her strength, I felt my arm snap.

A scream escaped my lips as pain laced through me. But Sheila didn't relent. She lifted my head up with one hand, still holding my broken arm in the other. "I told you, crippled bitch, you don't belong here," she whispered in my ear before slamming my head down into the stone.

CHAPTER 34

CHANCE

Cold water assaulted me. I jolted upright, blade in hand before I could even assess what was happening. Carran stood in front of me, a wicked grin spread across his face as he held an empty pitcher—water dripping down its sides.

"What the fuck do you think you're doing?" I demanded, wiping my face with my now-soaked sleeve.

"Waking you up, boy." He smirked.

Rage consumed me, begged to be freed. I shoved it down inside and forced my hand holding the knife to relax. Carran was one of our own. My comrade. My peer.

"Perhaps you could find a better way to do that in the future, Dux Carran," I gritted out through a locked jaw. My temper was barely leashed. My head pounded thanks to the booze from the past several... nights? Weeks? Time held no relevance when wine was involved.

"I would have to agree, but honestly, you look kinda cute, like a drowned dog." Shae appeared from behind Carran, her hand covering her mouth.

"Shae?" her name was a whisper on my lips. She smiled and stood before me, healthy and whole. She looked good. Her once vibrant blue hair now had dark roots that faded to a washed-out greenish blue. Her skin, while not rosy, wasn't grey anymore.

I dropped the knife letting it bounce on the wooden table and pulled her into a hug. Her bony body was crushed in my embrace. Family. She and Holland were all I had left.

Shae squealed before pulling from my embrace. "You're wet and you stink, Chance. You need a good bath." She spoke as she scratched behind my ear like I was her dammed pet.

But I wasn't even annoyed, because Shae was here—alive, breathing, and her old self.

"Yeah, yeah, all in time."

"Ach! I can bathe you here and now, boy!" Carran's voice boomed, the timber of his voice making my head throb.

I winced as I let Shae go. The place was empty, no one aside from the three of us were in here. It would be nice if Carran could speak without shouting.

"What time is it?" I asked.

"Don't you mean what *day* is it?" Shae teased.

"Day?" I shook my head, clearing the brain fog.

"It's Tuesday, Chance. It would appear you've been drinking yourself into oblivion." Shae placed her hands on her hips and leveled a judgmental, but playful, glare at me. Even when she was trying to be menacing, all I saw was a little sister who miraculously could walk. One who seemed to have cooled off since our last fight.

"I didn't think you had it in you! Makes me proud of ya', lad!" Carran stepped forward and slapped me on the shoulders.

I could feel the heat in my gut rising, the power begging to be freed. No.

I shoved it deep inside me as I shook free of his grip.

"How's Holland?" I asked.

"Pissed. As she should be. She said you walked out on her. You can't shut her out just because you're scared, Chance," Shae said.

The vision of that nightmare began to take over. Shae, siphoning Holland's life...becoming one of those vile creatures.

"I'm with this one, you have to face your fears, not hide from 'em like a coward," Carran said, his voice pulling me from my thoughts.

Fear, no, pure terror began to sink in as I recalled what *could* occur, if my father was to be believed.

I took in a deep breath, Carran's magical scent was mild compared to Shae's. Hers was appealing...intoxicating. Her magic felt like my own, and was begging me to take it...

"It was the right thing to do. I don't want to hurt her." The honesty was something I didn't expect to give the giant in front of me.

"Chance, we're stronger together." Shae smiled as she linked arms with Carran. The sight was downright disturbing.

"This wee one is right." He winked at Shae and flexed his arm. "You must face your fears. Drive 'em out with love, no better way to do that than in the arms of a female!" A round of laughter shook through the large, unkept male—met equally by Shae who shared a knowing look with Carran. Had everyone lost their minds?

"Amen, brother!" Shae winked at him. "That's why I need to get my arse," she pronounced it exactly as Carran would, "down to the Northern Outpost to find *my* lady."

"Aye!" Carran shouted. "If you don't, from what you've told me, I may just have to—"

Shae elbowed him in the gut, earning a yelp.

"So, you two are what, friends now?" I stared at them, eyes wide. What the actual hell?

"Yeah, amazing what being knocked on your arse—" there it was again, *arse*, "—and placed on bed rest can do to a girl. Carran visited often, checking on me." Shae smiled.

"He did not, I would know if he did, I mean I was there—"

"Were ya now, my boy? From what I heard, you weren't there and when you were, well parts of *you* were there all right." Carran's eyes glistened.

"I believe he was," Shae added, devilry written across her face.

"What in the name of Mother Blood are you two talking about?" I demanded. I was sure my face was reddening from the force of pushing the annoyance back down into my gut.

All of this felt *wrong*.

"It seems like perhaps you were with Shae, but really you were with *Holland*. Ach! The story had me rolling." Carran wagged his overgrown eyebrows.

My eyes darted to Shae's pink-colored cheeks. "You were still unconscious!"

"Well, I may have regained consciousness as you two were, uh, *engaged*—" her accent thick, her eyes lit in mischief "—in activities. And the sight of it sent me straight back into oblivion!" she said dramatically.

"You watched?" I couldn't believe it.

"No! Of course not, but even when I closed my eyes I could still *hear*," Shae said, annoyed.

"Why didn't you say something?" I demanded.

"Because, when I awoke it was far too late and it looked like you and Holland were more than just fucking, it felt a bit...spiritual," she lowered her voice. A certain sadness seemed to rein in her features. "I didn't want to interrupt, so I did my best to give you the privacy that I could. I closed my eyes and tried to tune *you* out." She tipped her chin in the air defiantly.

"Ach! But from the sounds of it, *you* were loud!" Carran nudged Shae with his elbow. "This one is a good storyteller."

I swallowed. "Where is Holland?"

"Where do you think? She's been looking for you." I didn't miss the pointed look in Shae's eyes. "When Carran's men spotted you in here, we thought it best to check on your state before sending Holland in. And...it's a good thing we did," Shae said as she scrunched her nose.

Fine, I smelt bad. I got the message. The whole sight of her and Carran still felt foreign to me. I wiped at my face with my hands, repulsed by the dirt that marred my palms and fingers.

"I'll shower," I said as I strode from the pub. I could hear their footsteps following me.

What would I even say to Holland, to Shae? That they became vile creatures, and it was my fault? How could I even stop it? My father was pure evil, trusting him would be like trusting a serpent not to bite you when stepped on—not wise. But what other options were there?

Dr. Worshah. He would know the truth.

I stopped moving and Shae bumped into me.

"Ow! What the—"

"I have to go." I didn't wait for a response, but instead changed course and headed for the lab.

"Chance!" Shae called after me, her footsteps trying to keep up.

I would get some answers, perhaps I could even have this magic removed from my body. I could be me again. For the first time since the explosion, I felt hopeful.

CHAPTER 35
AETHER

Tate was still unconscious. I'd moved her back to my place, and she now lay on black satin sheets under a lush, fur comforter. Her head had healed, and her arm was in a sling. Thank blood for the Luna Tribe's magic.

Vala stood there, staring at Tate. "Fuck, Aether. I mean...she's in bad shape. How...how'd you let that happen?"

I shot her a glare. I had seen only red when Tate's arm snapped. The entire compound shook with my fury, even the dome fractured from the force of my wrath. And when her head slammed into the slab? I broke through the barrier and engulfed everyone in pure darkness. I willed my power to cradle her, to comfort her, and barely restrained myself from ending the person responsible. But then James intervened without warning Arithi was there, she was watching.

I pulled myself together even as Camella collected Tate from the floor, blood dripping from her head, and carried her from the dome to the Luner medical tent. Every one of her steps was painfully slow. If it weren't for James's restraints upon me, I would have fucking exploded. I could have torn through his binding in a second, but the reminder was enough.

I had to play my cards right to prevent any additional harm from coming to Tate.

But fuck, it took *too* damn long for me to get to her. And once I did? I wasn't going anywhere. Not as I scared Camella off, not caring that my words and actions looked like those of a psychotic overbearing male. Not thinking twice as I blanketed the room in black flames, a cyclone around Tate, myself, and James. I collected Tate and had James carefully blink us into my house, refusing myself the vengeance I craved.

My eyes were now glued to the goddess I'd just come so precariously close to losing. I ran my hand through my unbound hair, pulling on its strands in frustration.

My reaction was unwise. It was emotional. It was telling. I'd have to deal with its ramifications later.

A growl escaped me. "How long until she's conscious?"

"No way to know, well not without getting my mother in here to look in her mind, which I can do, but I figured—"

"No."

"That's what I thought. The potion should work wonders; I mean her eyes are already significantly better, they're not black and blue and swollen, and the gash on her forehead has already closed. Her arm will take some time, but she should be better soon. I'd say that in the next twenty-four to forty-eight hours, the worst of it will be over. The only thing that could speed it up is pure Untish blood, but given that the last time you did so, she was pissed, I'd—"

"What did she say to you about it?" My question was a whisper.

Vala just stared. "I'm not telling you."

"Excuse me?" I could feel the energy in the room, the molecules around Vala's body. With a mere whim, she could be suspended—the air choked from her lungs.

"Aether, there is such a thing as the *girl code*. I'm her friend, one of the few she has, you really want me to betray that?"

Fuck. No, I didn't. The look in Vala's eyes confirmed she knew she had me.

Tate stirred a bit, a moan and whimper escaping her lips. She looked so small, frail even. I was supposed to protect her, but how was I to do that without revealing who she was—to me and the Embassy? It felt like an impossible task.

"So, Aether, this isn't any of my business, but seeing as *most* of the Embassy knows about Ruby..." She left the rest unsaid.

I needed to tell Tate. But we were *finally* good—well goodish. Things were escalating. We were connecting. She'd accepted the bond, even if we hadn't actualized it yet. I swallowed back the guilt at yet another secret. Could Tate withstand the knowledge of who Ruby was to me?

"I know. I just, I don't know how to share it. If I withhold until we're closer, and she finds out anyway, it could ruin everything. If I tell her now, it could be too much, and she could run."

"You should trust her." Vala approached me slowly.

I sucked on my fang. Tate could handle this; she was fierce and brave.

"So...what do you have in mind for those assholes who did this to her?" I appreciated Vala's subject change. "Rumor has it, they don't particularly like Tate and may have been intentionally rough with her." Vala looked at me, hands on her hips. "I'd love to get my hands dirty again; it's been too long since I've gotten to properly kick some ass."

"We do nothing."

"Excuse me?" Her eyes bugged out.

"Vala, any further action will make Tate *more* of a spectacle, it will draw further attention from the chairs the regent, Arithi. We don't need them looking closer at her, wondering at my connection to her. If Tate wants retribution, I'll help *her* get it."

Vala nodded. "Jared said that your recent mission with him was successful?" She looked at me.

"Yes, we've confirmed that the Glenn is moving troops. James is preparing to leave on another recon trip to scout the Fern, Wataedge, and Yates, but rumor has it that there's been activity in the south. Specifically, that the Fern Vamp's troops have been moving."

Discussing *work* calmed me a bit, but it still felt oddly wrong to be focusing on it while Tate lay on the bed, broken.

Even war seemed so trivial compared to my new priorities.

"Will they postpone the Matching Ceremony then?" Vala asked.

I hadn't even considered it. The ceremony was held on the new moon, which was coming up much quicker than I would have liked. The idea of Tate having to attend made my stomach churn. But I could see why Vala was concerned. If we had to fight, Jared and Vala could be sent into battle, unbonded. That would mean waiting to be officially matched until the next full moon...upon winter season.

"I doubt it. From what my uncle told me, Arithi and some of the other chairs don't want to be involved. They want to watch the Vamps destroy each other."

"Isn't that against what we stand for, as a Untish people? Our values are to value *all* life. Not just let it wink out."

"Vala, if they create beasts and become them as well, perhaps it's best they eliminate one another." I ran a hand over my face.

"Jared said the same thing. I feel like I don't even know him anymore. Do you think..." She paused, leaning against the white wall.

I waited. Allowing the silence to encase me. Focusing on the flames flickering in the fireplace, the light from the moon washing the room in its red glow. I listened to the waves as they crashed in the distance. I became bathed in silence with only my brooding thoughts accompanying me.

Tate rolled over and whimpered again. I adjusted the pressure around her, tightening, in an effort to comfort.

"Vala, I think—"

"Do you think magic can be matched wrong? Like, that Jared and I aren't a true match?"

I froze, glancing at her. I didn't expect that question—wasn't sure I could mentally handle another's worries and concerns at the moment. Not when all I wanted to do was cradle the small female, my mate, who was lying on my bed, healing and recovering ever so slowly. No, I wanted Vala to *leave*. She'd helped Tate, gave us the potions, and now it was time for her to go. And yet...she was Tate's friend. What was my responsibility here?

I sighed. "Magic is sentient, but our interpretation isn't infallible. When I was matched to Cher, it was clear to us that our connection was strong. Clear to the chairs, so there wasn't any question, ever. Even with the slight age gap, her magic reacted to mine and it was obvious it chose for us." I cleared my throat. "We were a good match, Vala."

"But...did you love her?" She looked down at her hands and picked at her fingernails.

"Not at first, and never close to the way I feel about Tate." It felt like a betrayal of Cher to admit such things. She was a good female. My magical match, but not my soul's match. We both understood that then, and it changed nothing now. "In time I came to care for Cher. Love can bloom."

"What if it fades? I've only felt more and more disconnected from Jared since we've returned. He's pissed about our deal, thinks I'm wrong for agreeing to it and lying to the chairs. Believe me, he's made that abundantly clear...prick." She murmured the last word. "But I don't understand why he's blaming me? Why he's been avoiding me?" She bit her lip, her fangs popping out.

"I'm sorry." I had no other words to offer her. "If he's an idiot male, hopefully he'll come around."

Tate stirred. I jolted forward, moving toward her. Slowly she opened her eyes, the most gloriously mahogany hue, and smiled.

Hey, babe.

Her words had my heart nearly exploding.

CHAPTER 36

TATE

Aether looked down at me in wonder.

Mother Blood, you're beautiful.

If I could have snorted, I would have. But everything still hurt.

"Tate!" Vala appeared behind Aether, the smile on her face at odds with the troubled expression. "How are you feeling?"

"Like shit," I spoke through a dry tongue. I needed something to drink. As if reading my mind, which he probably was, Aether handed me a cup of water. "Thank you."

I could feel the room buzzing; my head still pounded and barely moving had my arm throbbing with pain.

"It will heal, soon hopefully. But blood can expedite it," Vala chirped.

Blood? I looked to Aether and my toes curled at his expression. I tried to feel his emotions, read his mind, but they were clouded in a heavy veil that felt heated.

"I'll be going." Vala winked at me before sauntering out of the room.

Blood, huh?

If you wish.

I stared at him. The scar just over his right eye was sexy as hell, his eyebrows lowered in what could only be explained as a sultry expression. And I swallowed as the air around me constricted in all the right places.

I'm surprised you didn't just give me your blood while I was still unconscious.

I didn't want to pick a fight, not really. But...part of me couldn't resist saying what was still on my mind. Healing took time, I supposed.

I've learned.

I smiled at him as he sat down on the edge of the bed, careful not to hurt me. I could see his pulse pounding in his neck as the tattoos on his arm danced when he flexed as he adjusted on the bed. Fuck me, he was hot.

Thanks, dear, but let's get you up to snuff first, eh? Blood?

My cheeks reddened as I wiggled my feet, my left leg throbbing. A reminder of my deficiency, my failure. I'd been humiliated in front of Aether. I'd been broken.

"I'll take some blood." I simply said, willing my thoughts to fall silent. Aether looked at me, his expression deepening. But he didn't say anything, didn't make me feel worse than I already did for what had happened, for my public embarrassment.

Instead, he offered his right wrist to me and scooted closer. His left arm reached around my body to brace on the bed while he leaned in, waiting. Gingerly, I took his wrist in my good hand and lifted it to my lips. The mere scent of his sweat had my mouth watering.

Ash and salt. Mystery and power.

Without hesitation, I punctured his wrist. His blood hit my tongue instantly—there was nothing but him, his blood, his life, his sacrifice. I pulled deeply and savored the way his blood interacted with my system, the way my every nerve seemed to be rapidly firing.

I could hear each of his breaths, the increase in his heart rate. I could sense his arousal, his physical restraint. His musky, ashy, salty scent was intoxicating. The flavor of his ancient iron, a ballad to my tongue.

Nothing had ever tasted so good, so right.

I moaned as I pulled again and closed my eyes, dropping my head back on the pillow, and pulled him with me. Soft satin engulfed me, warm skin atop my own. Our breaths were synchronized as our hearts pressed together. My other arm was tingling, as was my leg, and neither one hurt anymore. Instead, they felt fuzzy and gloriously free.

A smile pulled at my lips as I drank. And I drank. And still, I drank more.

I could feel Aether's sergeant saluting and suddenly I was hungry for something much different. Something far more exciting.

I yanked my arm free from the sling, savoring the movement of my limb once again, and pulled at Aether's back, shredding his shirt. I dug my nails in, scratching and marking him.

I needed more, needed to be completely consumed by him.

Fire erupted in my belly and the whole world was nothing but color. Black sheets, a symbol of depth and mystery—power. Red-gold blood and flowers, reflecting both life and lust. The cream accent pillows that matched the floor and walls—pure.

Everything had meaning, new meaning, deeper meaning. Everything was alive.

The black flames, a representation of Aether's brute force.

My inner lake's pink ones, a representation of—

A moan slipped through my lips, and again I pulled. And this time he removed his hand from the bed beside me and stroked the side of my face gently. My eyes flew open and locked with his dark ones. The gold swirled with desire and the breath in my lungs caught at the sheer lust in his eyes. I could feel my core tingling in anticipation. He parted his lips, ever so slowly, and leaned closer. The fullness of them was on my forehead, tender. Everywhere our bodies met, I felt friction and desire. Every single cell of my being was hyperaware, firing rapidly and overwhelming my brain with so much input that only one thing mattered: him.

I pulled my fangs free and cupped his head with both my hands. "Aether."

His name was a prayer on my lips.

One he happily responded to.

A moment later, the fullness of his mouth was on mine—devouring, claiming, and yet, gentle. I raked my hands through his hair and neck, and then deepened the kiss even as the center of my thighs constricted. I was on fire; in nearly every sense, I was pure energy.

I craved him. Needed him. Loved him. Trusted him.

The thoughts kept pouring forth and, likely sensing them, Aether just gave me more and more of himself. He stroked my tongue with his even as his hand gently caressed the side of my hip in equal measure. Tender.

Firmer, Aether. I won't break.

Tate—

FIRMER!

His kiss intensified, but his hand on my hip was gentle. I dug my nails deeper into his back, trapping him with my legs. I tightened all my muscles even as pink flames erupted from my touch and swirled above us.

Aether growled in my mouth before prying his lips free of mine and standing, leaving me on his bed, alone.

Are you sure you're ready? In a very real way, you were just beaten… badly. This can wait, should wait.

I growled as I sprung from the bed—amazed at how my arms, *both*, worked well. Even my headache and blurred vision had gone. I was fine. More than fine.

I alone decide what I can handle, and when.

I stalked toward him, pink flames tinting my vision.

Your blood worked wonders.

I could still see the hesitation in his eyes—the worry. I growled and lunged at him. He threw his arms out in alarm and caught me, holding me close to his chest like I could break at any second.

My heart pounded. My head did feel light. Dizzy even.

Why don't we just...rest.

I don't want rest, I want—

I know, but our joining will rock the world. And I don't want to hold back.

I curled my toes at what his words promised. I supposed we could wait—a bit.

Laughter from the city below sounded, voices that were embarrassingly familiar. The sneers, the mocks, the taunts...

I don't want to be here.

His arms tightened around me as he strode for the balcony.

Seeing the question in my eyes, he said, "I've got somewhere special in mind."

I was barely aware of him stepping through a portal, of once again being in that forest. He opened a door into a cave I didn't recognize and placed me on the edge of a fur-covered poster bed.

"Rest, my love." He strode over to the firepit, filled it with his flames, and returned a moment later, with a jug of blood and a bottle that suspiciously looked like whisky. "The best healing combo," he said.

"What?" Had he lost his mind?

He didn't respond, instead, he crawled into bed next to me and pulled a blanket over us.

Just, rest. Heal.

I bit my lip. This was *not* what I was craving. And yet...the idea of being held secure by a male who promised so much—life, protection, devotion, and pleasure—was overwhelming. Tears prickled at my eyes as I leaned back into his arms and snuggled against him.

"Want some?" he offered me the blood.

I took it and drank heavily, eyes flaring. It was good—not as good as Aether's, but it held a certain ancient note to it.

"Aged blood, laced so it doesn't clot. It allows the magical properties to heighten and increases the flavor tenfold." He smirked.

"Ah, why didn't you start with this?" I teased. Even with its flavor, I still preferred Aether's blood—his was that of pure power.

"I should have. But I wanted your fangs all over me."

"Mmm, I bet you did, you greedy bastard."

He laughed, causing his chest to shake beneath me. The sound of it brought a smile to my lips and made the tears in my eyes fall—I was happy.

Happy.

When did that happen?

"I'll always crave more of your touch," he growled into my hair. "But you should know that since we're bonded, my blood is much more potent for you specifically, as yours is for me. Which means that it can expedite your healing and restore your magical stores much faster than any other blood would."

"All I heard was that you want more of my touch," I teased.

I could hear him grunt in my mind at the same time he did so in my ear.

I'll always crave your touch.

In that case, let me show you what I can do with my hands—

Mother Blood, we need another bed.

He went to move but I snatched his arm, halting him. "Don't you dare," I challenged him.

His arms tightened around me in passion, echoed by his *excitement* rising within the sheets.

"The other bottle?"

He smiled, primal, and lifted a rosy caramel-colored liquid. "Aged scotch with bits of...blood."

"We don't have that in the Glenn."

"It's very, very hard to find."

I grabbed the bottle and took a swig. Fire hit my tongue, my tonsils, and my throat—it immediately ended with me coughing, fitfully.

My core tensed as I shook, trying to clear my airways. He liked that stuff? His chuckles met my ears as my wheezing ended and I shot him a glare, noting the way he tried to hide his smile.

"It's an acquired taste."

"I'll say." I shoved the bottle into his hand before nestling back against him.

He took a long swig, swallowing the scotch several times, before placing the bottle down and holding me in both of his arms. Safe.

I was safe.

The pressure in the room intensified as the door opened, revealing fat flakes of snow that fell from the sky. Each large clump drifted slowly, dancing on its way to the white, sparkling ground. The fire crackled in the hearth; the heavy fur blanket covered my body.

All of it was comforting.

But the male beneath me, surrounding me with his body—heat sinking deep into my flesh—was the most reassuring of all. So, I lay there, in the arms of my mate, embracing each sign of life as our heartbeats sang in unison.

CHAPTER 37

CHANCE

I slammed open the door to the lab, ignoring the protests, and strode directly to Doctor Worshah who was watching monitors, disk in hand.

"We need to talk," I demanded.

"Ah, Chance. I've been waiting for you," he said. His thick round glasses were smudged as he pressed them up his pudgy nose.

"Clear the room," I shouted. The varying scientists and arches hesitated, looking to Dr. Worshah. He nodded and they filed out, the last one holding the door open for Shae, followed by Carran, who stepped inside. "Shae, give me a minute."

"No," she said as she stepped beside me. "You need family."

I gritted my teeth. I didn't have the energy to fight her on this too.

"Can you get this power out of me, siphon it from me?" I asked Dr. Worshah.

"What?" He looked at me like I had two heads. "Dux Dale, you have a rare gift. A powerful one. One that could change the face of this war. Why in Mother Blood's name would you want to part with it?"

"It's not a gift. It's a curse. It brings death," I snarled. "Get it out of me!"

"I can't," he said with pursed lips. His disk, displayed in front of him, began beeping with alerts; the screens in the room showed various lab rooms, pits, beasts...

"Can't or won't?" I challenged. The whole place was organized. He had been working on this for *years*. Why would he waste my power when it was everything he'd been working toward?

Hate fueled me.

I allowed the power to surface, to dance across my skin. My anger flared, and bolts streamed out and struck three different screens, shattering them all. They smoked as their fractured bits fell to the floor.

"Amazing," Doctor Worshah looked at me, eyes wide. "The amount of control you have over it is unheard of. Have you been training?"

Fury overtook me as my hands flew out and wrapped around his throat. "Enough!"

"Chance!" Shae shouted.

"Leave me, Shae." I focused on the crazed scientist in front of me. "Can you get this out, or not?"

He didn't respond for a moment. I added more pressure until he nodded.

"Good, then do so. Now!" I dropped his body, letting him crumple to the ground. His disk clattered against the cold, hard floor.

"Chance! Stop this, you don't need to be afraid!" Shae shouted.

I whipped my head around, red laced my vision. I could see the fear in her eyes. She knew what I was. "Why shouldn't I be? You clearly are."

Carran stepped next to Shae in a protective stance. Was he serious? "Boy, why don't we just calm down and—"

"Get. Out. Now." I flexed my hands, forcing the energy to remain where it was. It begged to be freed, to reach out and consume Carran. He had no special power, no special magic—he was just ordinary. But even the average scent of him was appealing.

Shae however...I inhaled deeply. I could sense vast stores of chilled power within her. Similar to that of the seethings, but purer and clean. It beckoned me, asked to be tasted, to be devoured—

"No!" I shouted, cupping my head. Bolts shot out from my body, fracturing the control board.

"Dux Dale, there is no siphoning your power. Can't you see?" Doctor Worshah spoke from behind me. "Who would be powerful enough to *contain* your force? What you possess is rare. We've tried to create a strong enough controller, but we've almost always failed. Even those who are considered our success stories are dim compared to you, and if they siphoned your power, they would die, freeing the magic in a dark wave. Who knows what would happen, who would be impacted? The implications are numerous, it would be a tidal wave of energy."

My heart raced with every word. Stuck, I was fucking stuck.

"The only two who may be strong enough to take it, could die trying," Doctor Worshah said again. "So, no, I can't help you."

I threw back my head and screamed. My core burned from the tension of keeping my power leashed. Shae's scent became intoxicating. The more power I released the more I wanted her energy, her force.

Just a taste...

"The other two, the ones who are compatible, get them in here. NOW! I don't want this!" I shouted, even as red static began to halo around me.

"Chance, it's all right. You've got us," Shae said as she stepped precariously close to the static cloud now engulfing me.

"Stop! Shae, this power in me wants to *siphon* you. You need to leave, now! I should have never come back." The energy within pulsed, the cloud growing.

"Who are the other two candidates?" I shouted at Dr. Worshah. "Get them in here, now!"

"Dux Dale," he started, slowly stepping back. "The only other two options would be individuals with preexisting power stores, people who were exposed to the same wave of power as you were when the base exploded—and have survived the blast *and* the mutation. They'd have to be trustworthy and skilled. And...they'd need a long enough lifespan to hold the power." His lips curved in a smile as delight filled his eyes. "They'd have to be compatible with you and your magic, which usually means you on an unconscious level picked who you'd share your connection with while mutating..." Each of his words was a nail in the coffin.

"It's me, isn't it?" Shae voiced. "That's why Chance is reacting to my presence when using his power."

Doctor Worshah simply nodded. "Yes, you and Dux Holland are the only two options."

The room began to spin. My nightmare, the vision was becoming a reality.

"I'll do it," Shae whispered.

"Lass! I think you better not," Carran spoke, and for the first time today, I agreed with him.

"If it helps him, I can do it. Maybe if I just take a little bit of your power, you will be able to better control the force." Shae smiled—small and scared, but willing.

No. The vision of her siphoning Holland's life played out before me. Holland crying for help. Shae saying I could have stopped it. Dammit, I would stop it.

"No, this is mine. I alone will carry it." My eyes snapped to Dr. Worshah. "You knew. All along, you and my father knew I'd never subject them to this. Tell me now, did you manipulate this?" I spat the last words.

"How can one command magic? We've been trying to for years. When the blast occurred, the three of you were close enough to absorb it, but far enough to survive it. More importantly—" drool began to drip from the sides of his mouth "—you were exposed to a raw magic. We still haven't been able to replicate it. Many of the seethings that were also exposed now possess *new* gifts, they're changing in ways we only have begun to understand. There is no orchestrating that. Nor could we have ensured your unique genes had the potential to mutate." He clasped his hands in front of him and was practically jumping with delight. The asshole liked talking about this?! My misery, my power, was intriguing to him?

I lashed out with a small bolt and encased his body. He screamed as he began to convulse.

"Chance!"

"Dux Dale, stop it right now, boy."

But I ignored them. Ignored Dr. Worshah's shrieks as I pushed more power into the force now eating him. "Did. You. Manipulate. It?"

"Yes!" he said through teeth that were now broken, blood pouring from his lips. I released the lightning and his body shook freely as his clothes smoked, holes dotting the fabric. The lights in the room blinked in and out until the room went black.

"How?" I demanded. Red bolts began tracing across the floor toward Dr. Worshah.

"Blood!" he shouted, hands in the air—still shaking from the last strike. "I administered blood from each of the three of you to one another. From our research, we know it strengthens any bond. If you didn't survive, they wanted a backup. Someone who would be compatible and who could take your power."

"Who commanded this?" I seethed. The power within climbed, heightened.

"President Dale."

White hot fury consumed me. I didn't think before releasing my power out toward the injured doctor. Didn't hesitate as the light from my red lightning illuminated the mad scientist's face. Only when Shae jumped in front of me, hands out to shield her face, did I try to rein it in. But it was too late.

"Shae!" Carran shouted her name as she screamed from the impact of my bolts.

For a moment she shook, but then a blue aura surrounded her, and she grunted as she *pulled* at my power. She was taking it, siphoning it into herself.

No. I had to stop her. Panic raced through my veins. I yanked back on the magic fleeing my body, entering Shae. I clawed at the power as it was being ripped from my being.

Shae began to eat the red lightning, swallowing it with a cloud of blue energy. The relief I felt internally was good. Too good, too freeing.

I hated myself.

The image of Shae on the ground, becoming like those muscled controllers, once again flooded my mind—it was becoming a reality.

I pulled at my power, harder than before, and commanded it back. At first, nothing happened, but then I pulled again, and this time I could feel her draw stall. Feel the magic start repelling her.

More power.

I reached within, to the rage and the storm still brewing, and pulled against Shae. The power hammered back into me, sending me to my ass. But even still, I siphoned.

I would not relent.

I may be a disgrace to the guara, a Leviathan in many ways, but I would never turn her into one.

Shae screamed as I consumed and pulled, bits of her magic filling me with the return of my own. I pulled as her aura diminished, the blue cloud shrinking in size, until the energy didn't return to me in red waves, but instead was an airy, cold blue.

Shae dropped to the ground. Her aura blinked out. Gone was the crystal blue cloud.

Even still, her power still flowed into me, cold and delightfully calming.

"Stop!" Carran screamed.

Doctor Worshah laughed in the corner of the room, blood dripping from his mouth as he witnessed what I was doing to my best friend.

I closed my eyes and tried to turn the valve off, to stop the flow of power. But the flavor of Shae...of her magic, it was enticing. Delicious even. Fresh and—

I flew forward at the impact of a club to my head. Pain exploded inside me as my body hit the now-fried control board. Carran stood above me, eyes wild. "Enough."

Panic fueled me as I looked at Shae, shaking on the ground, crying in pain.

What had I done?

I slammed the door to my power shut, and the siphon ended. The whole room became engulfed in darkness.

CHAPTER 38

TATE

I sat there in bed, snuggled against the mountain of a male who was my mate. Mine. I allowed the thought to lull me to sleep the night before, and still even as the sun rose and the snowy flakes in the sky continued to fall, it echoed through my mind as I stayed cradled in his arms. Safe.

The sun peaked, then fell, and now the moon lit the flakes as they continued to accumulate on the ground. A gust of frosty air filled the room, and the flames rose to meet it, sending out a wave of heat to ward off the chill.

We'd laid together for a day, barely separating except for when we absolutely had to. Conversation had stalled. We were both content to simply just *be*.

Together.

I sighed, content. If only this time could last forever.

I'd been avoiding thinking about how we'd soon have to go back and face everyone—deal with the recent events.

"How are you feeling?" Aether asked, his voice gravely against my hair, even as the heat from his words settled into my scalp.

How was I feeling? "Whole."

We both remained silent for a moment. We both knew our time here would be cut short, and we wanted more…of that, I was sure.

I twisted in his arms and locked eyes with his. His earnestness and lust took my breath away. "Why did you take us here?"

"You needed a break from the Embassy." He spoke as he caressed my head, dragging his fingers down the curve of my neck.

"Yes, but you said more. You said our joining would 'rock the world'…"

A devilish expression crossed his face, but he didn't answer. Instead, he continued to stroke the column of my neck, even with his cock hardening against my thigh, and his throat bobbing, he remained silent. Then, he simply nodded.

"Aether, why did you take me *here*?"

"Because this is for us, and no one else."

I reached up and cupped his face with my hand, running my fingers over the scar that jutted down his cheekbone.

"For us," I repeated.

Are you sure you're ready?

His voice in my head was tender, yet full of heat.

More than ready.

I yanked off my shirt, revealing the light pink bra underneath, and then stood, and unfastened my pants. He watched, desire radiating from every feature—he white-knuckled the sheets, veins bulged from his forehead, and his eyes fully dilated.

Lust.

A small smile played on my lips—this reminded me far too much of a time not long ago. But this time, he'd join me—he would participate. I yanked my pants down and stepped out of them. He hissed as he drank in the sight of my lacy black thong. It hugged my curves just right, revealing and yet, concealing in the most sinister of ways.

Well? I arched a brow.

For a moment, neither of us moved. Not as his gaze roamed over my expanse of skin, pausing on my once broken arm. Not as he extended his power, wrapping around me and checking, ensuring I was well and truly healed. I reached out with my mind and felt it: the pure primal beast, barely restrained. In a fluid motion, I opened the door to my mind fully so he could sense every desire I had, hear every thought pulsing through me, feel the all-consuming need rising in my veins.

He swallowed as a new expression, a dark expression claimed his features—stronger than lust, purer than love. It was a look that promised a cleansing of my soul, a claiming of my essence.

He pulled off his black shirt and then stood, facing and towering over me in the process. His chest was heaving with sweat glistening over his skin, slickening his tattoos. Some curved over his right pec in an intricate pattern that began to move, forming new words that I could read:

Reverent.

Unparalleled.

Invaluable.

Possessive.

He stepped closer to me, chin high in the air—every motion that of confidence. He was not someone to be toyed with. And yet...

I smiled as I slowly unlatched my bra, allowing it to fall to the ground. My breasts hung there, weighted, full, and warm. I squeezed them in front of him, sending every delicious thought of what I wanted done flying down the bond.

His nostrils flared as his lips ticked up to the side in anticipation.

In equal measure, he unfastened his pants and then allowed them to drop, revealing a large bulge within the black briefs, now proudly on display.

Those are some wild thoughts, darling. Are you sure you can handle it? They're not nearly as gentle as—

I don't want gentle. I want you.

I could sense his beast roaring, swore I saw the slightest twitch in his shoulders, echoed in his black aura surrounding him.

Well, hello, I purred.

With a sudden growl, he was holding me, pressing me to his body.

His scent enveloped me, one hand roughly cupped my breast, while the other found the small of my back.

Exhilaration sparked within at the sensual promise in his eyes. I grazed a finger over his chest, playing with his tattoos, before finding his neck.

She writhed within, sensing his beast.

With a playful tug at my nipple, he urged me back toward the bed, and I sat on the edge, feet dangling with my right toes grazing the floor.

Kneeling before me, he picked up my right foot, swallowing it in his hand.

I share with no one.

Before I could respond, he switched to my left foot. Instinctually, I stiffened. I'd *never* had anyone sexually approve of my shortcomings. They've overlooked it and never acknowledged it.

When I claim, I take it all—everything.

He lowered his mouth and took my toes in his mouth. One by one, he sucked on them and pulled them in and out of his mouth. He slid his tongue in between each of them and nearly purred as he did so.

Tears pooled in my eyes.

No one had ever fully accepted me for who I was before. Just loved me for me, not in spite of my shortcomings, but to have my very deficiencies loved? It was a purer passion than I'd ever known.

Fucking perfect.

His words were a balm to my heart and the tears I'd held at bay fell freely down my cheeks. I'd never known love like this. He kissed away the rejection and the insecurities I'd lived with my entire life.

He released my toes from his mouth, teasing me with his fangs and playfully nipping them before kissing the top of my foot, up to the ankle. He paused his pursuit and reached up, wiping away my tears with his thumb. He pressed his thumb to his lips, devouring my pain.

Every part is mine. And I yours.

The dominance of his words awoke something *new* inside me. Broke something I'd always kept caged because it was too *primal*.

All of you is mine.

His voice was rough in my mind as he held me hostage, trapped in front of him, his arms now on either side, with his face mere inches away. It was a challenge, and my inner beast feasted on it.

Once again, he lowered himself, but this time he tugged my black thong off in one fluid, slow motion. Before releasing a wave of power and completely incinerating it. Gone was any barrier, physical or emotional, as my past shame and the mask I'd worn my whole life went up in flames.

With this male, I was free.

A wave of friction flowed over my breasts, caressing and teasing— air with the slightest black tint danced in front of me. Aether smirked, knowing full well what he was doing.

Expertly working me.

His hands gently gripped my left calf and slowly he pressed his lips to my flesh, kissing. One kiss after another, until he reached my inner thigh. He gently reached up to my hips and pulled me down, adjusting me so I was at the edge of the bed, head back with his palm on my abdomen. He licked the column of the sensitive skin up to my core before pausing there and exhaling—his breath had me tightening.

Mmm, so fucking wet.

I wanted him, all of him. I reached out and gripped his head, willing him closer to my exposed flesh, but he didn't move.

Instead, a wave of the most glorious, dense air nipped at my entrance, it blanketed the bud of nerves and constricted.

I bucked from the unexpected pleasure.

Oh, Mother Blood—

But my cry was silenced as his lips touched my wet center and pulled. More delicious tension cascaded over my breasts, my neck, my ears—he was everywhere at once, in every way—his magic an exten-sion of himself.

He moved his mouth with precision, moving slightly away toward the base of my thigh, using his magic to tease my bud, my center, my back entrance... My head lulled back into the bed, and I clawed at the sheets, desperate for more.

He smirked in my mind.

Slowly, he dragged his tongue down my thigh until he reached my knee where he then playfully nipped and kissed his way back up. All while still working me with his master manipulation of energy; he teased my nipples, nipped at my neck, and grazed my clit, even as his physical body was tasting every part of mine. I reveled in each touch, each pass of his tongue—an answer to a prayer I'd whispered my whole life.

He placed one gloriously thick finger near my entrance and just waited. Unmoving. At my whimper, he thrusted it inside of me and pumped once, then twice. All while wetting my thigh with his mouth, increasing the caress of every sensual part of my body.

A moan tore from my lips as I could feel the rising tide of release approaching.

He grazed with his fangs and hovered just to the side of my entrance, waiting...

I want to claim you in every sense of the word. I want to take you into my mouth, fuck you with my mouth and my cock. I want to dominate every sense until the only one you think of when you writhe with need is me. *I want to own every sexual expression, even this.*

His fangs pressed but didn't puncture as he waited for my approval. I laughed as pure pleasure erupted from the depths of my soul. This was what sex should be—not just fucking but love-driven acts of passion. I didn't need time to think, didn't hesitate as I nodded and shoved his head further into my thigh.

His fangs punctured and the pain was instant, but then just as quickly, the venom entered my system, and the sheer euphoria was unlike anything I'd ever felt.

I became disembodied, riding waves of an orgasm that was unending. He drew more blood into himself as his fingers plunged back inside me—at the same time the air caressed every tender part of my body. My neck and breasts were washed in a constant stream of pulsing tension. A constant tense grazing over my bud had me writhing against Aether's head, even as he drank deeper still.

The creaking bed was a physical tether as I became lost in a sea of bliss.

So perfect. You taste better than I'd ever imagined.

More. NOW. I commanded.

I could hear him chuckle in my soul, dry and lethal. He'd give me more.

A moment later, the tension coating my body, playing with me, intensified tenfold, and with it my orgasm heightened. Such ecstasy was unknown to me, I'd never experienced anything like this. He removed his fangs from my thigh and kissed the wound before dragging his tongue down my center, teasing the sensitive bud of my sex, in one drawn-out motion. I dug my hands into his hair and the sheets, claws coming out—I was sure the sheets had been shredded.

My inner beast roared, and the room lit with pink flames that danced about the cavern. The walls were covered in fire, but didn't burn from the heat, even as Aether's power rose to meet mine—pink mingling with black, intertwining and becoming one.

He played with my entrance with his tongue, flicking my clit with his finger at the same time before adjusting so he could take me further into his mouth. I bucked as he pulled, purely euphoric.

It claimed me.

It dominated my senses.

It devoured my being.

He drew me deeper into his mouth, and I whimpered from the bliss of it, still high on his venom. I was grinding on his mouth, tensing, and demanding. Purely insatiable.

He released me for a moment, the cool air shocking me, and then took me again, harder this time with his tongue dancing over my sensitive flesh, hitting the nerves just right before pressing gently with his fangs.

Too much, Mother Blood this was too much.

I'd never known love like this. Never felt things like this. Only one could elicit such a response, my mate.

I shook within as he sucked on me, eating me, as he stroked my stomach and the underside of my breast with his hand as he feasted. Stars danced across my vision.

Aether.

His responding growl and the building tension was too much.

I was ready to erupt.

One more pass of his tongue, and my core was clenching as I climaxed again. Euphoria flooded my system as I rode the waves of pleasure, all while I was held in his mouth. He worked me harder with his tongue as I writhed, pushing me further than I'd ever known possible.

This is what I'd been missing my entire life.

She roared within and a projection of her danced in the flames, mirrored by a black dragon. Their cries were deafening, and my blood boiled, firing rapidly. I felt his power enter my system. My very being was being claimed by his essence.

I was drunk on him.

He released me and slowly stood, satisfaction and lust coloring his eyes. He licked his lips, my blood dripping down the sides of his mouth, and my toes curled at the sight.

The beasts in the air roared, eliciting a flare of magic within my deep internal stores.

Mine, forever. Aether's thoughts reached my addled mind through the bond. His cock pulsed against the black fabric, and it was too much.

I flicked my wrist, willing some of the flames in the ceiling to pour down and devour the inhibitor of my pleasure. In a flash, the material burnt and ashy pieces fell to the ground, revealing a primed and smooth cock—his beast finally freed.

He was perfection.

I swallowed. I'd never wanted anyone like I desired him. Never needed anyone as much as I craved him. Even with my climax, I found myself not just desiring to come again but desperate to devour him.

Without hesitation, I willed the air around him, forcing him forward. His tip brushed my cheek and I didn't wait as I pulled him into my mouth, barely covering the tip, and grabbed his readied shaft with my other hand. He bucked at the contact and released a moan that competed with the roaring dragons. He began to step back and—

Ut-uh, don't pull back. You. Are. Mine.

I spoke the claiming words, giving into my most primal instincts.

My hair rose from my head as a cyclone of our magic filled the cavern, shaking the stalagmites from the ceiling and burning them to nothing but ash before they were picked up in the wind and circled around us in a show of pure power.

I flicked his tip with my tongue, savoring the flavor that was him. Just as I'd imagined and hoped: ash and salt overwhelmed my senses.

I feasted.

Holy fuck, he moaned and roared as I passed over his tip again, swirling and teasing.

A smile pulled at my lips as I held him hostage in my mouth, my hand still pumping him in tune with the movements of my tongue. I dipped into the crevice at the tip and was met with salty readiness. He thrusted against me and then gently rocked.

My veins filled with new power, high on his venom and the way he responded to me, and *she* took over. I willed the air to tease his back entrance, to cup his balls and squeeze. And still, I fucked him with my mouth.

My nerves screamed in pleasure as the missing pieces fell into place. The cavern shook and the stone around us cracked. The bed poles went up in the flames, and with it, the fur comforter.

Still, he stood before me as I became bathed in black and pink flames, unharmed. They were an extension of me—of us.

I reached behind him with my other hand and squeezed his ass, forcing him forward, further into my mouth. The sheer size took a moment to adjust to, but then I was grazing his cock's head with my fangs, squeezing his ass as I did so.

"Fuck, Tate," he whispered.

She roared at my name on his lips.

I want you in every sense...

I let the question hang. The responding 'fuck yeah' down the bond had me releasing him from my mouth. I commanded him to lie down on the ruined bed, the ashes and flames, before straddling him with my ass toward his face. Leaning over, I found the tender spot near his inner crotch on his thigh and my fangs found purchase. He bucked and hissed as I punctured and pulled. I released waves of my own venom and rode him as he worked me from behind with his hand.

Together we were swept away in bliss purer than anyone ought to be allowed. I pulled harder, deeper, and savored every cherry note of *him*. His blood, his person, his essence—they were all *mine*.

She writhed as I could feel myself grinding against Aether's hand.

I released him from my fangs, allowing my venom to fully enrapture him, and then took him harder into my mouth. This time I grazed him with my fangs while working his shaft and squeezing his manhood, and then he came. For a moment it was fluid shooting into my being, but then it was nothing but flames and power. I savagely inhaled it all.

I released him and he adjusted me so I was facing him, sex dazed and carried away in passion. He claimed my mouth again with his, tasting himself on my lips.

He was my missing piece, the note to my ballad. My entire life, I'd had to hold back, afraid I'd break the men I was with—

His growl was feral, and my eyes glistened in return. I could have fun with him, I could...

He lifted me up so I was hovering over his cock, fully hard again, in challenge. I didn't hesitate before impaling myself on him. Pleasure erupted and I threw back my head and screamed. The friction was too much, too powerful, the sheer size of him threatened to undo me completely.

But then I adjusted, and the fit was so right...it was as if it were ordained by Mother Blood herself. As if we were written in the stars, and he was custom-built for me. Every inch of him that entered was the answer to my life's plea. It stroked and filled every craving I'd had —every desire and itch that was never satisfied.

I rode him, meeting him thrust for thrust—my heavy breasts bouncing in a way that made every sensual part of me hyperaware. My core ached, and each pass of him soothed it, but then only left me wanting more. I increased my movement, savoring the length of him.

He could handle me. Fuck, he outmatched me. I didn't need to be gentle. Didn't need to worry—he wouldn't break. I slammed myself down on him harder, dominating. And then again, and again, and again. Each time our flesh fully met, our souls blended further.

I didn't miss the way he growled as he gripped my ass in one hand and somehow still reached the base of my neck with the other. Our bodies lit up in black and pink fire, fusing as one.

The slick motion of him inside me along with his outward caress sent me over the edge. I could feel him in my mind, feel his pleasure, his desire, his lust. His emotions mixed with mine and I became lost in a sea of love.

Desire overtook us as our very souls and essences became intertwined.

I tensed on him as I came. At the same moment, I felt him pulse, our moans synchronized as we *both* climaxed. Together, as it should be. I clung to him as he held me against his chest, our breaths coming in pants.

Overhead, our dragons roared and the magic that had pulsed to life was no longer in two streams of separate fire, but an intricately braided single flame of black and rose-gold. It encased our beasts as together they screeched and breathed fire that was made of the same flame. The entire cavern shook, the ashes that Aether laid on were blown away as the ground cracked and then, the air stilled. The beasts were gone and with them, the flames and sparks.

It was done.

I looked down at my hands and smiled. They were bathed in pink flames that held a black center.

We were bonded.

CHAPTER 39
AETHER

She lay atop me, cradled in my embrace. The gravity of what just occurred was still sinking in.

We were bonded.

It was more powerful than I'd have ever guessed and was nothing like I'd ever experienced before. It was transcendent.

I could feel the difference in my being, the extra power I now had that was purely Tate. My magic had altered and with it, my very essence.

I was wholly hers.

The primal instinct to claim had me practically taking her again, but the sweat glistening from her back and her even breaths told me she was asleep. Worn out.

Smug satisfaction raced through me.

A smile pulled at my mouth as I rubbed her back. I could stay like this forever, would stay like this if that's what she wished. But reality would find us. And if we were discovered like this...

My grip tightened at the thought.

I would never leave her. She would be safe. I just needed her to pass her upcoming assessments and then she'd be *my* active Untishee member, and I could take her with me wherever I was sent—no questions asked. I bit my lip, hiding a snarl as I thought of *any* who tried to stand in my way.

I'd fucking kill them.

Any and all who dared threaten her.

A soft snore escaped her mouth as she snuggled deeper into my chest. There were a million logistics that needed my attention, and several pertinent conversations I needed to have with Tate. And yet... she was so peaceful, sleeping soundly. I couldn't bring myself to wake her, to jar her from her glorious after-sex haze.

So instead, I held her close. I inhaled her scent and studied the changes I felt within. I had changed, for the better, of that I was certain, but with this new power came more responsibility. Namely, to Tate.

I forced an exhale through tight lips.

I would not fail her.

HOURS WENT BY AND EVENTUALLY, she stirred. I carried her back through the portal, her naked body cradled closely to mine, and strode quickly across my balcony to my room—our room.

She looked up at me, eyes wide and trusting. Instinctually, my grip tightened before I forced myself to release her so I could draw us a bath. I further heated the water with my flames before pouring in some lavender bath salts and bubble bath. She slowly submerged herself into the tub and moaned as the water engulfed her. If it were possible to be jealous of bath water, I was.

But instead of yanking her out of the tub and taking her again, I forced myself into the kitchen to retrieve a large pitcher of blood along with a block of cheese, and then joined her in the tub.

The water sloshed over the side as I entered it. Once again, I was grateful for the *large* Untish tubs.

"Here." I extended her a cup of blood and a chunk of cheese.

"Thanks." She took both, sipping the blood. "So...what now?" Her mahogany eyes were full of questions.

I forced myself not to focus on the way her breasts were barely covered by the bubbles, or the way her hair clung to her flesh and highlighted their swell. Instead, I looked into her rust-colored eyes and the faint splash of freckles that graced her perfect nose and cheeks. Cheeks that angled flawlessly, sharp but full, and brought out her perfectly symmetrical eyes. Eyes that were now lit with sensual promise and intelligence.

I could feel myself enlarging, only growing harder as she smirked.

"Right..." I cleared my throat as she shoved the cheese into her mouth, her moist and fuckable mouth.

She arched a brow at me.

I shook my head. "I've added you to the roster of trainees who will test out in the upcoming assessments. I want you out of basic and by my side as soon as possible. I've been watching you and Camella, you're getting good."

She snorted.

"Tate." I lifted her chin up. "What happened in the ring doesn't define you. We'll work on how to get out of being pinned like that."

"Really?" She looked at me, a deadpan expression claiming her features. "Aether, my ass was handed to me. They don't think I belong, and maybe they're right." She pulled her knees to her chest and wrapped her arms around them.

Anger rose in my blood as I recalled the cruel words they flung at Tate. Fuck, I wanted to slaughter all who dared speak ill of her.

"You belong here. This is yours. All of it, more than you know." I leaned forward and moved a stray lock of hair from her face. As much as the primal side of me liked her hair's black tips, I missed the pink ones that were truly *her*. "Vala says your magic is improving, and really, you'll only be expected to form a shield, even a small one, and light something on fire. After that, you'll be classified as an active member, and I can take over your training. We can be together as much as you'd like."

I swallowed; even after all we've done and become, I still feared she'd reject me. That she would discover my flaws and not want me. It was abundantly clear I didn't deserve her. And the secrets I still held...

She placed her hand on mine. "We're one now, Aether." We sat in silence for a few moments before she cleared her throat. "What do you mean by 'all of this' is mine?"

We were entering a much-needed conversation, and yet, I loathed having to worry her with politics. Still, she had every right to know.

So, there in the tub, I told her. "You are from the royal line, Tate. Pink is the color of the House of Blush—you are a direct descendant of Perry and Matias, the last living one within the borders of this realm. That makes you the rightful ruler of the Embassy."

She stared at me with wide eyes. For a while, she said nothing, the only sounds came from the splattering of water hitting the floor when it was displaced by each of her deep breaths.

"I think I knew deep down, after starting to puzzle it out once we got here," she began. "What does this mean?"

I could feel her fear.

"I won't let anything happen to you."

"I know," she said, but I didn't miss the worry in her eyes. "Aether, why am I the last living royal here, the last member of the House of Blush?"

I took a deep breath. "After the Great War, many Untishee returned to Mydant. But not all, some stayed to ensure peace and balance. When we didn't side with any one Vamp, together they decided we were dangerous and sought to exterminate us. Lilith Drago and her family stayed behind as royal representatives for the House of Blush, while everyone else fled to Mydant to secure its borders. But soon after, she and her son, Alistair, were murdered. Esme, Lilith's granddaughter, was the last member of the House of Blush, the Royal Tribe, and she took her father Alistair's seat until—"

I couldn't bring myself to finish. I was young then, barely an adult.

"Until?" Tate asked, manipulating the air around me.

"We were attacked, and she died along with her babe. No one from the House of Blush has since ventured into this realm. It was deemed unsafe and instead, as cousins to the House of Blush, the House of Iron has ruled here under the guidance of Mydant's Crown."

"Okay, but Aether—" she exhaled, my heart constricting at the fear in her eyes "—if she died and so did her baby, how am *I* here?" She bit her lip.

"I don't know." The admission stung. "But since you are a royal descendant, the Embassy is yours. The chairs will be obligated to answer to *you*, or they will once we stake your claim—if you stake it, that is."

"So, what you're saying is I'm *your* queen. I think I shall from henceforth be referred to as *Your Majesty*," she teased. But even with the lighthearted tone, I could see the strain in her features—feel it through the bond.

"You're not alone in this. And if you want, no one ever has to know," I said.

She arched a brow.

Ach-hem...

"*Your Majesty*," I added, love swelling in my chest for this female who had so thoroughly bewitched me.

"Thank you," she said in the best proper tone I'd ever heard. But her smile quickly faded. "What if I don't want the responsibility of power? What if I want to run away to the human realm with you?" She didn't take her eyes from the water, nervously playing with her hair.

"I'd leave in a second." And I meant it, every word. There wasn't anything I wouldn't do for her.

She nodded. "Good, well... Before we can run away, we need to deal with President Dale. What does Arithi have planned? I still haven't mastered my magic, but I'm more powerful than before and I can't hide here forever. It's time I stop running. What are we going to do?" She leaned forward, resolve in her gaze.

I smiled, crooked, but full of appreciation for the female in front of me. "I have a recon mission in a couple of weeks, I'd like you to come.

We can assess, report back to the tribe chairs, and then likely get an army to go and destroy those fuckers," I said.

"I like it," she responded smiling. "But...why wait? Why not go and destroy them now?"

Her presence in my mind, along with her perky, exposed breasts, had me practically agreeing to leave now, to kill and destroy whatever threatened her. But then my internal shrewd warrior took over.

"We don't know where all their bases are. We only had the location to the one compound, and we destroyed it. Recon missions have been happening and word is spreading about dozens of other bases just like the one we destroyed...not to mention, impending war. Things can get messy, fast. We'll need to be united in our attack and that takes the cooperation and planning from strategic leaders, namely the chairs."

"Ah," she said simply. "Aether, wasn't your *father* the Night Tribal chair?"

I gritted my teeth; I'd hoped she didn't pick up on that with the memory she'd witnessed not long ago. "Yes."

"So why aren't you?"

She voiced the question I'd been asked my whole life.

"I never wanted the responsibility. Never felt..."

I left the sentence hanging.

She cupped my face in her hands. "You are worthy."

Before I could respond, she kissed me, and all the semantics fell away. There was nothing but her.

Nothing in all the realms but my mate.

CHAPTER 40
TATE

I wiped sweat from my forehead wishing, yet again, that Aether would surround me with a breeze. But, as he pointed out this morning, it would draw attention. Attention we didn't want.

Camella raised her sword, and I mirrored her actions. We'd moved on to sparring with weapons a week ago. They were, naturally, a combination of wood and stone—still painful when struck, but not deadly. And they were very heavy to lift. My muscles groaned as I kept the sword suspended above my head.

"Good, your stance is better," Camella commented a moment before nodding, signaling the beginning of the match.

She charged, per the norm, and I deflected, meeting her blade in the air before spinning and offering a counterstrike. She was prepared for it and met each of my swings with one of her own. Once again, I found myself on the defensive, her strikes pushing me back, closer and closer to the ring's edge.

I ground my teeth at the force of her last swing, my muscles hurt, and my left leg throbbed.

Go on the offensive. Aether spoke into my mind.

He'd come to watch today and had been full of suggestions until I silenced him after he distracted me, allowing Camella to land a nasty blow to my shoulder. He'd been quiet until now.

I huffed and as she swung, I ducked, then stood and hit her calves. Not enough to send her down, but enough to earn a surprised look.

I smiled, after the many hours in this ring, there had only been a handful of times I was able to make contact with her.

Good. Her legs are often unprotected, next time swipe at her knees from behind and send her to her ass.

I erected a wall to block his comments, even as I made a mental note. The distraction cost me; with two calculated strikes, it was me on my ass—again—her blade at my throat.

"Not bad, but you got excited and that cost you. Keep emotion out of battle, unless it's rage, rage fuels your swings." She removed her sword from my throat and helped me up. I stood, a good six inches taller than her, but even so, I felt small.

"So, why the protective hawk?" she asked, nodding to Aether. She had acknowledged him earlier, but for the past two hours, she hadn't spoken of him.

"Males," I huffed.

She smiled at that. "One more match and then you're off to lectures."

I swore she enjoyed seeing the dread in my eyes, and the way I was pushed to my max physically and mentally every day. I couldn't wait to pass the assessment. Then, I could dole out some justice of my own. Aether could see to my training and...my toes curled in my boots.

Fuck yeah. I can get rid of Camella now...

I sent him the bird, mentally, of course, and he chuckled in my mind—his presence heated my very being. Since we've bonded, I could *feel* him with me constantly. The bridge between our minds was stronger, easily accessed, and constant. I didn't need to 'try' to send a message, I just did. In fact, even with my shielding, I couldn't keep him out. Something that would have bothered me more had he not had the same problem.

Several times when I'd been struck, I could feel him *wince* and knew some of the pain had echoed down the bond.

A secret smile claimed my lips as I recalled the way he looked at me this morning as we ate breakfast. The dirty thoughts that male had... and I heard them *all*. The look of embarrassment on his face when I voiced each thought aloud was worth its weight in gold...as was the *particular* breakfast we enjoyed right after.

"Begin," Camella said and then struck. I was ready for it, along with her counterstrike. I swung once myself and she spun out of the way before swiping at my feet. I jumped and then deflected her next blow. I dropped, turned, and struck her behind her knees. She went tumbling to the dirt. I was on her in an instant, sword discarded in the dirt beside me, a dagger at her throat.

"Well done." Her eyes gleamed.

My chest heaved as I moved from her and collected my abandoned weapon.

A gong sounded, signaling that it was—in fact—time for lecture. I sheathed my dagger and then wiped my sweaty forehead with a towel before grabbing my bag.

"Aether," Camella spoke as his scent surrounded me.

"Camella, her training is going well."

"It is, she'll be ready for assessment next week. Not battle," she paused and gave him a pointed look. "But she should be ready to become an active member, that I can recommend."

I suspected Aether had encouraged the one-on-one training, but from her comment, it was likely that he was behind the switch to weapons training as well.

"Good. Well done." He nodded at her and clamped me on the shoulder. "Time for lecture," he said, directing his gaze at me.

I waved goodbye to Camella, who merely smirked, and then walked toward the arena where lectures had recently been moved to. The salt and ash in the air were delightful, but I was fully aware a *large* part of that was coming from my mate beside me and not the sea beyond.

"I will observe lectures today and have already given Professor Darsew a heads-up. He knows I want you in the assessment next week and it's not uncommon for commanders to come and oversee so they can select candidates they want in their command."

The arena came into view, the sun lighting up the white stone in a glorious shade of pink and red. It *felt* right.

Without warning, Aether tugged my wrist and pulled me into an alcove, off to the side, before erecting a wall of darkness—pure flames —around us. His mouth was on mine before I could even blink and I savored the sultry taste of his tongue. I welcomed each stroke and the heat that built in my core.

I want you.

Pure desire pulsed through me, and my legs began to wobble as he intensified the kiss, further pinning me against the wall. His hand gently cupped my face and tilted my head back as my legs wrapped around him, perfectly lining up with—

Another gong sounded.

Aether broke the kiss with a growl.

Later.

My skin danced with anticipation as he slowly set me down but didn't release me. I savored the contact of his hands on my hips, thrived on the warmth and tension I could feel radiating from him. From here, I felt his heart pounding and saw each golden whorl spinning in his eyes. The gong sounded again and the fire in Aether's features threatened to consume the instrument itself.

I smiled.

He let me go and we entered the now-empty pathway, the flames vanishing. As we filed in, his hands left my hips, and I instantly missed his touch. I found my seat, next to Carly who looked nervous and was biting her nails.

For the first time since I could remember, I was well and truly happy. I had a home—Aether. I belonged. I was fully myself. Contentment settled in my bones as my inner dragon curled around herself, happy to sleep. I still needed to figure out how to awaken her and shift, but that was a problem for later.

"All right, today's lecture covers the types of shifters. I wish to prepare those of you who plan on taking the assessment next week. I've assigned some heavy reading that will help, though I know you'll no doubt be preparing tactically, I'd caution you to not neglect your studies as this has been one area I've seen the greatest of warriors fail in and, consequently, not pass." He adjusted his glasses before erecting his screen of white flames and projecting some points on it.

Three general camps came up—the mixing of species as he called it. Personally, I found it distasteful, but it was important in understanding our origins.

"Can anyone tell me the three types of Untishee?" he asked.

Carly's hand shot up, and Professor Darsew smiled as he called on her.

"Shifters, wielders, and supports," she answered.

"Good. And what do these groups entail?"

"The shifters can become dragons and are our warriors. The wielders fight alongside the shifters, also as warriors, but specialize in defenses. And the supports are in charge of population," Carly said, her voice dipping at the end.

I smiled in spite of myself. She really didn't like talking about sex.

"Population?" Professor Darsew pushed.

I didn't miss Perseus's smirk or the way he thrived on prodding Carly in public. How could magic match those two? All I could see was a future of abuse and unhappiness.

"Yes, they are the ones who provide the genes. The breeders," I answered. Carly smiled at me, visibly grateful.

"Very good, Tate," Professor Darsew said as he filled the screen with facts.

Aether and I had discussed his history into the wee hours the night before. After seeing the memory of his mother, I wanted to understand the different Untish relationship dynamics. My heart still ached as I thought of the female who had once been so close to her son, given so much, and was now viewed as an outcast. Worse still, she *rejected* her son after the death of her husband, his father.

"Untishees are created with the three camps of magic: human, vampirical, and Fae. The mixing of these bloods gives us a new breed, the Untish. As we saw with Perry and Matias, their magic blended when they bonded, and this gave Perry—full Fae—the access to human and vampire magic through their shared blood and connection. This is incredibly rare as usually it takes a child born of blood and magic to have the Untish gene trait—one that is primarily *magical*. Can anyone tell me *why* Perry received the gene?"

Hands shot up all throughout the arena.

"Shane," he called on a small male in the front.

"Uh—" Shane cleared his throat, still not transitioned to his adult male voice. "—because magic is its own power—it follows its own rules. As Perry herself states, '*The force was one that could not be undone. Could not be rejected. There were no choices. We were bound, even before our joining.*" He paused and ran his hand through his golden locks. "I would surmise that she became the mother of the Untish Tribe because of her purity of heart and the binding of her magic with Matias's. They were mates."

Several jocks laughed, Perseus included. I ground my teeth. What Shane had said was beautiful and it made so much sense to me. I knew, unequivocally, that Aether wasn't just my bonded...he was my mate.

Love blossomed in my chest along with an instant need for Aether.

Careful, darling, or I'll come down there and take you right where you are.

Chills danced across my neck and back at his voice—my mate's voice—in my head.

I'd love to see how that would play out...but I don't think it would be taken well.

I thought of Carly and her shyness. No, it would certainly not be handled well at all. A secret smile played at my lips.

Professor Darsew droned on about the combination of possibilities and strengths before calling on Carly.

"The strongest always come from one party who is pure Fae and one that is a half-breed, a human and vampire combination. Next would be a human Fae half-breed with a pure vampire and lastly, a Fae vampire half-breed with a human. Of course, this can vary depending on the bloodline's purity, as will any strengths and giftings present in the offspring." She closed her disk and lifted her chin in the air. I'd obviously missed an exchange she'd had with Perseus who now sat in front, glowering.

"Very good, Carly. Can anyone tell me if this ever changes?" Professor Darsew asked.

Everyone was silent.

"I thought so. Many think that genes and heritage are everything, and in ruling, they do matter, but magic is its own entity. In many ways it is sentient. It was suggested by the philosopher Cleo that our dragon forms are an expression of the magic itself, not us. That when we shift, we are held hostage to the powerful force of magic and we— as known by ourselves—become background, taking the passenger seat. She also suggested that if magic was its own *entity,* then it would entirely be possible for it to circumvent our understanding of genes as we know it and produce a new breed, a new expression of magic's self," he finished. Most of the class seemed glazed, Perseus was whispering to his friend—the obnoxious red-headed beauty. But a few of us were paying attention. A few of us leaned in.

"What would this look like?" I asked thinking of the seethings.

"Ah, well it's purely theoretical, but it could be a different form of beast, new powers, some even suggested a *new* gene marker could be formed. But again, we're venturing into philosophy and not history," he answered.

"Could it ever be harvested and...made *evil?*" I asked. Dark magic, that's what Aether had said made the seethings. But what was dark magic exactly?

"Mmm, your question is one many have posed: is magic wholly good? This is something debated by many of the greats, Cleo and George included. Some argue that magic is composed of various shades of grey, just as we are, and depending on its wielder, it can express itself in darkness, as evil. Still others argue that magic is *only* good and if it were to be used as evil, it would not be the magic but the wielder who made it so. As such, these people do not agree with Cleo's argument that magic is itself sentient and our dragon forms are controlled by magic, rather they believe magic unlocks our dragon forms that are merely variations of ourselves. Our most primal state. It's fascinating really," he began to ramble.

"My father said Cleo was a rattled lunatic," Perseus quipped, earning laughter from his squad of degenerates.

"Yes, he was never my best student," Professor Darsew said, earning a glare from the red-faced Perseus.

"So, what is dark magic then?" I asked, directing attention once again to the subject at hand.

"Dark magic, dear Tate, is something we do not discuss. It is forbidden. A violation of nature herself, taking what is not yours, holding it for too long, and forcing it into a vessel against its will." He cleared his throat just as the gong sounded. "That's it. Those of you who wish to test out, I cannot encourage you enough to read the material I highlighted for you."

The arena erupted in movement as many cadets began gathering their belongings and filed out.

You were talkative today.

Yes, well I have to learn, you big oaf. Knowledge is power.

The moment I said the phrase, images of Fletch flooded my mind. He had taught me that. He had tried to convey the importance of information in our last conversation. Tears pricked at my eyes.

I'm so sorry, Tate.

I sniffed and then exited the arena. I would make Fletch proud. We would defeat President Dale. I was nearly strong enough; my skills had vastly improved since I first arrived here. I just needed to play by these stupid rules a little longer and then I could *finally* do something to destroy the embodiment of evil and finish Fletch's mission.

We'll make them pay.

It was the darkness in Aether's tone that solidified the sentiment. A promise. The Glenn would pay for their crimes and the lives they stole. Power thumped through my veins, and I could feel the energy dancing across my skin as Aether joined me in the clearing.

They will pay, I confirmed.

He threw out a portal disk and then pulled me into his arms. A moment later we were back in *our* cavern. Safe and secure.

In the meantime, we have a few minutes...

I didn't respond, instead, I tore into his shirt with my nails and smiled. There were *definitely* perks to having a mate.

CHAPTER 41
TATE

"Good! You engulfed it without burning it. Well done!" Vala encouraged as she jumped on her feet cheering, fist pounding the air.

"Thanks." I smiled. My pink and black flames circled not one, but two elms without harming them. She'd been teaching me control for a while, but it finally clicked this week. Tomorrow was the assessment. Tomorrow I would finally be free to plan *my* revenge. And it couldn't come soon enough.

I was ready; Aether had agreed this morning, bolstering my confidence as he held me against his chest in the early sun's light. The honeymoon stage, that's what Vala had called it. She had, naturally, guessed we bonded and congratulated me immediately—which was, of course, followed by a series of improper questions.

"Can we work on shifting now?" I asked. I still hadn't shifted into my dragon.

"Yes, but it's not necessary to pass the assessment. You just have to be able to protect yourself, not shift. Which is good and thank blood for that! Because you still lack a connection to *her*," Vala teased. Even with her tone light, I felt the underlying concern.

"I will." This was something I had to do. I knew, intrinsically, it was paramount for me to not just shift, but to master it entirely.

"All right, well then let's go for it. Although honestly, Aether may be a better teacher when it comes to shifting. But for now, close your eyes and then picture that pool of power, find your dragon, and simply awaken her," Vala said.

She made it sound so easy. I huffed and nodded. This time, I sat down on the grass and dug my fingers into the soil, feeling my connection to the magic that was buried deep beneath the surface.

Inside me, my inner pool was there, glowing in pink flames with black twirling at the center. My magic, Aether's magic, blended together. It still gave me a thrill every time I saw our flames and knew it was a testament to the binding of our essences.

Beyond the smoke and fire, she lay there. Curled up in a ball, sleeping. Just like last time. And the time before that. And the time before that. The cord that I used to tug was no longer a light string, instead it was heavy...it was thick. I grabbed it and yanked, but it refused to budge. Frustration began to fill me. I had to do this. I needed to be able to shift when we attacked the Glenn.

I used that rage to pull harder and this time, *she* opened her eyes and looked at me. I smiled encouragingly and waved her forward, begging her to come, to claim my body and shift. But instead, she huffed dry steam and then closed her eyes again, nestling in on herself.

No! I controlled my body. I *would* shift. I tugged on the heavy rope and screamed internally as I did so—the air around me sparking from the energy swirling within. Her eyes snapped open, glaring at me; she shook her head and snapped at the air before turning around and then kicking me out of the pool. It became opaque and covered in flames. She was gone. Not only that, but *she* had forced *me* out.

Anger claimed me. What the hell? I was inclined to agree with Cleo's assumptions of magic being sentient.

"It's okay, Tate, let it go," Vala said.

But the air whipped around me, swirling and heating. I opened my eyes and saw I was in a cyclone of pink and black flames, the ground scorched beneath me.

"Tate..." Vala's voice was uncertain, bordering on scared.

The magic took over and the cyclone became bigger, thicker until I couldn't see Vala through the flames. The air sparked and popped.

Love, you may need to cool it down. I'm overheating over here and just burned the parchment.

His voice was a caress on my skin. I was in control. This was me. I exhaled and with it, released my hold on the magic—a hold I hadn't even noticed I held.

The flames winked out.

There you go. Save the heat for the bedroom, his voice sounded light, but held a certain edge of worry.

The storm vanished and left me sitting alone in a charred circle. Vala dropped her shield and smiled at me wearily. "Well, that could have been worse."

I gave her a side glare and then stood. "I'm done for today, take me back."

I LAY in Aether's arms in his bedchamber watching the sunset, dipping into the turquoise sea. In just ten hours, I'd be testing out—dueling and showing my powers. We'd gone over it again and again. It would be in the arena and one by one we would face off with a peer. We'd be given three chances and had to succeed in two of them—which meant either getting my opponent to tap out or survive for thirty seconds without being pushed from the circle, and then I would pass.

Next, we'd duel again, but this time with weapons, and I would have to either survive for one minute without stepping outside the circle or deal a death blow. We'd be given two tries to pass once. Assuming I passed this, I would go to the magic demonstration.

This would take place in a different arena and was, according to Vala, simple. Construct a shield. Block a magical projection—usually composed of flames or swords. And lastly, blast my power at a target.

This traditionally occurred in some game-like setting, witnessed by a large audience. The details were always hidden until moments before, but I just needed a small display of magic. Simple. I grunted as I shivered inside. If I failed...

You won't fail. You have this, you're more than ready.

His comfort in my mind was paired with his hands rubbing my back in slow circles. He breathed into the shell of my ear and shivers ran down my spine.

Still...I couldn't forget the pain I felt when I dueled Sheila, the fear when my head was held just above the ground with my broken arm pinned behind me. I could still practically taste the blood in my mouth.

"Aether, what if I'm not good enough?" I thought of my uneven footing, my shortcomings, and the many times I tasted dirt in training. If I couldn't face a trainee, how the hell would I defeat those vile beasts and the entire military strength of the guara?

"Hey," he adjusted his grip on my chin, lifting it so I could see his eyes. "You are more than good enough. You're perfection and you got this." He nipped at my lip with his fangs.

"But—"

His lips swallowed mine gently as his hands gripped my waist. His body was beneath me, around me; he was everywhere. He pulled back and began to nibble at my chin.

"What if I can't? What if I can't avenge Fletch and—" He nipped at my collarbone and neck, Mother Blood have mercy. "—save Shae and—"

His lips sealed over mine, and the air whooshed from my lungs.

My mind became blanketed by his presence there, surrounded by his musky scent, laced with desire. He kissed me deeper and the stubble on his chin scratched my cheek, eliciting a delightful pain, as he began to search my body with his rough hands. I moaned in his mouth, my fears forgotten. There was only this male before me.

My mate.

Say that again.

He continued to devour my mouth.

Mate. My mate.

He growled, both in my mouth and in my mind, before pushing up my short, silken nightgown, so it bunched at my waist. In one motion he was naked, gloriously nude in front of me. He knelt there at the edge of the bed for a moment and was fully ready. He waited, chest heaving. I reached around and cupped his ass and he bucked at the contact.

Aether, now. Please.

I tried gripping his hips and pulling him toward me, but he only gave an inch. He hovered just at my entrance, ready. I spread my legs wider, open in invitation. He stood there, pleasure within reach, but didn't move. He just drank in my spread legs and my exposed core with his eyes.

I willed the air around him to move him forward, but his magic rose in countermeasures, resisting it.

"No magic. This is purely carnal, just us." His voice rumbled over me.

"Aether," I growled his name as I lowered my hips until my center brushed his tip. Almost there...

He smiled at me, primal and full of control. It was clear he held the power here, and blood, did I crave him. He braced a hand on my stomach and hip, swallowing both simultaneously, and then began to gently prod me. Slowly, never actually penetrating.

He prodded my center, my upper thighs, my sensitive bud...

The pass of satin skin, warm and primed, had my neck arching. The dribble of his pre-cum, dripping down his manhood as he continued to toy with me, had me begging for more, gripping him with my legs. He ground his way up, avoiding my center and allowed the length of him to brush against my clit, eliciting the most delightful friction.

A whimper escaped my lips as I ground against him, viciously.

Aether, you fucking brute, don't play with me anymore—

In a fluid motion, he thrusted, and his hardness entered me. The hard velvet of *him* slid in easily against my wet center.

I threw back my head and moaned. This was everything I'd ever wanted, everything I needed. Him. All of him.

Aether...

He growled as he shoved in again before leaning over me, so his face was mere inches away. "Say that again." He began to kiss my jaw, behind my ear, and the sensitive column of my neck. "Say my name."

"Aether," I whispered, lost in euphoria.

I began to wiggle against him, demanding more, but he remained stoic—just playing with my ears and neck with playful nips of his fangs. My hips increased their motion, and he began to slowly pull out, halfway and then halted completely.

Say it again.

"Aether. Aether!" His name spilled from my lips as I bucked against him, demanding more.

His smile was sinister as he complied and gave me thrust after thrust of his hips, burying his manhood deep within me, and stoking pleasure I didn't know was possible. He was pure male.

He growled in the air and then leaned over me and ripped my negligee down the middle. I arched from his touch as his thumb gracefully traced the column of my neck down to the tip of my breast, all the while thrusting inside.

Mother Blood, this was too—

He slammed himself into me at the same moment he found my taut nipple with his tongue. In perfect unison, he worked me. I'd never experienced a *male* like this before.

Only me. No one else, ever again.

His growl within my mind sent shivers down my spine as he pulled back from my nipple and then nipped at it before expertly kissing the hurt.

Aether...

He lifted his head from my body and then gripped my hips, pulling me down closer to him. The air around my nipples moved, chilling and yet heated, simultaneously eliciting the most sensual emotions.

I rocked with him, intensifying the pace.

Impatient thing, are we? My name on your lips will be my undoing.

I dug my fingers into the sheets before ripping them free and clawing his shoulders, shoving him in further.

Aether, oh blood—

A moan erupted from my lips and silenced all thoughts. His friction increased and I tightened around him, savoring the glide of his skin on mine. The exhale of his breath on my neck and chest. The way his fangs hovered just above my clavicle.

He increased his pace and went deeper, harder, faster.

More.

It was the only plea I could utter. The only coherent thought I could think. And he happily obliged. My senses became overwhelmed. It was too much, and I tensed around him as I came. Euphoria pulsed through me as I began to buzz with both physical and emotional energy, pouring from me in waves.

My mate. Fucking perfect.

His words were gentle against my mind as we stilled, breathing heavily into one another. He pulled himself out, still partially erect, and then dropped to the bed next to me. He cradled me in a hug, so our faces were mere inches away. I stared into his eyes. The eyes of promise, the eyes of my future.

Eyes that were mine.

CHAPTER 42
CHANCE

*M*onster.

The word had been playing on repeat, living rent-free in my head. I nearly killed Shae. My friend, my little sister in all ways but blood, and I nearly siphoned her life from her. That fact, that fear, was the only thing that got me in this cold metal chair—much like the male who summoned me.

I'd been here for blood knew how long. Days or weeks? But what did it fucking matter?

I unclenched my fists, willing blood to flow in them again. Control. I needed to learn control. *That* could never happen again. Worse still, there was no way out—none that didn't involve turning Shae into the beast I was becoming. The hellish scene I'd experienced weeks before could soon become a reality.

Fuck. That.

The door opened and President Dale entered along with a few high-ranking members of the guara, Dr Worshah, and to my surprise, Holland and Shae. The moment her washed-out blue head appeared, I lurched in my chair. She was blocking the only exit. My heart pounded.

I could feel the pull of her magic, the taste of it lingering in the air, just a little...

I silenced the beckoning.

"What the fuck are they doing here?" I nodded toward the two females standing mere feet from me—the last two people in the world who mattered to me. "Both of you, get out."

"Tsk-tsk. I raised you better than that," my father responded. "Chance, you should have taken my help sooner. Things have...progressed," he said as he tapped his cane.

I didn't take the bait. I swallowed. I could sense the pure chill of Shae's magic, the wild calling of it.

The ancient and unknown power of Holland was a foreign scent that begged for me to explore it, to take it, to have it...

"Doctor Worshah told us that you've learned to siphon on command. Now, I by no means think you have control of it, but I think you *can* learn to master this power," President Dale said.

"Get. Them. Out!" I commanded through gritted teeth. Shae's magic was filling my senses, my nostrils, and my very veins pulsed with desire. I could feel my magic swirling in response, begging for more. Recalling her flavor.

Just a taste...

"It can be controlled," Dr. Worshah said through broken teeth. "The cravings, we have ways to control them. First off, *this* shot. It will numb the call. And second, *through* selective feeding, you can have controlled siphoning on proper individuals." The pudgy doctor stepped forward, syringe held between his hairy index finger and thumb.

I held myself back even as every fiber in my body begged to move, to remove that smug look from the doctor's face along with his hand holding the vial. Sweat pebbled on my forehead and back.

"You want it," Doctor Worshah said, eyes glistening. I could still remember the feeling of *him* frying. Perhaps we'd revisit that.

"Chance, all you have to do is ask. It's yours if you'd like to cooperate with the guara and submit to training. If you're willing, we can help you," my father said, sounding very much like a sympathetic leader and *nothing* like the male who sired me.

Evil begets evil.

"Please, Dale, let them help you." It was Holland's voice that pulled me from the fog of rage building in my mind. Her tiny frame filled my vision as her honey-brown hair, soft olive skin, and pleading eyes came into view.

Holland.

Her presence was reassuring. I could feel the gentle manipulation of my mind from her, pushing against my rage, caressing my inner child. Peace began to coat my senses, as did a wave of certain awareness. Her normal honeysuckle scent now held a wild note to it, a flavor unlike any I'd encountered. It smelt ancient. But it also smelt like something foreign, not of this world. It was truly intoxicating.

"The syringe please, Doctor Worshah," my father commanded.

I could feel my pupils widening, suddenly aware of every breath being held in the room. They were waiting to see what I'd do.

"Dale?" Holland asked. She reached out and touched my arm. The grey marks weren't on her forehead, no purple marks, no diamond. And yet...I could sense the energy turning within her, the ancient untapped power rising like a tidal wave.

I swallowed. "Yes, I'll comply."

Doctor Worshah smirked as he walked over and stabbed my arm with the needle, not caring that it hurt or drew a spatter of blood. He, no doubt, enjoyed that.

Holland reached out again to my internal being while giving me a reassuring hug. I allowed her in, allowed her power to engulf mine and to calm the synapses that were rapidly firing.

She tamed the beast within.

"Good, I've got you, Dale," she spoke as she looked deep into my eyes. The room was full, stuffy even. For the first time, I could smell the sweat and body odor surrounding me. My own stench hit my nostrils. Even still, Holland pressed her forehead to mine and swallowed my head with her small hands. The gentle caress was reassuring.

I was still me. I still had control. I exhaled, breathed in deeply, and then exhaled again. Grounded.

"I got you," Holland murmured against my sweaty forehead. Fuck, this female truly cared for me. How did I deserve that?

"Touching." My father's curt voice wrenched me from my thoughts. "If you're ready then, Chance, we need to take you to a secure part of the lab for the rest of this training. There are portions of this I'm sure you'd rather not show to the lovely Miss Holland," he finished.

"Dux Holland," she corrected him. "And I'm not afraid. If Dale wants me there, I'm there."

Damn, I loved this female. "Holland comes."

With a nod from my father, the room cleared out. Shae's eyes locked on mine. Sad, but...proud? She smiled and then left without a word. I'd hurt her.

Never again.

I allowed the silent vow to settle deep into my bones.

Holland straightened her back and together we looked to my father and Doctor Worshah.

"Very well," my father's disapproving tone grated across my skin as he spoke. "You were warned."

CHAPTER 43
TATE

I clenched and unclenched my hands. The written exam was before me, almost done. I should have spent more time studying the documents Professor Darsew had suggested, but I'd been distracted...

A knowing smile pulled at my lips. It had been the most delicious distraction—

A loud cracking sounded to my left as a cadet popped his knuckles, sweat visibly gathering at his hairline. This was a stressful situation for most, I would likely be perspiring like the Ironhead next to me if I didn't have my secret weapon—thank blood for Aether.

I bit my lip as I could feel him chuckle in my head. The next question was one, yet again, I didn't know the answer to...at least not fully.

Why do some Untishee lack the ability to shift even when they have all three bloods?

I paused, pen suspended over paper. Frustration tore at me. I should know this.

Aether? Why don't all Untishee become shifters?

A moment spanned by—a sign that he was distracted.

Sorry. It sounded like he was clearing his throat. *Not all have the right combination of each blood and power behind it. Magic isn't predictable. Even with all three blends of blood magic, it could be too mixed or from someone whose magic is too weak, or their connection to the planet feeble.*

I wrote down what he said, paraphrasing to make it sound like me. I answered the next series of questions on my own, but it was the second to last question that, again, gave me pause.

What does bonding entail and what are the levels of bonds?

I knew that Aether claimed we had a strong bond. I knew he was my mate…something I never thought I'd have. A fairytale and yet it was real, my life. But what were the exact levels?

Begrudgingly, I relayed the question to Aether and waited in silence. I thought back to Cher. He'd been bonded with her; I *hadn't* asked what type of bond he had with her, and I wasn't sure I wanted to know. Vala claimed it was nothing like the bond I shared with Aether, but she wasn't alive when Aether was bonded to Cher. And then there were the questions about Ruby that I'd still yet to ask. She looked so much like Aether, especially in her eyes. I suspected the truth but was happy to ignore the nagging questions. Or was I?

Jealousy began to creep up my cheeks.

Aether? I called out to him, again. Perhaps I'd have to guess on this one.

Sorry, love. I'm here. There are four levels of bonds that are widely accepted. The first is considered a basic magic bond. It is determined by the chairs during a Matching Ceremony and occurs when one person's magic is weak and doesn't find a strong connection with any other's magic. It can be bonded with any. In this case, the chairs decide what is best for the Untish Tribe as a whole—a fighter, a protector, etc.

I wrote basic bond with a brief summation beside it.

The next level is a moderate bond. This occurs when one's magic strongly prefers another. There is little room for the chairs to manipulate this, although sometimes, if the stronger magic prefers multiple, the chairs decide.

I continued to write as he spoke.

Got it.

The third level of bonds is considered a strong bond.

Very creative, I teased.

He laughed. *Yeah, well originality isn't our strong suit. But this level of bond occurs when both individual's magic is powerful and strongly prefers one another. This is nearly impossible to alter and produces the strongest warriors, though not always the strongest offspring.*

And the fourth?

The fourth is a soul mate bond. The mating bond. It is incredibly rare and occurs when both are evenly matched in magic and in strength of mind; they are drawn to one another physically, psychologically, and magically. It is a blending of the two. Like with Perry and Matias, and like...with us.

My heart warmed at the thought as Aether's pride flooded the bond.

Thanks!

I finished writing my answer and then looked to the last question:

Why is bonding important and what does it do to benefit the Untish Tribe as a whole?

I found myself re-reading the question over and over but couldn't focus. I realized I *wanted* to know about Cher, and perhaps from this safe distance, with several other cadets scribbling ferociously on white pages of parchment, I felt safe. I had the space to ask.

Aether...what was your bond with Cher?

I waited—biting my lip. I could sense a wave of tension down our bond from Aether.

It was a moderate bond. At the time my magic didn't compare to Cher's. Her stores were vast, and my magic just didn't blend well enough with hers. But when she passed, some of her magic remained in my veins and as I learned to wield it, it grew. It's sentient in many ways. And that is what I'm most grateful for: that I now had enough power to match you, my love.

I smiled. Even with the ache in my heart, I was relieved it wasn't a soul mate bond. Pressing the pen to paper, I continued to answer the next question, sure of what I'd say.

I set the pen down and noted the time, I had ten minutes left. I'd done it, taken the written exam. I was now educated enough that I wouldn't be a threat to the Untish Embassy or myself, as Camella often reminded me after she knocked me on my ass. It was for my own good.

I snorted.

The other students studiously wrote their answers down, a couple sat idly waiting out the time as I too did, now deep in thought.

Cher was a moderate bond.

I had a soul mate bond with Aether.

A mate.

My mate.

Visions of what our life would look like someday played out in my head. Aether and I fighting side by side, both as dragons and warriors. Taking down the guara, the Glenn, and President Dale—avenging Fletch and my mother, along with the countless others who were murdered under his wicked rule. Then, after we'd brought justice to the realm and ensured the seethings were disposed of, perhaps we'd relocate to our cavern. Maybe we'd spend a few glorious months in there, exploring one another...who knew, maybe one day, we'd have children.

Ruby.

Her name echoed through my mind. Was that from Aether? Or had my subconscious drummed it up? I picked up the pen and idly twisted it between my fingers, poking the tip into my thumb to the point of pain before releasing it. I needed to know. Or did I? What if the truth was what I suspected...what then?

My inner beast roared, heat filled every crevice of my being along with the urge—no, the need—to know.

Who is Ruby to you, Aether?

Silence.

I dug the tip of the pen into my thumb deeper, my finger whitening from the impact. Ruby had red hair, not like Aether. But her eyes...they were undeniably Aether's. That didn't mean anything though, did it? Plus, I mean, she couldn't be older than ten. Cher had died a long time ago, nearly a century if I recalled correctly. Perhaps Ruby was simply a niece or a granddaughter of Aether's...

I shook my head at the thought. Aether a grandfather? I could get on board with a *hot* daddy, but a granddaddy?

I cleared my throat as my grip on the pen tightened.

Things were definitely different here in the Embassy, that I knew. I also understood our lifespans were much longer than I'd originally thought, Untishee can live for thousands of years if our Fae blood is pure enough...but still, Aether couldn't be *that* old. Could he?

Panic laced through me.

Aether?

Through the bond, I could sense his anxiety building.

Tate, I'd rather have this conversation later...

Why?

I bit my lip even as my heart raced. Had he taken a lover since Cher? I thought back to the curvy female who cared for Ruby and the boy. Was she Aether's consort? Or worse, was Aether bonded to another like Perry was?

Aether, are you bonded to any others besides me?

No! I could sense his urgency, the panic building in him. *You are the only one for me, Tate. The only bonded since Cher.*

Okay, then who is Ruby? Is her mother your...consort? I choked on the thought as the tip of the pen punctured my thumb, drawing blood.

No. Aether sighed in my mind. *I wanted to have this conversation at a better time, but I won't lie to you, Tate. Can you please be patient?*

Could I? No, the questions would assault me to the grave. And with the combat and sparring coming soon, distractions could actually kill me.

I could sense his reluctance and then, finally, acceptance.

Tate, Ruby is my daughter.

Numbness washed over me as I sat there in silence.

*Ok...*I exhaled slowly through tense lips. *Thank you for answering truthfully. I just...I need some space to process.*

Before he could respond, I threw up a wall, blocking Aether, in an attempt to protect myself.

I laughed dryly. Too late to remain hiding in my willful ignorance. No, now the band-aid had been ripped off, the pain stung, and with it, the truth had been searingly liberated.

The bell rang, the test was over, and everything had changed.

CHAPTER 44

AETHER

Tate had gone silent—again. She'd erected her wall and was blocking the bond, a fact that annoyed me immensely while simultaneously made me proud of her progress. Still...fear gnawed at me.

I should have told her sooner. Should have trusted her instead of being selfish and enjoying every moment with her. There were so many things we'd yet to discuss, Ruby included. Based on our bond and Tate's intense emotions, it was clear she still needed space.

"I don't see how you can take her," my uncle said.

This conversation was getting on my nerves, more so now given the exchange I'd just had with Tate.

"I'm not leaving her. That's far more dangerous," I repeated for what must've been the hundredth time this hour.

"But you suggest bringing our *princess* into danger. Taking royalty into the field. It's been forbidden since the extermination after the Great War. You should leave her here under my care, and then when the gates open to Mydant, we can—"

"I'm not leaving her," I spoke and the papers from his desk went flying with the force accompanying my words. My power had increased significantly since I'd bonded with Tate, and I was still learning to control it.

Enzo's eyes widened. "Mother Blood, you've fully bonded."

I gritted my teeth as violence gathered behind me, the room became bathed in black flames with a tiny pink center. Vala had hid them via cloaking, but I revealed them to my uncle. He already knew and he *needed* to understand the level of bond I had with Tate.

His tan, worn skin went ghostly pale. "A mating bond."

I nodded and waited for his reaction—an asp ready to strike.

"I see. Perhaps *you* don't need to leave. I can see a way around it," he spoke, eyes full of reverence.

"No." I would not murder another family member.

"Aether it is the only way. You aren't just a high general, but you're head commander of the Shadow Tribe. It is expected for you to spear-head intel. To lead a tactical team, to prepare. You staying here any longer will raise questions. Hell, it has raised questions. Arithi is—"

A series of coughs interrupted his speech, causing a golden maroon blood to splatter on his pocket square.

"It won't be long now, my boy," he spoke kindly. "End it for me, and you'll take the seat. Your power is unmatched, and your blood entitles you to it. You can duel Juda, and we both know you will win. Then you can remain here until the time is right."

I saw the determination in his eyes. But no, I would not kill him. I would not end my uncle.

"I'm sorry, but no." I pulled my power back, the room lightened once again to its warm golden hue. "Tate will come with me, and I will train her. That is what I've decided. Every day, every single damn moment, that she stays here, we risk detection. Vala's updating the cloak daily, but since we've bonded, Tate's power is strong, nearly too much to conceal."

"*Her power cannot be contained. Cloaked, and yet, impossible to conceal—*"

"Stop."

"*With a cyclone of power, even nature attests to her birthright.*"

"I said, stop," I bit out.

"Pink flames and white light will reveal her and lead her to—"

"STOP!"

Enzo fell silent as my chest heaved and the room once again was swallowed in darkness. My power and flames devoured all.

I ran my hands over my face, willing myself to use the self-restraint I knew I was capable of. With a deep breath, I called the darkness back —again.

"What's the word on his majesty's condition?"

Without missing a beat, Enzo simply nodded—ready to move on. "Grave, I'm afraid. I don't believe he'll make it to the new moon ceremony in a few weeks time. We could be called back any day for a Crowning ceremony."

"Then we wait and when it's time, we get Tate back to Mydant, where she'll be safe."

"Agreed. But what of *this* Embassy chair?" Enzo asked.

"Let Juda have it when the time comes. But there's no rush. Hang in there, ancient one." I winked at him, and he snarled in return. I may be the alpha, but he still was the chair and his pride emanated it.

A gong sounded.

The written test was done. Tate would now move on to combat. I nodded to my uncle and then left, noting how stiff Juda was as I walked by. She no doubt wanted to know what my business was— always coveting the chair's seat. I wouldn't be surprised if she stabbed her own father in the back for it, but my power held her at bay—I would destroy her in a duel, and we both knew it.

Tate would be in the ring soon and I sure as fuck would be there for her.

I wished I could fight with her. If needed, I *could* do some manipulation, but she needed to hold her own. I knew the pride and confidence that came from defeating one's opponent and making the right of passage on your own. I wouldn't take that from her. Especially after what occurred with the last duel.

She needed a win.

Tate? I sent down the bond. My words were returned to me in force, smoldering. She was not in the mood to talk.

Fine, when the testing was done, there would be time to discuss Ruby.

So, slowly, I filed into the stands and took my seat at the front, waiting and watching.

Hours went by and then that glorious dark blonde was in the ring.

There's that hot stuff. I tried to lighten the mood. Yet again, my words were burned upon reception.

I swallowed back my annoyance. *She* was the one who pushed the envelope, asked and demanded to know, and now...

I exhaled. No. This was on me. How many chances had I been given to tell her the truth? To share with her my story? To trust her, fully, as she had me?

Her anger and confusion were well deserved.

I watched in silence as her lithe form took the ring. Even with her bone discrepancy, prominently on view given her limp, she was glorious. I wanted to gut every last person who sneered at her when she fumbled for footing.

Restraint. Restraint. Restraint.

The word was a chant in my head. Tate needed to do this alone, I could sense the intensity of the need last night. I just needed to keep my mating-anger in check. There would be time to dole out punishments later. With every new grimace or taunt, I made a mental list of *all* the extra training, toilet duty, and dragon pit duty each would receive. For weeks.

Tate lost her footing but quickly recovered. It didn't matter to her peers though, several were openly laughing.

Make it months for those motherfuckers. They'd be lucky if they ever had five minutes of free time, and they were especially lucky that I didn't just slaughter them where they stood. The thought was tempting.

Tate threw a punch-kick combo and the female she dueled, Claure, stumbled. In an instant, Tate had her strong-armed, ready to break it, if needed. Claure bucked and twisted but couldn't get free. She tapped out.

Tate won.

I sent shimmering pride down the bond and was met with an image of me fucking myself.

Oof.

More space, message received.

The second round was painful to watch, and while it was a fair fight, Micah used Tate's bone discrepancy against her and continually attacked on the left. After several smooth evasions, ones that even had my jaw dropping, Micah managed to kick her right foot out and Tate crumpled. Micah had her in a chokehold a split second later. Round over, Tate had lost.

Looked like Micah would be on night shifts and field cleaning for the next year. All that shit, all that stench, and it still didn't feel like enough of a punishment—yet, the rational side of my brain told me Micah had simply fought well, and that nothing uncouth occurred.

I locked my jaw as I focused on Tate; she held her head high even after taking a beating.

All around me, generals made notes and joked with one another about who they wanted in their command, and who they didn't. It was jarring just how many times Tate's name was raised, mostly as the one they *didn't* want.

Restraint. Restraint. Restraint.

I flexed and unflexed my fists, reminding myself of the many, many reasons why I couldn't openly gut them where they sat. Why I couldn't strangle them to death. Why I couldn't burn them from the inside out.

Tate. She was all the reason I needed. Her safety was my priority, not making my possessive mating bond a spectacle.

Another thirty minutes went by and Tate's name was called along with Ursa's. I disliked the female, but she was a fair fighter. Much better than Sheila.

Thank Camella for this pairing.

They both entered the ring, shaking their limbs out, and then found their stances. The whistle sounded and before it even ended, Ursa swung left followed by a right jab, and then left again. Each time, Tate evaded her by ducking or blocking, but she failed to land a single strike. Ursa charged her again with a strike-kick combo, and Tate barely missed it as she dodged to the left.

Tate threw a punch followed by a kick, and Ursa smoothly side-stepped and blocked both before counterstriking and catching Tate in the gut. Tate flew backwards and landed on the mat, panting.

Get up.

I clenched the sides of my seat but willed my face into a neutral mask. It wasn't lost on me that Arithi had chosen to sit a few chairs down, just to the right of me near the other chair heads, but not centered as I'd expected.

Self-control.

Tate stood up, one hand clutching her stomach and then without hesitation, she glided through the air. Ursa struck out with a punch, but Tate ducked before taking Ursa's feet out from under her and immediately pinned her down. Tate's forearm was at Ursa's throat, pressing. Pride swelled within my chest.

The clock hit thirty seconds and then Ursa tapped out. The match was over. Tate had passed basic hand-to-hand combat.

The tension in my shoulders relaxed some, even as Tate walked off the mat still clutching her stomach—her discomfort echoed down the bond, making my own stomach twist.

She succeeded. Just as I knew she would.

I could sense her pride, the feeling of accomplishment—even as several of the other trainees looked at her wearily.

"She did well," Arithi spoke from beside me, having moved to claim the seat next to me.

"Indeed." I nodded, not looking at the withered female.

"It seems you've taken a personal interest in Tate's welfare," she hypothesized, the threat covered in her honey-light tone.

"She's a member of my tribe. No matter what general is her direct superior, as high general and head commander, she'll be under my command. I feel responsible for her," I responded. Half-truths were always the safest way to lie.

Arithi merely nodded and then focused ahead on the next match. Weapon sparring would begin in the next hour and then finally, magic testing. Tate had made it halfway through the process.

I wanted to reach out, to congratulate her, but the instant I explored the bond, I felt her sweltering heat. I sighed.

My secrecy had earned her anger.

CHAPTER 45

CHANCE

We had gone down several floors, at least fifteen. Clearly, President Dale liked the stairs. My legs throbbed with every step we took. No doubt, this jackass's way of punishing me for allowing Holland to join.

We ended up in a large conference room, not where I thought he'd take us. A grand oak table sat in the middle, big enough to seat fifty, with black leather chairs surrounding it. It was oddly civil for a lab buried underground. Bits of rubies and turquoise stones were embedded in the table in a way that spoke of power and class. Perhaps this was where my father flexed for foreign governments.

My father turned to the glass wall that formed one side of the room and beckoned us to approach. Ever the presidential figure in his black pressed suit, red shirt, maroon tie and matching pocket square. With his ever-present cane, he looked regal—if not distinctly evil. I was acutely aware that the handle of his cane was that of a human head—mouth open, agape. I'd always thought it was at odds with the figure my father presented. He was sophisticated and collected, the cane was morbid and wild.

I stepped closer to the glass, Holland at my side, and peered into a large room. It was composed of solid stone, and it was empty. Darkness gnawed at it.

"What is this?" Holland asked.

"This, Dux Holland, is the *facility*. It is the place where the Glenn flexes its latest scientific breakthroughs, the place of duels, sparring, and displays of pure brute force," President Dale responded, wearing a smile filled with fondness.

I swallowed back the odd sense of respect filling me, allowing it to combat the stomach bile currently rising.

"So, this is where you bring the seethings to be displayed?" I questioned. Reminding us *all* of the lines my father had crossed. He'd broken his own oaths, his own laws.

"Yes. And it is where *you* will be tested, trained, and become *what* you were born to be."

I gritted my teeth. "You said I'd learn control, to sate certain... cravings?"

"In due time," my father turned to Doctor Worshah. "Doctor?"

My skin began to itch insatiably. I rubbed my head against my shoulder, attempting to scratch the ever-annoying prickling.

"Yes, I'll make this as simple as possible since it's my understanding you didn't do well in chemistry or any upper-level science courses," Doctor Worshah spat. His mouth now had a retainer with attached teeth to cover the ones I'd broken. It seemed his memory was still intact. Too bad the electricity didn't fry that. Too bad, indeed. "Dux Holland, forgive me if I dumb this down to where it's painful for you, but perhaps you can help Chance comprehend what I'm saying."

The little fuck. It was obvious that he chose not to use my title.

"Oh, I think he'll be fine." Holland winked at me. She was enjoying this? Oddly, I felt turned on.

"If you insist." Doctor Worshah nodded toward Holland and then fixed a gaze of malice on me. "I'll start at the beginning. Stop me if this becomes too confusing."

My father sneered at Doctor Worshah, who immediately had the good sense to look ashamed. "Apologies, sir, I'm afraid I'm a bit frazzled after being electrocuted." He pointedly looked at me.

"You'd do well to remember who you speak to. Dux Dale is my son, next in line for office, and a powerful male." President Dale tapped his cane in emphasis.

"Of course." Doctor Worshah tipped his head to me, revealing a balding top with sparse, burnt patches of frenzied hair.

I smiled smugly in return.

"Doctor Worshah?" I questioned. I was ready to be done with this, delaying the start was a waste of time. No matter that I enjoyed seeing the prick squirm.

"Yes." He cleared his throat. "When you were exposed to the sheer force of power that occurred when the base exploded, that energy reacted with dormant genes in your DNA resulting in the activation of certain genetic codes. These genes have several factors and they can alter not only your internal power structure but outward appearance. You, thus far, appear the same as before, which is quite unexpected—all other subjects tested prior to the explosion have displayed some sort of external change that mirrors the internal one. This means, either you've altered in ways we cannot begin to comprehend, or you haven't accepted the fullness of your change. You've halted the process."

"So, you're saying he could look like those *things*?" The horror in Holland's face reflected my own.

"No, not necessarily. We've seen several controllers merely have menial changes: veins sprouting, eye color changes, muscle mass, and hair loss are the most common," Doctor Worshah responded. "You yourself have demonstrated certain external changes, although they are very unique in that they pulse for a moment and then disappear. Rest assured, we are paying close attention to them, for your safety, of course, Dux Holland."

"The diamond," the words left my mouth before I could stop them.

"The what?" Holland asked at the same time Doctor Worshah nodded.

"Yes, the diamond appears to be a mark of Dux Holland's own changes. However, the power levels that we've detected from the labs show minimal changes. This would indicate that she didn't have dormant genes and is merely experiencing altered existing ones. While this can be powerful and helpful, it's not what we classify as a game changer, or the criteria needed to be a controller. The seethings respond to brute force. Pure power." Doctor Worshah looked directly at me. Both hate and acceptance warred on his face.

"What diamond?" Holland repeated her question.

"Uh, when you seized, I saw a purple diamond on your forehead," I answered lamely.

"Doctor Worshah, the video please," my father spoke, bored—he wanted this little session to move on.

"Yes, right away." Doctor Worshah pulled out his disk and projected a screen on the stone wall behind the table.

Images and videos of Holland strapped to a gurney appeared. The purple diamond was clearly seen along with purple-grey veins sprouting from it. Doctor Worshah tapped the video next to the images of the diamond up close.

In the video, Holland heaved as she fought the restraints; she was breathing heavily. She began seizing and then went still. Her frame was shaking rapidly, she appeared to almost glitch for a moment, as if she left and then came back, before she began to seize again. This occurred two more times before she became still, death-like, if not for her rhythmic breathing.

Holland looked mortified. "Why has no one told me?"

"When you awoke, you had no recollection. For our research, we determined it best to not mention it and thus allow for more organic results," Doctor Worshah responded.

"You mean, you wanted to see if it happened again without my interference," Holland snapped.

"Yes."

"As much as I'm sure this is surprising to you, Dux Holland, we need to focus on Dux Dale. He is the one with enough power to change the course of this war. The sooner Dux Dale learns control, the sooner we can save the lives of our guara." My father's voice held no sympathy. No room for argument.

Holland clenched her jaw. She wanted answers and knowing her, she'd get them, but she also understood the proper channels and the way things worked in the military.

She squared her shoulders and nodded.

"I've always known you'd be an asset to us, Dux Holland. Dr. Worshah, send Dux Holland all the files we have on her once we're done here," President Dale commanded.

"Yes, sir." Doctor Worshah swallowed.

"Please, continue." The command left President Dale's lips the moment his cane hit the floor.

"Right away." Doctor Worshah cleared the screen and pulled up an image of gene structures. "With you, Dux Dale, your genes have altered. They've changed and we've seen the power you now have, the pure waves of energy."

The video showed the DNA code changing, replacing itself, and cells altering. "However, this change requires fuel. Much like we, as vampires, need blood to survive, you now need energy and power to change."

"Siphoning," I said aloud.

"Yes, siphoning. What's really interesting, is that most of our controllers do not have that intrinsic understanding. They do not siphon right away. It is a painful process of learning, however you did it not once, but twice. It's as if your altered genes *know* exactly what they need. What they crave." Doctor Worshah changed the screen to show side by side videos of me siphoning from both Shae in the control room and the seethings in the pit.

Hate fueled me.

I could feel the power in me responding, building as rage flowed in my veins. Holland's gentle, internal presence tried to calm me, but I shoved her out. I was the embodiment of evil.

"You siphoned from them because you needed to in order to

survive the genetic changes you're undergoing. Magic is sentient, it too requires fuel and stores of energy. Since yours was dormant until recently, it's looking to grow its stores so it can express the fullness of its power. You will need to siphon, continuously," Doctor Worshah continued.

Siphon? "No."

"Son." President Dale approached. "It's just like feeding. Only, instead of blood, it's power your feeding from." His mouth ticked up in an uneven smile.

"It's forbidden, it's enthrawment," I spat. Images of Lucas's body filled my mind. My father had devoured his power. I was the devil's spawn, and evidently, I was just like him.

My hands began to shake.

"Not to us, it's not. It's forbidden for the public. We need control, and if everyone went around siphoning one another's power reserves, we'd have an unstable society; we'd be in a constant civil war. That is why this knowledge isn't accessible outside the high-ranking leadership. And now, you two." He said it as if it were an honor to know his dirty secrets.

"I am *not* like you. I don't bend rules to fit my needs. There has to be another way." The pounding in my head doubled.

"Son." He said that word again as he took a step toward me with a cold smile plastered to his lips, rage simmering in his eyes. "You want to prevent mass casualties? You want to *serve* the Glenn? This is the only way."

I refused to believe that.

"There must be an alternate path, perhaps if he just half siphons from several?" Holland whispered, her reassuring hand on my shoulder. All five feet of her was more comforting and intimidating than either male in the room. I inhaled deeply, and fear clawed at me as her wild, unknown scent filled my nostrils.

"My dear, that wouldn't work. Care to explain why, Doctor Worshah?" My father's placating tone wasn't lost on me. From the stiffening of Holland's shoulders, she was well aware of the way he demeaned her. In another life, she would have been the perfect wife—strong enough to handle the political undertones that my world was bathed in.

"A half-feed from a human will temporarily heighten your gifts. In extremely rare cases, it will perhaps be enough to *awaken* gene markers in your own coding. But as I said, this is rare," Doctor Worshah began, walking over to the window with a red dry erase marker in hand. "Half-feeding from vampires is exactly the same. It will heighten your gifts. But the notable difference is in the transference of powers. In a short feed, you could consume some of their power and make it your own—it's no longer theirs, and no longer your own. It becomes its own. It mutates."

"Then perhaps—"

"It's still not enough, my dear," my father said. Holland bit down on her lip. I could see her reminding herself that he was her superior, even if he was a giant sexist asshole.

"Correct. These gifts, while transferred, only offer temporary changes, only in extremely rare cases does the transfer of power remain. But as I said, it mutates. It doesn't fuel the changing that Dux Dale needs. No matter how many he feeds from, it will not be enough to sate his cravings. It will not last. He will need to fully consume the person in order to spike his own energy levels enough for his own mutating genes to proceed and meet the required threshold; to maintain the new levels of power." Doctor Worshah drew a third person figure. "Feeding from Fae will not solve the issue, but their blood is significantly richer in magic stores, so it could in theory be enough—"

"Say that again," I demanded.

"It could be enough, but it's fairly untested since most fled to Mydant after being hunted following the Great War—"

"No, you said *Fae*." The word tasted wrong on my lips. "They are foreign beings with no recorded vampire feedings or laws permitting said feedings."

Doctor Worshah smiled widely. "It is always my pleasure to correct that intentional misleading."

"Those files have been purposefully redacted, son," President Dale spoke.

Rage in my belly rose as Holland stiffened. We'd both been lied to. Again.

"How can we trust anything you say if everything you taught us is false?" I exploded. Red streaked across the room and hit the glass wall. To my shock, it didn't explode. Instead, it hummed as my red energy danced across it.

My father tsked before reaching out his hand and *pulling* the power into himself.

"Did you just—"

"Siphon? Yes, I did. And you will learn how to siphon expelled magic once you stop acting like a damn child and pay the fuck attention," my father snapped at me.

I could siphon expressed magic? Perhaps, if I learned that, I wouldn't have to siphon anyone to death. Holland looked at me, her internal gears turning—she was thinking the same thing.

"Fae. Tell me about them," I responded. I would not take the insufferable male's taunts and engage in what I knew he wanted, a pissing match. He wanted to express his own power, to be dominant in every way? Fine. But it wouldn't be fulfilling since I refused to engage.

"Well, they're originally from Mydant, but several explorers migrated here a long time ago, long before the Great War. We don't have records from that time, well very few, but what we do have shows they bred among us. With humans and vampires alike," he paused for emphasis. He picked up the dropped marker and began rapidly drawing tallies, making a pyramid. "Much like humans, their breeding among us created one-offs, gene mutations, new races. Humans had their own magic, but when mixed with Fae, it becomes much more potent and promising. When you mix all three blood forms—"

Spit flew from his mouth as he spoke, his excitement clear with his slurring words as his rate of speech increased.

"This—" he drew a blue tally "—is a Fae person. They bred with a vampire—" he drew a red tally "—and then we have this." He drew a purple mark. "This person," he jabbed the purple dash several times with the marker, "has mutated genes, possessing both vampirical and Fae power. But it doesn't stop there." He grabbed yet another marker, a yellow one. "This is a human. If our new mutated individual breeds with this human, we get a very unique breed—known for their power, fire, and shifting abilities." He drew an 'x' in pink.

Shifting abilities. Fire. "The dragon," the words left my lips along with the power in my veins. I felt faint.

"Exactly, the very enemy we hunt. The one you witnessed. The one who blew up the damned base," President Dale spoke. Tap. "The one *you* trusted, accepted as one of our own, is in fact, one of *them*." Tap. TAP!

Tate.

I recalled how she levitated through the air, a goddess on the wind. She abandoned us, flying off with a dragon. Nausea roiled in my stomach, I dropped to an empty seat at the table and cupped my head.

As if in emphasis, Doctor Worshah projected footage the compound had transmitted prior to the explosion. Tate's pink aura filled the screen as her small frame was pressed against a warehouse building. She flared, and with it, her body disappeared from sight, enveloped in a cloud of pink-golden light.

The whole ground exploded, and energy soared in every direction, incinerating several seethings and guaramen who were near Tate. Finally, the camera itself was swallowed in flames.

"What do we call this type of creature, this shifter?" Holland whispered.

"They call themselves, the Untish."

CHAPTER 46

TATE

My hand tightened on the hilt of the sword. I stood in the center of the sparring ring, feet locked in place, at the ready. The field was covered with ten different rings that had fights simultaneously happening. I understood now why Carly called this a performance as much as a test.

It was here that many candidates' rankings would be determined. That tribal leaders would select their warriors.

I tried to focus on the task at hand. When I was combatting Ursa, my focus was solely on her. But here, while I waited for the match to begin, I thought back to Ruby. Aether's daughter.

His *daughter*.

He was a father. And in all the time we've had together, he never told me. Not in the cave while we held one another for hours upon hours and discussed our lives; not in the Embassy as he helped me learn about the Untish ways. It wasn't even a prime memory for me to *find* when he opened himself up to me. So many opportunities to show me his truth, to trust me as I had him, and yet he never did until I directly asked.

I bit my lip as I waited for Perseus to step into the ring. Naturally,

I'd be paired with him of all people. He was at least ten inches taller than me and the sneer on his face was menacing. He selected the heaviest sword, of course, and then stepped in.

Carly gasped from beside me, "This isn't a fair pairing."

"It's fine," I assured her. But my gut swirled.

I could feel Aether's presence wrapping around me, the tension palpable.

"Ready to bleed, cripple?" Perseus sneered. I despised the nickname he'd coined for me.

"Get her good!" Sheila cheered from the side, standing next to Ursa who inspected her nails.

I just smiled in return and sunk further into my stance.

The bell sounded. My heart rate rocketed as Perseus raised his sword in the air—blade gleaming. He struck and I raised my sword to meet his, shaking in my core from the force of it. Dueling with Camella had been trying but with Perseus? It was nearly unbearable.

Still, I braced myself for his blade as he struck again. I just needed to stay in the circle for one minute of sparring. That or land a fatal strike, one that could kill if not properly controlled—part of the test, restraint. We were to land a fatal strike without actually killing.

Kill your opponent, you fail.

Don't land a fatal strike, you fail.

Step outside the circle, you fail.

He advanced again and struck, I blocked with my blade before twirling out of his way and striking with my own sword. He turned, prepared for my strike, and blocked. He continued to push, forcing my blade down. My wrist screamed in protest at the force, and my sword shook as I fought to keep it engaged.

He pulled his blade back and then struck again, before pulling out a dagger and swiping at my side. Pain erupted as blood sprayed red in the white dirt. He struck again with his dagger, but I twisted and swung my sword. He met my blade with his and then began to force me backwards, toward the edge of the ring.

Panic began to eat at me as my blood continued to mar the ground.

I ground my teeth and snarled. I refused to lose, especially to this jackass. I'd fought people far darker than this male, and I would not cower now.

I slipped into the cool mental place, my inner pool beckoning me forward, and my face slackened into its neutral mask—a mask I've worn on so many missions.

The mask of a predator. The heart of a warrior. The vengeance of justice.

Calmness blanketed my senses, numbing the pain and strengthening my resolve. He was just like the abusers I'd faced in the human realm. Arrogant, abusive, bigger than me in stature. He may have the advantage of speed and the giftings of the Untishee, but he was still just like my other targets: cocky.

Fire flooded my system, and I felt my inner dragon awakening, demanding to be unleashed. *No.* I commanded her. We weren't allowed to use magic in the sparring rings. Instead, I used the energy pulsing through me to fuel my strength.

I forced my will into my sword and pushed Perseus back, gaining a half inch. His eyes widened and then filled with hate. "You're nothing. You're no one, you don't even have two good legs. You don't deserve to be here," he sneered, even as veins bulged in his neck from exertion.

"Yes. I. Do," I gritted out.

In one push toward him, I dropped the heavy sword and rolled, putting myself behind him, I yanked my dagger free and stabbed his left side with my blade. He yelped and fell forward, his sword clanging to the ground. I didn't wait, I launched myself on him and poised the dagger at his throat—ready to slice.

The ire in his eyes intensified as the bell sounded. I'd won the match and made an eternal enemy. I smiled slowly in return before leaning in closely and whispering, "People like you will always lose to people like me."

I stood, slowly, and then sheathed my bloodied blade before stalking out of the ring—my own blood still leaking, trailing my path.

Several medics approached and began administering medical care.

My side stung as they began to weave the wound closed and then cover it with gauze, before giving me a healing potion.

I looked up and spotted Aether, even from here I could see the dark threat of death lacing his eyes. I could sense his energy, he was livid. It had been a while since I'd had someone *that* worried about me. Even Fletch would have been concerned, but angry? No. Not the male I knew.

A sad smile graced my lips. I missed him. Missed the person who was, in every way that counted, a father to me. But being here in the heart of the Embassy, I had no doubt he was proud of me.

I survived. More than that, I won.

That's my girl. Aether's voice and pride echoed down the bond, only for me to abruptly dissolve it—again.

I still wasn't ready to discuss things with *my mate* who was, in fact, a father. He had a daughter and he never told me. I sucked on my fang as I moved. I was a stepmother. The thought was as laughable as it was dire.

I found the bench off to the side where Carly waited, towel in hand. She threw her arms around me, "You did it!"

"I did." I returned her embrace, wincing as she squeezed my injured side.

"Sorry!" She pulled back. "I don't think I've ever seen anything more glorious than Perseus having his ass handed to him. Although, I think he *really* hates you now."

It was worth it.

"Do you know who you're sparring with?" I asked as I wiped at my forehead, grimacing when the white towel came back bloodied.

"Yeah, Toga. Should be a fair fight," she said. But her smile couldn't hide the nerves.

"You got this," I assured her.

"Carly and Toga, you're up!" Camella shouted.

I watched as they entered the blood-stained ring.

CHAPTER 47

CHANCE

U ntish. Tate was a member of the Untish race. This powerful magical being with all three types of blood—and she'd fooled me, lied to me.

"I don't understand, wouldn't our blood testing have picked that up? Shit, wouldn't her magical stores have been detected?" I asked.

"Ah, and now you see the questions that have guided much of my life's work," Doctor Worshah said, releasing a heavy sigh. "We suspect certain parts of the gene are not awakened until full maturity. We've calculated this to occur sometime after fifteen but haven't been able to narrow it down. Through our samples, we've gathered that once they hit this stage, their magic awakens and expresses itself." Doctor Worshah took a seat opposite me.

Awakens. Almost like how Tate was changing—a goddess in the air —in front of my eyes at the base just after the explosion. The sheer power she possessed...it was staggering. And she was our enemy. My gut soured even as my heart begged me to be wrong—recalled the free-spirited girl I'd once known. Was it at all possible that she didn't know she possessed such power?

"She lied to you, son. Her whole family did," President Dale spoke. "We've now confirmed the blood sample we received at birth and when she was sixteen were not her own. They belonged to another vampire around Tate's age. She played you like a fool."

My hands shook as red sparks flew across the table. My father simply waved his hand, and the sparks flew *into* him.

"Stop doing that!" I demanded, unnerved at my own power's *awakening*.

"Make me." The challenge was clear in his eyes. A challenge he won; I didn't know how to stop him. Fuck my own stupidity. Fuck that male for making me ignorant. Fuck all of this.

"Have you always known? Is that why you pushed them so hard when testing me? To see the true depth of my magic?" I couldn't keep the bite from my tone.

My father merely smirked at me.

"Answer me!" I demanded, more sparks flaring from my fingertips.

"Your mother was a Fae," he said simply, picking lint from his jacket. "I suspected you'd have larger stores of power because of that. This research that Dr. Worshah has been doing is not a *new* discovery to the Glenn. Leadership has long been aware of the role genes play in our power manifestation—much of the community is composed of halflings, mixed-raced vampires. Even beyond the veil, humans are not all purely *human*. We suspect—"

"What?" I interrupted. This was all so much, too much. My mother a Fae? "Is that why you married her?"

"Son," my father tsked. "Really, out of all that information, you get hung up on the sentimental?"

Rage doubled within my veins, as lightning darted across the room and struck the glass wall. She'd been nothing more than a breeding mare to him. It all made sense, the way he'd never really shown any grief with her passing. The casual ways he flippantly referred to her— my mother, died in childbirth, Fae first lady. She'd been a pawn to this evil male, the same as I was now.

I slammed my hands against the table and stood, throwing out bolts of power that merely grazed my father's erect shield.

"Dale…" Holland approached slowly, placing a hand on my shoulder as her calming presence begged to be let in.

"She was a means to an end. She had you and then died. Sad story, but it's over." My father glared at me as he stood. "Some of us care more about this country than we do pitiful love. She was a good female, but she's gone. And so yes, I expected more power from you. I had them push you further and further until they confirmed the power markers existed but were weak, just like you're acting now."

"You had them torture me!"

"For science! For the betterment of this country. And I'd do it again, and again, and again." He laughed bitterly, pulling my power into himself. "I never expected it would take that bitch to finally awaken what I knew was always there. But thanks to her, we are much closer to solving the puzzle generations before me have struggled with. We have a formula; we can awaken others."

Holland's hand tightened on my shoulder as I began to massage my temples. "How?" I asked.

"That explosion showed us many things, but simply put, we need a large store of *raw* energy, mixed with dark magic, and a kicker—like the explosion—to be introduced to our specimens." Doctor Worshah practically shook with excitement as he spoke.

"You mean the explosion that killed hundreds of guaramen? Soldiers, good males and females, didn't survive. Damaris didn't survive."

"A necessary sacrifice," my father clipped.

An icy calmness crept over me. He was completely serious. He'd kill tens of thousands of vampires just to awaken a few dozen magical beings.

"Dale's right," Holland began, not cowering in front of the monstrous male. "About a dozen of us guaramen survived the base explosion. You can see for yourself in the footage that several were incinerated by the force and power of the explosion. The very wave of power that ate the camera should have consumed not only the base but miles around it. How can you suggest recreating that?"

"You're very astute," my father focused on Holland. "Although I haven't yet determined if you're brave or very, very stupid." He looked her up and down before nodding to Dr. Worshah who opened his disk and refreshed the projected screen. "Contrary to what my son thinks, I'm not the devil incarnate. We can take what we learned from the explosion and recreate it in a safe environment."

The video showed an animated warehouse housing a specialized container—a hundred yards in circumference—with both seethings and vampires inside of it. A wave of golden energy poured into one side of the dome while a wave of dark energy poured into the other side, appearing to be sourced from dark energy, freed from several seethings incinerated by an explosive.

"When the explosion happened, magical stores were released from the incinerated beasts, vampires, humans, and from some of our own containers. That is what killed those beasts—*her* pulse combined with the force of the explosives formed a wave of energy that killed some while still allowing others to live." My father cleared his throat, pointing to the screen. "This is something Doctor Worshah is trying desperately to understand in full detail, something he better have a breakthrough in *soon*." I didn't miss the pointed look he gave the doctor or the way the small doctor's frame shook from the threat. "We have a general understanding, and Doctor Worshah's team has devised this as a model, but we've yet to understand the qualifiers for the raw magic *source*."

My head pounded as I tried desperately to understand the implications of what my father said. One thing was abundantly clear: he wanted to recreate the circumstances of the explosion to produce more magic wielders, people like me.

"So, that pulse wasn't just from the explosives?" I questioned, feeling stupid and slow all over again.

"No, no it was not. The sheer force of it was generated from the explosives, but it is our belief that the explosion was triggered by Tatealia's energy release of *her* magical stores." *Tap!* President Dale's cane clipped the floor as he paced over to the screen.

Moving quickly, too quickly for someone who couldn't stop shaking, Doctor Worshah pulled up another video with similar footage to what we saw before. Only this time it was from one of the buildings that was far enough away from the blast radius that it wasn't destroyed. A controller stood in front of it, a cloud of dark magic surrounded him as he clawed at an invisible shield. The ground shook, lights pulsed, and then the controller threw out his hands, breaking through the shield and blocking the building with a wave of his own power before clawing at the pink-golden energy. It was almost unnoticeable and happened in an instant. His frustration afterwards, along with the way the pink was repulsed by him, told me enough. He couldn't siphon her power.

"So, it was Tate's power that killed our men and the seethings, as you call them?" Holland asked, her face pale.

"Yes and no," Doctor Worshah answered. "The blast alone would have leveled several buildings and killed some. We've confirmed there were multiple charges. However, the extent of the damage and the way that those beasts near Tate, in the warehouse that exploded and with nearest proximity, were mutilated, tell us that it was a combination of her power and the bombs. But the magical release? That was *all* Tate."

"Magical release?" I asked, hating myself for not knowing this. Red static danced across my skin, salivating. Holland's own rage was palpable. I could taste it, I could...

"Yes, if you look closely." Doctor Worshah zoomed in and then circled the portion of the screen electronically. "You can see the beasts killed by the blast, some of their matter dissipates as is normal in this case given the heat from the explosion. However, the instant after the blast, there is another pulse. Here—" he circled another portion of the display "—you can see the air shimmer and take on a golden-pink tint. It's nearly indiscernible, but the instant the pulse is gone, so are the bodies. They are nothing but black goo and dried husks."

"Fuck," I said. "So, she siphoned them?"

"We're uncertain—"

"Yes," my father interrupted Doctor Worshah. "Furthermore, Tatealia Aaralyn's very unique magical pulse merged with the other forms of magic. All of which impacted *you* survivors. Some died after, unable to handle the exposure, some mutated, some awakened, and still, some did *both*." His eyes sparkled as they locked onto me. "Chance, you didn't just awaken. You instinctively *siphoned* that power into yourself. Like no one has done before." The smug look on his face was enough to send me over the edge.

Bile rose in my throat as I threw my power at the male who seemed too proud of the *thing* I was. He simply blocked it with a shield that protected him and simultaneously ate my energy. He pulled and more of my force flowed into him. Enough. I yanked it back, but he wouldn't relent. He wouldn't stop siphoning my expressed magic—something that was no better than siphoning contained magic in a vessel, both occurred without consent. He was just as vile as a controller—he should just fucking become a controller but wouldn't because he wanted the glory of a president—not that of a disfigured monster created by being struck by dark magic instead of willfully inhaling it.

I was lucky enough to be both: struck by dark magic when the base exploded, and yet, still willfully siphoned it at impact. Lucky, fucking me.

The mere thought of it, of all that had occurred, and of all the deception, the betrayal of all that was sacred, sent me over the edge.

I threw back my head and screamed as the room shook.

Then it was over.

I was standing above the male who sired me. He looked at me, and for the first time in my life, *he* was *afraid* of *me*. I smiled—all teeth, fangs bared.

The whole room was silent. One thing was clear, I was the alpha here.

"Teach me to control this, to siphon," I commanded, straightening my spine.

Holland cleared her throat. "Dale, maybe—"

I threw up my hand silencing her. "I want to control this, Holland." I sniffed in her direction. The sweet scent of ancient and new mingled, beckoning... "I want to siphon *you*, Holland," the words I spoke drifted on the wind. I was half aware.

My power reached out to Holland and inhaled deeply. Sweet honeyed notes.

Temptation.

With half a thought, I was pulling at her power—devouring the ancient scent. Thrill filled me as my veins sparked with newfound power, even as Holland's body shook and crumpled from the force of my energy. She became engulfed by my red bolts. They dug into her ears, her eyes, her nose...

She opened her mouth to scream, but nothing came out. Instead, my power filled the opening and urged more of her magic forth. Her skin began to crumple and dry up before my eyes.

Nowhere in time, and yet everywhere. I am infinity.

Her power was speaking to mine, binding itself. The euphoria of the moment carried me away. I was vaguely aware of Holland, dead at my feet. I could see my father shaking out of fear and pissing himself, but its meaning didn't register. I looked at the window and saw my reflection. I wasn't Chance Dale anymore—I was pure magic, pure hate, pure vengeance.

Red light flared from every part of my skin. My arms were engulfed in bolts of lightning, no—the lightning bolts *were* my arms. I was no more. I was pure power and a captive to its intoxication. I was—

"Dale?" Holland was kneeling next to me, cupping my face in her hands.

I shook my head violently. My hands were white-knuckled as I gripped the armchair. My throat burned and I realized I was still screaming.

The room was covered in red static, but nothing was harmed. I was still in control.

Holland was alive. She was here, trying to reach me. I could feel the gentle presence of her power against mine, the knock on my heart. I smothered the internal fire, the electricity coursing through me, and breathed deeply.

"Teach me to control this," my words came out hoarse.

My father's eyes were locked on me—calculating.

"Let's begin." President Dale tapped his cane.

CHAPTER 48

TATE

The goal was simple. I, along with the other trainees, would be on the field awaiting whatever challenge came next. All I needed to do was conjure a flame at some point, demonstrate control, and form a shield. Five minutes. I would have five minutes to do all of that.

I hopped from foot to foot, cringing only slightly from the pain in my side. Luner magic was impressive, their tonic and healing weaves had sealed the bloodied dagger wound, but it still hurt with certain movements. That would fade soon, or so they'd said.

Even so, my nerves were more irritating than the freshly healed wound. This arena was different from the sparring one. This one would be surrounded by spectators in coliseum seating—anyone in the Shadow Tribe, regardless of rank, would be allowed to watch. The stakes were much higher here than in the sparring ring; once you were in the arena, there was no coming out until it ended or you died.

I bit my lip, attempting to steel my nerves.

The door in front of me was shut. Any moment, it would open, and I would be expected to walk out and face whatever lie beyond. I had no idea who would be in there. Several other tribes had already tested through. If they did it, so could I, right?

Breathe, darling. You've got this. I'll be in the stands if you need anything.

I followed Aether's pull to his calming center and inhaled. I wasn't alone, even in the dark hallway physically by myself, Aether was with me. Aether...my mate. And he'd lied to me, again.

I pushed back. No, I didn't want his comfort right now. I was still pissed as hell at him. He had a daughter—something he should have told me before we bonded.

Right.

Vala said your shields are almost as good as her own, that's impressive for anyone outside of the House of Luna. But given your blood, I'm not surprised.

I didn't miss the playful nudge at my mind. Still, I wasn't ready for the levity his tone implied.

Well, let's hope it's enough.

I'm sure—

I threw the shield up again. I didn't want the banter, not right now. Even with my mind blocked, I could sense him knocking on it—wanting in. My nerves were racing.

We will need to talk you know, I shot down the bond.

I know...whenever you wish.

I snorted. Sure, now it was on my time. When would secrets stop existing? Could I even trust Aether to be fully honest with me?

The countdown started overhead. The doors would be opening soon—my anxiety doubled.

I missed Aether. Missed his comfort.

That was the irony of it all. Six hours prior, I had felt so close. Now? Now I felt mistrust breeding between us. A chasm that would be hard to bridge. I replayed our conversation from the night before in my mind. The way he'd held me tight against his chest, warm and secure. The quiet had been just as comfortable as the conversation.

"Any idea who will be in the arena with me?" I asked, tucking my head further into his warm flesh. Savoring the way his scent engulfed me.

"Traditionally, they divide the test by tribes. The details are undisclosed and no one outside the tribe is allowed to witness the challenge prior so that there's no tip-offs. You'll be with the Shadow Tribe. And...traditionally because the Shadow Tribe primarily accounts for the fiercest warriors, the threats will be harder—they'll expect a show of brute force and flames from you," he responded, rubbing my neck and back in slow, comforting strokes.

I mentally nodded. Shows of brute force, flames, and control. I knew what to expect. I could do this. I'd prepared and I was ready.

I'd wasted enough time here; I needed to return for Shae and vengeance would soon be had—a certain president would finally be met with justice. Yes, I could do this. I was stronger now, skilled, and understood more about my magic than I ever had before.

A chime sounded once, twice, three times and then, the door opened, and light poured in.

Show time. I stepped into the light.

The arena was bright, eerily so. The ground beneath me was composed of solid black stone, not the white stone and sand I was accustomed to. Looking around, I didn't see any other candidates. Cheers sounded and one glance told me the coliseum was packed.

The sound was deafening, overwhelming to my senses. Thank blood I could use magic to silence it.

I weaved it around me, muting the noise and chaos as I looked for any threats. Walls, fifteen feet high, made of pure black stone were erected and formed paths. I could only see twenty feet in front of me. A small three-foot walkway led away from me on either side, disappeared around the curve of the dome. I began walking, listening for anyone nearby while muting the crowd. Nothing.

The path ended and I turned left, leading down another path five feet wide this time. It was a maze.

Unnatural screeches and roars filled the air, overcoming my sound shield, and sent me to my knees.

I knew those cries.

They were the thing of nightmares, my nightmares.

Seethings.

Aether, I spoke down our bond, lowering my wall, but he was silent.

I could feel a wave of pure rage pulsing through the bond.

Aether!

I tried again, but this time it was as if I sent it into a void. I felt it then: the ice settling over what was once our connection, freezing and blocking. The sky pulsed as a webbed energy flickered in the dome above. It was some type of shield, likely what was blocking my connection to Aether, somehow.

Panic.

Aether's fear flooded my senses.

Oddly, I was comforted that I could at least feel him still, even if I couldn't hear him.

I found my feet and squared my shoulders. I was not weaponless. I had trained, I could shield. Glancing at my hands, I willed my magic to the surface as I continued forward.

"Trainees, welcome to your physical magic test. Survive for five minutes while demonstrating control and power. Begin now," an overhead voice said, followed by a series of gongs.

Screeching ensued, closer this time. I had no idea which way to go, so I turned around and headed back to where I came from. I had barely made it fifteen feet down the path when it came into view.

It was massive, ten feet tall, with wings tucked into its sides and talons on each hand that were each at least a foot long. Unlike the other black and grey ones I'd encountered in the Glenn, this one was covered in milky white scales with red veins dancing across its body. It threw back its head and cried into the night sky, foaming spit hit the ground as it tossed its tongue side to side.

Shit.

I stood there, frozen for a moment as it charged. I had no physical weapons, no dagger or sword. But I had magic. And that was the point of this test, wasn't it? I threw my hands forward and simultaneously looked inward to the thread I'd become so familiar with, and then, I pulled. Fire, pink flames to my eyes, erupted from my hands and swallowed the beast whole. It screamed as it dropped to its knees and clawed at the flames.

I pushed more energy into it and a moment later, it lay there, dead. Its flesh was burnt and boiled over bones that looked completely misshaped.

Control. Vala made it clear the color of my flames would be concealed. And given that she reinforced the cloak on me right before I entered, it in theory shouldn't be affected by the magic-blocking dome above. If she was right, my flames should be blanketed to look black, but she could do nothing for the magnitude. I needed to *appear* average.

The flames winked out.

Screams sounded ahead. Without further thought, I ran *toward* the screams erecting a shield around my body as I moved. The countless hours of practice with Vala had paid off, it was now almost second nature to command a shield around myself.

Ahead I could see not one, but two wingless seethings attacking a small female. She was in a dome, but it was weak and fracturing; her pixie black hair a confirmation that she was a Darkling.

One seething swiped at it and the dome flicked out just long enough for the other seething to swipe in and slash the female across her gut, sending her flailing back into the ground. They stalked toward her in single file, the path too narrow for them to move side-by-side, and then raised their taloned hands in the air. I threw flames at them, willing the fire to surround the beasts but leave the female unscathed. Both seethings stopped mid-step and they turned; their all-white eyes locked on me as the one closest to me snarled.

I swallowed back the stomach bile threatening to erupt and instead forced more fire toward the vile beasts. The one in the front took a step toward me, and its scales began melting and falling off, followed by its flesh. The next one ignored me and continued toward the wounded female. She sat up on her elbows, tears streaming down her face, as her intestines began to seep through her fingers.

Shield, I needed to shield *her*. I could do this. I looked to the inner pool of power within me, I felt the connection to the massive energy stores beneath my feet, and in one swift internal moment, I pulled and projected.

The air in front of me shimmered and then pink energy flowed toward the female. I sent more flames at the beasts while simultaneously commanding *all* of my magic. The wave of energy hovered just above her head before encasing her and solidifying. A worthy shield. The seething roared as it swung at the dome, and then hissed when it didn't so much as flicker.

I did it! She was secure.

I sent more flames pouring toward the beasts and allowed the temperature to spike, the core of my flames became solid white. The seething closest to me continued to crawl on its maimed limbs before it succumbed first, and then the other one too fell. Their bodies melted and boiled. Gone.

I took a steadying breath. The clock on the ceiling read three minutes and twenty-five seconds. I could do this.

More screams sounded along with the roar of a...*dragon*? Someone was stupid enough to shift? It was a death sentence, Aether and Vala told me to avoid doing so as it would not only get you disqualified, but if you hit the grid guarding the arena, it could kill. I looked up and saw the serpent hovering over the center, black wings gloriously spread out. But its shifting was premature, it was flashing, and I could tell they were having a hard time maintaining their beast form. They needed to go higher, but I doubted they could—especially with the additional shield the chairs had enforced.

The dragon threw back its head and roared, black flames struck the shield above before pouring down. It tried to fly higher but hit the dome and shrieked as it was repelled downwards. The impact undid it and before my eyes, it shifted from a dragon into a male, free-falling through the air. The seething's roars echoed from below. He was as good as dead, even if he survived the fall, the seethings would devour him in seconds.

Manipulation of space and energy.

The words played on repeat in my mind.

I reached for the air around the male and willed it to come into my command, for my power to fill the space. Nothing happened. I gritted my teeth as I began running toward the falling male, weaving my way through the maze. I had mere seconds before he'd be dead.

She screeched before scratching her talons down the walls of my internal well of magic. She was awake now? Now that I couldn't shift, wouldn't shift, she decided to acknowledge me and participate? Her rage fueled me, feeding my confidence.

I snorted. I could do this. I didn't give myself a chance to second guess or to consider the fact that I was impacted by my inner dragon's influence. Instead, I forced more of my energy into the air, visualized the threads, and attempted to weave them. I could *feel* him then, falling with my power surrounding him. I yanked on the inner thread and opened the floodgate. The male froze midair, not more than ten feet above the erected stone walls of the maze. Seethings snapped at him as they lunged, talons swiping and barely missing.

He was safe. He too would live.

Sweat dripped down my temple and into my eyes as I dug my feet into the ground and willed the magic from the stone to seep into me with every step. I could feel the drain on my power, my energy, and it became consuming. Maintaining the shield around the female and keeping the male suspended in air took significant concentration and power. Vala had said I was capable of more than I knew; I still hadn't explored the new pool of power that was from Aether, and I wasn't sure *now* was the time. I needed to appear normal and messing with his power could be risky, especially if I couldn't control it. Shit, I may have already done *too* much.

She roared within, begging to obliterate the entire compound.

I heard screeches from behind me and chose to keep moving. I went left, then right, then left again. Another dead end. I retreated and made another left, weaving my way to where I hoped was the perimeter. One more turn and I realized my mistake—I had moved to the center of the maze. In front of me was a wide opening that poured into a field composed of black pebbles.

I felt their power before I saw them. At least half a dozen seethings were gathered in the center of the maze with a platform erected just before them.

These seethings were larger than the ones I'd just encountered, at least two feet taller and they *all* had wings. Without thinking, I threw out my hands and commanded my flames to end them.

They used their wings to cover their bodies and blocked my fire. Images from the compound and that monster seething flooded my mind. It too had blocked my flames with its wings.

The six of them stood, in one motion, and threw back their wings before projecting red flames at me. I threw up a shield, blocking their fire.

The male suspended in air shrieked as my hold on him faltered and he dropped so he barely hovered above the stone walls.

In the distance, a female screamed as I felt my power slipping from the shield guarding her.

Screeches sounded from all around, I didn't need to turn to know there were more seethings behind me. I forced my focus onto the shield that was now being swallowed whole in red fire.

The flames stopped a moment later and the seething closest to me smiled.

"We've come a long way," it spoke revealing razor-sharp teeth. "All this is for you, a test designed to reveal what and who you really are."

Everything fell silent for a moment before *she* roared within me, thrashing violently in the pool of power.

I needed more control.

I could feel my shield shaking from the force of the seethings pounding on it. I pulled from the ground below me and tried to refill my stores while leaving bits of myself closed off. The giant seething growled and then as one, the six beasts sent another wave of red fire that consumed the shield and managed to heat the air within.

My inner beast began surfacing, stirring, and building my magic within. It would be so easy to free the well of power writhing inside...

Control. I needed to control.

The fire ended and for a moment I just allowed myself to breathe. Fear and panic would cost me, I couldn't allow myself to feel, not right now.

The clock on the dome showed two minutes. I only needed to survive for two more minutes. I'd already shielded and demonstrated control and flames—now I just needed to wait it out.

I began breathing in practiced rhythms, thank you Fletch, and lowered myself to my knees inside the dome. Mentally, I reinforced my shield making it stronger, even as the seethings assaulted it. The leading one screeched, enraged that I was beyond its reach.

One minute and thirty seconds.

More screams sounded, some Untishee and some beastly. I bit my lip as I swallowed back the sour taste in my mouth.

One minute.

I would make it out of here. My power grew, reassuring my survival, and became a tidal wave begging to be released.

Thirty seconds.

A shrill scream came the same moment the beasts in front of me took a unified step back, highlighting a path directly to the erected platform in the center. A platform that now had a giant seething atop it with a small female in its grasp. Whisps of green hair blew from her pale face as she was held by her neck, dangling over the edge. Other seethings gathered below her like a bunch of hungry jackals.

She screamed again, flailing her limbs.

Carly.

Time stilled.

I didn't have to try to reach for my power, it was just there—a being of its own. With half a thought, my dome burst forth, the power of its blast brought the seethings nearest me to their knees.

Without another thought, I reached out to the matter surrounding the beasts in my path and suspended them, locking them in place.

I didn't even have to raise my hands before a wall of pure energy erupted in a wave of pink-black light. Everything that stood in its path was incinerated, nothing remained. Nothing but stones and pebbles and the vertical tower holding Carly, with a few remaining beasts below.

Another swell of energy rippled forward, and those seethings too were gorged, fully annihilated with nothing but scattered bones to mark their presence.

Carly wailed, but it was strangled as her face began to turn purple and then blue.

"You've shown yourself. There will be no redemption," the seething spoke.

Before I could react, it plunged its talons into Carly's abdomen. Blood gushed out, pouring down to the ground. A scream clawed through my throat but came out a mere whisper: *Carly.*

But the seething wasn't done. It ripped its talons free, cutting through her flesh before plunging again and lifting her into the air. It dropped her to its mouth, its fangs sinking into her side, and drank. She didn't react, she just hung there, limp. Gone.

Rage consumed my senses and I shined brightly. The seething became momentarily blocked and then *I* could see through the light. See the seething frozen, shock across its face.

It dropped Carly and as she plummeted toward the ground, I reached out and stopped her fall, willing the air to gently lower her.

My inner pool became a cyclone of energy, Aether's power and my own magic violently turning within—barely constrained. My inner beast roared as she snapped at the flames now shining bright inside me. I could feel *her* fighting her leash. The desire to shift became nearly undeniable, but the tether remained heavy and unbudging. It didn't matter, even if I could shift, doing so in this dome would be a death sentence.

And I didn't need to shift.

I was more than enough, even in this form.

I wanted to inflict pain on that seething and enact revenge.

Me.

The cripple.

The outsider.

The avenger.

My power responded to my fury and wrapped around the seething. I willed it to slice, and the beast's wings were cut from its back. Its shrill screeches filled the air. Bolts made of flames speared its gut, its neck, its crotch. Grey blood poured from its open wounds. As it cried, I willed the matter around the seething to become a blade and cut the serpent tongue from its mouth. In a tornado of vibrant pink flames, I encased the mutilated monster. I seared the air from its very lungs until even its screams died out.

It was nothing but a charred corpse of manipulated power. Evil had been vanquished.

A light grey and red cloud hovered above its body, sparking with energy that beckoned me:

Take me, I'm here. I no longer have a master.

It swirled as it spoke and showed images of pure power and lethal carnage. Dark magic.

The things we could accomplish...

"Never."

It laughed, pulsing with the movement. *I am power to be wielded. You could use me for good. Together we could end all seethings. I wasn't always this beast crumpled before you. I once was like you, a Untishee who faced unspeakable things. Renew me, revive me, save me....*

It reached out in a wave, dancing through the air, until it was touching my fingertips. Fingertips I hadn't realized were extended toward it, until now. Tentatively, I brushed against the energy.

My system jolted as images of power, the destruction of all seethings, the vanquishment of evil played before me. The mist conjured image after image.

Renew, revive, retaliate...

The mist began to envelop me and poke at my skin, begging me to let it in. Showing me a throne, a crown, a purpose.

I wasn't always this way. I was captured and tortured. They forced me to become this thing. Your own leaders have left the path of truth and abandoned the teachings of Perry.

My head lulled from side to side even as my energy continued to build, a wave meeting the mist.

"I...I can't," my voice was but a whisper as I became enchanted with the energy's promises.

Oh, but dear, you've done it before. I can smell it on you.

"What?" My head snapped straight. "I have not, I would nev—"

Images of Judge Rollins flooded my mind. I could see pictures of his corpse, no, his *husk*. Had I taken his energy? Was that what that was?

Help avenge me. Help me get justice.

The sweet melody flowed around me, weaving its magic.

I can help you...

My feet began to dance as my eyes rolled back into my head and my body swayed, following the notes of the power before me.

I felt a snap within, a burst of power.

SHE ROARED.

Pink flames escaped my mouth and ate at the mist, devouring it and destroying it.

SHE DEMOLISHED.

Fire consumed and shattered the power floating in front of me. The dark energy screamed as it tried to flee back toward the dead corpse of the seething.

SHE CLAIMED.

A new torrent of liquid flames left my lips, spewed toward the corpse, and ravaged it until it was nothing but bones—disfigured and abused—and then even those too succumbed, becoming ash.

With a final roar, even the ash was wasted and became no more.

The flames ended and my breath whooshed from my lungs as my vision and mind cleared.

Carly's body rested on black pebbles and scattered bones. Tears sprung free from my eyes and my feet were moving before I could register their motion.

"No!"

Carly was before me, pale and blue. I knelt down and touched her body. A cry ripped from my lips as I beheld her mutilated state.

No! I refuse to let you go too, I shouted to her mentally.

I cupped her head in my hands and held her there, staring at her and willing her to live. I couldn't lose another friend, I wouldn't.

Her body began to hum, pink and gold energy swirled over her skin. Then *Carly* began to shine and the gaping holes in her stomach stitched themselves shut with new strings of flesh, covering the once deadly wounds. Color began slowly returning to her cheeks.

Come on, Carly, you can do this, I commanded her.

In a burst, the light dancing on Carly's skin blasted outwards and then was pulled right back into her, sinking into her skin and her very being. She lay there for a moment, unmoving.

I heard nothing but my heavy breaths. And then, Carly opened her eyes.

They were glazed for a moment before slowly finding me.

"Majesty," she uttered before her eyes rolled back into her head and she was unconscious once again. Her words barely registered as my emotions danced within.

Carly was alive.

CHAPTER 49
AETHER

Violent emotions raged within. Fury and betrayal at what Tate was being exposed to, put through. Anger that our bond was somehow blocked. That shouldn't be fucking possible.

Awe at Tate and the way she handled herself. She demonstrated mastery of skills and control that were practically unheard of for trainees.

And then horror at Carly being used as bait to draw out Tate's power. The moment the dome became nothing but blinding light, I knew she'd chosen. Chosen to save Carly and expose herself.

I felt more pride than I knew was possible for my mate.

Grief overtook as the whole audience saw Carly plummet toward the ground. And then I felt it, Tate was rallying her power. My soul heard her silent plea for assuagement for what she was about to reveal. Without a thought, I pulled from my internal power, and the whole dome became shadowed, bathed in black flames. Nothing inside the arena was visible, Tate was concealed.

Tate! I called into the void for the hundredth time.

Nothing, we were still blocked. A growl escaped my throat as I looked to where the chairs sat. All their eyes were on the dome, all but

Arithi's. Her cold maroon eyes were focused on me—analyzing. It took all my restraint not to attack her, to prevent my inner beast from unleashing.

Instead, I steadied my breath.

Agonizing seconds ticked by. Anything could be happening in that dome. Tate could need help.

Trust. I needed to trust her.

Trust her in a way I should have all along. The way I should have given her the full truth about the bond, about Ruby, just...all of it. I should have been completely open from the very beginning. I couldn't change the past, but I could learn from my mistakes.

So, I gritted my teeth and waited. I'd *felt* Tate's rage, her power sparking my own. I'd *felt* her expending energy in purposeful bursts. And then, then I'd felt numbness. Confusion. And worst of all, fear laced with desire. A foreign presence scratched at the bond, sending panic lacing through me.

Trust her. Just trust.

I reminded myself, even as I could still feel the tickle of foreign magic...and then, I could sense the rising of a new expression of power from Tate:

Primal. Lethal. Uncaged.

It clawed at the bond and demanded more simultaneously. Instinctually, I fed it. I gave it more and more of myself until it peaked and then vanished.

A full thirty seconds passed, and I allowed the flames to clear.

My eyes found Tate on her knees in the middle of the maze next to Carly, who lay there, unmoving.

For a moment nothing happened. And then, the doors screeched open as several medics clad in white rushed in searching for survivors. The fact that there were survivors at all was a testament to Tate.

Screams from the audience echoed all around, parents' panicked cries.

A test rarely went this far.

The audience was instructed to remain calm and see their trainees in the Luner medic bays. I glanced to where Arithi had been sitting, her chair was now empty.

Fuck that.

I began to storm down the stands to the field, but Tate was already walking into the underground hallway, led by several medics. My chest heaved. She was okay. Fuck, she was more than all right, she was amazing.

I shouldered past several shocked staff members and made my way to the basement. Following the pull that I knew was Tate, my internal bond's compass, I stormed through several hallways, stairs, and more hallways. My shadowed energy and flames gathered at my back—my dragon barely contained. Even with my attempts at restraint, concealing the expanse of my fury was impossible. My mate was almost fucking killed. She was exposed to those vile creatures and I had to watch. I was helpless, and in those moments, my ire would not be bound.

Now, even as I stalked down corridors, my darkness engulfed and claimed. Gasps and panic reigned, taking with it any mourning silence from parents or medics.

It wasn't until the pull in me tripled outside a door, that I took a steadying break. My mate fucking dominated that field. She was worthy, so worthy. Not of my ire, not of my wrath, but of my worship. I pulled the darkness in and then pressed the door open.

Tate was there, before me, sitting on the bed with her knees tucked into her chest. Her arms wrapped around her calves, and her hair draped over her body

Hey there.

Her head whipped up, mahogany eyes wet.

Aether.

I sat on the edge of the bed and pulled her into a hug, embracing this mighty female. Relieved, I released a breath—she didn't shut me out and demand I leave.

Instead, she allowed me in. More than that, I could sense that she *wanted* me here. So, I held her and savored the way her lush form pressed against my body. I wanted to taste her, to devour her. But she needed my presence right now, my comfort—not my lust.

That was some pretty amazing shit.

How much did you see? Does everybody know?

I stroked her head, feeling the nervous energy radiating from her. She was scared.

Nothing is known. Carly is alive, and no one knows how.

That fact still held me in awe. Carly had been dead, she looked it, and yet when medics had reached her in the field, her wounds were healed, and she was *alive*.

Yeah, I may have somehow commanded that from her...

I chuckled into her head. Only Tate would command and will the very life back into someone.

You were—

Too obvious. I'm sorry, I tried—

"Hey." I tilted her head upward. "You were amazing. I've never been prouder to be your mate."

Her eyes shimmered and then the silent tears she'd held at bay fell. I leaned in and kissed each one from her cheeks before once again cradling her head against my chest. I warped the energy around her, demanding it to compress her pressure points and massage, offering the comfort that I *knew* she appreciated.

"Aether, what now?" she asked, sniffing as she did so.

"Now, we wait. The chairs called a meeting directly following the trial. Everyone has questions. Namely, who designed this challenge and allowed those *things* into the maze. And then yes, there are questions as to how you have the power you do. But..." I paused and gave her shoulders a reassuring squeeze. "I blocked the ending, so no one saw you revive Carly, or defeat the giant seething. We still have some secrets." I winked at her.

She snorted. "Don't I know it."

And there it was. The elephant in the room. "Ruby was born just after Cher died."

Tate's eyes locked on mine, the mystery in them was laced with pain and curiosity.

"So, who then? An ex-wife?"

"No, Cher gave birth to her."

Tate tilted her head, disbelief coating her features. "Aether, that's not possible."

I swallowed. "Cher was well into her second trimester when we were called into battle. It was the second to last battle of the Great War. She was a high general, and I, her general—there was no dissuading her. She was a fighter and insisted our young would be too. But when..." I exhaled, averting my eyes from Tate's. "When she fell, there was no reviving her. No saving her life. She was bleeding out and the medics were too far away. But we had a Luner with us. A strong wielder. A protector. Cher asked her to save the baby, and she did."

I could sense Tate's shock and remorse. I closed my eyes.

"I'm sorry, that's horrible. I didn't know." Tate cupped my cheek with her hand. "But I still don't understand, the war was over a hundred years ago...Ruby doesn't look more than ten."

"She's nine actually." I smiled in spite of the tension filling the room. "Luner tribe members are gifted in various ways, but to preserve Ruby's life, a large force of magic was used. Magic from Micah, the Luner, and magic from Cher. She gave her remaining life force to cloak Ruby. Micah froze her in her premature infant state and she stayed that way until the time was right to remove the cloaking."

"Cloaking?" Tate exhaled.

"Yes, it...it was the only way." My words were failing me. "Nine years ago, we uncloaked Ruby and with the medics and their advancements here in the Embassy, they were able to save her life. James and his wife, Uley, agreed to raise her as their own."

I could sense it, the slight judgment from Tate. Old guilt surfaced —I'd abandoned my child. I was a horrible person, a selfish bastard.

You were hurting. Her voice in my soul sounded.

I am unworthy. I failed Cher and I couldn't raise Ruby alone. She deserved to have a mother.

"Hey," Tate said as she pressed her forehead to mine. "You did what you thought was right. Ruby seems healthy and happy. You gave her a family with two parents. My mother did her best, but take it from a child who grew up without a dad, there were times my mom simply couldn't be there for me logistically, and the stress she felt..." Tate tensed. "She needed someone. Fletch was her person, my stand-in dad in many ways. Ruby has two parents *and* you."

I pulled her into a crushing embrace, inhaling her lilac and lavender scent.

What else do you want to know?

I was done keeping secrets.

I'm not sure. Can we revisit later?

Absolutely.

I stroked her back and held her in silence. Our breaths were the only sound in the small space.

"How long until we hear from the chairs?" She sniffed.

"I don't know."

I hated the admission. Hated being powerless. But until I knew where the chairs stood, where Arithi stood, we'd be acting blindly. Rage refueled my belly as I recalled the terror I felt from Tate when she saw the seething.

Arithi put those beasts in there. Whether it was her command or another, she was the head of the Embassy. The very female I'd spent the last several decades following and respecting, put Tate in danger and nearly cost Carly her life.

Flames sparked from my hands, barely contained. It had been a long time since my power got the better of me. Control had been my gift, but now? When my mate was almost ended, forced to relive some horrific moments in her life by the mere presence of those seethings? Now, my inner beast was edging closer and closer to the surface.

Tate began to hum, quietly as she rubbed my back in slow circles and together, we sat there for a moment, unmoving. There would be time for vengeance later. Right now, Tate—my mate—just needed me.

"Did you see how I kicked Perseus's ass?" Tate said, lifting her head slightly to look at me.

"I did indeed. He did *not* see you coming." The fear I felt when I watched Perseus's knife plunge into her side still made my stomach turn. I'd felt a mimic of the pain down the bond, and my beast rose with it—begging to end the one responsible.

I tightened my arms around her. She was safe. She was alive.

Aww, you big overprotective brute. I'm right here.

She poked a finger into my ribs and wiggled it, eliciting a chuckle from me.

I'm always going to be an overprotective brute where you're concerned. But I'll try to...restrain myself.

I inhaled her scent and laughter. I wasn't a fool, I knew we'd still need to discuss things further where Ruby was concerned, but for now, what was paramount had been said. She knew the truth. I had no more skeletons.

She nestled her head deeper into my chest, contentment radiating down the bond.

"Aether, those seethings were different. They talked like the ones at the base, but they had power. They didn't just kill with their talons, they had flames and seemed to be waiting for me."

I sucked on my fang. "I know. I plan on getting answers."

A knock at the door sounded. I jolted upright before Juda stepped inside. "Aether." She looked at me—judgment clouding her eyes. "Enzo has requested your audience."

About fucking time.

CHAPTER 50
CHANCE

My stomach turned, even as I sipped from the large stem of bloodwine. Doctor Worshah had brought in two pitchers, one for me and one for Holland. It appeared we'd be here for a while.

"Would you like to know why I broke the sacred rules of the Glenn? Why it is so *important*—" my father's eyes shot daggers at me "—for you to learn how to control your power?" His voice wafted up from the pit below through the sound system. "This is why. Behold what will fall upon our country should we not act. Should we play by the rules. Simply put, we would be devoured."

A sound buzzed as Doctor Worshah hit a button on his hologram control remote. At least that was something I couldn't destroy. I laughed dryly, earning a concerned glance from Holland.

Several doors opened all at once throughout the dome. Large creatures, moving on two feet, stalked through. Their milky white skin was the first thing I noticed. Their wings were the second.

"Behold, the creatures of the Fern," my father spoke as he marched toward the largest of the beasts directly in front of him.

The creatures were surrounding him with methodical steps. He was outnumbered, seven to one. My gut clenched. Was it possible that my father *was* acting according to the greater good?

The creature roared at him and then began running. My father planted his feet and held his ground. "We discovered leaks in their research three years ago. It took us one year to understand the implications and to fully decode it," my father spoke as he threw out his hands.

The giant beast launched itself upward, beating its massive wings, it raised and began to fly. It directed its hands toward my father and red flames poured from its palms in powerful streams.

It would have incinerated him, easily killed him, had my father not shielded. The beast dropped in front of the dome, landing in a crouch. It stood for only a moment before my father dropped the shield and engulfed the thing in a cyclone of wind. No, not wind, energy. The beast screamed as my father *ripped* its magic from him. I stood there in awe, watching the male who sired me drain the beast.

The other six creatures screeched as they charged him. He was outnumbered. Even with his power and ability to siphon, he couldn't siphon from them all at once, could he?

The closest beast sent flames flying at my father, but he evaded them by dropping and rolling, before shielding once again.

"You see, we are not up against nature. We are not facing a traditional enemy—we are facing dark magic evolved," he spoke, his voice strained from the force of holding a shield that was now being engulfed by flames from the six remaining seethings.

"Dale..." Holland said, understandably at a loss for words.

My jaw ticked. I didn't know what to believe. It was clear that these things were far different from the beasts we'd encountered.

The shield around my father flickered out as he ran toward the closest beast who was recovering from his last projection of flames. And a moment later, he stood between two of the six large creatures. He extended one hand toward each and siphoned viciously. They contorted before my eyes and began to crumple in on themselves.

The four other creatures screamed as they charged my father. He shielded before they could reach him. But they continued their assault. Instead of fire, they used their large silver talons to claw at the dome.

"We have been attempting to create our own army of the dead, an army of dark magic that can compete against these things. Things our enemy is generating by the masses. But we are behind in research," his voice broke in a grunt as the shield began to flicker and crack. "We're behind in development." Sweat poured in his eyes as he dropped to a knee. "We are outnumbered, severely." His chest heaved from the effort of maintaining his protection. "Their intelligence alone is something we've yet to successfully replicate, all except for those who were at the base when it exploded—"

His voice broke as the beasts struck again, with talons and flames.

"You can hide, but you will die," the beasts spoke as *one*. Shivers raced down my spine at the sound of their voice. Even the three crumpled on the ground spoke, voices high-pitched and hoarse.

"That is why we've been researching genes: human, vampirical, and even Fae. Our lack of intellectual advancement with our seethings is why we need controllers. Why we need *you*," my father said, nodding to Doctor Worshah.

Doctor Worshah hit another button. Four more doors opened, and black and grey beasts—seethings—poured through the openings. Mostly on two feet, but some on four. None had wings. None looked half as sophisticated as the creatures currently attacking my father's shield.

The seethings raced forward, unfocused. They frantically snapped their teeth and spread out. The milky beasts paused their attack on my father.

"Pathetic," they spoke as one.

Two stayed near my father's dome, still attacking, while the other two raced toward the seethings. They clawed into them with their talons, longer by several inches, and tore them apart with half a thought.

The seethings, dozens of them, had hectic attacks. They lunged at the beasts, but barely made an impact. The beasts swallowed them in flames, and two to three at a time, they dropped. Moments later, the ground was littered with corpses and piles of black goo. Not a single seething remained.

"As you can see, we are severely behind our enemy. Or we were, until we discovered one major factor," my father said as he once again signaled to Doctor Worshah, who in turn hit another key.

One last door opened. Seethings poured out. All on two feet, marching in pairs of two. Their black scales glistened against the red flames currently pouring from the beasts in warning. These seethings didn't run uncoordinated. No, they filed in and then stopped. One lone figure entered next. It was tall, at least seven feet, with muscles built upon muscles. The controller. Its eyes were red, and purple veins spread out from each socket covering every part of the male's nude body.

It tilted its head and the seethings began moving in organized motions. They surrounded the two beasts closest to them, talons at the ready. One beast began to shoot flames at the seethings nearest them, but the seethings pivoted, avoiding the flames as the untargeted ones attacked.

Unlike the scene from seconds before, where the seethings were being incinerated, they now held the advantage. The moment the beasts adjusted their targeting, the other seethings attacked. The seethings' talons sunk into the beasts, tearing a wing off here, plunging into their sides there. Even as the beasts engulfed a few seethings in flames, they weren't given a chance to recalculate as more seethings swarmed them and began ripping apart their flesh.

Moments later, both beasts lay on the ground, ripped to shreds. The seethings rushed the remaining beasts, both the three injured on the ground and the two uninjured ones, and they utterly destroyed the incapacitated beasts. The two remaining beasts launched into the air and flew toward the seethings teaming on the ground. They shot flames down and attempted to engulf the seethings. A few fell to the flames, but I stood in awe as the controller stepped forward and outstretched its arms. The beasts' flames stopped short, and then as if an invisible force directed them, the flames turned around and began to engulf the beasts midair. They screamed as they began to slowly become incinerated. One plummeted to the ground as its flames died out, and the seethings devoured it—they sunk both talons and fangs into the beast and slaughtered it.

The remaining beast's flames flickered out midair, and it too, fell. Only, the seethings didn't approach this one. Instead, the lone figure—the controller—stalked forward. The beast scooted back, snapping its teeth at the controller.

"Your time is up," the controller said.

"Your time is coming," the beast replied.

In a fluid motion, the controller pulled at the beast's energy and its magic fled from the beast and hovered above both controller and beast in a cloud of grey.

My father dropped his shield. "I am powerful, siphoning is one way to destroy these beasts." He gestured to the beast's energy hovering in the cloud. "But to command *our* seethings, to capture each of their fragile minds and make my will their own? I would need a tether to them, a commonality, to be forcefully exposed to dark magic in waves like they were—like *you* were when the base exploded, and that my son, is too great a risk for the president."

My father approached the controller. He moved past the shredded limbs of the beasts, the piles of black goo, and then stood in front of the now writhing beast. The grey cloud spun and then flowed toward my father.

"I am still powerful. I will lead. I will rule. I am the PRESIDENT."

He siphoned the energy.

The whole arena was quiet. My father donned his mask, the mask of a leader, and looked up. His eyes locked with mine. "You see, Chance, this is your destiny. Combine the power of *your blood*, your *status* as my son, and your mutated, awakened genes, and you are the fiercest weapon we've yet to witness. You are the Glenn's hope."

CHAPTER 51
TATE

The moment Aether was gone, the room felt cold—empty.

Aether? I called as panic swelled.

Here.

His voice and emotions soothed me. We still had our connection.

I stood and walked into the room's adjoining shower, ready to wash the dirt, sweat, and seething blood from my body. The water's forceful spray was a welcome relief. My arms still bore crisscross scars, the representation of what was lost—who was lost—Fletch.

I sniffled as tears threatened to spill over, again. Grabbing a bar of soap, I gently scrubbed at my body, noting once again the number of marks that marred my flesh.

So gruesome. So ugly. So violent.

Beautiful, Aether's voice filled my head.

He'd never said anything about the scars—never made me feel ashamed, and yet—staring at them now, how could he see anything but them? And what they represented: my failures, my loss, my flaws.

I was a broken person.

I reached for the shampoo and my foot slipped, the discrepancy in my height was just another reminder of my fractured state.

I'm about to rip some heads off over here, but if you don't stop the self-deprecation, I'll put this on hold and come over there and show you just how perfect I think you are. In many, many different ways.

He sent a quick image of his tongue dancing across my body, covering each scar and kissing each mark. Of his hands gliding across my bare skin as he continued to taste every inch of me.

I blushed even though I was alone. A small smile pulled at my lips as the suds washed over my face. I grabbed the conditioner next and squeezed a generous amount into my palm.

*Mmmm. I really am a total mess, a total clutz...*I teased.

We still had much to discuss, many hard conversations ahead of us. But for now, I had enough answers. There would be no more secrets, or there would be no us—I'd make sure Aether accepted this new *rule*. I still had no idea how Ruby was here, given that she was born nearly a hundred years ago, a child from his late wife, and only nine years old. At least she was not an illicit love child as I'd feared. I could live with this.

Stepmother? I laughed dryly.

After rinsing my hair, I towel-dried before stepping into the tunic left for me. It wasn't grey, like the trainee's tunics, it was black. A representation of the Shadow Tribe.

My tribe.

His tribe.

Chills rolled down my back as Aether moaned in my head.

"Tate Aaralyn," a voice nearby had me jumping. "Sorry, I should've knocked," a small female with wiry red-tipped, brown hair spoke. She looked to be just shy of adulthood.

"No, I should be more aware and not lost in thought," I said. "Do you need something?"

"Yes, I'm to take you to your post-trial documentation." She nodded toward the doorway, her green eyes round and full.

Apprehension filled me. I didn't want another discussion. I wanted to go home with Aether. I wanted to sleep. I wanted to *not* sleep with Aether.

Everything all right? I'm getting mixed signals and a variety of emotions...

I smiled, Oops.

Yes, just being called for post-trial documentation?

Normal.

I nodded, both to Aether and the girl in front of me. "Lead the way."

She smiled, before leaving the room, practically hopping from foot to foot.

We walked down a series of hallways and then the small girl pushed open a very large door. Inside was a chamber. Ancient. Old. Powerful. An arch lay ahead, with a solid iron door that swung wide open. She approached the door and then motioned for me to enter. The room inside was a dome, like much of this city, it was made completely of white stone. She stepped aside and didn't enter, her nervous energy increasing.

I squinted past her into the room. Strange marks were painted on the floor and on the doorframe.

"Just inside, she'll be with you in a moment." Her voice squeaked on the last word.

"Ok..." I only paused a moment before I stepped through. The moment I passed the doorframe I felt it, the magic. Its presence settled on my shoulders and skittered across my nerves.

Aether...

I sensed it then, a foreign presence—a parasite. The connection was not our own. It was being monitored...somehow.

As if in response, I felt Aether's apprehension and warning.

Say no more, he warned and then the line fell silent.

The door behind me swung shut and then locked, the sound intentionally obnoxious. I was locked in. I swallowed as I took several more steps into the room. In the center were two chairs facing each other, carved of stone, and covered in strange marks. The skylight opened in two different spots allowing the sun to pour in and rest on each of the chairs.

I walked closer and hesitantly ran my hand over them. I could feel their power, the sting of some, and the calming presence of others, the moment my hand made contact. I yanked it back.

"They're runes," a cool, withered female voice said.

I looked up to meet the dark glacier red and white eyes of Arithi. "Please, have a seat." She moved gracefully to her seat, her red tunic fluttering across the floor as she walked.

I didn't move. Panic began to course through me, and I could feel Aether's power rising in response. I quieted it immediately. I didn't know much about runes, but just the feeling of our bond being monitored made this whole meeting dangerous. Not to mention the trial that I just went through a little over an hour ago.

"You did well today," Arithi began. "I've not seen such a gifted wielder in many decades. Especially not one as young and inexperienced—" her hands traced the armrest, "—as you." Her eyes locked onto mine. "Very few outside the Luna Tribe have been able to use the shields you used today." She left her statement hanging as if it were a harmless accusation.

"I had a good teacher," I replied.

She smirked. "Indeed. Perhaps we'll have Vala start training all the new recruits. But I have to say, the fire-wielding you did...Vala doesn't possess such a gift."

I could feel it then, the probing at my mind. I reinforced my mental walls, brick by brick, just like Vala taught me, and then tried to enact a shield around me, but the shield didn't form.

"The runes, my dear, won't allow for shields. There's a reason we sometimes debrief in these rooms. It allows for more...transparency." She smiled as she said the last word.

I remained silent, willing my heartbeat to slow. Memories of the last time I was interrogated, of a cold stainless-steel chair and white room, assaulted me.

"I'm not sure I understand." I squeezed my hands together and tried to focus on the female in front of me and not the hellish memories of the past.

"I think we both know that's not true," Arithi spoke each word slowly. "For example, the runes on this chair allow me certain heightened gifts. Temporary, if only for a brief moment, but ever so *enlightening*. Do you know much about runes?"

I reinforced my mental walls again and pictured a brick blockade protecting my bond with Aether. "No, I can't say that I do. They don't really teach much about magic in the Glenn."

Arithi nodded, an eerie smile still claiming her face. "Runes are like magical power bursts; I think of them as borrowed magic. They can do many marvelous things. Add strength and fire, provide protection, like a shield, and not just a physical shield, but one that can block powers. Have you noticed anything strange since you entered? Aside from not being able to form shields?"

I paused mentally, taking stock of my body. I felt blanketed, quieted.

"The doorframe has blocking runes that prevent the use of power such as fire and shifting. In here, you and I may as well be mortal. Well, that is if there weren't *other* runes also in here." She caressed a large mark embedded in her chair's forearm. "This one," she chuckled dryly, "now this one allows its user to sense magical bonds and essences. Mind you, I can't read thoughts, but I can *feel* the presence of magic. And this rune," she gestured to one on the other side, "this one allows me to feel the depth of magic. The stores. And you know what, Tate?"

I swallowed, stepping back toward the bolted door.

"Your stores are deep. Unnervingly deep. Not to mention, mixed... ancient, dark, and yet, somehow bright." Arithi's eyes got a distant look as she focused on something, and the knot in my stomach doubled.

"I'm lost," I said as I tried to feign a calm demeanor. "This is all new to me. Magic, runes, powers...I didn't even know this existed until a couple of months ago."

"That may be so, but the power you demonstrated today confirmed what was already suggested about you, my child. As these runes also do so now. You are not normal."

"Is that supposed to be an insult?" I tilted my head at her and took a step forward.

"Please, you think I didn't crosscheck your blood to make sure you had the Untish gene? Of course we did. Especially since Irene was always so cagey about you. I'd had my suspicions, but after initially meeting you and realizing you had zero knowledge of your magic, I brushed the thought off as paranoia. I didn't look any further, at least not at first." She paused, caressing a rune with her left finger. "But what we found once I started digging was a bit alarming." She sighed and pulled her hands from the chair, eyes slitted as they settled on me. "Who are your parents, Tate?"

Her question startled me. This was a new direction, something I wasn't ready to confront. So similar to my first encounter with this female...

"As I've said *before*, Irene was my mother and she never spoke of who my father was." I knew he had to be of royal descent given my bloodline, but that wasn't something I'd share with her.

"Yes, so we thought. And your father, Irene truly never spoke of him?" Arithi asked, toying with me.

"I believe that's what I just said."

She snorted. "You see," she idly stroked another rune on her chair, "I thought it must've been Claus, he and Irene were close and stationed together in the Glenn, including around the time she would've gotten pregnant with you..." She paused. My heart pounded in my chest at the name of my potential sire. "But your DNA didn't match his. And that was odd."

I stared at the cruel female in front of me, noting the way her eyes lit up with clear amusement at my discomfort. "My heritage seems to be of great importance to you for you to waste time and resources on me," I bit out.

"It is, more than you know. Silly, isn't it, the people we trust?" Her statement was yet another misdirection.

"Excuse me?"

She smiled, a predator playing with its prey. "You see, I might've let it go had I not received a tip that perhaps there was more to you... strongly suggesting that we should *dig*. And so, we did. Funny thing about digging, you can uncover some pretty gnarly bones." Her fingers landed on a new rune and tightened. "Your DNA did *not* match any male DNA in our records, but more intriguingly, it didn't match Irene's."

My breath caught as the room seemed to slow. Surely Arithi was fucking with me.

"I can tell from your face that this is news to you," she mocked me with a placating look. "Please, sit and allow me to tell you more."

I looked to the chair covered in runes. She wanted me to sit—there had to be a reason why. I should be focusing on that, instead all I could think of was that Irene may not be my biological mother.

"Tate, more information can make you sick and you already look quite pale. Please, have a seat, now," Arithi commanded as she gestured to the chair once again.

"How do I know this is real?" I asked. "That you're not lying about my mother?"

"Dear, why on earth would I do that?" She pursed her lips.

My chest heaved as stars filled my vision.

Irene. Not my mother? The female with eyes so unlike mine, who never shifted in front of me, who shielded me from so much...

I recalled the other female in the vision I saw months ago, in the warehouse, the one made of pure flames. She was not Irene, and yet the familiarity of her voice...

A voice that was so similar to the female who'd been holding a younger version of myself, the one I'd seen while I'd been in the pool; how had I not made that connection earlier?

"I don't...I don't understand," I whispered.

Arithi said nothing, she simply waited for me to sit. Frustrated, I took a step forward and lowered myself onto the seat.

The sting was instant. The chair lit up and glowed bright pink and with it, Arithi's eyes widened.

"It's true then." Her mouth slackened, and she trembled. "You're royal."

I sat there, stunned at my own stupidity. How could I have sat down?

"I'll need to notify Mydant immediately, Your Highness. You mustn't tell anyone of this and will stay here, under my care, until we can secure your safe passage to Mydant." Arithi stood and strode for the door, nose curled in a snarl as she walked.

"That won't be necessary, I'm no one," I feigned. If only I could make her believe that.

"Dear girl, that may be true in many ways, but alas, your blood entitles you to certain power that some would kill for. There's a reason your line does not dwell here in *this* realm." She swallowed and then bowed, a shallow and stiff motion.

I sat there, frozen and unsure what to do.

"I'll have the guards escort you to secure chambers," she said.

Before I could respond, she left, but I didn't miss the ice building in her eyes or the way her hands shook.

Aether...she knows.

The fear and rage I felt in response chilled my very soul.

CHAPTER 52

AETHER

Enzo sat behind his desk, legs propped up and hands behind his head.

"You really expect me to believe it's a coincidence that they tested Tate with those beasts?" Frustration gnawed at me. Tate had been silent for far too long. Whatever questioning was occurring was not standard.

"No, I don't. But most of the chairs believe it was just a test that went too far, got carried away in the name of preparing for impending war. Arithi has confirmed her Head Commander became overly enthused and crossed a line, something she has made clear she will remedy."

"And that's it?!" I exclaimed, flames pouring from my hands and scorching the stone walls nearest me before I pulled them back.

"No, there will be a meeting with the Iron Head Commander and *all* the chairs will pass judgment. What occurred today was reckless and caused unnecessary death. Carly nearly died."

"And how do you think that Carly, the only friend Tate has in her class, ended up in there? She's a Liver!"

He raised his hands, placating. "I know. We're looking into it."

"Not good enough." I took a challenging step forward. "That *thing* declared they were intended to uncover who Tate is. I'm convinced Arithi must know, or at the very least, highly suspects." A wave of dark matter surrounded me, matching my mood. I didn't have time for this, especially as I felt new apprehension rising from Tate through the bond.

"The chairs are conducting a thorough investigation into how those *things* were added—we're interviewing everyone who had a hand in the event, both planning and participating. If Arithi was involved and is lying to us, we'll find out. It would be grounds for her dismissal as Regent."

I gave him a deadpan look. We both knew Arithi would sooner kill her High Commander to cover her tracks than relinquish her seat.

Another pang flashed down the bond from Tate, shock and disbelief coated my tongue.

"Is that why Tate is being debriefed with magic measuring?" I hated that I could feel her turmoil. Hated that someone was searching for magic stores and bonds. Even if it was in the name of uncovering the responsible party. I was just grateful each tribe handled its own debriefs amongst its own members.

Enzo's eyes widened. "I didn't authorize that. She should be with Juda, being debriefed without the meddling of magic."

Fuck. There was only one other person who could override a Tribal chair: the regent.

"I need to go."

"You can't barge in there. It will only complicate things for Tate, give Arithi grounds to detain her under suspicion." Enzo locked the air around my feet and suspended me.

I snarled.

"I know." He raised his hands. "You're mated and *we're* sworn to protect her, but trust me, you going now will only worsen things."

I tugged at the air and whipped it from my feet before reaching out and suspending Enzo in his chair. "I will not leave her to Arithi."

"I wouldn't ask you to. In fact, you both need to leave, tonight. It's the only way to keep her safe at this point. Do not return until we're called back to Mydant."

I released Enzo, who gracefully re-manipulated the air around himself and lowered slowly to his desk. He bent over, unlocked a drawer that was bound with runes, and then pulled out a satchel and tossed it to me.

"I'll send Juda to collect Tate when her questioning is done. She will bring her safely to the Night Tribal quarters, and you two will need to depart immediately—her life depends on it."

Another wave of panic from Tate, bordering on pain, crashed into me.

"Fuck that, I'll go get her now."

"No!" Enzo rose from his desk, alarm written across his features. "Regardless of what Arithi discovers about Tate's heritage, she would never act directly against Tate. It would be treason; she'd be signing her own death sentence. After *your* display of flames today, concealing the dome, some of the chairs have voiced concern about your involvement in the testing—suggesting that you played a role in adding the beasts."

"You mean Arithi accused me," I snarled. I'd known there would be consequences for my choices but fuck they complicated things.

"Aether. Given that Arithi wants you questioned by the chairs, if you step foot into the Iron Tribe's debriefing room or jurisdiction, she will have you detained. If Juda goes, and waits for the questioning to end, then Arithi will have no grounds to stop her."

My chest heaved. I wanted nothing more than to storm in there, kill any who got in my way, and rescue Tate from Arithi's talons. But he made sense. I hated it, but he was fucking right.

His pupils returned to their normal size, and Enzo nodded. Apparently, I was easy to read. He gestured to the satchel.

"What's this?" I opened it and peeked inside, grateful that my restless hands had something to do.

"I held onto it for Her Majesty, Esme. She knew her time was limited, especially after the first attempt on her life. She asked me to hold onto this and return it to her or the rightful heir upon their rise to Mydant. After she and the baby were assumed lost, I merely hid it and held it as a form of honor. I wouldn't have dug it up had Tate not returned to us."

Impossible.

I unclenched my hands, willing my nerves to steel. "You expect me to believe that Tate is related to Esme? Esme was pregnant and expecting *seventy* years ago. Legend has it that her babe was born when she was fleeing and that neither survived the attack on the cliffs." My chest burned at the thought of Tate being hunted like Esme had been. "It's far more likely Tate's dad was of royal descendant, a cousin or half-cousin of the crown, someone who stayed at the Embassy without being noticed."

Not to mention that it was incredibly rare for Esme to have a successful pregnancy at her age—few ever even achieved pregnancy once they passed a hundred years, let alone at two hundred and thirty-two.

"My boy, you and I both know the power she wields could not be from a watered-down bloodline holding a faint connection."

"Magic is its own entity," I countered. "How are we to know anything!?" I was unwilling to truly consider what he suggested.

"Esme's journal is in there as well. Along with a certain necklace from the archives; it's listed as belonging to Irene, but I think we both know that's not the case. And the photograph I think Tate will find... important. She and Esme share many physical similarities." He paused. "Not many know this, but when Esme fled, the Luna Tribe chair, Lux at the time, along with myself, honored Esme's wishes and washed the memory of her appearance and whereabouts from all those here at the Embassy. A reframing spell. Many know of Esme, but only Lux and I remember what she actually looked like. That is the only remaining photograph of Esme found here on Shappa."

A calmness settled over the bond from Tate, and I took a deep reassuring breath at that.

I shook my head. "I'll bring it because it belonged to Esme and is

Tate's by her connection to the Crown, but not because Esme is her mother."

"Aether," he said placating. "Look at the picture."

I grunted and with a sigh, I opened the satchel and located the picture. It was next to the locket Arithi had dangled in front of Tate's face back in the Glenn, the one Tate had longed to keep. I'd be proud to give it back to her. Slipping the photo out, I stared at it. Frozen, if only for a moment, by the striking similarities. Esme had the same facial symmetry as Tate, and her eyes...they were identical to Tate's.

"I may be old, but I am wise," Enzo began as he bridged his fingers together. "I know you're well educated; you know about the prophecy—"

I silenced him, constricting the air around his throat.

"I don't believe in prophecies," I snarled. A moment later I released him.

We both stayed silent for a long moment. My eyes, of their own accord, lowered to the photo. The resemblance was irrefutable.

"This doesn't prove anything," I warned.

"Perhaps, it will offer more comfort than proof, at least for Tate." He swallowed and ran a hand over his tired face. "Aether, I have been watching Labs and Research. They've pulled Tate's DNA. They ran it against every male Untishee in our database along with Irene's, and you know what they found?"

I didn't and wasn't sure I wanted to.

"Not a single match. Not even Irene."

My stomach dropped. Fate kept dealing Tate an unbearable hand. She had just listened to me recount the birth of my daughter with my late wife and previous bonded. How much could a person take? It wasn't fair. Wasn't right.

"They tried to compare against royal bloodlines, but thanks to Esme's warning before she fled, I deleted those from the database here. Only those in Mydant can access royal DNA logs. But my dear nephew, *Arithi* knows about Tate. They just don't have the proof...yet. You must leave tonight."

My grip tightened on the bag. "I'll take her and we'll—"

"Go to the location written on that parchment," he raised his hand as he interrupted. "I do not even know its location as it's hidden in runes and only a drop of royal blood can activate it. Once the location is revealed, the beacon will be ignited, and the direction will become plain." He sighed. The sound was wet from the blood rising in his throat. "Do not tell me. They will come for me, and I cannot know."

The realization hit me. He knew that when we left, Arithi would seek answers. They would interrogate. This could be the last time I ever saw the male.

"Come with us."

"No, I've lived a good life here. A long life. It is an honor to help a member of the royal line. Especially, if it's connected to the prophecy." He held up a hand and beseeched me with his eyes to not strangle him again. "And it is an honor to have kept my promise to Esme."

I could see the resolve in his eyes.

"Tate should be free from questioning any moment now. Go. Juda will bring her to you, but you must move quickly."

I nodded and bowed in reverence to the male who'd been more of a father to me than my own. "May Mother Blood be with you."

I raised from my bow and then exited. I would honor him with a warrior's exit.

CHAPTER 53
TATE

I stepped out of the chamber and guards surrounded me, ushering me down a hallway.

"She's all mine, boys," a familiar voice called out.

"Ma'am, we have orders—"

"It's *high general* to you. Practice it with me. High gen-er-al," she said each part of the pronunciation with emphasis that belittled the guards, guards who had the good sense to look embarrassed. "I said she's mine. The chair himself sent me. Be gone," she commanded. Her white-blonde and black hair had been recently cut to a point, the longest black tip barely reaching her sharp chin on the right side. The left side of her head had been shaved. Gone were her long braids. Now, half her hair was black while the roots remained pale blonde.

The guards looked at each other and then left after a moment of hesitation.

"Come with me," Juda commanded.

"Yeah, no thanks." I turned to leave, but she gripped my arm and yanked it behind my back, pressing my face against the wall.

"I'm Juda, high general of the Shadow Tribe, House of Shadows, and leader of Darklings. You will come with me." Her pressure increased for a moment. "I don't know why our chair thinks you're important and worthy of my escort instead of some grunt, entry-level Untishee, but I'm here and dammit you're going to come with me." She released the pressure but kept my arm behind my back as she began escorting me down the hallway.

"I don't wish to stay in Ironhead housing." I sounded pitiful, and I hated it.

Aether, where are you?

Waiting. Go with Juda.

Frustration filled my veins, but I did as I was told and let the beastly woman lead me through the hall.

"Here?" She tsked. "We're going to the Shadow Tribe, sweetheart."

I yanked my arm free, and sidestepped her, earning an alarmed, but appreciative look before walking beside her. "I can walk myself." I tilted my chin up. Where was this coming from?

The logical side of my brain knew I'd just received life-altering news. Irene was not my biological mother. Arithi knew I was royal. I was utterly fucked. So perhaps I was lashing out?

I huffed a dry laugh.

Shae would know or have some insight. Pain stabbed my heart at the thought of my best friend. A friend I had abandoned. I would go back for her, I promised myself I would return for Shae, and now I could. I would.

"This way," Juda said as she turned down one hallway and then another.

I followed her as we entered an outside courtyard. She moved in the shadowed alcoves until we reached another tunnel. I kicked at a large pebble and watched it bounce freely, as I followed the large-footed female.

We entered yet another courtyard, this one darker than before, and headed for the stairs at the back. Juda stopped abruptly and put a fist in the air, a moment later she had my back against a pillar with a shield in place. Bullets rained down, biting into the stone and mortar at my back.

"Keep your pretty head down!" Juda spoke as she returned fire, temporarily lifting her shield to do so.

Panic filled my veins. Arithi hadn't even known about me for an hour and already I was being shot at?

"Backup requested in the Shadow Tribe's main square. One shooter. Sniper," Juda called into the comms at her shoulder.

I'm coming, now.

I had no words, just pure fear. It swallowed me as Aether's emotions mixed with mine and flooded my system.

Shield! he commanded.

I closed my eyes and pictured a shield. I then willed it into a dome. A moment later I could hear the *ping!* of bullets hitting the barrier.

"Nicely done, can your shield move with you?" Juda asked.

"I think so."

"Think? Not good enough. Yes or no, Aaralyn?"

"Yes."

"Good, then don't drop it." She surveyed the shield, moving her foot slightly and the bubble followed. Pleased, she gave a tight nod. "We take it slow, and you do as I say," she commanded.

I nodded.

"Follow me step for step. Left!" she barked. I stepped left with her. "Right!" I stepped right, behind another pillar.

We continued until we reached the stairs which were, thankfully, empty.

"Down, two at a time!" She leapt down while holding my elbow. I followed her, barely keeping my feet under me, until we reached the bottom, nearly losing my footing as we landed. Damn my uneven legs and her colossal strides.

The hallway was also empty. A few more turns and we made it to the 'safe room'.

"Roger," she spoke into her comms. "Secure. Awaiting the High Commander and then I'll join you in the hunt."

I swallowed. Hunt. I was being hunted.

"I owe you an apology," Juda said.

I blinked several times. "What?"

"I shouldn't have questioned my chair's choice of guard. I should have been more careful."

I stared. "It's all right."

She nodded and then turned and faced the door, weapon trained on it.

Almost there, Aether's reassuring voice filled my mind.

Isn't that your motto?

I sent a quick image of him struggling to come, thrusting and face turning red with effort.

Really, darling, at a time like this?

I smirked in return, even as my nerves fired rapidly. Humor was ever the good defense.

"Why use guns? I mean with the sheer amount of power I've seen trainees using, I imagine an assassin would have even more available to them?" It had been bothering me since the first bullet missed.

"Because anyone can use a gun. You use power? Magic? It's a calling card and practically identifies you," Juda snorted. "Cowards. All of them."

I sniffed, the dust in this room made my eyes itch. A loud crash from the hallway outside sounded and then a body came flying through the door. Dressed in solid brown. Hooded.

Juda fired at the corpse repeatedly, but it didn't so much as twitch. Aether appeared behind it, shield already blocking Juda's bullets now trained on him.

"Enough, it's me," Aether growled. He moved into the room protectively, stepping over the body, and pulled me into a tight embrace. We didn't speak for a moment. His hand tightened on my head as he inhaled my scent deeply.

"Right, my team has one other assassin. Dead. In brown," Juda spoke interrupting my stupor.

"Brown? That's not one of the House colors?" I voiced.

"That's kind of the point. Harder to identify." Juda rolled her eyes. "Real bright one, this one."

"Watch how you speak about her," Aether growled, hand at Juda's throat, magic restraining her body.

"Why?" Juda sneered at him, hate simmering in her eyes.

Aether's grip tightened and Juda started to turn red.

"Enough." I placed my hand on Aether's shoulder. "She saved my life, even if she's being rude, that's her prerogative. Come on now, no more overprotective brute, remember?"

He released Juda and she dropped to her feet before spitting at the ground, mere inches from Aether's boots. "I'll ensure the grounds are secure, but I don't need to tell you that your house is likely compromised since you've been shacking up with that one."

Dear blood, Juda had a death wish.

"Aether." I met his wave of power with one of my own, blocking Juda.

She raised a brow at me and actually smiled. "Perhaps I misjudged you." Without another word, she strode confidently through the door.

"We leave, now." Aether cupped my face with his large hands, his lips a mere breath away. "I promise you this, I'll get you out alive."

CHAPTER 54

CHANCE

I sat in a room much like the one I woke up in when I discovered the horrid thing I'd become. Only this time, I didn't feel like a vile creation. I felt oddly justified. I could be a monster if it meant sparing the world from those beasts.

Holland had left a while ago and...I was thankful for the reprieve. She supported me, no matter what, but I could see she was unnerved.

I inhaled. For the first time in a while, I wasn't being suffocated by her tempting scent...by the desire to consume.

"We'll start small and work our way up," Doctor Worshah instructed. The room was empty, save for the two of us. My father had other things to attend to, and after his display, he stalked away smugly. More powerful than I'd ever imagined.

In many ways, I felt like the small boy I once was. Admiring his father, fearing his sire, desiring his approval.

"In order to strengthen your internal power and feed your newly awakened magic, we need to give it fuel. So, you simply need to siphon." Doctor Worshah looked at me through thick, smudged glasses.

"Understood," I replied. I could sense my magic awakening as if sparking in anticipation. "How do I do that?"

"You've done it before; you'll figure it out. Just follow its pull."

I nodded and approached the door he'd indicated. Slowly it slid open, I stepped inside—alone. It was a double-door system. One I'd once thought was used for only the most dangerous of prisoners. I never would have imagined it would be used to cage beasts of our own making.

The door slid shut behind me and for a moment there was nothing. It was just me in a small, confined chamber. The only sound was my breath, pouring through tight lips. Odd how I found it comforting.

Golden sun-kissed skin shown from beneath a black tank top. Blonde hair in a high pony tickled her back as she looked at me from behind her shoulder—mahogany eyes piercing my own.

"Coming?" she asked.

"What do you think?" I retorted, my blond curls falling in my face.

She winked at me before stripping out of her jeans and then pulling off her tank. Her bright pink bikini barely covered her generous swells.

"Ladies first," I said gesturing.

"Chicken," she teased before taking an uneven step to the cliff's edge. The pool of water below was deep, at least twenty feet. It was dangerous, but highly unlikely to be fatal...for us. "See you down there." Her feet left the edge as she threw herself into a freefall and squealed.

She was fearless.

I shook my head at the memory. The door in front of me clicked and as it opened, the door to my past closed. Tate was no longer that free-spirited girl I fell in love with. She was the enemy. She not only lied to me, but she'd lied to her country—betraying us all. Even if she, like me, hadn't known about her *true* wells of power, when she fled with the enemy she chose *him*. Yes, it was time to forever close the door to my past.

Tatealia Aaralyn was a traitor to the Glenn.

Inside the room, I could hear the scratching of claws, the snapping of jaws. Seethings. I stepped into the eerie space.

It was dimly lit and inside there were three beasts, restrained by metal chains at each of their four feet. They looked at me like I was dinner. Pure beast, that's what they were. Whatever and whoever they'd once been, they were no more.

A click sounded behind me, and I was sealed in—this was the fate that awaited me. I swallowed back the nerves and allowed the magic within to surface.

Red lit up the stone walls and reflected from the beasts' black eyes. They were relatively small compared to some I'd seen. I reached out toward them, and I could *feel* their magic within. It was untethered, swirling within their skin but undirected. With a simple tug at the beast nearest me, its energy ripped from its skin and flew into my hands.

The moment it entered my system, I staggered back. It was darkness. It was wrong. It was manipulated and borrowed and not natural.

But it was mine.

I closed my eyes as I engulfed the energy. Unlike the last time I'd siphoned from seethings in the pit, this was intentional—I wasn't enraged, but fully in control of my willful actions. My internal pit began to fill, eating up the power and transferring it to my magical stores.

More.

Without hesitation, I reached out to the other two and pulled. Their energy hit me in twin streams and the room became engulfed in red bolts of lightning. It flared as I siphoned their power, pulsed, and then the flow stopped. Their magic was empty. There was nothing on the ground but small, scaley husks. I'd drained them fully.

"Well done, how do you feel?" Doctor Worshah's voice filtered through the room's sound system.

"Starving."

HOURS HAD PASSED and I'd graduated from small seethings to larger ones. The last dozen had been a foot taller than me; even so, draining them had been easy. Too easy. My nerve endings fired rapidly as I paced down the hallway toward the outer courtyard.

I felt oddly sated and yet, ravenous. Perhaps I was becoming an addict.

Control. I needed to master this and not become its puppet. Doctor Worshah suggested mastery came with practice and time, and that I should take a break and get some fresh air. From the laughter sounding beyond the doors, I could see what he intended: practice with temptation.

Shae sat on a bench with her head tilted back in laughter, eyes tightly closed with tears slipping out. Her roots had grown out more—darker even. Carran's hearty laugh encased hers as he stood behind Shae looking at Holland who was, in fact, the source of their entertainment.

Her small frame was gesturing wildly, a smile on her lips. Joy blossomed in my heart, and I allowed it to smother the accompanying feeling of envy.

Family. They were family. It was to protect them that I would become this vile thing.

Danger. Destruction. Death.

The words coursed through me as fear gripped my heart. These dear people could be easily killed by those beasts. Milky scales, silver talons, fire-breathing beasts that could shred through Shae's fair skin. They'd devour Holland's small frame, and even Carran would be no match for their flames.

My body began to shake as fear took over.

They would not die—I refused to allow it.

Holland's eyes snapped to mine through the window and she motioned me out. I could do this; I was in charge—not my power. I pushed open the door and stepped into the fresh air.

"Ach! There he is! The supermale Holland won't shut up about!" Carran joked as he moved closer to Shae in a protective stance. The last time he'd seen me I was siphoning from Shae.

"Chance!" Shae exclaimed as she shot to her feet. She looked good. Thinner than before all this shit went down, but healthy.

"Come sit with us," Holland said. Her eyes were far too keen, as if she could sense the battle within.

Shae too waved me over, her steel-blue eyes trusting. How I earned that trust, I'd never know. I was nothing short of a bastard.

Still...I took a step closer, mentally checking the walls that encased my power. The gate was locked down—hard.

Shae's scent hit me in the face. *Ice. Power. Exciting.*

I could recall the flavor of her magic. So much purer than those vile beasts I'd spent the day siphoning. Her mere scent filled my gut more than draining a dozen beasts did. Perhaps just a taste...

A calming breeze reached my internal war—its honeyed scent quieted all thoughts.

Holland.

I locked eyes with hers and she nodded, gesturing to the seat beside her. I swallowed back my own self-hate and moved to stand near her. Not too close, but not too far—even from a few feet away I could sense her ancient power. It was known and yet foreign. Unlike Shae's, it was purely untethered, and I knew a taste from Holland would never be enough—I'd consume her.

I locked the gate down further even as sparks formed at my fingertips.

"You good, boy?" Carran asked, his hand resting on the hilt of his club.

"Fine," I snapped. Sweat poured from my brow.

Just a taste...

"Holland tells us you've been training. How's our new secret weapon going?" Shae teased. "I'm told you will single-handedly save the Glenn."

"It's going. Draining," I said not finishing the thought. It was draining for the vessels I emptied and still, somehow, tiring for me.

"Good. I knew you'd master this." Shae's eyes shown with pride. How the fuck could she look at me like that?

I cleared my throat. "Shae, listen, I...I'm so sorry. I never meant to hurt you, and I swear it won't happen again."

Carran's eyes narrowed on the pebbles of sweat dripping down my cheek. "No, it won't."

"Chance, I'm fine. We all are." Shae pulled out her disk. "Hey, so the disk I had in the base attack was fried, along with all the footage I was deciphering for the mole hunt. But I got my backup and I've been trying to hack that footage again, but obviously, things have dramatically intensified around here, and the new Internal Intelligence Team is kicking my *arse*. I haven't been able to break through, yet. But I will and—"

"Shae, let it go," I commanded with a half-smile, trying to soften the blow.

"What? No, I was so close—"

"Shae, it doesn't matter. We know it was an attack from the Fern. We know Tate was working with Mardi and his team to infiltrate. Right now, we have more pressing things to consider. To prepare for. The Fern is developing their own beasts, that's our concern right now."

"You just want me to give up?" Disbelief covered her features.

"For now," Holland said rubbing my back with her hand in reassurance. "The things we've seen Shae, it's bad. Our focus needs to be on preparing for possible war."

I nodded, grateful for Holland. Shae opened her mouth and then shut it, clearly annoyed but accepting.

"We may get to kick more arse, little lassy! Maybe you can show me how you use your drone to eliminate the scum!" Carran shouted, returning to his merry mannerism. I knew whatever relationship he had with Shae was purely platonic. But I also knew he'd protect her. Odd how things have evolved.

Shae simply nodded. "I'd love to show you." Her eyes lifted to mine. "I just got word from Nora. They just arrived at HQ. She mentioned there's concern of an attack. If you get sent there, bring me with you?"

"I'll see what I can do," I responded.

Shae adjusted her jacket, and a cream piece of parchment fell out. Bending over to pick it up for her, I could see a worn envelope. Shae's name was scrolled across it. The handwriting was undeniably Tate's.

"What's this?" I asked.

She did this. She made you this.

My grip tightened on the worn paper. I swallowed back hate even as my eyes saw nothing but red...

"Oh, nothing. I'll take that back, Chance." Shae reached for it, but I lifted it out of her reach.

Was Shae in on this, too? Was she an accomplice?

My veins began to thrum with renewed energy, I could sense the fear in Shae that only increased her icy scent...so tempting.

Carran stepped closer to me and began to unsheathe his club. Holland gasped even as a red bolt began to dance in front of me, directed at Shae.

Enemy. Traitor. Manipulator.

"Control!" Holland spoke, her voice cutting through the cloud of rage. What was I doing? I didn't even know what the letter said.

I tore it open and my jaw clenched at the familiar handwriting.

Shae,

I'm so sorry. I wish I could explain, but I have to leave—it's the only way to keep you safe. Please forgive me. You must leave immediately, the guara is not who they say they are. It's not safe—

My anger flared and the electricity zapped the letter, igniting it in flames before I could finish reading it. Tate warned Shae?

"Shae, why didn't you show me this sooner?" I snarled.

My hip buzzed—several of our disks went off.

"Shit," Holland spoke as she looked to Carran who nodded.

"What?" Shae asked.

I looked at the message. It was a red alert. HQ was under attack.

CHAPTER 55

TATE

We'd been flying for hours. Once again, I was in Aether's clutches. It was just us in the sky—the silent companion to our quiet journey.

When we'd first fled, he'd asked for a drop of my blood and placed it on a parchment that swallowed it in pink flames: a beacon, he said. It would lead us to safety. Safety from the threats at the Embassy, my homeland, where I was now being hunted.

The forest below grew denser as we continued our flight. I had no idea where we were going. After seeing the assassin in brown, my whole world had shifted. My inner beast was simmering, but still not ready to make an appearance. Ironic, seeing as mere hours ago she was begging to be freed, and now? Now, she was coiled in on herself, quiet rage radiating from her.

I exhaled, inhaled, and exhaled again; rhythmic breathing designed to calm. I'd been mulling over Arithi's words forwards, backwards, and inside out. I kept looking for an alternate explanation—that Irene *was* my mother, and Arithi was gravely mistaken. She had to be wrong. And yet...

Irene's eyes were green. Mine were mahogany.

387

We both had blonde hair, that's true, but was that enough? I tried to recall what her nose looked like...did it tilt up slightly as mine did? Were her earlobes free as mine were? Did she have a splatter of freckles like I did?

The air whipped past me, and I was grateful that Aether didn't try to block it. I liked its feel, savored the bite of it—a reminder that I was alive.

Living.

Aether banked left and began to lower toward a valley surrounded by gargantuan pine trees. They were easily twelve feet in radius at the base of their massive redwood trunks. Ferns covered the canyon walls, and I could see various rivers branching out below.

Vibrant.

Slowly, Aether approached the ground. I became acutely aware that the silence, along with the space to think, was soon going to vanish. In mere moments, I'd have to talk about it all—Ruby, my mother, Arithi. All the things I wanted to avoid.

All the things.

ALL of them.

Aether's taloned feet sank into the valley's floor, and its resounding shudder testified to his presence. He heaved deep breaths; each one heating the space and had his chest moving closer to the talons holding me in place. Below me, the grass swayed and crickets chirped. I closed my eyes and savored the warm sunshine and the faint floral scent that hovered in the moist, misty air.

Aether shifted and almost immediately, my boots hit the lush grass. He held me in his arms, silently reassuring me as he pressed his forehead to mine. Here, it was just us. His nude body was a reminder of how close to our bare essences we truly were.

All around us, nature sang. Our hearts pounded, a steady beat to its song. The chirping of birds, the keys of a piano playing a tranquil tune. The rustling of branches, cymbals in the melody. Creation's music, woven together.

I savored the warmth of Aether's bare skin, pressed tightly against my body. The scent of ash and salt engulfed me, comforted me, quieted me. Home.

He was my home.

Even knowing my heritage had been exposed and that I was actively being hunted, I allowed myself this moment of peace. I wiggled my boots in the grass until they hit the wet dirt beneath, and I savored the way the mud parted for me. The way the grass bent to my will...almost like it *knew* me.

I relished the embrace of Aether, to simply be with him. If just for a moment. His heartbeat pounded against my chest, and his arms tightened around my waist. Once again, I was hit with a wave of passion, love, and appreciation.

My mate.

We stood silently interlocked for several minutes. Our hair was tossed in the breeze of this private valley. Everything was so perfect. Except, it wasn't.

Things were messy. Things were broken. Things needed to be remedied.

"What now?" I asked, looking into his golden chocolate eyes.

"Now, we move. We finally go on the offensive." His eyes darkened as he spoke, and the golden whorls turned.

I smiled. "About damn time."

CHAPTER 56
AETHER

After throwing on a pair of extra trousers I'd kept in the travel tote Tate carried, I led her through the forest and a mile up the mountainside. She followed me, walked beside me, but remained silent. I kept my mouth shut and ignored the presence of the satchel against my side—along with the urgency I could feel building within.

Much had changed.

We would be pronounced as enemies of the state. Any moment now, if she hadn't already, Arithi would hold a meeting—calling us traitors to the Crown, calling for a witch hunt from the very chairs who were sworn to protect Tate. Only, they didn't know that. I was undoubtedly sure that Arithi would bury Tate's bloodline and set Enzo up as a fall man, ensuring his word would be nulled and her mess pinned on him.

She was as meticulous as she was cruel.

I breached the hill, following the beacon on the parchment, the arrow of pink fire that had directed us our entire journey. The closer we moved, the more on edge I became. I could *feel* a powerful presence. Like that of a wall, or a portal, or a veil...

We moved closer, and the presence tripled before an audible buzz filled the air. The arrow pointed straight toward the source of power, whatever it was. I squinted and noted a soft blur—barely noticeable. I extended my hand toward the energy and the sting was immediate, undeniable.

A second veil.

I had assumed this realm had only *one* veil, not two. I was wrong.

I glanced at the parchment, and now in place of an arrow, runes were drawn along with symbols—all in the same pink flame.

I pulled at the surrounding energy and drew the runes in the air before lighting it with black flames. The veil blinked, pulsed, but remained shut. It rejected my runes. I glanced at the parchment, and the same runes burned brightly in pink. Pink fire. Tate.

"I think you have to unlock it," I said.

She simply bit her lip and looked at me. I could feel her apprehension along with her acceptance. More than that, I could feel her courage and anger.

She nodded and then drew the same runes, but they were crafted in her pink flames—a royal's flames. The curtain shuttered and then a doorway opened. I looked at Tate, her eyes wide. Sometimes the truth was easier to swallow in small doses.

I nodded and together, her hand in mine, we walked through.

The instant we cleared the veil, the gate shut. We were secured, sealed in, safe.

"What is this place?" she asked, her voice quieter than usual.

We stood in a large basin, surrounded by cliffs and mountains with a forceful waterfall pooling into a glorious lagoon behind what could only be described as a castle. Ancient stone pillars on top of stone walls stood majestically in front of the glittering falls. Glass walls formed a large part of the castle along with towers upon towers, topped in pointed roofs—each with a large metal spike rising into the sky.

"A haven," I responded. Even I couldn't keep the awe from my voice as I beheld this stronghold. It was glorious.

Tate nodded and released my hand as she strode forward on the stone path. It was elegant, no weeds marred its existence. Everything appeared to be in a frozen state—flowers in full bloom, roses blossomed in bushes that were maintained and trimmed. Her feet padded across the cobblestones as she reached out her fingers to caress the stone railing. It was gloriously free of moss, and roses along with butterflies were etched into it.

The closer to the castle we got, the air became sweeter, and lilacs and roses filled each breath. Royalty's display of power—common in Mydant but unheard of in this realm. The markings and scent were undeniably that of the House of Blush, rulers of the Untish.

Pink roses, flamingo-colored daisies, fuchsia blossoms on bushes; *blush* claimed every object, every space. Even the stone railing had morganite inlaid in it, declaring unrivaled power. Every single detail of this place was majestic.

"I..." Tate began. "This place feels familiar..."

I waited for her to say more, but she remained silent. We made it to the main courtyard and strode past a fountain that had crystal clear water gushing from it, with a basin covered in pink diamonds and morganite. Gold lined the edge of the bowl along with each of the three tiers. Tate extended her fingers to catch a bit of the falling water and to my shock, it *danced* at her touch. A cloud of mist formed, and butterflies made of nothing but water flew in the air before returning to the fountain where they perched.

Amazing.

Tate looked beyond the fountain to the massive iron doors at the entrance. Gargoyles stood perched on either side of the path, eyes flaming red, as we walked and approached the colossal entrance, doors that dwarfed even me. Tate pressed her hand to the rose gold handle and it hummed. Then, of their own accord, the doors swung open.

As her feet crossed the threshold, the place went from dark to gloriously bathed in light. Mage lights lit up the ceiling in bursts of pink. Pink flames poured from the wall sconces as pink sapphires inlaid on the floor began to shine and illuminate the ground. Every step she took, the room got brighter and brighter. This palace wasn't just responding to Tate—this palace was *hers*.

"Aether, this place...I feel it." Tate looked at me, wonder showing in her mahogany eyes.

I nodded. "It was only accessible via your royal blood, so it doesn't surprise me that it's responding to you, even if it is amazing to witness."

She smiled sadly and continued to stroll into the massive room. It was at least twenty feet high and a hundred feet wide. Banners hung on the walls representing each of the seven Houses, with the House of Blush's banner in the center, three times the size of the rest. The mere image of Arithi on the wall representing the Iron House made my skin crawl.

"Maybe I should check the palace out first, just to be sure there's no one else—"

"No." Tate put up her hand, silencing me. "We do this together."

I swallowed before continuing forward. It would take hours to explore and properly sort through the entirety of this castle. I reached within and pulled at my power, willing it to explore the palace—to detect any other magic or life forms.

Immediately, I felt a shocking jolt of power, but further assessment confirmed what I suspected—it came from the palace walls itself. This place was doused in magic. I felt no other forms of power, no life forms aside from the potent magic that coated every inch of this structure.

We went from room to room, passing through a large dining hall that could easily seat two hundred, and a smaller dining hall that could still accommodate at least seventy-five. Each held a large mahogany table with chairs composed of gold and blush cushions surrounding it. Large windows graced nearly every room and not a single item had dust on it.

Tate gasped as we entered the largest library I'd ever seen. It easily competed with that of Mydant's royal tomes. Bookshelves lined the entirety of the place, three stories high. It fed from room to room, to room. Each with the same enormity of tomes and scrolls, books old and new. Tables were scattered throughout, cozy but large enough for a small conference, with pink mage lights hovering above each one. A large hearth filled each room, lit with pink flames. Large cream rugs covered the mahogany floors and fat chaises with thick cushions were sprawled throughout, each with a cream or pink blanket on it.

"Mother Blood," I whispered. I wasn't much of a reader, never made time for it outside of the mandatory reading, but this place made me want to change that. I wished to read for pleasure.

Tate laughed as she heard my thoughts. With our bond and her growing mastery of her magic, there would be no secrets. Ever. A fact I was more than okay with.

"I've never seen so many scrolls," Tate spoke as she ran her fingers across several tomes on a shelf. "Aether, some of these date back to a thousand years ago...the amount of knowledge here is staggering. I mean, it's pure power."

My appreciation for my mate grew even further. Even after all she's endured, the lies she'd been told, the truths she'd confronted—and still must face—she found wonder in simple things like old scrolls. I smiled, confounded and speechless.

Tate continued to walk through the library, room to room, occasionally climbing a ladder to reach the higher shelves on the mahogany bookcases. "I mean, wow. This one dates back to three hundred years prior, and it's all about the history of Shappa. Do you have any idea how many questions this could answer?"

"A lot, I imagine," I mumbled. This place, while awe-inspiring, could easily drain weeks of our time. Time, we didn't have. "We need to keep going, there's much to—"

"Eeeek!" She pulled at a scroll and nearly lost her balance as she yanked it off the shelf, recovering by grabbing one of the rungs on the ladder. She jumped down, mildly faltering, and extended it to me like it was gold itself. "Aether! This is an actual journal from Perry herself! I've been searching the database for it and *nothinggg*. Not a single authentic, untouched excerpt." Her eyes shown with wonder. "And now I have her very journal!" She squealed, holding the tome close to her heart.

"That's great, I bet this place has more, *much* more, to offer." I placed my hands on her shoulders, drinking her in for a moment. The excitement etched in her large features. The huge smile sprawled across her lush lips—it was one I could drown in. "But we need to finish the tour. If you'd like to stay here, I can—"

"No," she sighed. "I'll come." She shoved the tome in her bag and then reluctantly led the way through the remaining library chambers until we were once again in a large hallway. Windows lined one side, each shaped like an arch, and several held stained glass depictions of various people, all with roses or blush accents.

Every part of this place had been carefully crafted and well maintained. Every detail declared omnipotence.

Hours went by as we meandered through the palace. Room after room of luxury and design that boasted not only wealth but power. Often, Tate would stop and stare at the blatant wealth or admire the intricacy of the décor. We'd made it through the main level, the basement with the dungeons, and most of the upper levels as well. We'd entered the west wing, and I was unsurprised to see it was composed mostly of bedrooms, as was the east.

Tate went to open a door and then abruptly stopped before turning and walking straight to the end of the large hallway, ignoring the rest. She briefly paused outside of a large set of double doors, accented in golden leaves and rubies, before pressing her palm to one. It swung open. Immediately, she stepped inside. Unlike with the other rooms we'd explored, she didn't curiously look around—not even a cursory glance. Instead, she moved with a clear path in mind.

I followed her through the parlor; it was like most of the others, but the sitting area was easily double the size of the rest. Large chaises, tables, and couches filled the room. A shelf with books also graced this lounge, but Tate bypassed it all and went into the adjoining room—yet another entertaining space. This one had a conference table along with what appeared to be a small eating space. No weapons, no threats. As

I'd done with every room we'd entered, I scanned for any possible harm. A balcony was opposite us, large enough to rival the one outside my own home—the perfect place to shift.

But Tate paid no heed to it, not even the large bookcase near the patio door. Instead, she walked into the bedchamber, as if being pulled by an internal string. This obviously was the royal suite. Even with its rich furnishings, the gold inlay four-poster bed, the golden floor with crushed pink sapphires, the rose gold framed doors, Tate ignored it all. She walked straight to a small single door at the back of the room and entered the space beyond.

My breath caught as Tate abruptly stopped, like she'd found what she was searching for.

"This place," she whispered. "I recognize it. It was my home."

I placed my hands on her shoulders—offering the silent support I suddenly understood she needed. Before us was a tiny bed, etched with white lace, and crafted of mahogany wood. It sat in front of a large mural depicting a mother, Esme, holding a small babe. Both had blonde hair, and both had the same-color eyes: mahogany.

CHAPTER 57

TATE

The room called to me. I'd felt it the moment I entered the west wing. Inexplicably, I knew this place. I was meant to find it. I ran my fingers over the small bed, it was cool to the touch. The smooth wood felt oddly familiar, like a piece of me I'd long ago lost. On top of the mattress were cream cushions and sheets along with a small teddy bear. I gasped as my fingers grazed it. It was soft, warm, comforting...known.

I looked up to the mural beyond. The female had blonde hair cascading down her shoulders, ending in brilliant pink. A crown of white and pink sapphires graced her head and her eyes...they were *my* eyes. The shape was undeniably that of my own. Her nose held the same curve mine did and her cheekbones...

I shivered.

I looked identical to her in many, many ways. The babe in her arms was swaddled in a pink lacey blanket and clutched to her chest—the image of love. I recognized this female; I could nearly hear her words echoing in my mind.

"*She won't make it!*" a female voice had cried.

"Yes, she will. She's as stubborn as you. She will be strong enough," a male voice spoke, I could see his shadow forming in the room—

The painting in front of me *moved* and came to life as the memory faded.

"My darling." The female reached out, cupping my face in her gentle hands. *"How you've grown, Tatealia. Blossomed, as I knew you would."*

I couldn't stop the tears from pouring down my cheeks. Esme pulled me into her embrace, no longer holding the babe but instead, she held me.

"This is the truth. It's within you. The heart knows even when the mind doesn't." Irene's words echoed from the female in front of me. Only she wasn't Irene, and she wasn't a stranger.

I pulled her essence into a hug and willed her to hold me, to save me from this truth. But nothing met my hands as the female settled back into the wall once again.

"Follow your truth, Tatealia. Find the chamber." Esme was a painting once more. Holding the babe in her hands.

"Tate?" Aether's voice brought me back, jolted me from my daze. He looked at me, eyes filled with worry. "Tate?" He gently shook my shoulders.

I became aware that I was openly weeping while clutching the small teddy bear. "She's my..." I sniffed, trying to force myself to calm down. "Aether, Esme was my mother."

AETHER HAD SAT by me for hours, rubbing my back and just being a reassuring presence as I processed it all. Princess Esme, of the Embassy and Mydant, was my mother. Impossible, and yet, my reality. I blew my nose into a tissue, ever the picture of composed grace, before tucking my head back into Aether's chest.

"I just don't understand how it's possible." The words left my soul feeling void, empty.

"We knew you came from royal descent, but this is much closer to the throne than I'd suspected. There are ways in which it is possible though, Tate." He continued rubbing my back in idle circles as he nuzzled his chin over my head.

"Yeah?" I snorted. "How?"

"Well." He took in a deep breath. "Ruby. She was cloaked and frozen for nearly ninety years. And then when the time was right, when I was sure James and Uley would be good parents, the right parents, I uncloaked her."

I closed my eyes. This was all so very much. More news, more magic, more learning. I was ignorant and it was beginning to really sting. "How?"

"The cloaking usually has a time restraint, depending on the level of magic being contained and used, it can last for centuries or mere decades. Sometimes it's a set time, while other instances it just needs a trigger. In Ruby's case, it was my blood that broke the cloak." He constricted the air around me in comfort, even as I could feel him swallow. Hear his heart hammering.

"I see." But I didn't understand at all. This was all so foreign to me. "And this is a common practice?"

"It was, a millennia ago. Primarily it was used by the royal bloodline to ensure the right successor, a guaranteed heir, and reduce the risk of bloodshed."

It was barbaric, that's what it was.

"So, let me get this straight. What you're saying is that to prevent fighting over a throne, they'd cloak potential heirs?" My tone was dry.

"Yes," Aether said. "But in my case, it was the only way to save Ruby. I wasn't ready, she wasn't ready. At that time, she was so premature that she would've died. And then, even with medical advancements, I was the one who wasn't ready. She needed two whole parents, not a singular fractured one."

I grabbed his hand tighter and gave it a reassuring squeeze.

"But for you, Tate, there was likely a very good reason why you were," Aether cleared his voice, "cloaked."

I shivered involuntarily. Cloaked. I was suspended in time, frozen, and now I was what, supposed to just pick up where my mother left off? Why the hell was I cloaked? "What happened to Esme?"

"We're not sure. My uncle, Enzo, was close with her. She disappeared, and it was alleged that after an attack, she and her baby had died. I only recently realized the extent of certain…concealed truths." He paused, clearing his throat. "No one really knows what happened to her, just that royals were being hunted at the time by all the Vamps and, as some of us have suspected, by our own—the superstitious, power-hungry Untishee. Esme fled and was never heard from again. She was decreed dead five years later by King Owen and there was a grand funeral procession."

My mother's funeral had happened, and I wasn't there.

Sensing my thoughts, Aether gave my hand a gentle squeeze. "I do have something for you, though." He adjusted, sliding out from under me, so I was sitting on my own, before picking up his dropped satchel and extending it to me. "Inside is a packet my uncle gave me. Esme asked him to keep it safe and give it to her heir." His eyes locked on mine. "It's yours."

I gingerly grabbed the bag, my fingers clinging to its worn leather. Slowly, I opened it. Inside was a journal and a locket. No, not just a locket—*thee* locket. The one Arithi had toted was from Irene, the one she withheld until I had proven myself. Once again, I tried to open it, but it flared and then remained shut. No amount of force would open it.

Disappointed, I looped it around my neck where it could at least be close to my heart.

My skin warmed from its contact.

Next, my fingers brushed the journal.

A journal.

I may yet still have a chance to get to know her, to understand what happened, to learn my father's name. I opened the journal and a photograph fell out. I picked it up and smiled. She was even more beautiful than the painting. She was my mother, Esme.

"Thank you, Aether."

CHAPTER 58

CHANCE

The circuit jostled violently. It veered right and pulled my body back into the old leather seat. I hadn't known this direct line existed. It appears I wasn't high enough on the totem pole to know about it...until now. Holland sat next to me, her head resting on my shoulder. Carran was at the other end of the car with his men and, to my annoyance, Shae. It shouldn't bother me that she'd made a friend. But somehow it *felt* wrong.

Erroneous. Mine. Betrayal.

I shook my head. Territorial bullshit was not who I was.

I unclenched my fist and exhaled. In time, I'd make it right with Shae. When I wasn't a threat to every person in this blasted tin can.

Last time I was on a circuit, we were en route to the S.O. while I was bleeding out. Shae was totally fine, and my biggest concern was a mole hunt with the potential implication of dark magic. I chuckled dryly. How far we'd come in such a short time.

Eight hours. We'd arrive at HQ in eight hours. Little was disclosed about the attack. Well, very little except that it was believed to be the work of the Fern. Beasts had been spotted. I could only hope that

Mother Blood shielded our citizens and that there was something left to protect when we got there.

We should have relocated there the moment the threat was realized—it infuriated me that it took an actual attack to get my father to move his *army*.

Holland nuzzled her head deeper into my shoulder, and her mysterious scent filled my nostrils. Even still, my power merely turned within, but was thankfully quiet. It seemed feeding *did* help sate my desire. That and the pure horror that awaited us at HQ. I needed to preserve my strength. I may very well need to lead a bunch of seethings into battle, and I had zero practice at it.

"I seem to remember a time in a car like this where it was just you and I, and we had a bit of fun," Holland murmured into my arm. She gave it a gentle kiss.

I squeezed her hand in my lap. Much had changed since then. I wasn't afraid to acknowledge what was between us anymore. She was mine and I was hers, even with the beckoning to consume her power— I had found ways to make it tamer and hold it in check. Almost like blending our bodies somehow blended our magic...or in some way, my magic respected hers—even if it did want to devour.

My disk buzzed. A quick glance told me I was summoned to the presidential car.

"Got to go." I stood.

"I'm coming."

"Holland, you weren't summoned. I'll be right back. It's going to be—"

"I'm worried about you, Dale. You seem barely in control. I can *sense* your turmoil, more than in others, and I seem to be able to soothe it. Allow me to come?" Her brown eyes were wide.

How could I deny her?

"Fine, but first sign of trouble and you're back here where I know I can't hurt you." I bit my tongue before I said more.

I could feel my magic awakening, anticipating a feed. Never from Holland. Never.

We stalked past Shae, questions in her eyes, and Carran, suspicion in his. We moved through ten cars until we reached the presidential one. It was, oddly, in the middle but toward the front. I would have guessed it would be at the very front, but evidently, my gut was wrong about a lot lately.

At the head of the car, was my father. Two vessels were at his side with fresh puncture marks. One was in a beautiful haze, her eyes dazed, while the other was painfully aware—fear shown in her eyes. My father liked to do that, reward one vessel with venom for pleasing him and punish the other by giving her none. Sometimes I suspected he'd do it just to fuck with them.

Across from him sat Luina, perched atop a male vessel, and currently partaking in his blood. Next to her was Doctor Worshah, looking immensely pleased with himself for having not one but two vessels, a male and female, that were doting on him—visibly high on his venom.

And lastly, at the back of the car was someone I'd hoped I'd never see again, Rusty. He, naturally, had a scantily clad vessel dressed in patches of black lace perched on his lap, writhing her hips as she played with his lapel. He gripped her ass in both hands.

"You wanted to see me?" They jolted at my voice, oblivious of my entrance, and Rusty shoved the female from his lap, laughing as she crumpled to the floor.

I swallowed back my hate for these people. They were my equals and higher-ranking officers. We were at war. Lines blurred in times like this. The soldier in me knew this even if my soul soured at their mere presence.

"Yes. Luina, please inform Dux Dale and, it would appear, Dux Holland of the news you just shared," my father spoke, sinking deeper into the presidential car's red velvet sofa, bloodwine in hand.

"Reports have identified the attackers as mostly beasts from the Fern with a few vampires among them—in a one to twenty ratio from what we can detect. Our forces are holding strong, our seethings are fighting, and the Northern Outpost arrived a day before the attack.

Together, they are doing well at keeping the enemy at bay." She read off a transmission of numbers and head counts, all while remaining atop the male vessel who was actively sniffing her. "We've lost about a hundred thousand civilians thus far. And their remaining troops are estimated to be around thirty thousand. The majority of which are fire-breathing beasts."

"Fuck," I said.

"This is why we will need you, Dux Dale. We need you to fuel up and feed. We have some...advanced seethings that you will be commanding in battle. But they respond to strength and you, as strong as you are, do not have the brute force or magical stores to command them. That is, as of yet," my father spoke, eyes narrowing on mine. I could feel him looking at me as if he were gauging my stores. "Doctor Worshah said you did very well feeding from seethings, but they don't seem to be fueling you as they should. We believe you may need a different," he paused and swirled his glass, "type of magic source."

"Different?" I asked. Holland looked to me, and I didn't miss the way she swayed a bit from foot to foot. A clear sign of nerves, and that was unlike her.

"Yes," Doctor Worshah answered, keeping a hand on each vessel. "As we briefly discussed before, there are four main sources of magic. We've explored dark magic from the beasts, and that seems to have given you a boost and helped in controlling your appetite, but it's not enough. You need raw, wild magic. We suspect you need *human* magic."

"Excuse me?"

"Don't look so surprised, son. We feed from them to sustain us—" he smirked at the very alert vessel next to him "—and we get more than just nutrients from their blood. With every feed, we get trace amounts of their magic. Just imagine what siphoning them to death can do." He swatted the vessel's ass before extending his hand in clear expectation for her wrist, again. She swallowed but complied. A smile played at his lips as he patted his lap, demanding she sit, and like a damned dog, she did as she was told.

It shouldn't irritate me as much as it did. She was human, beneath us.

"That's against the Glenn's code," Holland spoke up.

"Miss Holland, do not mistake your allowed presence here as an invitation to speak," my father snapped.

"She has a point," I retorted. "Why the fuck do we have rules if we can break them when we want? We are not above the law."

"Don't be naive," he responded. "We *are* the law."

"Damn straight!" Rusty pounded his fist on the side of the metal car wall, purple spit flew from his mouth as he spoke, landing on the floor near his drugged vessel. He was more beast than male at this point.

"What the fuck happened to you, Rusty? Playing with nature's laws too much? Or perhaps, the misguided thoughts that *we* are the law is what drove your actions and turned you into this *hideous* thing," I snapped at Rusty.

His nose flared as he lunged at me and then stopped mid-step. It seemed he hadn't lost all his scruples. He kicked the vessel, earning a sharp cry from her and a gasp from Holland, before sinking back into his seat—glaring at me with hate-filled eyes. He kicked her again and smiled as Holland covered her mouth, visibly uncomfortable with this kind of cruelty. Cruelty I was raised in and knew only too well.

"Dux Dale, you will siphon from humans, or we will not survive. Do you wish to betray your country? To allow civilians to be slaughtered because you have an issue with some of the ethics we employ here?" my father asked.

"It's not that simple," I retorted.

"It actually is. You saw those beasts, those were just a few that we managed to capture. Imagine an army thirty thousand strong. Do you really think the average vampire—one who can be killed by flames—stands a chance?" Doctor Worshah spoke, leveling an admonishing glare at me. "It's frankly remarkable that we've survived as long as we have, even with our seethings. I suspect the Fern is holding back, for what, we don't know but—"

My father cleared his throat, silencing Doctor Worshah.

I exhaled through gritted teeth. The truth was never clear. The right thing was always so damned murky.

"I see you understand our point. But...why wait? Siphon her—" he jerked the alert vessel "—now." He threw her to the floor, still holding her wrist in his hand, and gave me a pointed look.

"Dale," Holland whispered. "She has certain rights; we are to protect—"

"Protect who, Miss Holland?" my father hissed. "Humans—the equivalence of livestock—or our own? Who do you choose, Dux Dale? Do you value this slut's life above that of your country? Your sworn duty to protect? The vamplings in our city who are defenseless?" With every word, my blood boiled. With every implication, the temptation grew, and my magic took new moral ground until I *wanted* to siphon from her.

Her eyes pleaded with me as tears covered her cheeks. "Please, you don't—"

My father's slap silenced her as she flew to the side, crashing into the floor. Blood leaked from her skull. She was already dead.

"Now or never, *son*."

I moved away from Holland and then extended my hands, sending streams of red lightning to probe her body. It was too easy. One moment, nothing. And the next? The next, a tiny aura of white flowed from her and into me. Her body began to crumple in on itself, until it was done. She had nothing left. Guilt filled me as I recalled how mere seconds ago she was full-fleshed and alive, and now was nothing but a husk.

The worst part was, the high felt good. Too good to be remorseful, especially if this was what it took to keep the Glenn safe.

"Doctor Worshah, take Dux Dale back to the containment car," my father commanded before adjusting in a leisurely position next to the other unaffected vessel, still high on his venom. He continued speaking with Rusty and Luina in a calm, unaffected tone.

"Very well," Doctor Worshah began. "Stay," he commanded his

vessels and then headed for the door that led to the cars closer to the engine.

Luįna looked at Holland and smirked. I hadn't forgotten she was the one who ordered Shae's death. She was a hypocrite and a traitor. I would see to it that she was punished accordingly. But first things first, I needed to be powerful. In that, my father was correct. I wasn't nearly strong enough. Even with the small taste from that vessel, she didn't have much to offer. No, I needed my internal power stores to be vast, larger than anyone in this car, even that of my father. If I wanted to stop this war and make a difference, it meant more than simply ending the enemy beyond our borders. It meant cleaning house.

I followed Doctor Worshah, Holland close behind, as we passed through two cars until we entered a heavily guarded third one. Four guaramen stood at attention as we passed. I could sense their fear—both at what lay beyond those doors and at the sight of me. I clenched my jaw as I stepped into the car after Doctor Worshah.

Dozens of vacant faces appeared. Humans, all chained to the side of the car. All being held in violation of the rights that we promised them as residents of the Glenn.

My stomach soured.

The high from moments ago tasted rotten.

Several scrawny humans looked at me through hollow eyes. They were practically unresponsive and young. Much too young to be here; they were barely adults. The fattened humans, too, stared at me, nothing intelligible in their gaze.

They were livestock that had been immobilized.

They were a means to an end.

They were delicious...

Taste.

"Dale, you don't have to do this. I know you value fairness and ethics. It's why we are such a good match. There must be another way," Holland pleaded.

Their magic wafted through the air—free, new, uncertain.

"Holland, you saw what I did. We don't stand a chance against those beasts."

"But are we any better if we violate life and the promised protection for our own citizens?" she questioned.

"They're only human, Holland."

"They're citizens protected by the No-Kill law. You're better than this, Dale." She placed her hand on my shoulder. I could sense her magic; it was nearing her surface. The closer it got, the stronger her scent became.

Old, yet futuristic. Pure power.

I could almost feel part of my own magic in her. The temptation was great.

Feed.

"Get out, Holland. You don't need to see this too," I whispered. "I'm a servant of this country. Right now, we have civilians being slaughtered by walking evil. By beasts. Sometimes it takes a greater monster to end bloodshed," I said as I turned to look at her.

I could see her veins pounding with force as blood flowed through her perfect body. Without hesitation, I placed my hand around her waist and pulled her to me, tipping back her head. Her lips were soft, wet, as mine swallowed them. She tasted like home, but also like something unknown. That was one of the things I loved most about her, she was never simple.

She moaned in my mouth as she fisted my shirt in her hands and intensified the kiss. Her tongue swept in and teased before she playfully nipped at mine. I could feel the swell of her breasts pressed against my chest, and hear her breathy pants as she continued to possess my body. This was all that mattered. She was what mattered.

For her, I would become anything...be anyone...do anything.

I ripped my lips from hers and staggered back. Her missing presence, a coldness in my soul. "I choose you. I choose us."

Before she could respond, I stepped further into the train car. I released the power inside, cracked the gate, and allowed dark red bolts to fly and connect with a dozen humans at once.

Wild and raw magic met mine and with a gentle pull, it flew into me. I could taste notes of earth, of iron, of flowers, and of water. But more than that, I could taste freedom. It was as if their power was unstructured, primed for manipulation.

I willed it to the empty spaces in my own magic, a covering for my internal wounds and a bridge to my missing genes. It melded with my own power. Immediately, I could sense the difference. Their power was strong. It was *exactly* what I needed.

I could feel it heightening my senses, growing my own abilities. I *saw* the well inside me, the source of my red energy, being richly filled and fueled with raw power.

The distant sound of a familiar gasp accompanied a dozen thuds echoed throughout the space. But nothing mattered, not with the energy coursing through my body demanding more.

I looked at the remaining humans and smiled.

CHAPTER 59
TATE

Aether had left me in the library hours ago. Last night had bled into this morning, with us scouring the shelves for language textbooks until he reluctantly informed me he had to go—without me.

I bit my lip in frustration. I understood he meant well, but that didn't give him the right to tell me when to stay and when to go. And yet...I had been too drained to fight him. Too emotionally spent, so I'd merely ignored him as he excused himself.

The books under my fingers were precious, old, and full of knowledge. I had managed to pull six volumes from the shelves thus far. A tome containing the royal history and bloodlines, two more of Perry's journals, a book about magic and its different forms and expressions by Cleo herself, another book about the mysteries of Mydant, and the last one I still held in my hand: *The Transformation of the Houses with the Untish Gene.* And yet, none of the books I'd found contained what I looked for: an expansive look at languages.

When I'd first opened Esme's journal, I'd hoped to gain great insight into my parents. That hope had quickly faded as I realized that, aside from the initial dedication page confirming it was, in fact, Esme's journal, the rest was written in a cryptic language I'd never seen before.

Even Aether couldn't understand it. We'd spent most of the night searching for language textbooks to try and identify *which* language it was. After hours of searching, we'd found one book concerning *other* languages, but not the one Esme used.

I grunted at the thought.

No matter. I was determined and stubborn as hell. I would unlock the secrets in Esme's journal, even if it meant tearing the entire library apart to do so.

The prospect excited me. How many mysteries and secrets could I unlock from these tomes? Even with the disappointment of not being able to read her journal, I was secretly relieved. If I couldn't read it, then I couldn't be hurt.

It was cowardly, but for now, I allowed myself the dalliance.

My hand tightened on the tome as I perused the books on the nearest shelves one more time, looking for anything useful in decoding my mother's journal. Nothing. Several books concerning history and customs caught my attention, but nothing pertaining to lost languages. Even so, I was thrilled by the vast amount of knowledge surrounding me. At how much I could learn. I would no longer be ignorant or dependent on Aether or Vala. I could finally hold my own. And given my bloodline, I needed to be *well* educated.

I placed the book in my satchel and then moved higher up on the ladder, still searching. At least I could read *most* of the titles, they were generally written in languages I knew—though, not all were. I skimmed through several more titles and once again wished I under-stood the organizational method. It wasn't alphabetical. It did appear to, at least in part, be organized chronologically, but also by topics and I'd yet to find the section on *communication*. I blew a stray piece of hair from my eyes.

I pulled at a tome and paused. *Maps.* I smiled, it wasn't what I was looking for, but perhaps if I understood where my mother originated from, where my ancestors lived, I'd be better able to guess what language she used. Lowering myself to the floor, I walked over to the table in the bay window where I had set up for the day and sank into the large, cushioned chair. I set the two additional tomes down and paused. In all the books I'd selected, they offered insight and partial clues as to *who* Esme was, what lost languages she may have known.

I suspected the royal family were well versed in *many* dialects, which meant the more I understood about their history and customs, the more likely I would understand which language Esme used.

Where to start?

I hovered my hand over the titles and felt a pull to several at once. Apparently, my magic wished me to know everything. I huffed dryly as I closed my eyes for a moment—focusing on what I *felt*.

I'd start with something safe but helpful, *The Royal Bloodline*. I cracked the ancient book open and began reading, grateful it was in a language I understood—an old language, yes, but one I knew. Thank you Fletch for insisting I study the 'dead' languages. The thought of him brought joy to my chest. It was the first time since he'd passed that I could think of him and it didn't *only* hurt.

A few chapters in and one thing became glaringly obvious: the bloodline was *heavily* manipulated. I had assumed that it just took the mixing of three bloods, but the more I read, the more I understood that it was important in *how* those bloodlines mixed. For example, a full Untish with all three bloods can procreate with another full Untish, but it is hypothesized that it will water down the genes. In this case, which ones prevail? And even then, the different Houses are genetically predisposed to certain gifts and traits, but the strongest expression of them—shifting and magic wielding—isn't a guarantee. Several questions rattled in my head as the book voiced more and more opinions.

Given that Untish shifters were rare even with the right bloodlines, Perry's court recognized the purpose of intentional breeding with carefully selected bloodlines—a point of contention for the queen, but in the end, it was deemed unavoidable if she wished to maintain control of Mydant. The pure Fae must mate with a half-vampire and half-human—a halfling. A Untishee must breed with a full Fae if possible, or at least, a halfling of a Fae vampire mix. If there were any other type of combination, the shifting gene wasn't guaranteed to manifest.

I sighed, why hadn't Fletch taught me all this? Even after all my time at the Embassy, these concepts were foreign and difficult to grasp.

Aimee, daughter of Perry and heir to the throne, was a shifter. Her first bond was to that of a halfling, and their child was born strong and full of magic. Unfortunately, he could not shift. After bearing yet another son who also couldn't shift, and instead was gifted in various ways—shields, magical wards, and healing—it was determined Aimee must re-bond in order to produce shifters. Her previous offspring would not inherit the throne.

What the hell? Re-bond?

Aimee was paired with a full Fae, Choven, and together they bore twin girls: Maege and Sheriah, both dragon shifters and the greatest of their kind. In turn, it has been decreed that any royal heir must mate with a pure Fae to have the highest chance of securing the shifting gene.

This however did not stop other Houses from attempting to create their own dragons, their own shifters. After the death of the infamous Iron Dragon during a duel with Aimee, the other Houses agreed to further submit—even while still producing their own dragons. This, in theory, could benefit the Crown, but only if controlled. And thus began the evolution of the Matching Ceremony. Where before, the ceremony was designed to strengthen House ties and maintain each House's integrity, now it was a way for the royal bloodline to maintain power. In this, not only was dragon creation controlled, but any pure Fae from any House had hope of being matched with a royal Untishee, and as such, produce an heir to the throne.

The House of Blush established an eternal royal rule.

Aimee's daughter, Sheriah, was younger by three seconds and therefore not the direct heir in accordance with royal customs. She bonded in secret with a halfling from the House of Iron and bore a son, Zachiaz. In spite of his genes, he was able to shift. This has led to many discussions on the entity of magic, and with it, confusion reigned.

Since then, it has been mandated that any royal heir must be able to shift. A direct heir must bond with a full Fae, but any non-heir royal may select a mate of their choosing; however, if their offspring can't shift—they will never be a contestant for the throne.

Every direct royal heir must produce at least one eligible heir or forfeit the throne to the next in line—this maintains the royal bloodline's rule.

Okay...so, royal heirs who wanted to rule had to submit to arranged marriages and produce a child who could also shift. Not the worst thing, it certainly wasn't unheard of, and yet, it did seem archaic. But, then again, even the Untish Embassy had Matching Events, and they weren't royalty.

Maege could shift and as the eldest daughter, her son, Owen, who could shift, was entitled to the throne.

Interesting, was he the same as the current King Owen?

Ultimately, chaos ensued when Aimee's offspring from her first bond produced shifters—who was entitled to the throne? This caused the Great Uprising and once squashed, the Challenge to the Throne was established. This is to occur upon the passing of a Crown. In this, anyone with royal blood who can shift is allowed to compete unto the death to become the king or queen of Mydant. The last one breathing, wins. All will swear fealty to them.

With Maege's passing, Aimee's first offspring from her first bond produced two challengers, Aimee's granddaughters, along with Zachiaz and Owen. All of them were from the Royal House. In the end, Owen won and became the royal Crown for all of Mydant. And thus, the custom of royal challenging was established.

I pinched my forehead. Too much, so much, overwhelming.

Everything all right, dear?

I sent confirmation back down the bond to Aether but didn't respond. Instead, I stood and shook out my legs. So...a royal challenge would occur with any passing of a Crown. Any shifters with royal blood could fight for their chance to rule. But what of the other Houses? And did direct heirs not matter?

I took longer strides, driven by the many, many thoughts, and began pacing through the library, allowing the data to sink in. Hours had passed, the sun had risen fully in the sky, and it was now midafternoon. I walked through the archives and idly followed various paths.

The door to the garden was just ahead and I didn't pause before passing through it.

The sweet air hit my nose immediately. *Peonies. Lilacs. Roses.* I smiled. This place felt purely right. I ambled past several flower beds on the cobblestone path, noting several fountains boasting pink sapphire basins, and then found myself moving toward the back of the garden near the waterfall.

Aether's anxiety rapidly flooded the bond followed by a blanketing silence, almost as if he were blocking me.

I reached down the bond and was met with singeing anger. I bit my lip as I sighed. Dammit. If he wanted privacy, I could grant him that, right? Even if I didn't understand why *he* was annoyed.

He was the one who made it clear *he* wanted space today, wanted to keep me 'safe' from unnecessary risks as he gathered intel. The prick.

My previous annoyance returned, and I found the perfect pebble to take it out on by kicking it down the path. As I moved, I noted the internal pull I felt...it was almost as if I were being led. The sunshine beat down on my head and my bare shoulders but didn't burn. The mist in the air thickened and I could hear the pounding of the water getting closer. Turning past several large bushes, I found myself at the base of the glorious falls. The water pooled into a turquoise lagoon before flowing out in several places, forming rivers that spiraled away. A pink rainbow arched over the water and ended at the cliff at least three hundred feet above me.

Breathtaking.

I removed my boots and let them tumble to the small river rocks, before limping into the water. I inhaled sharply and then savored the way the coolness met my skin. A smile pulled at my lips as I spotted several schools of small fish swimming away from my toes. I stepped in deeper and crinkled my nose when my flesh met wet moss that squished with my movement.

I waded in further until the water was up to my waist, then my chest, and finally my shoulders. I continued to swim and then allowed myself to sink in fully, the water covering my head. In the full submersion, everything was serene. The waterfall pounding the lagoon was a soothing, constant, drum to the otherwise calm—

A flash of deep, agonizing pain screamed through the bond from Aether and sent my heart racing.

I instantly tried to breach the surface, preparing to check on Aether through our bond, when two hands gripped my legs and pulled me *down* further into the pool.

I searched for the force, for the perpetrator who was yanking me deeper and deeper into the water, but I didn't see anything—just crystal-clear water. And yet *something* invisible controlled my legs.

I went to scream for Aether, feeling a new flash of his pain, when the force holding me tripled until my chest burned from the excessive pressure on my body.

I kicked and twisted, but it was pointless. I couldn't even see the enemy.

Aether! I...

I managed the silent cry but was unable to finish as my entire body was flattened against the bottom of the lagoon, and my consciousness weaned. My head throbbed and my vision spotted—my ears stung as my lungs begged for air.

I wrestled against my invisible enemy, fought, but my head was whipped down. No, not down, to the side. I could see the faint outline of a door, set in stone, directly under the falls.

Come find me...I'm here, an ethereal voice hummed through the water.

The pressure vanished as did the hold on me. I pressed off the rocky bottom with my hands and then my feet, and sprang upwards. So, so far from the surface.

Tate! Answer me, are you okay?

I could feel his panic coursing down our bond, blending with my own. My eyes blurred as I fought with every ounce of my remaining strength to reach the surface above. Nearer now, just ten more feet.

I swam, I kicked, I scooped as I fought for my life. Just as my lungs were about to burst, my head breached the surface, and I inhaled greedily.

I panted heavily, gulping in sweet oxygen while trying to keep my face above water. I was close to the waterfall, much too close. I used my remaining energy to swim to the beach about fifty feet out.

Slowly, so slowly, I kicked until my right foot touched the mossy bottom and then, my left. I crawled onto the beach on all fours until my entire body was free of the water and then I collapsed, chest heaving.

Alive. I'm alive.

CHAPTER 60

AETHER

I massaged the back of my neck, the sweat on my skin slick. James stood in front of me, a map in hand.

"Here's where the troops are attacking." He pointed to a large spot on the map right outside the Glenn's HQ. "And here," he placed a dot on another small settlement marked 'S.O.', "is where the president and his heir were, directly before I left. But my understanding is that they are relocating to deal with the threat to HQ as we speak."

I nodded, adjusting my stance on the worn wooden planks—this cabin had seen better days.

"And who is assumed to be attacking?" I asked. "Who would have the strength and desire to face the Glenn with its creatures?"

"The Fern," James said. "But Aether—" he cleared his throat "—they have monsters of their own."

My eyes snapped to his. Images of the white seethings from the arena flooded my mind. "White with red veins?"

"Yes, and wings. *And* they can manipulate fire." James ran his hand through his surprisingly wind-blown pompadour.

"This changes things, it—"

"You can't get me!" Clarence shouted through giggles as he

zoomed from the adjoining kitchen into the dining area with Ruby hot on his heels. "Na-na!"

"You are going down!" Ruby chased him, soot covered her face in a smear—a face that was reddened in ire, growing brighter with every passing second. Her unbound curls were bouncing wildly off her back in a tangled mess as she ducked under the table and then slid out catching Clarence's foot, sending him crumbling to the ground.

"Ow! Mama, Ruby hurt me on purpose!" he wailed, clutching his skinned knee.

"Did not! You're just a baby!"

"Am not!"

"Are too!"

"Am—"

"Children." Uley walked into the room shooting us an apologetic glance. "Out, now."

Slowly, they obliged. Clarence crying as Uley scooped him up in her arms and Ruby smirked as she stalked out of the room, dirty face held high.

That girl...I couldn't keep the smile off my face.

"She's spirited," James whispered under his breath as if reading my thoughts. Ruby was so much like Cher, boasting the same wild nature. Cher would never let anyone get the better of her.

Shame swallowed me at the thought—I'd failed Cher, I would not make the same mistake with Tate.

I sighed as I reached out to the bond. I felt her—she's happy...until she recognized my presence, and then bristled, shoving me away. Still pissed that I left her behind, I supposed.

Guilt gnawed at me as I thought of *how* much more pissed she'd be when she learned of the prophecy—bogus or not, she deserved to know. Needed to know. I'd tell her...soon. Just as soon as I had an opportunity where she wasn't dealing with the latest blow or being bombarded by truth. Even the strongest of us had a breaking point.

"Okay, so what would your course of action be? What is Arithi planning?" I asked. I'd messaged James just after we departed, instructing him to take his family and meet me here. I had no idea whose abandoned cabin this was, but it was close enough to teleport to the border of Tate's veil, and more importantly, it was far enough to not draw attention to her.

"I don't know. Camella will be meeting us here, soon I hope, with Vala," he replied. "Aether, the more important question is *why* are we here? Why are we not with leadership? What has occurred?"

I felt the tension rising in my shoulders.

Here we go.

"There have been some developments and, brother, while I trust you, I'm not sure I can say more." I leveled a look at him, at the male I've fought beside for decades—the one I trusted with my daughter, *Cher's* daughter, too.

James just held my gaze.

"Aether, why does this feel like treason? I need a damn good reason for this, for uprooting my family and risking everything." I could see the fire building in his eyes.

"Tate, she...she's not safe there. Arithi is threatened by her," I began. James crossed his arms and looked at me, willing me to continue. "She's a royal, James. She's a member of the House of Blush, a descendant of Esme, and a possible heir to the throne."

My power built, one wrong move from James and I'd crush him— father to Ruby or not. To my shock, his eyes widened as his face cracked in a smile until he was bent over laughing, hysterically.

"What the actual fuck, James?"

His chuckling only intensified. My magic flickered, unsure of how to respond to this display of...whatever the fuck this was.

"It's just...who would have thought the female who bewitched you —the one who once thought you were the devil, the one *I* had to drag your ass to retrieve from Gari's clutches, is a royal!" He slapped his knee before righting himself. "No, *the* royal."

My anger rose at his last insinuation and my tension intensified tenfold. This was *not* how this conversation was supposed to go. "This is a serious matter, James." I couldn't keep the bite out of my voice, nor the black flames from beginning to swallow the room.

"Aether, calm down." He lifted his hands innocently. "I knew she was your match, your equal." He sighed, and with it, all signs of merriment were gone. "Congratulations, brother."

I stared at him speechless. "You knew?"

"Of course I did, I knew she was *something* special to you that day on the balcony when you wouldn't let me within ten feet of her. You *never* act like that. Then there were your delayed missions, and of course, the *way* you look at her. But most of all," he drew out the last word, "your demeanor is different. I noticed it the moment I picked you up in the forest. As unlikely as it is, you seem regal. Reverent of someone else besides yourself, awed by her."

He's known for hours and never said anything? My flames died out as the energy vanished, and with it any threat James posed. He looked truly happy for me.

"She's a hell of a mate."

"Thank you," I said stupidly. This whole exchange was unexpected.

"Uley and I will protect and serve Tate, as a member of the Royal House. But more than that, as a member of this family."

I nodded, loosening a breath along with the tightness coiled in my shoulders.

"Now that we're open about you landing yourself a *princess*," James wagged his brows with the title, "what's the plan?"

"The plan indeed."

We waited for several more hours until, at long last, the wards surrounding the cabin were triggered and James blinked out before returning with both Vala and Camella in his arms. Camella lost her footing when he set her down, sputtering colorful words at James who seemed to enjoy the effects his teleporting had on everyone but him. Vala stood next to him, bent over, huffing heavy breaths. Her short hair was pulled into a high bun at the top of her head, the white contrasting the dark of her roots—ever the proud Luner.

"Right, let's not waste time," I began.

"Clearly," Camella huffed, annoyed at being blinked here.

"What's wrong, can't handle the shifts?" James cooed.

"I'll show you what I can't handle—"

"Guys, seriously?" Vala interrupted. "Aether, what's going on?"

All eyes turned to me. Here it was. The moment of truth. I'd messaged them to meet me here. They were the ones I trusted the most to get me the intel I needed.

I released a sigh, Vala already knew in part. And I suspected Camella had an idea based on her comments and long hours of training with Tate. With a deep breath, I began explaining to them Tate's bloodline.

Vala's smile only widened as Camella's face remained alarmingly neutral. My power was continuously building, I could feel the energy wrapping around every person in this cabin—every potential threat.

"The prophecy," Camella said, awe filling her voice. Vala's eyes widened as she realized what Camella was implying. "Aether, she could be the missing—"

"Enough." I released a wave of dark power, knocking all three of them over. I could feel it hovering over their bodies, wishing to demolish, but instead, I pulled it back and swallowed my own energy.

They stood, slowly and warily.

"I am not about to allow my *mate* to become some pawn in a superstition. I don't believe in prophecies, and neither should you."

"But, Aether, I mean...if she's Esme's daughter, then that means she's Lilith's heir, the last one here on Shappa, and   "

"Vala!" I snapped. "I will not say this again, Tate's bloodline will be known to only us. We will get her back to Mydant where she won't be hunted for her royal blood, and she can blend in with the House of Blush."

"How do you suggest that actually happening? All royals are acutely aware of one another. You can't just sneak her in and expect no one to notice." Camella gave me a dead-eyed look. "You're smarter than that, even if you're a complete jackass."

I bit my lip to stop a snarl.

"She's right, Aether." James took a hesitant step toward me. "Tate needs to go to Mydant. I'm in agreement with that, but with the upcoming challenging, there's no way to sneak a *royal* in unnoticed."

"I...I don't have it all figured out. But her tips are black. Perhaps, we can sneak her in and just find a home on the outskirts, far away from the palace and all the political bullshit." I ran a hand through my hair.

"OK..." Camella hedged. "Is that what *Tate* wants?"

I didn't answer.

They all stared at me, waiting.

"She does know about the prophecy, yes?" Camella arched a brow.

Still, I didn't answer.

"Aether, fuck." James braced his head in both hands. "You can't make that choice for her. You can't take that from her."

My anger built, a cyclone ready to decimate. I could do this without them.

"Hey." Vala's hand on my shoulder startled me. "Tate can handle this. She won't face this alone."

The wave of energy shuttered inside me, melting and stewing, a storm brewing but...calming.

"She's right. We'll all stand by her." Camella gripped my other shoulder. "She has our loyalty. Her will is our own."

James nodded, as I returned a gentle squeeze to both female's arms and then cracked my neck.

"Fuckkkk." I loosened a breath, and with it, I accepted I may not be able to control this. "I'll tell her, just...not yet."

"Ok...but, Aether, where is she?" Vala asked.

As one, she and Camella looked around, skepticism clear in their features.

"Tate is secure. We will see her once it's necessary, but not before."

"Protective jackass," Camella muttered.

"You have no idea," Vala chimed in. "Like, he—"

"Agreed." James's voice rose over both of theirs. "But there are many pressing things to discuss."

"Where is Jared?" I asked.

"Coming. I sent him a message with your directions to meet us here. I'm sure he'll arrive at any moment," Vala chirped.

"Have you spent a lot of time with him lately?" I hedged.

"I mean, not as much as I'd like, but sure, when he's here and not out on a mission or working on reports or sleeping, or—" Vala's mouth snapped tight, anxiety clear in her features. They'd been matched but not bonded, at least not yet.

"James has confirmed the Glenn is under attack from the Fern, beasts on both sides are at play." I began. "Camella, what was the environment when you left the Embassy?"

"Not great. You and Tate have been labeled persons of interest in two Ironhead's deaths, and have been accused of being responsible for the presence of those *things* in the arena during the assessment. Arithi has issued public statements that you are to be brought in for questioning by the chairs and Enzo is…unavailable. I suspect he's been detained by Arithi as there are rumors *he* is also behind the deaths of the two Ironheads," Camella finished, squaring her shoulders. "Aether, the stage is set for you, Tate, and Enzo to be declared traitors to the Crown. What would you have me do?"

I paused a moment. "Any news on upcoming missions to the Glenn or of their attack?"

"None."

I nodded. "Then we do nothing for now."

"Aether, won't Tate want to help, to fight?" Vala asked, her words emphasized by a knowing look. She'd spent a lot of time with Tate and understood how badly Tate wanted vengeance. But still…

"She needs to be safe. That's what matters. She can't help if she's dead." I silenced all questions, before reaching down the bond and feeling Tate's joy—she was absolutely the brightest spot in my life. A spot I would not sacrifice, would not fail, would not lose.

"Aether—"

CRASH! The windows shattered as milky white beasts flew through them.

"Get down!" James shouted as he flipped a table over for coverage and Vala threw a shield around the group, blocking the glass shards. I didn't have to look to know Camella already had her weapons at the ready, to know her force had been called to the surface.

I threw my hands out and suspended the nearest three beasts in their spots before pouring dark flames of liquid fire at them. Only, they didn't die. They blocked the flames with their wings as even more beasts came crashing through the windows, splintering the walls as they continually barreled through the wood, none using the door. Camella suspended one as she shot flames at several others, but it also did nothing.

The beasts smiled as one, their red eyes brightening as their maroon veins began to actually illuminate. "Now," they spoke in unison.

Red flames poured from their hands—like in the arena. I leapt out of the way and blocked while holding my grasp on the other three. Vala further shielded herself, the children, and Uley, locking them away in a dome. I locked eyes with Ruby's wild black and gold ones just before the seething in front of me lunged, swinging with its talons as it poured its flames into the ground surrounding me. I quickly evaded and with a calculated strike, its head was severed from its body.

The entire cabin was consumed in living flames, smoldering and smoking from the heat. Camella grunted next to me as she tucked and rolled, decapitating one seething only to be attacked by two more. We were being swarmed.

I sliced my blade through the center of one beast while reaching out to grab hold of another half dozen. Even with nearly twelve in my control, frozen and restrained, more were pouring in. Sweat surged down my forehead and began to fall into my eyes.

Smoke, so much smoke.

I met their flames with my dark ones and attempted to beat them back. The beasts in my control were actively fighting, trying to wrench free of my grasp—to use their magic that I was currently suppressing. In a wave of fury, I ripped and pulled at the dozen in my hold—suppressed and tore, until they were nothing but corpses with severed limbs on the floor.

But it was still not enough.

Not nearly.

More were pouring through the building—a building that was crumbling, bouncing from Vala's shield, and plummeting through the wooden floor.

The children cried, huddled next to Uley, safely encased in the dome that Vala was actively reinforcing. James battled two beasts at a time. He stabbed the first, then blinked behind the second, stabbing it, before reappearing and beheading the first. It was a skillful maneuver, but still, the beasts multiplied.

Camella's shield was beginning to fail and her flames were not killing; she used her tactical maneuvers to fight the beasts, killing some, but with their sheer number, the deaths of two made little difference.

The creatures kept pouring into the building.

I locked eyes with James, and then with a nod, I turned and threw myself out the window, landing on the ground. The beasts surrounded me in an instant. I willed all my power to the surface and became a living torch, my weapon now lit in black flames.

And then, I danced.

I stabbed one creature before pivoting and decapitating another. A blast of red flames swallowed me whole, but my own power beat it back, and then projected. There were too many beasts to stop them all completely. So instead, I manipulated the air around them, suppressing their magic; sweat poured from my brows at the vast energy required to stall their flames. Even as I held their magic at bay, they attacked with talons. I dodged several swings before slipping into the numb state of a warrior, the waltz of death.

All around me, corpses covered the ground. And still, I was swarmed. Still, I fought.

I was vaguely aware of Camella fighting in the near distance, holding her own against half a dozen seethings.

I dodged the swing of one beast and plunged my sword into its gut, my flames eating its insides, before retracting it and plunging it into the side of another. A howl sounded from behind and instant pain flared as talons sank into my flesh.

A wave of fury and anxiety flared from me, echoing down the bond.

My shoulder screamed in protest, but I dropped and rolled, taking the beast with me before standing above it and slicing its arm from its body, leaving it maimed. With another strike, it was dead.

I could feel Tate reaching out, but another beast simultaneously attacked, and my anger flared. I cut the air from its lungs and then sliced its head from its body.

"You cannot win," they spoke in unison. "We are many, we are strong."

I smiled. "Watch me."

I sent a volley of flames targeted at them, but they blocked with their wings. It didn't matter, the distraction was what I was counting on. I commanded the moment, and was instantly before the beasts, slicing their wings from their shoulders, maiming them. I cut their feet from their legs, amputating them, and then, in a burst of power, I pulled the very air from their lungs and strangled half a dozen in a single instant.

They screamed as one before dozens more attacked. But I wouldn't relent. I killed one beast. And then another and another and another.

I erected a shield and paused briefly to refill my stores, drawing energy from the planet.

"You will not win!" their shrill voices filled the forest's air.

But I tuned them out as I dropped my shield and my feet moved across the ground, crushing pinecones and severed limbs alike. I sliced into one seething, cutting it in half, before turning to the next and cutting off its leg, then its arm, and then, finally, its head. I ducked, rolled, and then plunged my sword into the belly of yet another beast, watching its oozing, puss-like blood cover my boots and the grass below.

I pulled again at the molecules surrounding several beasts and tore the air from their very lungs. I silenced the flames of others as I slaughtered them.

I became one with violence until only two remained. They stood in front of me, panting.

"This isn't over. You were said to be easy, but have proven formidable. Our information was incomplete."

They flapped their wings and prepared for flight; I too tried to shift, my beast *clawing* at me, demanding to be freed, but a wave of pain knocked me to my knees.

Staggering pain claimed my entire essence.

The talons in my back—dark magic. The beasts began to fly. I could hear James cursing as he blinked in and rushed to my side.

"Get this fucking thing out!" I shouted, eyes still trained on the beasts' forms.

"Right," he spoke as he gripped the severed limb. "Here we go."

Before I could respond, he ripped the talons from my flesh, and I felt my muscles and skin shredding. I shook him off and stood.

"Are they secure?" I asked, looking toward the house that was now nothing but flames and ruin.

"Yes."

Good. And then I shifted, the agony instant. I flapped my wings and became airborne, but each movement threatened to be my last and tore the wounds open further. But those things came too close to Ruby, to Tate. They were sent to kill, assigned a mission.

I needed answers. And I would get them.

I leaned into the rage. In this form, it was easy to get lost in the *pure beast*.

I lifted my head and roared, dark flames engulfing the sky. The beasts noticed and began flying faster—trying to escape me. They turned their heads, almost unnoticeably, but I didn't miss where their focus had been. Or the way they seemingly paused a moment before making an abrupt turn in the opposite direction.

My beastly part wanted to follow, to devour and destroy, and yet my mind demanded I focus on something different. I forced myself forward, huffing from the pain of each flap of my right wing, until I could see two small figures in the distance. They disappeared almost immediately, but I didn't miss the ruddy red hair on the one skinny figure.

Pure rage enveloped me as I realized who it was that betrayed us, betrayed Tate.

I turned my attention to where the creatures had been, but they vanished, blending in with the sky and clouds. I freed a roar that matched my fury as I turned around and prepared to reunite with James.

I felt it then, *her* pure terror. The fear. The pain.

Aether! I...

I sensed Tate's fear increasing and I reached out to her, willing her to respond.

Tate!

No response, but the bond became murky, almost hazy.

Tate! Answer me, are you okay?

I felt a strangled cry and dread pooled in my stomach. I cried out to her again through the bond, feeling a tightness in my chest.

James was below, waiting for me, blade at the ready.

I shifted and in an instant was on my feet, running toward him. My legs trembled and I fell but recovered quickly, ignoring the blood gushing from my shoulder.

"Take me to her, now!" I commanded.

James reached for me, prepared to blink us there in an instant.

Alive. I'm alive.

Relief filled me at the sound of her voice in my head, but it was swiftly followed by panic at what those words entailed. I didn't waste another moment before gripping James's extended hand and vanishing.

Coming. I'm coming.

CHAPTER 61

CHANCE

I smelt the smoke the moment we deboarded the circuit. The sight of the buildings on fire was shocking. My home, the one I was sworn to protect, was in shambles. Several buildings were already nothing but rubble. It appeared the fighting had occurred mostly in the outer district of HQ, near the capitol building.

From where I stood, I could make out the dots of thousands of tents in the distance—roughly twenty miles away. We stood here, waiting. The sun shone overhead and bore down on us, reminding each guaraman of our own fragility.

"Right, so you want to send in the seethings and controllers, and then have the rest of our men follow and clean house?" Dux Jooxa asked.

"Correct," Anax Graff spoke. Her presence here was one of the only comforting things about being on the front lines and fighting a war I'd only ever hoped to avoid. "Seethings and controllers, then those with giftings will be next, followed by skilled duxes along with a few arches. And lastly, the arches and dokimoses squads will charge."

"Is it really wise to be expending such a large number of our forces?" Dux Jooxa questioned. I didn't know her well; from what I'd heard she was tough but fair. She was, as Shae had told me, Nora's commanding officer. "As you know, we've been fighting for the past twenty-four hours, Anax. And while we've held our own, we have lost a lot of our skilled warriors. You yourself have seen the devastating losses we've taken."

"This is war. We've fought well, and I recognize all you've done. I've been here coordinating this defense since the beginning of this attempted siege. We now have reinforcements. It is time to go on the offensive." Anax Graff rolled out a map in front of her.

"Dux Dale, you will be the second in line concerning the advanced controllers. Ahead of you, we have controller TZ2. Behind you, we have controller TZ3, with other controllers sprinkled throughout. Understood?" Anax Graff turned her gaze to me.

I nodded. I had no bloody idea how to control these things. I'd never even tried, but I was powerful. Of that I was certain. I could sense the new magic still blending with my own and was oddly excited to see what I could do now—to exercise my new stores and abilities.

The meeting continued with various instructions and questions, but all I could hear was the power thrumming through my veins—the sweet call to release it, to taste, to devour, to—

"Very well, we move on my signal. Positions," Anax Graff commanded.

I blinked, unmoving for a moment. Right, that was *my* cue to move. I stalked forward, eerily aware that all the other guaramen were walking *backwards*. The bodies of seethings were lined in rows upon rows ahead of me. Thousands of seethings. We had thousands. My jaw nearly dropped; all this time, so many creatures—so much magic.

I swallowed back the desire to *take* and instead focused on what lay in front of me. In the back, several moved like dogs on four feet. They snapped at me as I passed but remained in position. Their black scales glistened against the sun and their foaming spit bubbled on the ground as drool poured from their mouths. Mouths that were ajar with four oversized fangs. I spotted a few controllers amongst the beasts, and I nodded to them as I passed—I only received a slight blink from their eyes—they were completely focused.

I continued to stomp forward, certainty and power fueling every step. Several of the train cars had either contained humans or seethings, and I only made it through three of the human cars before I had to stop—the energy was nearly too much. Holland had begged me to stop on the train. Even as I moved to the next car and continued to siphon the humans to death, I could hear her telling me to use restraint. That I was enough as I was. After a while, she just stopped. Stopped protesting, stopped asking; instead, she nodded to me at the end like a soldier to a superior and excused herself. When we arrived, she was directed elsewhere and merely told me to be careful. I knew she wanted more…fuck, I wanted more. I craved another moment with her, longed to savor every curve of her glorious body. But we didn't always get what we wanted. A bitter laugh escaped my lips.

She was safe. As long as I was out here, she was safe. She may not agree with my methods, but I was doing this in part for her. With time, she'd see that.

My blood crackled in anticipation—the magic around me swirled, I could practically taste its vitality.

I was halfway through the throng of beasts, and they were now standing alert on two feet. They were larger and the closer to the front lines I got, the bigger they got. I began to become dwarfed in size. Even still, they moved out of my way as I passed.

"Dux Dale, come in," Doctor Worshah's voice sounded in my ears. At least the coms were working.

"Here."

"We can track your movements and vitals as you fight. I have Dux Holland with me. Should we need to, er, calm you down, she will be here to assist," he paused. "Continue forward until you're equally between TZ3 and TZ2."

I didn't respond but instead kept moving.

I spotted TZ3 up ahead. The controller stood, back to me, focused dead ahead. She was a female, smaller than I would have thought, and nearly nothing but muscles upon muscles. Her body was contorted, purple flesh covered in black veins. Red hair hung in patches from her scalp.

I passed by and nodded. To my surprise, she returned the nod—green eyes far too keen. Is that what I'd become? A monster with full awareness? Would Holland be repulsed by me after today?

Power. Strength is attractive. Brute force.

I reminded myself of the male mantra. If Holland hated me after today or was completely disgusted by me, I'd fucking deal with it; this would be worth it.

I felt a subtle change in the air around me. It became charged and far too staticky to be normal. The beasts just ahead were giant seethings. About a dozen of them had wings and they weren't just large, they were a different breed entirely. They stood on all fours, crouched and at the ready. They had tails that were spiked and deadly in appearance. I was inconsequential compared to these seethings, if they even were seethings at all. They were at least eighteen feet in length, not counting their tails, and their wings were composed of scales and muscles. Unlike the beasts from the Fern, these did not look sophisticated. Their wings looked like muscles simply grew over snapped bones and continued to multiply.

Each one of their legs was restrained by chains of black energy, coiling around their limbs, anchored deep into the ground. They tugged against the manacles as they sniffed at me.

"Those twelve are for you to control," Doctor Worshah spoke into the coms.

"Fucking hell," I exhaled. I was not ready for this. I may have felt formidable, but in the presence of these beasts, I was nothing.

"Dux Dale, you will make your country proud. These beasts *will* respond to you, son," my father said, using both of my titles.

"I'm not so sure about that," I mumbled as I moved to stand in front of the creatures. Their yellow eyes all narrowed as they focused on me, but they didn't move—I doubted they could given their restraints.

"We've been administering your blood and bits of your power to them since the explosion. They are genetically modified to respond to you, Dux Dale," Doctor Worshah said.

I stood there speechless. "And if they don't?"

"Then you won't live to remember it," my father said.

"How does one control them?" I really wished I'd had a chance to practice prior to being sent into the field—into a blood-damn war.

"Just like siphoning, you reach out to each of their power threads and simply commandeer it. You do not inhale it, you do not steal it, but simply put, you make it your bitch." My father's voice broke into a laugh at the end. Odd for him to be so informal. Perhaps, he was finally seeing me as a Dux and not merely a boy.

Pride swelled in my chest even as my magic stirred.

"Think of it as a lasso, just wrap your power around each of them and your will becomes their own," Doctor Worshah spoke slowly. "Believe me, as someone who's been on the receiving end of your power, it's no joy and not something these seethings will take lightly."

I smiled as I recalled flaying him with my electricity. Some things were worth it.

"Just call me cowboy," I half-heartedly joked. I could do this, I had to.

"Dale...I...I'll be right here," Holland's soft voice crackled through my coms.

"Hey babe," I responded. It was the first time I'd called her that, but it felt right. Even as my power swelled in my veins, foreign as it was, I knew I loved her. If we survived this, perhaps we'd wed.

"Babe?" she choked on the word as she responded.

"Yes?"

"Go get 'em." Her voice was tender, fond even.

No goodbyes. No last wishes. I would survive this.

"All right, on my count. We'll march in two minutes," Anax Graff's voice interrupted us.

A round of confirms told me that the line was open, and the

majority of leadership was now aware of Holland and my personal relationship.

Fuck 'em.

I smiled as the countdown began.

My power stirred and I opened the door halfway. I could sense it spilling out and scratching its back against the walls of my mind, a cat making itself at home.

Red covered my arms as static and bolts danced across my vision. I allowed my senses to open fully, and I could feel the beasts around me. The twelve strongest ones also smelt different—they smelt like lilacs and fucking lavender. They smelt like Tate.

CHAPTER 62
TATE

I sat there, silently shaking. The water had mostly dried off, but even sitting so close to the roaring pink flames, even with the plush blanket I had secured against my trembling body, and with Aether near—I still felt cold. Afraid.

"Tell me again," he demanded.

"Aether, we've been over this," I said as I lifted my hand to massage my aching temples. "I went for a swim, was pulled under by an invisible force, and then I saw a door right before I swam up to the surface."

"And have you *felt* that force since then?"

"No." I bit my lip. "Yes? I don't know." I dropped my head into my hands.

"I've searched for any foreign presence here, but nothing was detected. Nothing. I've scoured the water, dove in it myself—fuck, I even shifted, Tate, and flew above searching, but I still found nothing." He gripped the mantle tightly, knuckles turning white. "Whatever it was, it's gone or hiding from me. If Vala were here, maybe she could find it as a Luner, but..."

I could sense his fear through the bond, see the anger on his face.

"Aether, I'm all right. Oddly enough...I don't think it was trying to hurt me, necessarily."

Aether's eyes darted to mine. "Meaning?"

"I think it wanted me to see the door. I felt a *pull* that led me to the falls to begin with. I followed it and felt *beckoned* to step into the water. I think I'm supposed to go down there, to investigate, to open that door." If only my words weren't feigned confidence. By Aether's expression, he could sense my nerves.

"I don't care what the hell it wanted, you're not going back down there."

I raised a brow. Where did he get off?

"I just," Aether swallowed and averted his gaze. "I can't lose you. How can I protect you from an enemy I can't even see?"

I felt his frustration, it was mirrored by my own. And yet, I would not hide. So much of my life had been dictated by the fears of others— by secrets and half-truths.

"What happened to you, Aether? I felt *your* pain through the bond when I was in that pool."

I surveyed his body carefully. Most of the initial dirt and blood he'd been *drenched* in when he arrived had been washed off when he explored the lagoon, but his nudity still showed his wounds. He had a gash at the base of his neck near his shoulders, and what I could have sworn appeared to be faint, freshly healed claw marks slashed across his chest. I'd seen the gouges in his back, five pink puncture marks. Even with superior healing to that of vampires, the marks had barely healed.

"We were ambushed. Those *things* you fought in the Arena swarmed the cabin; they attacked in full force, by the hundreds."

"Mother blood." My face turned ghostly white. "Where's everyone else? Where's Vala and Ruby?"

Sensing my rising panic, he moved from the hearth and sank down onto the couch near me, pulling me into a tight hug. "Alive. Everyone is fine. No one was seriously hurt."

I arched a brow into his shoulder.

Really?

I mean, I was wounded, but I'm fine.

You didn't feel fine. You felt—

He tilted my chin up with one hand and gently kissed my lips. Slowly, tenderly, before pulling back.

"I'm still learning things about our bond. This *level* of bond is new to me, too. I'm sorry you felt my pain, perhaps we can find a way to mute it for you—"

"Not a chance."

He smiled at that and then caressed my cheek.

"So, when do they get here? I can't wait to show Vala this place."

"They're not coming. I can't trust them."

My eyes bored into his. "They're your closest confidants; Vala has trained me, you call James your brother and he's raising Ruby, and yet, you can't trust them?"

Silence. The crackling of flames.

"Aether."

His back tensed at the sound of his name on my lips.

Aether, talk to me.

I could hear his breath release, the air spilling from his lungs as the room's energy both intensified and simultaneously dissipated.

As I said, we were betrayed. Ambushed.

I bit my lip even as my heartbeat increased.

By whom?

I waited, willing it to not be Vala—silently praying it wasn't the one friend who truly knew me and that I'd confided in.

Jared.

My head swam. He was Vala's bonded, her mate. How could he have betrayed her?

Does Vala know?

We haven't spoken.

Well, bring her here then! We need to talk, to figure this out and—

No.

I clenched my fists and stood, throwing off the blanket. I was suddenly very warm. "Why not?" I demanded, opting to use my voice. I needed to physically release my energy, my building fury.

"It's not safe. Like I said, we were betrayed, and I don't have all the facts. I don't know who we can trust." He stood and looked at me, his eyes hooded and laced with nothing but the promise of death—my vengeful warrior.

"It's not safe here either. But I know one thing with certainty, we need our people. We cannot do this alone. I don't want to do this alone. Bring them here, Aether."

I stepped toward him. His eyes scanned me for the hundredth assessment since he arrived—reassuring himself that I was indeed unharmed.

"Tate, I can't..." He clenched his jaw.

I pressed my finger to his lips as my eyes locked with his. I let him see me, see my internal fire, feel my energy, my power and passion, my desires—I poured my emotions into my eyes *and* down the bond.

No more secrets, Aether. We do this together. Bring them here.

I can't lose you...

I cupped his cheek in my hand. "Then don't. But don't push me away either. And never hide me away."

He snorted. "I couldn't if I tried."

"Blood-damn right." I winked at him before rising to my tiptoes and lacing my fingers behind his neck. "Now, are you going to tell me more about the ambush? Or perhaps what you were doing *before* that occurred?" I had a fairly good idea.

"Maybe," he spoke as he rubbed my back in small, soothing circles.

His mere touch did such delicious things to me. The brush of his fingers on my lower back, the warmth from his breath on my forehead, even the nearness of *him* had my core throbbing with need.

And he was naked.

Gloriously unencumbered.

I felt him enlarging from the mere press of our bodies, and I leaned into him further.

I swallowed as I looked at his lips. So perfect, so full, so ready...

"I have a better idea," he whispered as he leaned down and his hands tightened on my waist. His nose nuzzled my neck, and my legs became weak.

"Such as?" I feigned ignorance, but I was very aware. Highly conscious. Desire coursed through me as I recalled every savory moment we'd shared. He began kissing the column of my neck and shoulders.

I dug my hands further into his hair and he growled as I simultaneously moaned when his fangs rested on an old lover's mark. "Aether."

"Mmm," he murmured into my neck. "You have no idea the power you hold over me, Tate. Just my name on your lips has me completely in your thralls."

I smiled as the insatiable need continued to build. I wanted his lips on mine, his body on mine. I wanted to run my hands over the soft expanse of bare flesh—to take, to claim, to devour.

I'd fucking love that, darling.

My toes curled as his voice echoed inside my head. I claimed his lips with my own, soft at first. Gentle.

Slowly, his lips parted and then closed over my mouth. Sparks flew through my blood, my body, my mind. I pulled him closer even as his hands tightened on me and slipped under my shirt, exploring.

I deepened the kiss, demanding more.

Needy little thing, aren't we?

Only in the best ways.

I could feel him chuckle in my mouth a moment before his tongue swept in and explored. I met him, stroke for stroke with mine even as he wrapped one hand under my hip and picked me up, smoothly moving me so I was lying on the couch, his body pressed against mine. I could feel the rise and fall of his chest. His warmth surrounded me.

I dug my fingers into his neck and back, carefully feeling the mostly healed wounds.

So strong, so brave, so very *male*.

I sensed his smirk in my mind as the length of him grew harder... longer.

The energy in the room was pulling at me, but different than before —it was similar to what I'd felt earlier. It was—

Aether paused his pursuit of my mouth and adjusted so he looked down at me—coyness in his eyes. He was going to play with me?

I arched a brow in challenge, even as I greedily ogled every lethal part of him. He didn't need a weapon to be deadly, *he* was a weapon— carefully crafted to disarm and conquer, both on the battlefield and in the bedroom.

You flatter me.

Aether's eyes twinkled as he gazed at me with an expression that closely mirrored that of adoration and love. I swallowed.

Love.

I'd never said that one word, not to my first and never to a fling. The idea of love, true love, seemed so foreign to me. I'd accepted the bond, this mate. It was a more powerful expression of love than I'd ever known possible. It was the marriage of our souls. And yet, until now I'd never considered it to be the same as love. To call it love felt insufficient, like it diminished what we actually had. No, what we had surpassed love—what we had was a soul bond that no word could encompass.

Mate, Aether's voice rumbled in my head, heated and full of promise.

Mate, I echoed.

Without warning, he leaned down and once again devoured my lips, pulling them into his in an act of skilled passion. I returned the kiss and wrapped my legs around his waist, trapping him against me. I began to flex my hips against his and he hissed before moving with me.

More. I needed an abundance of him, pure greed for every ounce of my *mate* rose within.

I dug my nails into his neck, savoring the way his skin felt beneath my touch—pulling him closer. There was still too much space between us. Sensing my rising need, Aether picked up his pace as his hands began to explore. I groaned at the mere contact of his fingers as they grazed my breasts.

All I could hear was the sound of his breath. Hot and heavy…

All I could see was his nude skin, mere inches away. Warm and inviting… His enlarged crotch held my attention—there were big things I needed to take care of…thoroughly.

Aether groaned down the bond.

I pivoted, using the tension in the air to manipulate our bodies, until I was atop him. He looked at me with surprised eyes and I flashed him a snarky smile.

I too could play.

Tease.

Withhold.

At the last word, his eyes bulged as his nose snarled.

I blew him a kiss as I stood and paced over to the curtains hanging from the ceiling. I ripped off the tasseled cord from one of the drapes, and then the other.

I walked back to him before stripping from my still-damp clothes and then posed in front of him, wearing nothing but my black bra and lacy thong. Tilting my head, I allowed my hair to fall over my shoulders, knowing the pink flames from the hearth gave me a goddess's silhouette.

He swallowed as pure primal need claimed his features.

"I seem to remember a certain image…perhaps, we play with that now?" I ran the tassels through my fingers before snapping the cord like a whip, hitting the couch cushions near him. His nostrils flared.

"On your knees."

He obeyed.

I grabbed one of the tasseled cords and tied his wrists together, cinching them tightly. I reinforced it with magic, earning a sharp look from Aether who now kneeled in front of me, trembling with restraint.

I pulled back the tasseled end and slashed it across his unharmed shoulder. He flinched.

Fuck. This is so much better than the vision.

I smirked at his voice in my head before delivering another playful pass of the soft tassels.

Aether's moan had my knees begging to give, but not yet...

He needed to understand one thing clearly: we were equals.

We both could play. We both could fight to defend those we loved. We both were powerful.

His eyes sparkled at the inner dialogue I'd allowed him to hear.

I'm on my knees before you, oh powerful goddess.

I pulled back the tassel and slowly dripped it across my chest, the strands tickling my breasts and stomach, before I dragged it across Aether's bare skin. He shuttered from the contact. The room became bathed in black flames and bands of thick, black energy, my pink ones rising to meet his.

Do you want me?

I gripped his chin with my free hand as I cooed down the bond.

Do you need *me?*

He swallowed, pupils fully blown, as I manipulated the air to raise his hands above his head and then lowered myself to my knees in front of him.

I released a breathy moan as I said, "Aether."

He snapped. In an instant, he was free from the loose bindings, free from the magical forces holding him at bay, and was on me. His fangs tore my bra from my body, and he pulled the taut tips into his mouth, one at a time, and then again. And again. And again.

My head lulled to the side as I became caught in euphoria, fully engrossed in our passion. He moved lower and reached for my thong and pulled it off, burning it as he did so. His cock was ready, more than fucking ready, it was wet with desire, and he didn't wait another moment. He thrusted inside me, and my entire world shattered.

I was everywhere, and nowhere. I was here, but not.

I could see us, as if looking down from above like an apparition. His broad expanse of skin, glowing with black energy. My body humming in pink flames beneath him.

We writhed together, and pleasure engulfed me. There was nothing but him and his body. There was—

My magic jolted, shuttered, and flashed. Images of a gate, of desperate people clawing at it and screaming, filled my mind. The sound of beasts snarling, and children's cries shook me.

I shoved Aether off of me and began sprinting for the door. But Aether was faster, he stood in front of my path.

Someone's here. They need in.

I can sense my wards being triggered by James; I have no idea how long it's been going off...I was a bit distracted.

"Get them in here, now." A growl erupted from my lips.

The sensation of panic and desperation clawed at me through my magic, and the castle itself seemed to shutter from the impact of despair.

"Now, Aether. Let them in. Now."

CHAPTER 63

CHANCE

These were her creations. I knew without a doubt that if I focused closely, I'd see the beast who had called Tate its maker. She was a fucking traitor. The hate coursing through me flared and cost me a bit of my control. Red bolts of lightning struck the ground ahead of me, haphazard and uncontrolled.

The massive creatures howled in response, stirring against their restraints. I mentally threw out a tether to each one and seized control. A few resisted, but I simply pushed more of my power down the cord. Moments later they were all mine. I could sense their minds within my command—my grasp, wrapped in my lightning.

Leader.

Things.

We have names. We know not what we were or who we were, but we know we were.

I wasn't expecting them to be fully sentient. To communicate.

Then, what shall I call you?

A moment went by, and through the tethers, I could tell they were communicating. The tale-tell firing of synopsis. Interesting.

Call us, the Tarragon.

As in, the little dragon?

We like the connotation, and we look forward to squashing all, even our cousins—the dragons themselves.

Fuck yeah.

"Dux Dale, we're going to release them from their restraints. They're yours to control now. Good luck," Doctor Worshah spoke as the vines of black illuminated chains vanished from the Tarragon's limbs, freeing them.

They didn't move, instead they looked at me—awaiting my command.

I laughed as the countdown ended. It was time to attack.

The seethings in front charged, TZ2 leading them into the fray. In the distance, I could see the beasts attacking, charging in organized patterns. No controllers were present on the enemy front lines. I gritted my teeth as white-hot hate fueled my actions.

More.

The Tarragon liked my malice? I shouldn't be surprised, they were, after all, the spawn of the female known for her ire—the one who wouldn't justify her actions but would, now and forever, be the bitch who lied to her country. To me.

Now?

I could sense their eagerness, restless steps emphasizing their desire.

Not yet, I commanded.

The seethings reached the line the same moment the beasts did. Instantly, the day got brighter as a line a thousand long lit up in pure flames. The seethings who a moment before were charging into battle, were now retreating—or trying to. Their controller forced them forward, and by the dozens, they sacrificed themselves to the fire. Their screams echoed even from miles away.

Hundreds more charged, all the while TZ2 and a few other controllers stayed back.

I swallowed back the bile rising in my throat—the feeling of injustice swelling in my chest. These things were vile. I should feel *nothing* over their deaths. And yet...the seethings' death cries echoed in my soul.

Enough! Be free.... My magic beckoned me, begging that I act. A sentiment I could tell the Tarragon shared. But I held their leashes tightly.

Leader...we can stop this, the Tarragon spoke as one in my mind.

I flexed my fists. My coms were still silent.

"Permission to advance," I requested. Silence. "Command, permission to take the second fleet of seethings in?"

More silence. Static sounded and Rusty's disgusting voice filled my ears. "Not yet, boy!" I could hear the spit hitting the mic as he spoke. "We'll tell you when."

My magic roiled in me. The seethings ahead were now climbing on decomposing corpses and clawing to the top. Some were breaking through the line of beasts and jumping beyond them. Finally, we were attacking—not just dying.

Now, let us move, now! I could feel the Tarragon snapping at the tethers to their minds—attempting to break free.

Our kind is being slaughtered!

I gritted my teeth; they weren't wrong. We were out here to ensure the beasts didn't advance. It was quite frankly a miracle that the Glenn had managed to hold its own as long as it had.

Not a miracle. It's thanks to our kind. Tens of thousands gave their lives —whatever they were—in battles days before.

I didn't miss the tone they used. Didn't miss the way that, even though they didn't know *what* they were, they knew they were—they were elite, and yet, they still cared for the smaller creatures. It was unnervingly noble.

"Command, come in. Requesting permission to move forward," I feigned into the mic.

Their voices broke through, but I spoke over them. "Moving in, now."

I didn't wait, instead, I began to move.

Now, I commanded the Tarragon.

As one, we stalked forward and then began to run. In moments, we'd be upon the front line.

Allow us to be airborne, they requested.

I could see it playing out in my mind. All of them airborne and me left to fight alone on the ground. I played through each and every option in rapid succession.

Half of you, fly and attack from above. Do not die. If you are failing, retreat, regroup, and then attack once more. The other half, stick with me on the ground.

I could sense not only their excitement but also my own thrill—my magic swirled in response. I sent signals to six of the Tarragon, and they didn't wait before launching upward. Their wings shadowed over me, massive and terrifying. Had I not seen a dragon, these would be the fiercest beasts I'd ever set eyes on.

Red streaked across the ground with every one of my steps. Webbing out from every place my feet touched. The ground crackled. I willed my lightning forward, weaving between seethings and striking the hearts of beasts.

They screamed at the impact and dropped dead.

Fuck yeah.

The high took over and I continued forward, through the throng of seethings and through the gap I'd made where dead beasts now lay crumpled on the ground. The Tarragon surrounded me, in the air and on the ground, before swiping their talons into the beasts nearest them. When streams of fire became targeted at me, the Tarragon blocked it with their scaled wings. To my shock, they didn't burn. Instead, they merely repelled the flames.

Pride swelled in my chest; *my* beasts were winning.

Not yours. And not beasts, they spoke as one into my mind.

I smiled, lopsided and strong, before throwing out my hands and unleashing bursts of red lightning. In coordinated attacks, the Tarragon swiped with their talons, swung with their barbed tails, and blocked the beast's flames. We were invincible.

Seconds passed, then minutes. Around me lay hundreds of corpses

—too many to count. And still, we pressed on. The beasts kept coming. Several leveled their flames at me, the Tarragon blocking them from the ground, and I threw up a wall of lightning.

Air coverage, now! I shouted to the airborne Tarragon.

They complied immediately, my will their own.

The fire punched through the lightning, and I went flailing through the air and landed on my ass. Several beasts stalked toward me, flames shooting from their hands—this was it.

Three Tarragon pounced in front, shielding me. But more beasts came. They overpowered one of the Tarragon—I could feel its agonizing cry as the beasts' claws sunk into the Tarragon's wing and ripped.

Terror. Fear. Pain. Strong emotions shot down the connections I shared with all of the Tarragon.

The first of their kind was maimed. The rest honed in on the injured one, attempting to save it from the beasts attacking it—but without its wing to shield, the Tarragon became swallowed in flames.

One down, now only eleven stood with me.

I didn't miss the cries and mournful wails I felt in my soul from all the remaining Tarragon. They'd lost more than a comrade. Their screams echoed through the night and through my very being—I could feel their loss and noted the moment the thread connecting me to the dead Tarragon went silent. Gone.

More beasts poured onto the battlefield in front of me, some going airborne. Rage filled my veins as the Tarragon began to fight, ripping wings from the beasts and gutting the closest ones. Still, we were vastly outnumbered.

We can win. My magic whispered.

Without another thought, I fully opened the gate guarding my power, and allowed it to flow, unleashed.

I could sense more than I'd ever thought possible. The fear in the air, the rage coursing through nearly every creature on the field, the pain from those who were injured. But what was more, I could taste something different. Something ancient wafting through the field. I inhaled deeply, even as several red bolts swallowed all the beasts within a hundred feet of my lightning, frying them from the inside out.

I tasted it then—the *wild* in them.

Their corpses fell to the ground, but I didn't retract my power. Instead, I followed its probing to a little kernel I could sense at the center of each of the beasts...their magic. It was protected, hidden, but powerful. I pulled on it and siphoned it with half a thought.

The moment their power began to flow into me, my lightning brightened—thickened in strength—and red became all I could see.

Leader! the Tarragon roared.

I sensed *my* red enveloping every blade of grass, every insect on the trees in the valley—I felt it covering every creature before me, both my Tarragon and the beasts. What was more, I could sense the *vampires* who'd been hiding in the throngs of beasts. My magic pulled at me, begging me to allow it complete and total reign.

And I surrendered to the sheer greed and euphoria: I became its puppet.

My power engulfed the hidden vampires and struck them where they stood. I pierced through their shields and located their magic flame, burning deep within.

Forbidden... my conscience whispered. But was it?

I smiled as I snuffed out their flames, inhaled their energy, and left them as nothing more than mere husks. Suddenly, I couldn't see anymore as the power I siphoned filled my stores and altered every-thing before me. My body was encased in red static, beads of energy that were vibrating so rapidly I wasn't sure *I* was material any longer.

The thought was jarring. I wanted to still be me. I was out here for *her*. I longed for Holland's honeyed scent, her light brown hair, and the way she scrunched her nose when she talked. I craved the taste of her on my lips.

Remember Holland, Shae, the guara.

I slammed the door to my magic shut. In an instant, the field returned to its normal hue. Which, even in the day, felt dark. Every-thing seemed to be ten shades dimmer. The dead surrounded me. In every direction, all I could see were the bodies of beasts and vampires. My Tarragon stood around me, a shield of scales.

I could hear the roaring of footsteps, the sound of an army a hundred thousand strong retreating. In the distance, their forms were running from us—from battle.

It was over. We'd won. For now.

CHAPTER 64
TATE

After quickly clothing ourselves, Aether and I rushed to the Veil where I opened the gate, revealing a desperate James holding Ruby and Clarence. He rushed through and dropped them in a heap at my feet, before grabbing Aether and blinking out once more.

I carried the two scared children from the clearing back to the castle, where they'd be safe and warm by the roaring fire—stoked by my anger. Someone was trying to hurt children. Children.

They were both covered in mud and blood. Even with Ruby's grumbling, I could see the fear. Clarence's lip quivered as he pulled his legs to his chest.

"Quit being such a baby!" Ruby nearly shouted, even as her shoulders shook.

"I'm not being a baby!" Clarence swiped at his nose wildly, willing the snot dripping down to disappear.

"Hey, hey." I waved at them. "It's okay, you're here now. Want to tell me what happened?"

Ruby squared her shoulders and tilted her nose higher in the air. "If you don't already know, then I'm not gonna tell."

I knelt down and pulled the small boy onto my lap, rubbing his back.

"They came from everywhere." He sniffed as he leaned into my embrace.

"Who did?" I gently asked the question while standing and moving to the couch, holding him tightly.

"Those things, they were—"

Aether burst through the door, Vala right behind him, and set an injured Uley down, before retreating back out again to join James. I didn't miss the sick thud of Uley crumbling to the ground, or the blood that gushed from an open wound in her side.

"Mama!" Clarence shouted.

I set the boy on the couch, tucked a blanket around him, and then rushed to the injured female's side. "Uley, it's going to be all right."

Was it though? I had no medical training, no knowledge in staunching the bleeding of gaping wounds. I had no serum. I had nothing. I felt completely useless.

"Vala, do you have any supplies?" I looked up to meet haunted chocolate eyes. They were void, full of pain, and unresponsive. "Vala?" I snapped my fingers and waved them in front of her face. She blinked.

"Tate?" Her focus was fleeting, with eyes glossing over again as her lips slightly trembled.

"Do you have a kit? A medic bag? Anything?" I searched the area where they'd been dumped. Nothing.

"N-no," Vala whispered. "They followed us, somehow, they found our new safe house and...they just..."

I quickly looked her over, no visible signs of a head injury. Nothing fatal that I could see.

I turned my attention back to Uley, pressing my hand into her wound. Blood seeped through. Too much. The floor around me was already soaked in maroon, and Uley's head lolled back—she'd lost consciousness.

"Ruby, hand me that blanket," I ordered looking at a wrap folded up on the chaise.

Ruby stood there frozen, face pale.

"Ruby, the blanket," I commanded firmly. She blinked and then rushed to retrieve the blanket. I maintained pressure as I waited.

Too little, too late.

Too little, too late.

The words echoed in my mind as my fears swam. Ruby couldn't lose *another* mother. Aether couldn't handle that. Uley had to live. I pressed harder.

Ruby came back with the blanket, and I wadded it up before pressing it to the wound.

No response came from Uley, the blood flow seemed to be slowing and her lips were pale, bordering on blue. No. I refused to let her go.

"Mama," Ruby's voice broke from beside me.

I met dark eyes that filled with unshed tears—her red curls matted around her head, dirty and disarrayed—but nothing was more disturbing than the look of shock and anguish that claimed her features.

No one should have to witness losing their mother. Flashes of Irene's face came to mind. I was much older than Ruby, and yet her loss still marred my soul. I never got to even see her body, but her being taken from me was cruel. No, Ruby would not lose her mother.

I wouldn't fucking allow it.

Following nothing but instinct, I threw aside the blanket and pressed my hands into the wound. Just like with Carly, I allowed my magic to pour from me. The room became illuminated in a pink aura, with shadows slithering within. I could feel my skin humming, buzzing with energy. I pulsed with power, willing the magic surfacing to pour into Uley. I didn't know what I was doing, but I simply followed the tug from my power.

"Live, Uley. Live!" I spoke more to myself than anyone.

I exhaled as I closed my eyes. I could feel the energy doubling, and from the red behind my eyelids, I knew that the room was getting brighter; my limbs tingled, and my power was everything and everywhere. Hair whipped across my face, and Ruby gasped, Clarence whimpered, and the wind howled.

I opened my eyes to see I was in a cyclone with Uley. The rest of the room had faded, there was nothing but Uley and myself, encased in a cloud of pink flames. Energy poured from my hands, siphoned from the air around me and the ground itself, in rivers flowing directly into Uley. Her body flinched, and then, her eyes opened.

The power instantly winked out. The cyclone ended and Uley just stared at the ceiling. For a moment I feared she was still too far gone, but then she began coughing and Ruby rushed to her side and bent over, crying into her hair, "Mama!"

Uley smiled and stroked Ruby's head. "Hey, baby."

I sat there for a moment and then my eyes locked with Vala's— wonder shown there. Clarence crawled off the couch and rushed to Uley's side, throwing himself into the fray as they all held each other tightly.

I didn't understand what had happened—how it had happened. But I did know one thing: they didn't lose their mother.

Ruby didn't lose another parent.

I stood, noting the large amount of blood covering my clothing and arms. I was covered in Uley's lifeblood.

James blinked in, depositing a grumbling Camella, nursing an injured arm. "Thanks for opening the gate further." He blinked out and then back again with Aether, covered in mud and blood. A thump sounded as the head from a beast hit the ground next to James's feet, dripping blood and white goo.

Lovely.

I turned and raised a brow to Aether. He merely smiled. "It got a bit messy."

I laughed in spite of myself. Perhaps the amount of expressed magic had altered my consciousness, but I found the scene ridiculous.

Blood covered the floor, a mother held her two children and James rushed to their side, inspecting Uley's now healed injury.

Aether stood there, blood and mud splashed across his face and covered his loose tangled bun. Camella was also caked in gore and hadn't stopped spurting choice words.

Vala remained silent, still in shock.

And then, there at their feet, was a grotesque, milky white head of a beast, its serpent tongue hanging limply out of its mouth as it dripped goo all over the iron-stained floor. A floor that was pristine just moments before and was now marred with violence.

More laughter bubbled from my lips.

Aether looked at me, smiling while simultaneously looking unnerved. I could sense him reaching out through the bond, inspecting me—looking for any injury. This only made me laugh harder. I doubled over, tears pouring from my eyes.

Impossible. This was all impossible.

Me, a royal? Unreal. The milky head of a new species of beast? Unthinkable. Uley's wound healed and her life spared? Out of the question.

My laughter turned to coughs as the air around me seemed insufficient—I couldn't access enough oxygen. I crumpled to my knees as I tried to calm my erratic heart.

I'm here.

His voice down the bond immediately calmed the rising tide of panic; as did his body brushing against mine, encasing me with his arms.

Let's get out of here.

What about them?

The panic began rising as I thought of all the new responsibilities I had, of the people who were here *because* of me.

"Is everyone all right?" Aether's voice was but a faint whisper as his arms tightened around me.

"Yes, brother. More than all right. We're alive," James responded.

I could feel Aether nod as he picked me up and cradled me against him. "Camella, there's blankets over there, tons of guest suites just up the stairs and to the right. And down the hall to the left, you'll find a fully stocked kitchen." His voice hummed against my chest, soothing my wild heart.

"Got it," Camella replied.

For a moment no one spoke, Aether just held me tightly against him—his body a reassuring force.

"Aether, we're good. Go take care of her and please, do us all a favor and clean up, you look disgusting," James chirped, his voice full of mirth—a juxtaposition against the blood and terror still staining the room. "Especially given the pheromones you're releasing, you really ought to bathe—"

Camella elbowed James in the gut, silencing him.

I was vaguely aware of them filing out of the room, of the quiet sound of the fire crackling and distant footsteps. And I didn't question Aether as he carried me from the study. His mere presence was loosening my tight chest. I leaned into his warmth; into the body I'd become intimately familiar with.

We moved through the library, room by room, until he had reached the staircase several stories high, with landings leading to each floor. Up and up he went, until, at last, we reached the royal wing and entered the royal chamber, Esme's chamber. But he didn't stop there, instead, he carried me out onto the patio and sat down on its lush furnishings. The cushions groaned from his weight as he leaned back, cradling my still-shaking body against his.

I was breathing, deep steady breaths. Aether murmured reassurances into my ear, his breath tickling its sensitive shell.

This is real.

Real. This was my reality now. Silent tears streamed down my face. Pain I'd been blocking exploded in my chest: Irene was not my mother. I was being hunted. I was a fucking royal with no desire for the throne, but my mere blood was causing others harm.

I sniffled as I swatted angrily at the tears.

"It's time I stop hiding, Aether. We need to act. Uley almost died." The weight of what had occurred wasn't lost on me. Those innocents were in danger *because* of me, because of my lineage.

Not because of you, but because of greed and Arithi. This isn't your fault. They almost died, Aether.

But they didn't. You saved Uley, just like Carly. It is an honor *to serve you, Tate.*

Aether continued to hold me as my tears subsided and my being stopped quaking. Several moments passed and a new resolve filled me—it was time to go on the offensive. Time to make our move.

Aether nodded in agreement, and his body's warmth began to heat more than my skin—it sank deep within, reaching my internal being and filling me with newfound need. I ignored the reason in my head that said I had things *to do*, to learn, actions that needed to be taken. Instead, I indulged myself as I nestled further into my mate, a pure wall of muscle. I savored the smell of his ash and salt, even through the stench of blood and gore coating his hair and clothes—it somehow increased his sex appeal. He was a warrior, lethal as hell. I reveled in the small circles he drew on my lower back with his hand while his breaths caressed my neck.

This moment was mine. It was ours. The rest could wait.

I tilted my head up and took his lips in my own, greedily.

He tasted of pleasure, of power, of victory.

He growled in my ear, and I realized I'd sent that image down the bond. *Our* bond. He was my equal in every way. Something in me broke at the reminder that I had someone I could fully trust—a mate. My other half. My magic rose and met Aether's, intertwining above us in a burst of black and pink flames. Even as my hands locked behind his neck and I adjusted on his lap to straddle him, our magic danced and grew. I was acutely aware of his presence, both in my mind and around my body. But it was more than that. My *magic* was aware of his—as if he was an extension of myself. Another shade, another layer, a shell of protection that was rooted deep within.

His hands roamed across my back, my hips, my waist. Everything in me cried for more, begged for more. He began kissing my cheek down to my neck, slowly and sensually, eliciting a moan from deep within.

"I believe we have some unfinished business," he purred in my ear before playfully nipping at it. "But let me clean up first."

"No."

"No?" He growled in my ear. "Does this turn you on?" He gestured to his bloodied hair and streaks of mud across his cheek.

"And if it does?" I leaned in closer to him and sent an image of us fucking after our final victory, over the corpses of the vile, and celebrating in the most carnal ways, down the bond.

The resounding rumble from Aether silenced my thoughts. "Fucking hell."

"Mmm," was the only intelligible response I could offer before his lips took mine once again.

His presence in my mind rolled like that of thunder, sending chills down my spine that only increased as his hands tightened around my hips. Burning need consumed me. I began rocking against the length of him and savored the way his magic purred with mine. Every inhale was that of ash, strength, victory, mystery, and sex. Every exhale was that of trust, devotion, passion, and love.

I broke the kiss only long enough to give him a demanding, pointed look.

So impatient.

On the contrary, I've been more *than patient.*

He chuckled aloud and in my mind simultaneously, before setting me down and standing in front of me—all male. The flames around us sparked with renewed life. I was vaguely aware of the aura, our melding magic of pink and black haze, dancing across the stone balcony. But my eyes were focused on the male disrobing in front of me.

His ruined shirt dropped to the floor, revealing tan skin that still sang of battle, displaying bits of dirt and unwashed blood. Tattoos covered his sculpted body, each one telling a story. Stories I dearly wanted to hear. I reached out a tender hand and traced his tattoos— the intricate pattern crawled over his right pectoral muscle and up to his collarbone before peaking at his neck. He had a twin tattoo on the other side of his neck, and ink also covered his lower left arm. I didn't miss the way he tensed under my touch or the static I felt from our mere contact.

Even after the moments we've shared, the intimacy we've experienced together, I was amazed that a simple graze of my fingers across his skin elicited such excitement in me. In him.

My mouth watered in anticipation as his eyes deepened with lust.

I smiled coyly. "Any ideas as to what we could do next?"

He didn't respond, instead, the air around me intensified and tightened as the fire surged. He sprung forward, embracing me, and then lowered me to the chaise—laughter escaped my lips at the sudden weightlessness and the playfulness of his gesture. He leaned over the chaise, eyes drinking me in, even with my worn, bloody trousers and tunic.

Beautiful.

A shudder crawled up my neck at the intensity in his gaze. He wrapped his thumbs around his pants and then pulled them off in a fluid motion, revealing a warrior's body, a very *excited* one. His manhood was fully alert, but he didn't move, he waited.

I smiled; I *could* toy with him.

His growl confirmed he heard that down the bond. I chuckled darkly. Pure need pulsed within, and the tic of his jaw was my undoing. I commanded my flames to *burn* my clothing before grabbing him and pulling him down, our bare flesh meeting. His mouth claimed my neck savagely and our magic flared with the passion we both shared.

Mine.

I smiled against his back even as my fingernails sunk into flesh. He hovered over the lover's mark, waiting in question. I nodded and then his fangs sank in, slow and burning.

Euphoric couldn't begin to explain the emotions that overcame me. My entire body became hyperaware and buzzed with unchecked desire. Every place our bodies met was purely aflame, internal fire burning so brightly that he didn't even need to enter me for my body to climax. Waves of pleasure rolled through me, and my head lulled back giving him greater access. I released a moan that had his hands tightening on my hips as he pulled deeper with his fangs.

Aether? I silently asked, waiting for permission to also partake.

The resounding image was more than enough confirmation, dirty and full of promise. I leaned forward and sank my fangs into the tender spot between his neck and shoulder. He jerked beneath me and then relaxed as his blood met my tongue. Just as I remembered, rich and full of power. The iron dripped down my throat in waves of glory. I was suddenly unaware of anything tangible, there was only him.

The air around me tightened to the point of near pain and then dissipated in a wave of release. He was in me. My hips met him thrust for thrust, increasing the pleasure with each silken pass of *him*. He growled against me as he removed his fangs and began kissing the fresh wound, and then every part of my exposed shoulder.

I pulled again, savoring his unique flavor as he dominated every sense, every part of my mind. Aether.

Aether fucking Brychan.

Mine, he growled down the bond.

Mine, I confirmed as I released my fangs and took his mouth in my own.

We were no longer on the chaise. In fact, we were no longer on the ground. Our entangled bodies hovered in a cloud of flames as we continued to ravish one another. His hands roamed across my skin as we continued to revel in the passion. My core tensed around him, preparing for release. He teased and pulled out, breaking our kiss, and then claimed my neck, my breasts, and my naval with his mouth. Every part of my being screamed for additional contact, further friction, added pressure.

A plea he happily obliged. Sweet tension coiled around my body, teasing every tender spot and eliciting ecstasy.

The sky lit with a show of fireworks and sparks as he hovered at my entrance, earning a whimper from my lips.

Aether, I growled down the bond.

In one motion, he complied and the fullness of him had me fracturing. I screamed his name as my nails dug into his flesh, piercing his skin, and my legs tightened around him.

I shattered.

Pure bliss engulfed me. I could sense him constricting and his moan was confirmation that he too had climaxed.

In a daze, we clung to one another, breathing heavily over our sweat-slickened flesh. I looked around, we were no longer surrounded by flames, but were encased in pure light—rose gold with swirls of black. Our bodies began to lower to the ground, the terrace coming back into view a hundred feet below.

Aether's eyes locked on mine—dark and full of promise. *Mate,* they seemed to say, appreciation lacing them. Slowly we lowered back to the solid ground, toward the many things that awaited us. The many challenges and truths I'd need to face, but not alone. Never alone.

I smiled at the male whom I'd come to depend on, the male who was in fact, my missing piece.

"Together," I murmured.

"Together," he agreed, and our feet reached solid stone.

CHAPTER 65
CHANCE

"What the fuck was that?" Rusty spat as I stalked through the leader tent, heading straight for the barracks to shower away the blood and sweat currently coating my body.

"Winning," I retorted.

Thriving, the Tarragon answered. I still held their minds in my tethers. Somehow, it felt right. Like they completed me, were made *for* me.

"The fuck it was. You ignored direct orders. You were told to stand down," Anax Graff spoke through pursed lips.

I leveled a glare at her. She was beneath me.

We are stronger. We don't need them.

I silenced the Tarragon. I needed my mind clear.

"Well done, Dux Dale," my father's voice was accentuated by his clapping. "Perhaps, he did violate the chain of command. But I've never seen a display of power like that. You were death embodied, son."

The way he accepted me had my fury spiking. Red danced across my hands. So, this was all it took. I just needed to be a powerful wielder and then my father would have my back, respect me? Claim me proudly as his *son*.

I narrowed my eyes at him.

He's strong, leader. But not as strong as you, certainly not with us.

I could sense the Tarragon's restlessness. They stood just beyond the war tent, hunched over on all fours like damned guard dogs.

My magic flared and I allowed it a cursory inspection of my father. His magic was...wild, old, new, and yet, somehow oily, sullied.

"You'd do well to remember who sired you and who's been wielding longer, even as strong as you are," my father spoke. I felt it then, the lightning *zing* of his power shoving against mine, pushing me back. But he didn't stop there. He stalked toward me as his power reached out and scraped its talons against mine, begging to be let in.

I shoved against it and a red aura met his grey one...the tent was lit with our power, dueling it out before abruptly vanishing.

"Anax Dale, everyone. Please acknowledge Anax Dale." My father's cruel smile spread across his face.

I stood motionless, momentarily frozen. Anax Dale? I'd dreamt of this day my whole life. My whole existence was building toward this. Becoming an anax and then, if Mother Blood allowed, one day president.

"Anax Dale," Rusty spat as his purple veins bulged against his grey skin. His crimson eyes flared. I could sense his magic; rotten, like the male itself.

"Anax Dale." Anax Graff nodded at me before abruptly turning her attention back to the projection showing troops and coordinating the guara's next moves. "We have them on the move, now is the time to plan."

"Agreed. How would you proceed, Anax Dale?" my father asked, as he too turned his attention to the screen.

I could see the enemy troops in red, covering the hills and spanning out over the next several hundred miles. Even with this recent battle, they still severely outnumbered us. They'd retreated, but they didn't flee. They were regrouping. As we should be.

I flexed my fist, coated in dried blood. "I say we advance. We wipe them out. We kill every single one."

The craving for more blood grew as power thrummed in my veins.

Yes! We can do it. We Tarragon are ready to claim vengeance for our lost one.

Even my magic bucked within me. *More*, it seemed to beg. I was capable of so much more. *Pure power.*

"I applaud the stance, but we must be careful," Anax Graff hedged. "We've survived this long based on skill and careful measures. Even with your...talent, Anax Dale, we would not be able to take them all down. Not as we currently stand. Their beasts outnumber ours thirty-to-one."

Ghouls. They're ghouls. The Tarragon spoke into my mind.

"They're called ghouls, and they have a hive mentality. I believe we can take them down if we strike the correct members. When I hit one, the rest responded. I think that if we locate the strongest and knock them down, the others would fall too." I slammed my fist against the tent post.

"An interesting perspective," my father spoke. "But, risky. What do you propose, Anax Graff?"

"A peace treaty meeting. We send our strongest along with myself to negotiate their removal." Anax Graff leveled her dark eyes on my father. "It is the only way to save lives. We must try."

My father's jaw clenched.

No, we can take them. I can take them... My magic swirled within.

"Very well, we try it your way, Anax Graff. If that should fail, Anax Dale will have free rein to handle this as *he* sees fit." My father spoke and the entire tent shook with the excitement coursing through me as red static flew out and danced along the canvas. I pulled it back, before turning and heading for the showers. A certain short female consumed my thoughts.

Exquisite.

A smile played at my lips.

CHAPTER 66
TATE

After rinsing off, I dressed in a gauzy lilac gown from the closet nearby. It had a plunging neckline in both the front and back. The gossamer strips were elegantly clasped with pink sapphires that formed a rose at each shoulder, and matching jewels formed a belt at the waist. Beautiful, but definitely not practical. It appeared royals lacked tactical clothing. That or it wasn't kept in this wardrobe. Frustration gnawed at me as I continued opening drawers and cupboards searching for shoes. I was about to give up as I limped about the room when I felt a tug toward a dresser in the far corner.

I sighed, this tug-and-pull was getting old. Even still, I followed it and opened the bottom drawer. Inside was a pile of tactical clothes, in both black and pink. I ran my fingers over it, amazed, before I noted several pairs of shoes: high heels, slip-on slippers, sandals, and tactical boots. My breath caught. It wasn't the obscene number of shoes that had me frozen, no, it was the fact that the sole of each left shoe was modified with a thicker base. They were made for me.

I stared at them, dumbfounded, before finally reaching in and retrieving a pair of deep violet slippers and stepping into them. They fit like gloves.

"Gorgeous," Aether said from the doorway.

I twirled around to meet his gaze and felt suddenly at a loss for words. "They fit, I don't know how, but they're...perfect."

Aether smiled. "It's not too surprising since this place is yours. Magic has a way of...altering things."

There were many things I needed to learn, but appreciation for magic wasn't one—it came effortlessly.

Aether cleared his throat. "We have many things to discuss, but right now I'd like nothing more than to tear that gown from your body and lick every, perfect, delicious inch of you..." His eyes hooded.

I smirked as I could see him playing the scene out in his mind.

Such a dirty imagination, I teased.

You have no idea.

My face heated as I brushed past him into the hallway. "Fill me in as we head down?"

His resounding growl and dirty thoughts poured down the bond. All of them had him *filling* me with different things, *not* information— a finger, the hard length of him, his tongue—

I laughed at how insatiable he was, at how much he desired me, and then immediately suppressed my smile. Males were sensitive when it came to their manhood.

Even still, he cleared his head and his steps sounded and then he was striding next to me over the deep maroon carpet. "James is gathering intel on the Glenn; he should be back with an update soon. In the meantime, we need to determine next steps. Vala is a mess over Jared and well..." his voice trailed off.

I paused mid-step and turned to him, eyebrow lifted. "And?"

"The king, it seems, he may not last the week. It's time to start planning your return to Mydant."

I swallowed and kept walking. I was still adjusting to the truth of who I was, what I was. And now I was supposed to stroll into the capital city of the Untishee, of Fae lords and ladies, of dragon shifters, and declare myself a royal? I didn't even know what that meant.

Not alone, Aether reassured.

No, I wasn't alone.

We continued to walk in silence until we made it down several flights of stairs into a large conference space that was richly adorned. The mahogany table was covered in pink sapphires ground into the wood itself, overlayed with glass. The large hearth, big enough to fit us all standing in it at once, was lit with pink flames that held a black center.

I could sense Aether's pride as he too noted the change in the flames. Mates, that's what it testified to. Vala stood, staring out the large window to the waterfall as Camella sat, legs propped up on the table, whittling a piece of wood with a blade. Her eyes locked onto us, and she abruptly stood, straightening her posture, and then bowed.

Bowed...before me?

The sight was unnerving. She stayed like that and Vala too knelt, eyes on the floor.

I felt a knock on the veil and immediately recognized the foreign presence. After the recent ambush, I realized this castle's magic connected with my own and bent to my will. It was mere instinct to form commands and weaves after that. With half a thought, I lowered the veil and James blinked in. Without missing a beat, he joined Camella and Vala by kneeling on the ground.

Aether cleared his throat, and I only then noted he too was on his knees.

I could get used to this. You on your knees. Perhaps in a different—

Darling, we can make that happen right now.

He sent several images down the bond, some replaying our previous encounter with the drape's tassel, and some filled with other suggestions of what we could do...

My face heated and I blinked. "Uh, rise," I commanded lamely. This was all too much, and I fumbled for the right words—I had no idea how to do it properly. And it felt wrong—I was their peer, far more than I was their *royal.*

Don't you dare lower yourself, Aether growled.

I merely bit my lip, unsure of what to do or say.

"I really appreciate you all coming, it means more than I can express, but really this formality is unnecessary—"

"Your Highness," Aether started, "it is your blood that we are sworn to protect."

"To protect and serve," everyone in the room spoke in unison, right hand over their hearts.

They all stood and then took their seats, leaving the one at the head of the table vacant. I paused, for just a moment, and surveyed my team.

Vala, eyes full of pain and determination, sat next to Camella who sat across from Aether, James at his side. Each one of these people left their lives for me. Sacrificed for me. I felt inexplicably unworthy. Who was I to take so much from them?

"Your Highness," Aether spoke slowly, nodding to the chair.

I bit back my retort; if they wanted me to embody what my blood said I was, I could at least try.

"Uh, yes. Begin." I sat next to him, sinking into the chair's thick cushions.

Also, you'll need to seal the veil again.

Right.

I swallowed, and I reached out to the magic coursing through the very air itself, willing it to shut, to once again lock us in and keep the outside *out*.

"James, what news do you have?" Aether began.

James grunted in response. "Well, shockingly, the Glenn has held their own. I could see the Fern's beasts outside the city limits, camped for the evening. The battlefield is littered with bodies, lots of black goo, and white bones." He paused, clearing his throat. "I did sneak into the guaramen's camp and overheard the conversation of a few duxes. Allegedly, there is a meeting that will take place tomorrow evening. A peace treaty conference."

I mulled it all over. "The city, is it still..." Images of tiny bodies, all the vamplings who were in Fletch's class came to mind. They were innocents.

"Standing," James confirmed. "But I'm not sure for how long."

I nodded. War was bloody. The seethings and President Collin Dale needed to be dealt with. He made those monsters, and brought them into the city, into the heart of residential areas. He was purely evil and we needed to banish the darkness—that included washing my hands in Collin's blood.

But to battle in the city? With mortals and children who were helpless? There had to be another way.

"Any news from the Embassy?" Aether asked.

James cleared his throat. "Other than King Owen's impending death, we've been officially listed as traitors to the Crown. It will make sneaking into Mydant even harder."

"And Arithi?" Aether continued his questioning, ever the high general.

"From what I gathered she wasn't even at the Embassy, but away at some formal meeting," James spat the last few words.

"Formal meeting?" I asked. That made no sense, not unless... "Could she be working with the Fern?"

Aether's eyes were keen, shining with appreciation. "That, Your *Highness*," he said as he winked at me, "was exactly what I wanted to know. After we were attacked by those creamy-eyed beasts, the same Arithi brought in for your testing, I began to wonder how she was connected. Did she merely capture them? If so, why not study them? But to subject trainees to them? No, she was definitely familiar with them."

"And?" I asked, ire beginning to rise in my belly.

"When they attacked us, and we identified our leak, the traitor ___" he cast a sympathetic look to Vala who remained silent "—his work with Arithi confirmed it. I still don't understand why she's working with the Fern. I mean, when we were sent to get *you* it was because she was leading the chairs in building an army to defend Mydant from President Dale's seethings, if it came to it. But now? I'm not so sure." I didn't miss the way his jaw flexed. He was visibly agitated.

You're not the only one who was lied to. My values and life were abruptly turned upside down, too, he rumbled down the bond.

I bit my lip, I'd been so wrapped up in what *I'd* been going through, I hadn't even considered Aether's life changes.

I'm sorry. I—

No need. I'm just saying, it's messy.

I nodded.

"I say we wait here and then smuggle her in when the borders open for the king's funeral. It could be any day," Camella said, straightening her back.

"That would be the wise thing to do," Aether hedged. "James, any word on Enzo?"

The look in James's eyes spoke volumes. I felt sick. "He's being held as a traitor to the throne. Juda holds his seat now."

Aether merely nodded once. "Then we're on our own. We will wait it out here and make preparations to return to—"

"No," I spoke, and all eyes landed on me. "We cannot simply leave. The Glenn is full of innocents. I will not leave them to be incinerated by one beast or another."

"Tate, I understand where you're coming from, really I do, but we cannot risk it," Aether spoke, challenging me with his eyes—pleading with me to agree.

"We have no other choice," James agreed.

I looked to Camella, who to her credit didn't shrink back. "Fleeing is the wisest course of action, Your Highness."

I ran my hands over my face. "The Untish are sworn to protect. To care for and guide *all* life forms. We are made of the three. I will not retreat to Mydant, and declare myself as royal when it means turning my back on things here. Aether, you gave me your word *we* would get vengeance. I will not leave until President Dale no longer breathes."

The room fell silent.

Please, Aether, you know I'm right.

It's not safe.

Safe for whom? Those innocents will die! Children. Vamplings. We have the power to help.

Tate—

Aether.

He growled out loud, everyone looking between us with uncertainty, almost like we'd lost our minds.

I'm your ruler, yes?

Yes.

Then, find a way for us to complete this mission and then *we will go to Mydant. Fletch and Irene deserve justice. My wrath has yet to be assuaged.*

Aether gritted his teeth, muscles flexing at his jaw. "James, anyway you see that we can accomplish what Her Highness desires?"

James remained silent for a moment.

Before he could respond Camella spoke, awe in her voice, "The prophecy."

Aether snarled and slammed his hands on the table, standing. "Fuck the prophecy."

"What prophecy?" I asked.

Camella stood, all five feet of her, and met Aether's glare. "She has the right to know. She deserves to know."

Pain exploded in my chest at the insinuation.

"Aether," I snapped. "What fucking prophecy?"

His jaw ticked and he remained silent, refusing to speak—eyes boring holes into Camella with dark flames rising at his back. Had he lied to me again? More half-truths?

"Camella, enlighten me. Now."

Her eyes ripped from Aether, and she looked at me in appraisal. "Yes, Your Highness. There is an ancient prophecy about an heir, *thee* heir, lost here in Shappa only to be found and returned to Mydant. It is said she will reunite the worlds, secure the realms, vanquish evil, and—"

"It's BULLSHIT!" Aether roared as a wall of energy pulsed, ready to engulf Camella.

I met his wave with one of my own and beat his power back.

Aether's eyes zapped to mine as he poured more of his power into his wall, combatting my own.

Aether, it's all right.

His inner turmoil only tripled down the bond, along with the distinct taste of fear and panic growing in him, reflected in manic eyes. Instead of leaning into my own anger and betrayal, understanding claimed me as waves of love filled the bond.

Shhh, I whispered to his soul.

I sent him an image of us embraced, overlooking the sea, hand in hand. A team. Impenetrable. Strong. Equal.

The wall of dark flames vanished, and his power dissipated. With a heaving chest, Aether dropped to his knees before me. "I'm sorry. My love, forgive me."

I placed a hand on his shoulder and then lifted his chin with my index finger. Terror still pulsed from him.

I can't lose you.

"A little old prophecy cannot separate us." I looked into his eyes and willed him to see the earnestness there. "Now tell me about this."

You're not angry?

I'm upset, but I also can see your intentions, I can feel your response to the prophecy and somehow, I understand. Help me understand this further?

He nodded and with my gesture, he stood and then took his seat next to me. The entire room was silent, eyes fixated on Aether and myself.

"The prophecy," Aether began. "Is, in my opinion, hocus pocus written by a crazed prophetess and promoted by Cleo."

"Aether—"

"It claims that a lost heir will be found and that she will restore balance. It's a lot of gibberish, and if you wish, we can search for the exact verbiage, but essentially, it suggests she will defeat evil, and her reign will bring peace to all realms."

"Okay...and why do you think it's about me, Camella?"

She swallowed and bridged her hands. "I only know what the prophecy means, or what I've been told it means. As far as what it specifically says, I don't have it all memorized, but this is what I do recall." She cleared her throat. *"The heir will rise from the ashes, will have survived from annihilation. From the blood of forgotten royalty, bonded with that of darkness, concealed until ready, exposed by the highest death, and raised in a pillar of fire, she will be called home. Her reign shall bring peace and justice to all realms and evil will be vanquished."*

Everyone fell silent. I could hear the pounding of my own heart accompanied by Aether's own turmoil, actively screaming down the bond.

"Sounds like I may be a badass," I half-heartedly joked—still not believing it was about me. Even if I *was* from forgotten blood, that of Esme, and *did* bond with Aether, the high general of the Shadow Tribe with distinctly *dark* flames, that didn't prove anything. "But the second half makes no sense. Just because I'm Esme's forgotten child and bonded with Aether doesn't mean I'm the heir spoken of in the prophecy."

"Tate," Camella spoke slowly. "'*The highest death*' has often been understood to mean the death of a Crown. The King of Mydant is expected to die any day now."

Oh. Well fuck, that did seem to change things.

I will protect you. You don't have to be anything you don't want to be.

I savored Aether's words, inhaled them deep in my soul.

"Well, we still have no idea who this prophecy speaks of, and honestly, I'm inclined to agree with Aether, it sounds a bit loopy." Aether's visible sigh released some of my inner tension. "Let's focus on the here and now. Let's talk about how we can end this war and spare innocent lives."

No one spoke.

"You heard Her Highness, what options do you see?" Aether spoke, ice in every word.

James cleared his throat. "Well, only a stealth mission would work given the size of our team. But it's unlikely we'd survive it. It would be a death sentence."

"Camella?" I asked.

Her eyes locked onto mine. "I'm sorry, but James is right. With just us, there's no way we could take on the Glenn's army, or even sneak in and take out the president. Those beasts alone are strong deterrents."

Frustration gnawed at me. The Glenn was at war with the Fern. Vile beasts from both sides would slaughter thousands of innocent citizens.

I was a Untish royal, sparing life was my responsibility. Even before I learned of this potentially bogus prophecy, unnerving as it was, I had always been justice-minded. Prior to understanding my blood's inherent rights and responsibilities, I had always felt an inexplicable urge to protect those who couldn't save themselves.

I growled aloud. "Okay, what if we used the two armies to our advantage? What if we sneak in during their battle or treaty meeting and eliminate Collin Dale then?"

"That could work, but from what I gathered, only his son and Anax Graff will be the Glenn's representatives," James said.

I could feel my blood boiling. "Any news of Shae Drew?"

Shame claimed me as I realized I hadn't asked about her until now.

"Who?" James asked, confusion written on his features.

My dear friend. I hadn't checked on her, hadn't thought of her in ages, and now...now I had no idea how she was or *if* she was. My stomach tightened. I would not leave her, not again. A dry laugh worked its way through my clenched teeth. She would have answers, suggestions, ideas. If only I had her here. If only...

If Shae were here, she'd tell me to use my wits. To observe. To allow myself to *fit* the role assigned to me. Here, among these loyalists, I was royalty. But in the Glenn? I was no one.

"What if we were to intercept the representatives?" I asked.

The quiet table got even stiller, if that were possible.

"I mean, what if it was a simple abduction...then return."

"Wha—who?" Aether asked, confusion marring his features.

I smiled. "James, how many can you blink at a time?"

"It depends on their magic and my strength, reserves, etcetera, but probably anywhere from two to four," he responded.

I nodded. "Camella, have you ever secured a 'package' before?"

Her eyes gleamed. "Oh, a number of times."

I smiled. "Is the compromised cabin still standing?"

Aether's puzzled look widened. "No, it's in ashes. But the foundation stands."

Perfect.

"I think this just might work."

CHAPTER 67
CHANCE

evour. Destroy. Claim. Change.

Magic poured through my veins, spilled from my fingertips, and charred the ground with every step I took. Red danced across the walls, flowing in webs. I followed the steady call of Holland's magic. Of her lure and pull.

I smiled, or perhaps I laughed, my awareness was waning. I pounded through the hall and savored the way all arches and duxes avoided me, pressed their pathetic bodies against the walls, and tried to become nothing.

As they should, the Tarragon roared in my mind.

My connection to them now felt second nature. I made a left down the hallway, through the barracks, and then a right into where I was told Holland's room was—but more importantly, to where I could feel *her*. I pushed open the old metal door and slammed it shut behind me, securing it with red bolts of lightning.

Holland gasped as she turned and spotted me, "Dale, you're..."

"Anax Dale," I said as I puffed out my chest.

"An-Anax?" She looked horrified. Anger rose in my belly and bolts shot out and swallowed the room, every inch except for a two-foot circumference around Holland.

"I did it. I finally made my father proud. More than that, *I* have power. We can change things, Holland. You and I." I stepped forward and she took a reflective step back, flinching as she did so.

"Dale, this isn't...I mean, you're not this..." Words seemed to fail her as she looked me over.

"What? Am I not good enough now that I've become what I must to save this country, the Glenn, to save *you*!?" I spat the last word, my lightning strengthened and closed in around Holland, leaving only a foot of clear floor surrounding her.

I could feel her presence reaching out—attempting to calm my mind.

I snarled as I zapped the connection. "I'm not out of control or some rabid dog. I'm Chance Dale. Anax Chance Dale. And you're *mine*." I prowled forward.

Holland swallowed and a certain sadness filled her eyes. "Dale, I... we can fix this." She nodded, more to herself than me.

"Holland, I don't need fixing. Maybe for the first time in my life, I'm right. I'm whole. I'm strong." How could I explain this to her? How could she not already understand? "This is who I am."

"No." She stepped forward, her feet grazing the bolts that didn't harm her—they crawled up her leg, swirled, but didn't hurt her, I wouldn't allow it. "Dale, this isn't who you are. This is the dark magic talking."

I snarled. "Holland, accept me or don't, but don't act like you're better."

She paused, flickered, and it almost looked like she flashed in and out. I could have sworn she left for a moment, but there she was, standing in front of me and extending a tentative hand. "Dale, look at yourself."

Hesitantly, I turned toward the mirror—driven by some inexplicable urge to please this female. My breath caught in my lungs. The male in front of me had changed. He still had icy blue eyes but they were haloed by a bright red around the rims. My wavy blond hair lifted from my shoulders, curls knotting in on themselves, with red light pouring from every strand.

I was sexier than ever. Lethal too.

My veins illuminated a red shade that matched that of the lightning shooting out from my very essence. I was *different*.

When I turned back to Holland, I could tell she saw the truth there. Rage fueled me as I saw fear in her features. She was afraid? Of *me*?

"How could you?" I demanded. "You and I are together. We have an understanding. And you dare act afraid of me? I became this for you!" I couldn't keep my voice down as I began screaming at the female who, to her credit, didn't cower. "Everything I've done, become, has been for you! To keep *you* safe. To please you! To become strong enough to deserve you!"

Her presence sliced through my shield and wrapped around my mind. *Here,* it seemed to say, as if soothing a wild animal.

"Dale, you and I *are* together, we're something special." She smiled. "But this," she again gestured to my body, "this power, this magic, it is changing you. The male who had such a strong moral compass would never have drained those humans—chained humans—in the train car. If you can't see that, perhaps your mind's been badly warped already."

"Warped?" I snapped. "It was a necessary evil, one that allowed me to destroy those beasts, the ghouls, who would have ripped apart our citizens if they'd broken through our lines."

"Where does it end? You justify small acts and then big ones, and before long, you'll be siphoning from our own."

"Really?" I snarled and laughed a dry, humorless laugh. "That's what you think of me? I can't believe you; I thought you'd respect me. Honor me. *Thank* me. *Worship* ME!"

My anger pulsed.

Leader, should we annihilate the female and show her who you can be? Should we put on a show and make her watch as we tear apart this realm?

My magic swirled in response to the Tarragon—the temptation was great.

"Dale, I am thankful for you. But you cannot excuse what you did, I can't forget it—I won't." Her lips quivered.

I'd seen it in the train car, the judgment. I thought she'd come around, come to see it was the only way. Perhaps I was a fool.

"What comes next? Will you siphon from me?" Holland placed a hand on my bicep, it tensed on reflex beneath her touch. "Will you siphon from *Shae,* again?"

Guilt began to build in my gut as I thought of the vampires I'd just siphoned—beasts as well. I'd taken their magic, snuffed out their flames, and hadn't been bothered in the least.

Enemy, the Tarragon reminded me.

They were my enemy. They were a threat to Holland. I did it for her.

I didn't respond. Instead, I wrapped my arms around her and pulled her close—nearly crushing her in my embrace. My lips savagely claimed hers even as her magic's scent tempted me, beckoned me to simply try a *little*...

I refused my magic and deepened the kiss as my hands began to roam over her petite body. Hard muscle, soft flesh, so fucking hot. I ripped her shirt from her body, and she pulled back, gasping.

"Dale, I—"

I tugged her back into my embrace, clamping my lips over hers once again. My hands moved of their own accord, seeking her pants which I quickly ripped down. Holland pushed against me as she tore her lips free.

"Stop it, Dale. STOP."

But I couldn't, I wouldn't. She wanted me, I just had to remind her.

She shoved against me, but my magic lashed out and bound her hands. Suddenly, I wasn't in control of myself. Not as I threw her back onto the bed. Not as I crawled atop her and yanked off my shirt. Not as I reached down, cupping her ass in one hand as my other reached for her bra and—

"I believe she said stop," a voice came from the door. A male voice.

How had he gotten through my bolts? Had I dropped them?

I snarled as I looked up, meeting the gaze of Carran. He stood there, club drawn and at the ready, eyes full of intensity. He didn't flinch as I shot a bolt of lightning toward him, he merely evaded it. "Boy, this isn't you."

How dare he. I withdrew myself from Holland and stalked toward the male. I was going to enjoy this. Very, very much. I threw a missile of lightning at his feet; he jumped out of the way. I threw another, and he jolted left. I smiled. I was a cat toying with a mouse.

Holland whimpered behind me, "Dale, please, I know you're in there."

But I ignored her as my magic pulsed and engulfed my vision. I saw nothing but red. I released a stream of lightning at Carran but he evaded, far too fast for a lumbering male, and then he swung, his club coming precariously close to my head. I growled and lightning coated the floor and wrapped around his wrists, holding him in place. He was no match for me.

I sniffed, my magic *inhaled,* and I could taste his small flame within. Barely any magic, but perhaps enough to satisfy my craving. "You really shouldn't have come," I purred.

Carran shrieked as I began to siphon his life force.

Holland screamed in the background, begging me to stop. A small part of my mind asked me to listen, to heed Holland's pleas and end this. But my rage was too great, my appetite too strong. So, I pulled.

Carran wailed again, dropping to his knees.

"Enough!" Blue ice shot out and hit the bindings holding Carran at bay, before continuing forward and hitting the web of lightning covering the floor. The water shot through my magical connection and sent me flying backwards into the wall. I crashed into it, through it, and landed in a pile, shaking haphazardly. My vision blurred as my limbs twitched.

Leader! the Tarragon cried.

I shot out a bolt at the door, to the figure now helping Carran to his feet. It met a wall of ice. Irritation filled me as I struggled to my feet. More ice flew toward Holland's bindings, and I jolted from the contact of the frosty water. Holland launched off the bed and strode for the door.

"Are you all right?" a female voice asked. I knew that voice.

I forced myself up again and willed my body to stop trembling. My eyes cleared and I locked eyes with grey-blue ones, filled with resolve.

"Chance, this has been more than enough." Shae looked at me, arching a brow.

I blinked as the magic in my body begged me to act. I looked around the room. The bed with Holland's torn shirt, Carran being supported by Holland and Shae—a sickly grey pallor to his skin. The fear in both female's eyes, along with judgment.

Shame filled me.

I shoved the door to my magic shut and instantly the red illuminating their faces ceased. I was suddenly cold within. The Tarragon's tethers had snapped and I wasn't connected to them—I felt empty.

I took a step toward them, and they flinched. I swallowed and looked away. What had I become?

"Excuse me." I stormed from the room without another word. My shoulder brushed Shae's and I jumped, attempting to avoid contact with all of them.

"Chance!" Shae called after me, but it was all too late.

Too damned late.

They were better off without me. Far, far away from me. I should have left a long time ago and never come back. Guilt filled every step, even as the magic began to slip from my control and spill from the door I couldn't seem to keep sealed. I was in trouble.

Big fucking trouble.

CHAPTER 68
TATE

This was a risk. A big risk, but one I felt good about. Aether continuously grumbled in my mind, but I paid him no heed. We would succeed; we had to.

Vala worked next to me, drawing ward marks on the ground. She'd shown me how and now we worked together...in silence. Unbearable silence.

Once it was clear that her magic had sputtered out back at the castle, she'd been hysterical. That was, until *I* realized it was due to a blood-oath she took with Aether, and Jared's betrayal of it. In that moment, I'd never agreed more that magic was sentient—it knew who it *was* a violation to tell and who it wasn't. Vala had been allowed to tell her bonded by Aether, and when Jared told Arithi and she acted on it, magic sought to satisfy its price—Vala's magic.

After that, and a few choice words with Aether for making Vala agree to such a thing, it was a matter of releasing her of the oath with another magical tie. Slowly, her eyes filled once again with their ethereal hue as her magic was beginning to restore. Aether said it would take time, but she should be at full capacity within a day or two.

Even still, hours later she was a ghost of herself—some wounds cut so deep, that I often surmised they altered our very being, that we'd lose part of ourselves.

I didn't want that, not for Vala. Not my bubbly friend who'd been nothing but kind and honest to me, who cheered me on even when I struggled to produce a single flame. She'd helped me in so many ways, and now I wanted to help her...if only she'd let me.

I cleared my throat. "I'm here if you want to talk."

She didn't respond, just kept working on her marks in steady, undeterred strokes.

"I know it must feel horrible; I've been betrayed many times and it's not...it doesn't get easier. But you're not alone."

"I'm not?" she snapped at me, yanking her eyes from the bloodied mark on the ground. "Tate, I'm completely alone. More alone than I've ever been. My *bonded,* the one I was supposed to be with, the one *magic* chose, the one I was matched with and would have wed in a few weeks' time, betrayed me. Jared turned on me," her lips quivered as she spoke.

My mouth went suddenly dry.

I knew Jared didn't like me, but the fact that he turned on Vala was still unbelievable. Sobering even. I couldn't help but feel a kernel of doubt in my own bonded relationship. What did I know about bonds after all?

"He screwed up, big time," I started, turning my eyes back to the task at hand. "But when he realizes what a colossal mistake he's made, I'll take him back if you will."

"You would?" Vala's eyes looked like they'd just about pop out. "Why? He literally just sold you out. Sold his *betrothed* out. How could you ever trust him again?"

I knew the feeling too well. "Fletch was murdered in front of me the night before I met you on the circuit."

Vala went deathly still. I continued to work, ignoring her as I focused on my ward marks.

"He lied to me. My entire life, he lied to me. I knew he wasn't my father. He was more of an uncle, a guardian. He was a vampling teacher. *Harmless.* Or so I thought. It wasn't until that day that I'd learned he'd betrayed the Glenn, my country, his country." I paused, loosening a breath I didn't realize I was holding. "Vala, I may never understand why he and Irene lied to me, but I know they loved me. I know that Fletch thought he was protecting me by keeping me in the dark, even as he instilled Untish values. I can't say it's the same for Jared, but we can only assume his motives."

Vala smiled sadly. "You really think he could have possibly meant well?"

"I don't know." I placed my hand on hers. "But if you're given the chance to ask, I hope you can find the answers you need."

She nodded at me, giving my hand a squeeze before surveying our work. "We're done here."

"I think so, too," I said with a smile.

Darling? I cooed down the bond. *How's it coming?*

I could feel his sense of humor battling his annoyance, and I knew he was likely suppressing a smile.

Fine, darling. *Almost there. You?*

All done.

I nodded to Vala, and we began walking back toward them.

"That's so weird and special, you know?" Vala began, sounding like herself for the first time since the attack. "Like, you can just talk to each other in your heads. No matter space. No matter time. It's nearly unheard of."

I chuckled. "What, you guys don't have advanced walkie-talkies?"

"What?"

"They're devices you can communicate with from afar, like cell phones but not as sophisticated."

She gave me a deadpan look. "You know what I mean. This form of communication, the one you share with Aether, it's like in your head... in your magic. It's so cool and *sooo* rare." She fell silent again, likely her thoughts had turned back to Jared.

I linked my arm through hers and we marched through the forest. Pinecones crushed beneath our feet reminding me of a time not too long ago when we were in a forest, and *she* was the one practically dragging me. Things had changed. I bit my lip as I thought back to *how* much had changed. How much was at stake with my plan. With a heavy sigh, I squared my shoulders in resolve—soon we'd have the upper hand.

We continued until we finally breached the hill, and I spotted Aether with James and Camella. He was surveying the rings we'd made; his muscles flexed as he crossed his arms, determination written across his face. His features were wild and firm, eyes dark and focused. Even his hair was pulled into a warrior's bun. He was the embodiment of a lethal, alluring angel.

We could abandon this entire half-baked plan...and you and I could just fuck.

Ha. Nice try.

I chuckled even as he shrugged, as if to say it was worth a shot.

"Well?" I asked the other three as Vala and I stopped just outside one of the circles.

James grunted. "It's set. But if you're not sure about this, it's not too late to back—"

"We are doing this," I interrupted James. "I can't let innocents die without at least trying to stop this."

James shook his head but said nothing more. Camella simply nodded, donning her warrior face.

"All right, you've done your part, Tate. James, it's time to get Her Highness back to the warded location," Aether said, gesturing for James to come get me.

James approached, but I stepped back. "Are you sure you don't need me to stay?"

Aether's jaw flexed. "Tate, you have every right to be here, you're powerful as hell, but you're still manifesting your magic. And you're still learning to shift. It's too soon for you to be subjected to this. Do you trust me?" His eyes filled with earnest hope. "Together, remember? We each do our part and bring President Dale down *together*."

I nodded. This was the agreement we'd struck, that I'd be relocated to a *near* but safe location, hidden by runes and shields, while he handled the meeting. He'd wanted to send me back to the palace, to lock me away in safety, but we were in this together. This was my plan. My people. My vengeance. I would not be sheltered inside a castle while their lives were in danger executing my will.

Together. If I suspect anything amiss, I'll be here—

Tate. You need to—

Aether. We are a team, yes?

James stepped closer to me. I didn't miss the tightening of Aether's jaw as he nodded to me and then James.

It had to be this way.

It was the only way.

James wrapped his arms around my waist, and together we blinked out.

CHAPTER 69
CHANCE

I sat staring at a blank screen, awaiting orders. My magic cried from within, begging to be freed. I pressed it down. I'd hurt them, hurt *her*. She may never be able to look me in the eye again; fuck, she shouldn't. She deserved better, so much better. I cradled my head in my hands and let the obscenities fly. What was wrong with me?

I exhaled in frustration. This was all *her* fault. Tate made those vile things. Tate lied to me and betrayed my country. She set those damned explosives off and turned me into this fucking power-crazed thing. I wrung my hands tightly, making my knuckles white.

"All right, we've received confirmation." Anax Graff strode through the open tent flaps. "We meet in six hours, at an unoccupied field about four hours from here via transport."

I looked at her. "Why so far?" The enemy was literally within eyesight, just over the bluff.

"It's common for Vamp leaders to gather in locations further from their armies, it gives a sense of equal footing." She shrugged before carefully eyeing me. "Are you sure you're up for this?"

"Fuck yes."

I swallowed back my fears. One good thing about it being so far away was that Holland would be safer, and so would Shae. I shuddered as I recalled the look in her eyes and the *power* she now had. Ice magic. I didn't even know that existed.

I bit my lip as I stood, running my hands through my annoyingly long hair. My knuckles caught in its tangles and stung. Perhaps I'd cut it sooner than not. "When do we leave?"

"In thirty minutes. Refuel. We want to arrive early to stake the area out and get ideal positioning."

Traditional tactics, finally something I understood. I reached for the pitcher of bloodwine and poured myself a large glass. I practically inhaled it, not realizing how hungry I was, before downing another. And then another. The pitcher went dry, but before I asked an arche to bring more, I noticed not one, but three additional full pitchers.

I smiled as I helped myself to more. The mind-numbing fruit took over and I allowed it to lull my thoughts to sleep. To quiet the guilt eating me alive. It would be easier this way; soon I'd be gone, and we'd be meeting with the enemy. If worst came to it, I would release the core of my power and incinerate them—or better yet, feed from them.

Yes...

My magic stirred within me. Soon, I promised it. Soon.

CHAPTER 70

TATE

James set me down on the bluff nearby. It was about a mile out, and high up, making it the perfect vantage point.

"I don't like this," he grumbled for what must've been the hundredth time. "I'm with Aether's original plan, it's not too late to take you back to the palace you know?"

"Then it's a good thing that *I* outrank you both." I winked. I was still uncomfortable with the *royal* title, but it did have its perks. Moving toward the edge, I gazed out at the valley below. From this distance, I was still close enough to see the outline and vague details of Aether, but far enough to hopefully avoid being noticeable myself.

"Are you sure I can't—"

I silenced him with my hand. He remained quiet and simply ran his fingers through his unusually frayed pompadour and nodded.

"James?" He looked up when I called his name. "Have a little faith?"

He grumbled some response and then bent over and began carving ward marks and runes. We didn't have long, but it would have to suffice. I helped him, as best as I could with my brief training in magical markings, wards, and runes. After he carved each one into the ground, I dropped my blood into the symbol and willed my magic to lock it in place.

"There, if you decide to stay here, no one will find you," James gave me a pointed plea.

"Thank you. You really are a bit dramatic." I nudged him playfully. "Just be sure to retrieve me when everything is secured."

"Now I know why my buddies called me a 'damned dog' when my power manifested," he muttered.

I laughed lightly. "Well, if you're a good boy, perhaps we'll get you a treat or a belly rub."

The disturbed look on his face had me laughing harder.

"Relax, James. This is all going to work out." I feigned confidence I didn't fully feel. My plan wasn't infallible. It was cocky and impulsive and could get any one of us hurt or killed.

But it was the only way. We needed to end this war, these beasts, before more innocent lives paid the price. I nodded to James who offered a prayer to Mother Blood and then blinked out, leaving me alone to my devices.

Hours passed as I waited. I practiced my shields, I called forth fire and made flames spark above me, beside me, swirl around me. Control was something that took time and practice, as Vala continuously reminded me, but I was a quick learner. I looked within and tried to awaken *her*. She still was slumbering, ignoring my calls. Almost as if she were punishing me for not releasing her when she wanted to finally make an appearance in the trials. I snorted at the thought. Even if I wanted to release her then, I couldn't have—I still wasn't sure how to. The intrinsic string I *used* to pull to shift into a raven was heavy, buried, and completely inaccessible. At that thought, *she* raised her head and glared at me.

I blew a stray piece of hair out of my face. Fine, I'd deal with *her* later.

I began to pace back and forth in my dome, noting the changing of leaves and the breeze blowing the dead ones scattered across the ground in a swirled pattern. The path I paced became noticeable and my feet began to ache. Slowly, I sat crossed-legged, and toyed with a stick. The satchel at my waist hummed with power, its weight bearing down on me. I tried to ignore it as I idly traced shapes and patterns on the ground.

But as time droned on, that too got boring. The sun was beginning to set, and I knew I didn't have that long, but still...

I pulled off my satchel and opened its leather flap, revealing the journal and a few scrolls I'd tucked inside. Slowly, I pulled out the journal as the breath whooshed from my lungs.

With no one around to witness my potential humiliation, I opened the pages of my mother's journal. My mother, not Irene. I ran my hands over the scrawled writing, reveling in how it *felt* alive. I longed to know what it said. I flipped through the pages and cut my finger, blood dripping onto the lettering.

"Dammit," I grumbled, sucking my thumb. The journal hummed, and then the letters glowed, changed, and then rearranged. The content shifted and I froze. It was a note, to *me*.

My dearest daughter, Tatealia Aaralyn Bloom,

How I wish I could say this to you in person, but I fear time is not on my side. The poison has taken effect and while we've made every effort possible to negate it, soon my breath will still. You deserve answers, and I wish to give you as many as I can.

I was poisoned in my eighth month of pregnancy. You were delivered early and miraculously survived. The effects of the poisoning were extreme. At times, I lost my sight. You, however, were spared...the doctors surmised it was because you were delivered quickly after the initial poisoning.

Not only did you live, but you flourished. We dwelled together in secrecy for three years, thanks to the Luner potions and antidotes.

I froze. Three years? I was three when she passed?

I've cherished each and every moment with you. I had thought the effects of the poison had been fully negated, that we took you soon enough. But I was wrong. Magic mixed with poison can be as unpredictable as it is cruel.

After the incident, I fear you may never walk again—not on two equal feet. I fear further for the implications on your magic. This is why I've decided to go through with the cloaking. It will freeze you in time to allow your magic to heal—and only when you are ready, when your magic is ready—will it thaw, and time start anew.

The Luner doctor was helpful, through her magic and potions, I've been assured you will have every chance possible to flourish. For now, she has devised a lock on your shifting...you will still be able to shift, upon the initial awakening of magic at early adulthood, to that of a bird, but until your Changing is complete, you will not be able to shift into your true form. This may take time; magic has a will of its own—do not be dismayed if it takes longer than normal for your Untish genes to fully express—even by several years. But when it is time, my sweet girl, find your way home, for only the truth of your bare feet upon rightful soil, will unlock your ability to fully shift into her glorious form. Then, let them fear you as they should a royal.

It would be perilous to not warn you: court life is not safe. There are many who will swear allegiance, who will offer support—but they are all vipers. Just like the cousin who struck out against me with power and greed in her red eyes, I fear they will come for you. It is with this in mind that I beg Mother Blood to forgive me for this falsehood. I will pass you to my handmaid. She has a daughter, young enough and not a close acquaintance of mine that she would be a safe mother figure for you when you likely will emerge from the cloaking.

It is with a heavy heart that I do this. It is not easy, but my body is failing, and the longer I live, the longer the binds I have to you pull you down with me. Always live with your heart, trust it, and know its truth. It alone will guide you.

Be free, my sweet girl. Be smart. Survive.

I love you,

Your Mother,

Esme

I stared at the pages and blinked. My entire life had been summarized to this? A couple of pages that changed literally everything? The memory of me falling and hurting my leg had been with Irene, hadn't it? Suddenly, I couldn't see the female's face. I couldn't see my mother's face.

"It hurts, Mommy!"

"Shhh, all will be right with time, Tatealia," a female cooed. Her face was hidden in a ring of light, rose-colored light.

I began breathing in rapid pants. How had I come to this? I thought I was ready for the truth, but potions and Luner magic? To be faced with the realization that my *mother*, Esme, blocked my shifting ability and then gave me an entire false mother in the name of safety? I'd been wrong. I wasn't ready, not even close.

I closed the journal as I furiously rubbed my hands against my face. How many more falsehoods would I endure? Irene had lied to me about my origin and taught me nothing of magic—in a world where knowledge was power, she and Esme left me unprepared and vulnerable.

I cursed under my breath as I threw the journal back into my satchel and stood. The hills hummed in quiet anticipation.

Movement to the left caught my attention. A transport, a surprisingly large one—especially given that we only expected a few representatives—rolled through the forest on a dirt road in the distance. Dust filled the air along with an engine's distinct hum before it abruptly stopped. It was showtime.

I swallowed back the fear clawing at me and reassessed my bond with Aether.

Any news?

Arriving now. Will keep you posted.

I nodded to myself. The transport's door swung open and a tall, lankly female emerged. Her black uniform was pressed and proudly bore the pendant of the guara. If memory served me, the shrewd-looking female was Anax Graff. The doors behind her swung open and half a dozen guaramen poured out. But it was the figure cutting in front of the rig that caught my attention. I'd recognize the messy head of curls anywhere—a golden beacon. He prowled forward and froze mid-step, his head turning toward me.

For a moment I panicked, could he see me? But his keen vampirical eyesight gazed *through* me, unfocused but in my direction—the shield was still in place. Even from afar, I could sense something turning in him, an untapped power I never knew he had.

Guilt filled me as I recalled the way he looked at me in the S.O., the way he tried to make things right. I'd fled, leaving him to the beasts after the explosion. I abandoned him, I abandoned Shae.

Anax Graff said something to Chance, I couldn't hear from here, but he appeared to nod. Then as one, the two leaders led their pack of guaramen forward to where the cabin's ashes awaited. I could sense a tightening down the bond, Aether had spotted them as well. Only time would tell if my plan and calculations were correct.

They strode forward, and the moment they entered the perimeter of the first ring, I heard a distinct shriek and the evening sky lit up with red bolts of lightning.

I was sprinting down the hill and toward the screams of rage in an instant. I hurled myself toward the storm of red. Toward a situation that I suddenly realized I'd gravely misunderstood.

CHAPTER 71

AETHER

The male roaring in front of me was pure power and fury. His eyes were haloed in red and illuminated red static writhed across his body. Two of the six guaramen lay dead at his feet; in his crazed state, he struck them with pure energy, and with a shriek, they crumpled to the ground immediately. Lifeless.

The female, Anax Graff, stood far away from Chance Dale—eyes wary. "What is this?" she called, looking me over.

She didn't know who I was.

From the bolts that continually attacked the shield, it was clear Chance remembered me. "Filthy piece of shit!" His voice was nearly otherworldly.

"Chance." I smiled keeping my face neutral. I glanced to my side and spotted Vala. Her eyes were wide as she reinforced the dome's power with her own, even from her weakened state. Our plan hadn't accounted for his deep stores of magic—this was a complication, to say the least. The shield would only hold for so long, our timeline had been cut in half. If that. "Nice to see you again," I drawled.

He clenched his fists as twin bolts hit the dome just in front of my face before webbing up and coating every inch of it. Vala gasped from the side, and I became acutely aware that Chance's force was eating through the wards and Vala's magic quickly; far too fast for her to keep up with it alone—especially when she hadn't returned to full force yet. I began to reinforce the shield with my own power.

We may only have minutes, not the hours we'd anticipated.

"Where the fuck is the bitch who holds your balls?" Chance drew, spitting on the ground near his feet. "She deserves you, you know that? A monster to match her own."

I swallowed back the rage growing and kept my mask in place: cool indifference.

"Anax Graff," I looked past Chance, whose eyes flared as he realized I wasn't taking his bait, to the female who kept her chin high. "We understand you are here to meet with the Fern in an effort to eliminate further bloodshed. We are here to broker that deal."

Anax Graff narrowed her eyes but tilted her head in a clear sign that said *continue.*

"We propose the complete demolition of your seethings and in return, the Fern will destroy their beasts as well. Both sides will hand over *all* research regarding their creation to me, a representative of the Untish Embassy." I didn't miss the fear that swelled in her eyes when I announced *where* I was from. "We will end all ongoing studies of dark magic and destroy any existing knowledge of the seethings' creation. We want to avoid bloodshed, to save lives, to spare *your* citizen's lives."

"I see," she began. "You must know that won't happen, even if we stand down and the Fern returns with their troops. We have no way of ensuring they dispose of their beasts, their ghouls. You cannot expect us to release the only thing keeping them at bay. To destroy our defenses." She huffed but stepped closer.

"We will ensure *all* creatures on both sides are eliminated. That is a promise. It will happen, with or without your compliance." As I spoke, black flames swallowed the dome—in a show of power, yes, but also to reinforce its magical holdings. My eyes swirled with wild energy, and I became acutely aware that two swords of black flames were in each of my hands.

Chance Dale stilled and Anax Graff froze, eyes wide in terror. I fueled her emotions a bit, adding additional frenzy and acquiescence to her internal wildfire—noticeable in the quivering of her lips. But with Chance, my attempt was rebuffed in an instant, leaving a putrid taste in my mouth. Interesting.

"As I said, one way or another, the seethings will go." My flames flared in emphasis as I spoke.

Chance laughed bitterly. "You think you can threaten us? That I fear your pitiful power and flames? It's all bark and no bite."

"Perhaps you'd like to find out." I tilted my head in a predatorial way as I called back the flames so they were transparent, before reinforcing the magical bonds surrounding the dome with my own power.

"I know what you're capable of, I saw you in your *other* form, but you must now see that I have changed. Things have changed. I have the Tarragon and it won't be long until they get *their* vengeance." His eyes flashed with red static, illuminating the inside of the dome and the horror on Anax Graff's face.

"Anax Dale, you were to leave them behind!"

"Anax Graff, you no longer give me orders. They are connected to me, and my will is their own. You'll soon see." Chance smirked as he flexed his hands and plummeted the shield with his bolts. My flames flickered in response, as I pushed more power into the barrier—attempting to hold his magic in check.

Glancing beyond the dome, I nodded to Vala, *Go.* We needed an update on how things were going with the other half of this happy convoy.

"Surrender your research and allow us to destroy the seethings. Send them all into the field, twenty miles outside the city by nightfall tomorrow, or risk our wrath." I met Anax Graff's eyes. Unease filled my gut as I realized my words held no power with her, not even as I fueled her fear. It seemed that Chance's—no, Anax Dale's—threats about the Tarragon held her captive, not the fire-wielding Untishee in front of her. I locked my jaw and Chance looked smug as he also realized his newfound stature.

"As I said, I have more power than you could imagine, *Mardi*," he spat my name, earning a rich chuckle from my chest.

The action put him on edge, causing him to prowl forward while Anax Graff took a step back. "Surrender everything, and your city—HQ—will see no more bloodshed. Innocent lives need not be destroyed." I repeated the threat, the plea, to both their ears. Anax Graff swallowed, but Anax Dale merely smiled.

He opened his mouth to respond when his eyes snagged on something behind me. His nostrils flared as his lightning shook the dome.

I felt it then. I felt *her.*

I twisted around to see Tate, gorgeous as ever, approaching quickly, dressed in midnight black. Pink flames claimed her normal mahogany eyes and she lunged the last several feet down the hill, landing in a crouch beside me. With a quick survey, she evaluated the situation and then threw a hand on her lush hips, before leaning in—accentuating her curves and ample cleavage.

What the fuck are you doing here?

Helping, darling. A team, yes?

She winked at me as she slowly strutted forward, her shoulder brushing mine. "Chance," she began, toying with him. "I see you've changed, but when was the last time you've had a haircut?"

"What?" He blinked, clearly unnerved. "You little bitch, I should—"

Tate clicked her tongue. "What would your mother say?" She turned in one motion and looked at me. "Sorry to keep you waiting, *babe.*"

Before I could respond, her lips were on mine in a savage kiss. Her arms reached behind my back and her fingers dug into my hair as she breathily moaned. "We'll finish later," she said loud enough for all to hear.

Chance stiffened as his eyes narrowed. A primal smile played at my lips.

"I'm going to electrocute you until you're nothing more than a whisp, a husk before me," Chance snarled—red lightning crackled with every step he took until he braced his hands on the shield.

The remaining four guaramen surrounded Anax Graff on the opposite side of the dome. Wise, I realized, as Chance was quickly losing control.

"Please, you have a difficult time getting hard for anyone, let alone summoning enough courage to actually prod them to death," Tate laughed.

You're marvelous, I whispered down the bond.

She patted me on the shoulder before turning toward the dome. Every one of my instincts told me to intercept her, to force her back and protect her. But she could handle her own—she needed my respect and support, not fear-addled coddling.

In the distance, I could see James blink in and shove two unsuspecting diplomats into the adjoining dome. The Fern representative had arrived. James blinked out and then back, this time with Vala and Camella. The former giving me a tight nod. It was now or never.

"I was telling them, darling, that they need only destroy those abominations and hand over all research, and we'd spare them—along with the countless innocent lives of the Glenn."

"Yes, and what has Anax Graff said?" Tate asked, tilting her head in a predatory motion.

Any progress?

Not too much, she fears Chance more than she does us.

We'll have to fix that. Perhaps you should show her your other form.

Not yet.

"Anax Graff is not in charge," Chance snapped. "I am."

"You," Tate snorted, "the mighty Dux Dale thinks he's in charge."

"It's Anax Dale," he snapped.

The Fern representatives took several unsure steps back, deeper into their own dome at the sight of Chance's power flaring. Lightning struck haphazardly and his body shook from barely contained pulses of power.

"Anax?" Tate laughed, dry and lacking any mirth. "Did Daddy

finally give you his approval? Or was the promotion mere posturing for the foreign government?" She took a step closer, a mere breath away from the shield.

Tate—

She silenced me with a look, eyes intense and full of warning. I forced myself to breathe and release every instinct that told me to whisk her away to safety.

"I earned it!" Chance shouted, bolts stabbing the ground as his anger grew. "He finally recognized the title that was mine by merit."

"Whatever helps you sleep at night," Tate said. "But if you're done with your tantrum, let the grown-ups talk."

Chance began shuddering, his remaining restraints rapidly crumbling. "You are a traitor to the Glenn. You turned your back on your family!"

"I suppose I learned from the best." She regarded him coolly. "Now, Anax Graff, while I can see Chance's power may make you nervous, I assure you it is nothing compared to what *I* am capable of. To what he," she nodded at me, "is capable of. The Untish are real. Dragons are real. We can end your life with half a thought, and the Glenn's with it. But our goal is not death, it is life. You know those creatures are vile and that they need to go. Do the right thing. Save those innocent vamplings, elders, and citizens."

Tate's body lit in pink flames, haloing her as she touched the dome and it *boomed!* from her mere contact. Pink and black flames erupted over both domes, swallowing them whole as an image of a dragon danced in the sparks, breathing fire that passed through the barrier and warmed the faces of Anax Graff, Chance, and the other diplomats. I watched in wonder as their clothes began to smolder and as Chance's shirt burned from his body, falling to the ground in scraps.

"Do the right thing," Tate's voice rumbled as the dragons lifted their heads before looking down at each dome and releasing liquid fire into the dirt. The two corpses from the dead guaramen were incinerated almost instantly.

A moment later, the flames were gone. The dragons were gone. Power filled the air, and I couldn't keep the awe I felt for this female from my face. She side-eyed me and smiled, winking.

Fuck, I *was* angry that she put herself in danger unnecessarily. But that display? I shook my head in appreciation. She was in more control of her magic than I'd realized.

"What would you have us do?" The Fern diplomats dropped to their knees, cowering. "We've done everything you've asked of us. We will retreat now. The beasts are yours; they've always been yours."

Confusion crossed Tate's face and was surely mirrored in my own.

Anax Graff stepped over the now burned bodies, nothing but piles of ash, and cleared her throat. "The Glenn is willing—"

"To destroy you," Chance interrupted, smiling like he knew something. "Interesting, isn't it Anax Graff, that *our* enemy claims the ghouls belong to the Untish? That they belong to Tate and have been doing her bidding?" He prowled forward.

I glanced at Tate, her expression was guarded but I didn't miss the doubt that crept into her eyes or the tightening around her lips.

"I know the truth. You made those things and now you want us to surrender to you. This," Chance gestured to the other dome, "is all a ruse."

"Chance," Tate's voice was quiet, and for the first time, scared. "You're better than this. You used to value life and rules. You can save your citizens. You can save Shae."

"Shae?" Chance laughed wildly—the sound unhinged. "Do you even know how she is? What you did to her?"

"What?"

"I'm not the only one affected by your magic, by the explosion. I may have *awakened*, but your dear best friend—the one you left for dead, the one you betrayed—suffers effects from *you* too. She—"

An explosion sounded, coming from the forest beyond. The protective wards had been triggered. I whipped my head in time to see plumes of smoke rising, billowing in the air. Another blast sounded and shook the ground, this one coming from behind. I didn't need to turn to sense the shift in magic. To sense the presence of beasts.

"Meet your creation," Chance purred, "the Tarragon."

CHAPTER 72

CHANCE

The chains holding me back shattered. I snapped. I could see Tate wavering from the impact of my words. It satisfied me even as my blood boiled at the sight of her with *him*. He was a reminder of who Tate really was, what she'd become, of what was at stake.

I glanced at Anax Graff who stood behind me, shaking in her boots but holding her resolve. I understood how she'd maintained her position for the past several decades, even with my jackass father dictating roles. All around me, energy pulsed. I could sense the magic rolling from the guards near me, from Anax Graff herself, from beyond the shield, from *her*.

I allowed the magic to course through me, to run wild. I ignored the barbed looks Tate shot at me, the looks imploring Anax Graff and the Fern leaders to see reason.

I was about to open my mouth when I felt them. A smile pulled at my lips—about fucking time. Thank blood I was sober enough to reconnect with my beasts before I departed HQ. My connection had grown faint, the further we went, but I could still sense them. Now, it was strong. They'd be here any moment.

A nearby explosion sounded and a dry laugh escaped my lips.

I locked eyes with Tate's wide ones, still spinning with an unnatural pink hue. "Meet your creation, the Tarragon."

Mardi began shouting orders to the rest of his small crew. I looked around searching for more soldiers—but saw shockingly few. This couldn't be all of them, could it? As if in answer, another explosion sounded from behind. The ground shuttered from its force and plumes of black coated the sky. What the hell?

I didn't know who that was, but I didn't have time to find out. I pushed against the shield and willed it to break. It flickered but resisted. I grunted in frustration as I poured more of my power into my attack. Red bolts shook the dome, engulfing it from the inside, but still it stood. I locked eyes with Tate and noticed she was pouring her magic into reinforcing the shield. That simply wouldn't do. The fear all around me grew as my lightning got richer. The calling to take and devour whispered in my ear.

I could sense my creatures, the Tarragon getting close. I could see them flying in the distance, specks becoming larger with every passing second. Tate was no match for them...at least not until she fully unleashed herself.

"You nearly killed Shae!" I shouted, not caring that my voice sounded less and less like myself. "She was in a coma for days, her skin a sickly grey. I thought I'd lost her. I thought you murdered her."

Tate's magic faltered, just enough for me to know I'd struck true. Mardi growled from beside her as figures darted about in multiple directions. A tall one approached, his hair in an alarmingly neat pompadour. I inhaled. Him. He was the one from the pub, only this time I noticed his ears—pointed. I laughed dryly. Apparently, Fae could *glamour* themselves from vampires, just as we could from humans. And they'd infiltrated our *home,* our military.

I snarled. "You're all a bunch of hypocrites! You come here begging for peace, to save innocents, when you're the ones who shed blood!"

Mardi gripped Tate's waist, stopping her mid-step as she began her approach. "He's not worth it. Tune him out."

Tate's eyes turned to his, looking deeply. They stood there for a moment, no words were spoken, and yet they somehow seemed to communicate, to understand one another intimately. The pompous male reached out, his red hair gleaming brighter from the bolts I continually hurled at the shield trapping me, and then he wrapped his arms around Tate. She nodded and a moment later, they disappeared.

No! My nostrils flared. I would not be denied my retribution!

Soon...none will escape.

I grunted at the shared sentiment with the Tarragon. Soon, but not fucking soon enough. They were still too far out. The other female also disappeared, leaving only Mardi and an unknown figure in the distance.

My magic bucked against my control. There was only one way out, I needed more power. I looked back at Anax Graff with eyes full of apology. Her breath caught in her throat.

"It's the only way," I said.

The moment my words left me, I reached out and siphoned her power, pulling deeply and without hesitation. She screamed as she dropped to her knees and swatted at the aura leaving her body. The remaining guards stood frozen a moment and then turned on me. With half a thought, my power flayed them—sucking their energy in streams that flowed into me.

"Your sacrifices are honorable. Your country will not forget," I spoke the lines said in reverence for fallen guaramen at a eulogy.

A flash of darkness occurred outside the dome, glaringly bright and yet somehow dark, and then it was gone.

I siphoned more power, ignoring the strangled screams coming from my comrades, until at last, their energy ran dry—I'd emptied their wells. The newness of their power filled my veins, fueled my steps, and I turned to face Mardi. Only, it wasn't Mardi's eyes I locked with, but the golden-black ones of a dragon.

Leader! We shall take him!

The ground shook as the Tarragon landed, one by one all around the dome and the dragon. The dragon lifted its head and roared, shaking the magical dome itself. My Tarragon released a cry of their own before charging the beast.

Half in the air, the others on the ground, I commanded.

Before waiting for a response, I threw out my hands and unleashed the torrent of power coursing within. In a blink, the dome was nothing but red static, my power burned through it, until at last, the dome shattered. It burst outwards and struck the other dome, incinerating it as well. The red wave crashed into a black wall of flames surrounding the dragon and was repelled, flying into the trees nearby and destroying them.

Bark fell to the ground in clumps of fire as the ground all around looked like the aftermath of a bombing. Black marred everything, not a single strand of green grass could be seen. Not a single tree within a half-mile stood.

The dragon's flames stopped for a moment, as did my wave of power. It looked at me, intelligence in its eyes. Its throat lit up and then it opened its mouth as streams of black flames came pouring out. I quickly evaded, and a Tarragon jumped in front of me to block the flames with its wings. The dragon turned and sent its flames at my remaining beasts.

They too withstood his flames.

Fool, my beasts could not be killed by fire.

As if sensing my thoughts, the dragon launched into the air.

Follow it! I commanded three of the eleven Tarragon. *The rest of you, with me. Except you three,* I felt their tethers within my grasp, *find the girl. Find your maker.*

An instant later, the six of them were gone. Three air-bound, and three leaping across the ground in strides that easily covered ten feet at a time. Thunder cracked against the sky as power shook. I strode toward the Fern representative. They were huddled together in a pile on the ground.

"Please, it wasn't us! It was—"

A roar rippled through the air, ceasing all words. The blackened ground shuddered from massive steps.

I glanced behind the three cowering Fern representatives to meet the blood-red eyes of a red dragon. It prowled closer. It was smaller than the black dragon, but its tail was barbed, and its fangs were pure yellow.

The group cowering at my feet suddenly turned to me for protection. I raised my brow. Were they serious? They were as much my enemy as was the dragon in front of me.

"Save us!" they cried out to me.

"No," I simply said and then met the eyes of the beast in front of me. I was acutely aware that the remaining five Tarragon stood beside me—a show of strength.

The dragon merely nodded at me, and I turned on my heel. My magic screamed at me to finish off the enemy, to devour their power, to attack the dragon. But that dragon? I'd never seen a red one, let alone a beast with such shrewd eyes before, and it wasn't any more my enemy than those vampires were. Let it devour them and then, if needed, I'd devour it.

What now? the Tarragon asked.

Now, I smiled, cruel and cold. *Now, we follow her. Now, we fight.*

They roared, deep into the night, agreeing with my sentiment. Behind me, the ground warmed from the heat of rich flames. Shrill screams from the Fern representatives claimed the chilled air, echoed by the snapping of bones. They'd met their end.

Sometimes, justice was served.

CHAPTER 73
TATE

I hated that Aether sent me away. Hated that I had to say 'no' when he asked if I could shift. I was disgusted with myself. I knew I was a liability if I couldn't shift, I saw those things coming. They were more evolved than I'd ever seen—much like the one in the settlement, but even from a distance I could tell they were bigger. And there were so many.

Still, I loathed leaving him there. Even now, I couldn't remain still. I paced back and forth, ignoring the looks Vala gave me as she reinforced the shield with her magic—magic that was still not fully restored, and she was using it for me. My guilt doubled.

James had blinked out again for Camella and they were 'relocating' nearby to protect. Bullshit. They were trying to keep me from battle. The whole thing was absolutely laughable. As a royal, *I* was supposed to be the most powerful. Have the rawest magic. But I couldn't fully control it. Thank you, Irene and Fletch.

I still couldn't shift.

Thank you, Mother.

An angry groan poured through my lips as I pulled at my hair.

A roar sounded in the near distance, or perhaps it was thunder—

either way, the ground shook and I didn't miss the way the dark sky turned bright red.

Chance.

Chance had power. He had magic. The moment I saw the red static dancing across him, my heart sank. He claimed I'd done this to him. That I'd turned him into *that* person. And what he said about Shae... was it true?

I bit my lip. I was shaken, and Aether knew it. It was the only reason I didn't protest more when he sent me away—I felt his fear and knew he sensed my inner turmoil. I looked within, begging my inner dragon to find a way to break the chains—to fully awaken.

I spotted my pool, lit with pink flames and burning brightly. Inside, I could feel her pacing, snapping at the tether holding her. I willed the binding to break, screamed at *her* to do something. But she only roared within, causing my skin to brighten, but nothing more.

I growled.

This had to be from the spell, the *lock* my mother had spoken of in her letter. Why could nothing be simple? I was supposed to break free of its binds on my shifting ability with the Changing, and yet, *she* wouldn't budge. What was I missing?

Only the truth of your bare feet upon rightful soil will unlock your ability to fully shift, the words rang through my mind as my magic purred, and *she* roared.

I blinked, completely jarred.

Bare feet? I'd been barefoot in the Embassy many times, I'd gone through the Changing, so why the hell was I still *stuck*?! I groaned aloud as I kicked a stone.

"Tate, it will come with time. You just need to be patient," Vala said, her voice tired, but sincere.

"Patient? For how long?" I demanded. "How long do I have to sit on the sidelines and be patient? I've been waiting and waiting for my power to completely awaken."

"Tate—"

"No! I was powerful that night of the base explosion, I held my own. I was a blood-damned goddess and now? I can call forth flames, but I can't shift—I'm missing a part of myself, and everyone keeps telling me to be patient while my entire world is changing." I couldn't keep the snap out of my voice. "My actions, and lack thereof, have consequences."

"You being here is something a leader would do. It's a sacrifice. By being here you're freeing Aether to fully focus and attack. That isn't nothing. That's selfless. That's huge." Vala stepped toward me, trying to calm me with her hands.

"Is that what you told yourself? When Jared was being attacked at that village and you were stuck with me in the dome, did that calm you?" Instant regret filled me as I saw the hurt in her eyes. "Shit, I'm sorry, Vala. I—"

"What I do is important. It is sacrificial. It is vital."

"I know, I didn't mean to—"

But my words were cut off by a loud growl, no, a loud *roar*, followed by the presence of a large beast, lunging midair toward us. It landed on all fours, with two closely behind it, and then, they looked up at me. Even from inside my dome, fear spiked through me.

"Hello, maker," one snarled.

"Tate, get behind me. Now! Call Aether," Vala commanded as she erected another shield and then another—we were in an onion of domes.

"That won't help," the beast spoke. It charged then, the two behind it moving in unison, and then they hit the dome. The shield shook, splintered, but it stood. Again, they attacked it, swatting with talons, swinging their barbed tails. The first shield was too fractured, it broke.

Aether!

Hold on—

But then the connection became muffled. Panic gripped me at what that meant. The beasts attacked the shield again and again. They continued to ruthlessly plunge their talons into it.

"Help me shield!" Vala cried.

I felt for the power within, willed it to flow out of me and into the shield. It stood strong. The beasts looked behind them and froze.

Hope rose in me as I thought of Aether.

But it quickly vanished.

The figure standing behind the beasts wasn't my savior, but a figure coiled in red vines of static. Chance.

CHAPTER 74
AETHER

I wrestled against the beast currently sinking its talons into my side. It was big, but I was much, much bigger. I twirled midair, as I sank my teeth into its hide. It screeched as I ripped it from my flesh and whipped it back and forth until its neck snapped.

I spat it out, wishing I could cleanse my teeth of its odious blood. The creature fell through the roiling clouds to the ground below. But there wasn't time to watch, instead, I turned my attention to the two beasts flying toward me.

While they were smaller, they were strong. Not dragon, not seethings...something else. Tarragon. That's what Chance had called them. I roared in frustration as I dove toward the two incoming Tarragon. I released a stream of dark fire, lighting up the sky, that engulfed the beasts. Not enough to destroy, but enough to distract. I snapped at the one, catching it off guard, and crushed it beneath my teeth. It shrieked as my fangs sank into it, black blood oozing from its neck and shoulders where I held it.

The other creature attacked from the side, digging its talons into my wing before moving under to my belly and swinging its clubbed tail up. I screeched in pain as I could feel blood oozing from the wound.

The Tarragon wound up again, preparing to strike. I tucked my wings in and rolled, spiraling down toward the ground with the one creature still locked in my jaw. The sickening snap told me its neck had broken and its body went limp. I waited, twisting as the ground became closer and closer.

Then at the last moment, I banked and flipped, facing the Tarragon in hot pursuit. I let go of the one creature and the other Tarragon didn't see it coming. It collided with its brother, the beasts smacked one another, sending them both tumbling toward the ground. I didn't hesitate before sending a stream of fire their way, marking their end.

Tate's anger was evident down the bond. She was pissed as hell that I'd asked her to stand down. But being the female she was, no, the leader she was, she agreed. She left with James and was secure. Soon she'd be in control of her beast form. Soon she'd have her magic mastered and be able to exact calculated strikes even in the face of death. Soon she'd be unstoppable. Soon—

Aether!

Tate's panic coated the bond, sending my own heart racing. I turned and began pumping my wings, heading to where I could feel her. Something was wrong.

Hold on—

Red flames engulfed me, blocking my vision, and sent me spinning out of control. I banked to recover but not soon enough to avoid the teeth of the creature attacking me. Large teeth, nearly the size of my own, sank into my shoulder—pain shot down my spine.

I roared as I pivoted, sinking my talons into the side of the beast. No not a beast, but a full-grown dragon.

A dragon I recognized without any doubt—a dragon I knew too well. Her red scales gleamed and were covered in blood. Her tail was barbed and arched through the air, swinging for me. I snapped at it and barely evaded it while using the motion to distract her and sink my talons into her chest.

She released me and roared, red flames swallowing the dark sky. In the near distance, red bolts of lightning rained down from the cloud-less sky toward where I knew a precious female was located.

Rage claimed me and I spewed fire at Arithi. I released my pent-up anger, blame, and ire. She put Tate in danger. Fuck, she *was* the danger. She needed to meet her end.

I flew higher, far above her shaking form, and then dove down straight toward her. She barely had a moment to turn, spewing flames my way, as my talons sank into her belly again and my teeth clamped around her neck. She was large, larger than most red dragons. The leader of the Iron Tribe. I used to admire her strength, her size, her merciless way of handling things.

Now I despised it all.

Lightning spun through the sky, streaking wildly and nearly hitting us, before darting toward the ground. Even from far above, I could hear the ground shudder—feel the force of the power and magic being released.

I didn't have time for this. It was time to end this dragon.

Coming!

Desperation gnawed at me as Tate remained silent. Only her fear and rage were noticeable via the bond.

I sank my teeth in deeper, and gutted Arithi further with my talons, even as she attacked me with her tail. From this angle, it was her only weapon. Her neck was too big for me to break like I had the Tarragon, but I sure as hell could injure her enough to leave her susceptible to a fatal blow.

She twisted in the air, sending me twirling with her, as her barbed spikes impaled my flesh, over and over again. The adrenaline must've been strong as I didn't feel, didn't notice the damage she was doing.

Only one thing dominated my mind: revenge.

And only one person commanded my senses: Tate.

I released a stream of fire while my teeth were on her neck, and let go at the last minute, knowing the flames had hit true by the wail coming from her throat. She dropped and began tumbling toward the ground. I pursued her, even as my heart raced at the sight of the sky reddening yet again—the static of more lightning swaying through the clouds. My chest tightened as Tate's emotions began to overwhelm my own, the scariest of which was guilt.

Arithi's wings branched out and she began to slow her descent, wobbly, given her injuries. I tucked my wings in tighter and dove faster, prepared for my final attack.

She was close, I could see her eyes widen in what I swore was fear. My talons were prepared to strike, my jaw opened, and my wings spread as I reached—

Spikes of pain erupted from my side and stomach as two beasts latched on to me and altered my trajectory. Talons and teeth began to sink in, drawing blood from me and injuring my already wounded shoulder. I ripped with my talons and turned my head to tear one off, but it evaded me. It released me before attacking my back and latching on with iron talons that pierced my scales, sinking deep into my flesh.

I loosened a roar of pain and fury as I tore one from my body before reaching the other with my teeth—yanking it off. I began to lower myself, my injured wing making it impossible to stay airborne, and prepared to end this thing's life.

Red lightning rose from the ground and simultaneously rained down from the eerie sky above, aimed straight for me. There was no time. No more quick evasions. No, the moment I realized the trajectory of the bolts, they were already striking me—right in the chest. Instantly, I had no control over myself or the beasts attacking me. They fell away from me as I plummeted toward the ground. My heart pounded erratically as my muscles spasmed and refused to work.

I crashed into the ground, and pain erupted from my wing as it snapped at an unholy angle. My left leg took the brunt of my fall as my body flipped over itself. Once. Twice. Three times and then I slid to a stop.

My consciousness ebbed, but the feeling of *her* forced me to keep my eyes open. To move. I was in a crater, black earth surrounded me. She needed me. Somewhere down the bond I could feel her, hear her even if I couldn't understand what it meant at the moment.

But I knew I would do anything, could do anything, for my mate. My Tate.

I forced myself up on my feet and then crumbled to the ground. I needed to shift, but my injuries were severe. Too severe to perhaps force a shift. But it didn't matter, I had to try. I willed my body to change, and intense agony erupted from deep within, causing my breath to hitch and my body to collapse.

I couldn't move. Couldn't breathe. There was only pain.

CHAPTER 75
TATE

He stood there, blanketed in crimson power. Five new beasts landed behind him, his Tarragon at the ready.

"You did this. Time for justice, Tate." He stepped forward and struck out at my dome with flashes of red. The shields shattered from the force, one by one until at last, nothing stood but the inner dome. A dome Vala was actively wielding, and I too was strengthening.

He called down his power and fury upon us, but the dome held. Slowly it fractured, but even still, it stood. Chance lifted his head into the night sky and screamed, lightning rising from his fists, the ground, and the sky before releasing it all, targeted at the shield.

Some hit true, but the rest hit a few feet away.

But still, our shield remained.

A feeling of fear and perhaps vengeance coursed down the bond, Aether would be here soon. He could end this. I could hear the distant roar of a dragon and knew it would be only moments before his arrival.

My magic within stirred. *She* roared, loosening new stores of magic that flowed into my veins. I let it surface and illuminate my face.

"What happened to you, Chance? This isn't you!" I shouted.

531

"You don't know anything, Tate. This is me, the best version of me. Better than ever," he said coolly. Momentarily, the lightning stopped as he looked to the sky in the distance.

I followed his line of sight and my breath caught. I saw not one, but two dragons twirling toward one another. They became a tangled mess as screeches along with two streams of fire, black and red, filled the evening air.

Aether.

My heart nearly seized in my chest as I felt his pain through the bond.

She burst against my chest, begging to be freed—stealing the breath from my very lungs.

And yet, I could do nothing to shift—the thread was heavy, leaden, and buried deep within. It was locked away, and *she* loathed it.

Chance looked at me again, maroon claiming his once blue eyes, and smiled. "We'll see how strong you are without your beast to fight for you." He nodded and two of the eight beasts took flight, aiming for the dragons.

Rage filled my veins, and the dome began to glow with bright pink flames that held a dark center. Every inch of ground radiated my light, basked in my power.

Chance cocked his head and then threw out his hands, torpedoes of red lit the sky streaking out toward Aether and the other dragon.

"No!" I screamed, but Chance only smirked.

"Not so strong now." He laughed.

"Stop this! What would Shae say if she saw you, and what about that other female, Joy H—"

"Don't you dare speak her name!" he snapped as he redirected the lightning toward me.

His action sparked something deep within and I smiled, crookedly.

"If she was into you, she may not be anymore...at least not when she sees what you've become. What you've done. Unless, perhaps, she too lacks integrity," I said.

He sent another round of angry strikes toward us, and the dome fractured at their impact.

Dragons roared in the distance, and I could see them still intricately intertwined. A cry of pain came from one of the dragon's throats, but the lack of emotion down the bond told me it wasn't Aether.

Chance looked up at the serpents.

"She really must be a piece of shit if you're into her and she likes you even after all you've done, the innocents you've given up on," I spat.

His nostrils flared as he threw out his hands and poured continuous streams of crimson energy at us. Red lightning rained down from the sky further cracking the dome.

I pushed my magic out, willing it to shield Vala and I. We became encased in a pink light that solidified into a new shield just as the other crumbled.

A dragon's roar sounded and suddenly, one was plummeting toward the earth. Chance snarled and noticed where my eyes drifted. *Shit.* There wasn't time to say anything else before he turned and called forth maroon streaks rising from the ground and pouring from the sky toward the uninjured dragon.

I felt Aether's pain *before* the bolts hit and noticed small lumps surrounding his body. The lightning claimed him, and his cry shook my very soul.

SHE SURGED.

Molten flames spewed from my lips, pierced the shield, and hit Chance—

Except, it didn't hit him, but was repelled by one of his Tarragon's massive wings, the beast shielding him.

Instead of his expected screams, Chance laughed. "You've always looked so innocent when in shock. You know that?" He stepped toward me. "Don't worry, I've sent all but one of my Tarragon to end him. He won't be in pain for much longer."

I looked around and alarmingly noted that all but one of the beasts, his Tarragon, were in fact missing. How had I not noticed that sooner?

I felt a jolt down the bond and could sense Aether's power failing, being expended in an attempt to slow him down—to survive.

Aether!

The world shook as Aether's body hit the ground. Even from miles away, my feet wavered from the impact of his body cratering into the dirt and rock. I lost my footing, and horror seized my heart at the sense of his magic fading through the bond—pure desperation and depletion.

I stood and snarled at Chance. "You're fucking dead!"

A mask slipped into place over his once irate features, collected and calm. Utterly terrifying. He reached out his hands and I braced for the impact of his wrath, preparing my own blaze of power, but instead of the full force of electricity hitting the dome, he began pulling at my magic, pulling at my dome. A choked cry clawed from my throat at the instant searing pain.

She bucked within.

I resisted, but the tearing pain dropped me to my knees. I willed my power to stay in place, to fight the pull of his. A scream erupted from my throat as I fought against Chance's siphoning.

Aether's panic and pain overwhelmed me at once.

Aether! I screamed down the bond.

I could sense a hazy awareness, but the bond was becoming cloudy, murky.

Don't you dare give up!

No response came, just a flicker of light through our connection.

SHE ROARED, and true panic gripped my soul at Aether's silence.

Aether fucking Brychan, answer me!

No response. I waited as I fought Chance's magic. But still, Aether didn't respond. Sweat dripped across my forehead as I wrestled Chance's pull. If I let go and dropped the dome, could I take him? What would happen to Vala?

I glanced at Vala and saw her crumpled to the ground. Over the course of my screams, I hadn't noticed she too had been impacted, her aura was drifting from her in ripples of white.

A new wave of Aether's pain dominated my senses along with the distinct need for power—his very life flickering in and out. I knew what had to be done, I could sense it in my core. Understanding, *she* stopped pacing and began to release all her pent-up energy into my accessible stores.

Mother Blood forgive me.

I pulsed the power I'd kept at bay. The force of it knocked Chance to his ass and the siphoning stilled.

Closing my eyes, I searched within, reaching down the bond and feeling for Aether. I *felt* his reserve; it was nearly empty. Then, following an inexplicable urge, I forced my own energy into his tank—through our connection—filling him with my power.

Chance grunted, but I refused to open my eyes. Loose rocks crunched beneath his boots, but still, I didn't budge. I poured more and more of myself into Aether, into his energy stores. I could sense his own aura brightening, opening eyes that had been forced closed—on the brink of a burn-out or death.

My sacrifice would be worth it. Aether must live.

I could hear Vala whimpering next to me, and I flinched as a soft hand enveloped my cheek. "What a fool you are," Chance whispered in my ear.

I could feel Aether's power riling, firing against mine and telling me to stop—to protect myself.

With one last blast, I poured all my available energy into him and sent out a final message:

I love you.

Aether slammed the door shut, stopping my flow and I gasped as my eyes flew open and I fell forward into the chest of a male I'd once felt safe with. A chest covered in red static.

Two hands jerked me away from him, forcing me to meet his now icy-blue gaze. There were questions there, curiosity that reminded me of the boy I once knew.

"Tate! Stop, you must—" Vala screamed as Chance struck her with a bolt of lightning and she fell back to the ground, motionless.

"Chance, please, leave her alone. Leave them all alone. Just...you have me. Call off your *dogs*. You wanted revenge, here I am," I spoke through lips that bled. My throat was hoarse and felt like sandpaper as my soul within quaked.

Tate, don't you fucking dare.

I smiled at Aether's snarl.

"Why?" Chance asked, reaching out and gripping my throat with one hand—writhing in bolts of red that tickled but, oddly, didn't hurt.

"Why what?" I rasped.

"Why give up? You could have resisted. I've never felt a fight like that. Never felt power like that. Why would you surrender?" He searched me with his eyes.

"Because," I said as I grabbed his hand on my throat with both of mine. A dragon's cry accompanied by dark flames filled the night sky. Aether knew. He understood what I had done. "He's worth it."

Comprehension flickered in Chance's gaze and before I could say anything more, electricity coursed through my body. I screamed as the pain increased until, at last, sweet oblivion claimed me.

CHAPTER 76
CHANCE

The wind whipped at my hair, sending it slicing into my face from all angles. I'd never ridden one of my Tarragon before. It was...strange. Unsettling.

It is an honor, the beast spoke into my mind.

Indeed, I said as I patted its scaled back.

Thankfully, this beast survived. I'd lost five of my remaining eleven Tarragon. But this one, the largest of them, remained unscathed and strong.

A familiar lilac and lavender scent filled my nose as the female cradled in my arms remained motionless. Holding her did things to me —things I wished I didn't feel.

Part of me reveled in the sense of personhood, the old vampirical me rising from the ashes. Odd, how even after all this time, her body felt right in my arms. Instinctually, I *knew* her—

Traitor. Bitch. Vile.

My magic sparked in me, reminding me of what she had done—of who she was. Images of Holland with the diamond on her forehead flashed before me. I replayed our last encounter and only saw

Holland's fear and disgust at what I've become. This was all *Tate's* fault.

I snarled as I dug my fingers into her sensitive flesh. Wet liquid dripped down the hand gripping her arm. I looked closer and froze. Blood.

I quickly released her, even as her blood dripped down my fingers and sprayed my arm, the wind making it a bigger mess than necessary. I swallowed. This wasn't who I was, was it?

Revenge. Taste. Devour.

I shook my head, quieting the unsettling thoughts and the call to partake in her blood...in her magic.

She smiled at me. "You know, this is forbidden."

I tightened my grip on her as I held her in place, her back to the glass palace wall. "So?"

"So," she poked a playful finger at my chest, "I thought the cowboy was too good a soldier to break any rules. What would Principal Andrews say, or worse, what would your father say?" She played with a piece of my hair, coiling it along one of her delicate fingers.

"I'm not worried about that, you...you are all I can see, all I can think of. Tate, you're all that matters." I kissed her, noting the way her mahogany eyes fluttered shut as she released a moan into my mouth.

Suddenly, I couldn't restrain myself, I released her lips and claimed her in the truest sense. My fangs pierced her sensitive flesh and drew her into me. I savored her unique flavor, so unlike any blood I'd ever partaken of.

Her head arched back as her fingers dug into my shoulder. "Chance," she murmured.

I shook my head. That was a very different time with two very different people.

Leader, should we eat her now?

No! I snapped back through my connection with them.

My emotions roared within, fighting. I still hadn't recognized all that had changed. The two kids that we once were battled with the reality of who we'd become. The desire to protect fought with one that begged me to devour.

HQ's towering buildings came into view, and with it came the pull of vile magic—somehow purifying. I needed a good feed. From seethings and vampires alike. My stores were weak after my battle with Tate, even with the high from draining Anax Graff and the guaramen, I was faint and fueled by hunger.

Take the food in front of you. Allow just a taste...

Tate's scent drifted to my nose, intensified by her blood, beckoning me to siphon and devour and enjoy and...

Leader, they sense our arrival. Shall we end any who question us?

I shook my head. In the near distance, there were several airborne fighters—prepared and ready to attack. The sight was alarming. In the Glenn, we opted for ground transportation as air was considered an 'evil' reminder of a dark past, namely, dragons. And since they were extinct, or so we thought until now, air support was practically non-existent. I didn't even know we had any aircrafts left as most had been destroyed after the Great War—or so I'd been told.

No. I'll handle this.

We approached slowly, my hands roaming over Tate's body with a mind of their own. She'd gained a few pounds of muscle since I'd last been with her. Clearly, more had changed than meets the eye. I threw out one hand, reluctantly letting go of her curves, before striking the sky in front of me in angry red streaks—announcing my arrival.

We continued toward the airborne fighters. I held my breath as I waited. For a moment, they just hovered. Held their ground. But then, they turned and headed back toward a distant battlefield. I smirked. My father had gotten the message.

Land.

Commanding the Tarragon now felt second nature. Slowly, the beast beneath me banked until a large field came into view with several tents and guaramen dotting it. Their magic hit me the moment the beast's talons touched the ground. So much power, so much energy, so much food stalking around unknowingly. I swallowed back my hunger as I jumped from the Tarragon's back, giving it a pat on its scaled wing, before turning toward the cluster of tents ahead. Tate's weight was marginal as I strode forward. She was, in many ways, an offering. To who, I wasn't sure, but I felt it in my soul.

Justice.

Rusty poked his nasty head outside the tent and was closely followed by my father, cane in hand. His eyes coolly assessed me and the female in my arms. I stepped as close as I dared, given the armed guaramen and the one controller surrounding my father.

I knelt before him, allowing my body to sink into the filthy earth. "Father," I began, "I bring you the traitorous bitch. The Fern referred to her as their leader. With her in our possession, we can do unimaginable things. We can win this war."

I laid her down, noting the sudden cold that encased everywhere her body had been. Leaving her lying in the muddy earth, I turned my eyes from her still form as I nodded to the other Tarragon who carried the other unconscious female.

"Another leader," I said.

"Well done, Anax Dale," my father said as he began clapping. The guards around him shared uneasy glances before they too joined in. "But I must ask, what of Anax Graff?"

I ignored how he didn't ask about the guaramen who accompanied us and instead said, "She was killed by this traitor."

"Mmm." He looked at me assessing. "And the Fern representatives?"

"Destroyed." I leveled a challenging look at him.

"Good." He motioned to the guaramen to pick Tate up. "Take her to the holding cell and ensure Doctor Worshah attends to her immediately."

They complied without further guidance.

"And her," I added pointing to the female lying face down next to Tate. "Make sure she's alive and somewhere Tate can see. Much has changed, but I still know that she'll make for good leverage to get her," I nodded to Tate's bloodied body, "talking."

My father smirked. "Do as *Anax* Dale says."

Another guaraman came and picked up the other female and stalked off, following the male who was carrying away Tate, and with her, the last traces of my past—of the male I once was.

CHAPTER 77
AETHER

I slammed my fist against the pillar again, this time it shuttered and fractured. The floor was covered in shards of glass, wood, and various debris. The library had borne the brunt of my anger, as testified by the pages currently dotting the floor in shreds.

I screamed as I turned and flipped a cherrywood table before yanking on a bookshelf and pulling it out from the wall. It groaned, resisted, and then like the rest of my life, it caved and became a total mess.

Tate was gone.

Taken, I was sure of it. I could feel her, but faintly. She was still alive, I felt this through the bond. She'd sacrificed herself for me. Gave me her power and then stood before that monster without any defense. I had done this. I had sent her away. And then, I was weak.

I failed her just as I had Cher.

"*Fuckkkk!*" I growled as I threw another punch.

If I had only trusted her, fought *with* her, perhaps she'd be here still. Instead, I was fucking losing my mind at the possibilities.

"Aether," Camella hedged, entering the room cautiously.

"What?!" I snapped as I slammed my fist into the stone fireplace, savoring the way my knuckles split and blood oozed.

"James is back."

I pivoted toward her mid-strike, she ducked evading me, and I hit nothing but air. "Where?"

"Outside." She nodded, giving me a wide berth to pass.

I stalked outside. I shouldn't be standing; I shouldn't be alive. Tate should be here. Safe. But instead, she was fucking abducted.

And it was my fault; *I* had ordered James and Camella to return to the domes and fight the beasts and the Fern representatives once they were sure Tate was secured and safe. It was my order, and as the leader of the shitshow it was *my* fault—even if they should've returned sooner, even if they were slowed down by Arithi and then the Tarragon for a few moments, they should've—

Fuck. This was on me. I'd failed Tate.

I stormed past the front door and into the garden. The irony that this place now *recognized* my blood wasn't lost on me. Tate had given me more than just her magic, somehow, she had altered the very curtain flowing through this place to allow me in—to respond to my will.

My chest shook and burned as my failure ate me from the inside out.

James stood, back toward me for only a moment before blinking out and then right in front of me.

"Well?" I bit out.

"I found her," he said.

I gripped his shoulders and squeezed. "Where?"

"Aether, we need a plan. We can't be rash here or—"

"Where!?" I growled as I shoved him backwards and let go of his collar. My inner beast begged to be freed. My power was well restored after Tate gave me everything. In fact, it was more than it'd ever been.

I shook the thought away and instead snarled at James as I strode toward him.

"She's being held captive in one of the main HQ buildings."

"Let's go." I moved toward the path but paused when I reached the edge and noted I was alone. "James!"

Camella stepped forward, head high, with James at her side. It didn't matter that he towered over her by nearly two feet, she was the one in control. "We *will* go get her. She is *our* royal princess of Mydant, and we are sworn to protect her. But we need to be smart. We need a plan, or not only will we fail and die, but she will suffer because of our impulsiveness."

I growled, not caring that I was acting like a rage-baked Neanderthal. "No. We get her now."

"Aether," James began, "you know we're right. If it wasn't Tate, you'd be the one with reason, not a rattled mate's brain filled with nothing but revenge."

"Let's get our girl," Camella said earnestly. "But let's do it and succeed. What's your plan?"

I paused. I wanted to destroy, murder, kill...but that wouldn't help Tate, not right now. I needed to get in and save her. I roared in frustration. "What would you suggest?"

Camella blinked, clearly not expecting me to relent. I knew she was right, but my mind was full of nothing but bloodlust. I needed someone with a clear head to plan this.

"Well," she breathed, "with only us, we definitely need a covert mission. No dragons." She eyed me. "And, from what we know of the king, he could pass any minute and then our window to get her back to Mydant will be excruciatingly short. If we miss it..."

She didn't need to finish for me to know the consequences. The only way for Tate to get back would be during the funeral and Crown changeover.

"Camella, what the fuck do you suggest then?" I urged. I didn't need a reminder of all that was at stake. Not when mahogany eyes were missing, were in pain, and were experiencing blood knew what.

I reached out once again, searching the bond for Tate. I could sense her, but nothing more. She was alive, at least there was that.

"We need a distraction, especially given what we now know about Arithi's involvement with the Fern," Camella continued.

Rage roiled through me, and I flung out dark waves of fire, reaching high into the night sky. I'd long suspected Arithi's interest in the wars and weapon development weren't purely to protect the Embassy, and I knew she craved power. But...the Untish were supposed to value life. Arithi had tossed all that to the side the moment her control was threatened—I now had no doubt she was involved in Esme's death, along with the other royals here on Shappa. And she was blatantly a larger part of whatever was going on between Vamps. Perhaps, she was even the one who instigated it.

And I'd nearly finished her. I had been moments away when those bolts struck true, and my life faded—likely would have ended—had Tate not stepped in and sacrificed herself for me.

"We've intercepted their past messages for the peace treaty, perhaps we do so again and *stir* things up," James began. "If the Fern attacks again, then the Glenn will be distracted."

"It won't work," I bit out. "They've got to know now that they were played; any carrier would have to be vetted...heavily."

"I know a way," James said. "I have a contact...we could get in one message. But only one."

"If that's true, then this could work, Aether," Camella responded.

But the lives lost? Would Tate ever forgive me for bringing war to her home? Forgive me for the countless lives that would be lost in a battle with civilians a breath away?

"How soon can you send a message?" I asked.

"I can deliver it within hours," James spoke with confidence.

Blood help me, but there wasn't a sacrifice too great to make if it meant saving her. My mate. Fuck, my life. She was my everything.

I nodded to James. "Do it."

CHAPTER 78

TATE

y head throbbed as I opened my eyes. The room was blurry. Bright metal and glass shined back at me. Pristine. Cold. Lifeless.

I bolted upright, pulling against the restraints clasped around my wrists. I'd recognize these cruel walls anywhere; I was in the tower at HQ. How long had I been out? A gasp from beside me sounded as hands forced me back into my chair. So many hands.

I whipped my head around and suddenly felt dizzy, queasy. "Hold her still," a male commanded.

"I'm trying," another grunted in response.

I blinked, searching for the source of the voices but it was all so blindingly bright, and every motion caused more pain—more disorientation. I felt a stab in my arm accompanied by a burning sensation. A needle dropped into the tray beside me with a single 'clang'.

"How long until it takes effect?" a voice asked. It was familiar somehow, odious.

"The last dose is still working, this was more of an insurance policy," the male responded. His voice was high-pitched and nasal. "And this," another needle pricked my skin, "will ensure she tells the truth. Just needs a minute or two to start working."

"And you're sure her magic is restrained?"

"Yes," the squeaky male responded, "it's worked on the others that we've tested."

"Good. You may leave."

"But—"

"Leave!" the voice commanded.

Feet shuffled and then I heard a door shut. I blinked rapidly, willing my vision to clear. I felt a tug inward and recognized it as Aether, I reached out, grasping for it, but met an iron wall. I screamed inwardly but it was muted.

Panic rose in me as I searched for my inner pool of magic—for *her*. If there was ever a time for her to awaken, it was now. But where my pool usually burned brightly in pink flames, it was nothing but opaqueness. I pressed against it, but it only caved a bit before springing back to its solid form, blocking me out.

The clicking of a cane sounded and then a chair wheeled over. A male sighed as he settled into his seat. "Tate, my dear girl, how did we get here?"

In my heart, I knew that voice. Even before my eyes cleared, even before I looked up, I knew what evil creature sat in front of me: President Dale.

"You." I lunged, but I didn't move. My body barely shuddered even with the full force of my will; I was being stilled. Hysteria coursed through me and warred with anger, but my rage won out.

"Please, save your strength. The drug we gave you mutes your muscles, your strength, and most importantly, your magic." He leaned forward on his cane. "But not your tongue, which is the only important part I'm afraid."

He ran his fingers, purple-grey skin that was oddly wrinkled, over the human's face on the cane—digging the tip of his thumb into its open mouth.

"Screw you," I spat at him, savoring the way spit did, in fact, fly across the small space and land on his pants.

He simply removed his maroon pocket square, wiped his pants, and then returned it to his pocket. "Well, now that you've got *that* out of your system...let's chat." He smiled cruelly at me. "My son says you've got impressive magic. Let's begin there. When did it manifest?"

A lie built in my throat, ready to be spewed, but it was silenced. "I only just learned about my magic," my lips betrayed my heart.

"Be specific," he commanded as he settled back into the office chair.

"I-I don't know, I mean maybe a couple of months ago, perhaps slightly sooner?" What was going on? My lips moved freely of their own accord.

Enough! I chided myself.

"And how long have you been working with the Fern?"

"I haven't," I replied. I snapped my lips shut and willed myself to stop talking, to be quiet.

"Answer truthfully!" he demanded.

"I am!"

"Clear the glass," he ordered.

The window in front of me, one I'd once assumed was a mirror, flickered and then faded, becoming transparent. The sight beyond stilled my heart. An identical metal chair to the one I was bound in sat in the middle of a white room, with a single figure strapped to the chair. She had metal manacles on each wrist and foot, and her head hung limply with her dark and light curls sticking to her face. Vala.

I tried to lunge in my chair and managed to move a fraction of an inch. "Let her go!"

"I see my son was right, you do care about someone other than yourself. You care for her." President Dale smiled, sinister, before he stood and paced over to the wall.

Images of a similar room, of him looking into a different interrogation cell, flashed before my mind.

Burnt flesh, charred remains, loss, and pain so unimaginable it nearly destroyed me...

My heart rate increased as I tried and failed to stifle a scream. President Dale turned, locking his cold blue eyes on mine. The bastard knew. He chose this intentionally. He was trying to rattle me, to unnerve me.

He wanted to break me.

I reached inward toward my magic, roaring at it to be free. I felt the tiniest spark, but nothing occurred—I couldn't realize it, nothing materialized. I reached out for Aether, but that too was silent. There, but...not.

"What does the Fern plan?" he asked, relaxing his shoulders.

"I don't know," I bit out.

"Remarkable, I was told you'd be truthful, but perhaps my scientists need some more time in the research lab, maybe even as the *test* subjects themselves." I didn't miss the way his knuckles turned white on the cane as he spoke. "What does the Fern plan, Tate?"

"Mother Blood, I don't fucking know!" I shouted at him.

The sight of Vala in a chair, identical to the one I'd last seen Fletch in, was making my blood boil. Unwanted tears began to spill down my cheeks. I was completely unable to control myself.

"Okay, let's talk about *dragons*. How many are there?"

I swallowed back the words, willed them down, and forced my lips shut. My chest burned with the effort and was accompanied by an ice pick, stabbing haphazardly throughout my mind.

"Release the gas," he spoke.

The room holding Vala hummed and then a fine, green mist began to pour from the ceiling.

"Stop!" I screamed. I couldn't lose her too, I wouldn't.

"How many dragons?"

"I don't know, dozens!" I hated myself for caving, for breaking, as I eyed the green gas swiftly approaching Vala.

"Be specific," he commanded.

I bit down on my response as I thought of the Embassy and all its children, of the innocents who *couldn't* shift. What would happen to them if I sold them out? If I answered his questions? And if I didn't, could I live with myself for sacrificing Vala's life?

"I don't know," I responded, voice breaking.

The gas hit Vala's legs and she jerked, her head flew up and her eyes went wide. A moment later she screamed.

"Enough! I'll answer your questions, just stop!" I shouted, my breaths becoming short.

"How many dragons, Tate?"

"I don't know. They can't all shift. I saw at least a hundred." Guilt raked through my body as I thought of the innocents housed in the Embassy. But they were not helpless. "Stop this! Free her!"

The dragons could protect, they *would* protect. No one was here for Vala, none but me.

President Dale went still even as Vala's screams rose.

"I answered you, stop it! Spare her!" I demanded, pulling against the manacles and actually gaining an inch. President Dale didn't seem to notice my newfound strength, good. Perhaps, I could break free and—

"Where?" he demanded.

My eyes widened and I froze. The words clawed at my throat; I pushed them down, even as my own agony grew. My chest felt like it was on fire and the pressure in my head built. Vala screamed again, writhing in her chair, fighting for her life.

I puked. The stream of vomit arched through the air and splattered right at President Dale's feet. Even still, he ignored it.

"Where!?" he demanded.

The heaves wouldn't subside, the pressure continued to grow, and my mind couldn't see anything, hear anything, think of anything but pain.

Pain. More pain. And still, more PAIN.

Vala screamed and my body seized as my muscles cramped, the throw-up finally ceasing.

"WHERE!?" A hand slapped across my face, throwing me back into the chair. My vision blurred.

"Next step!" he commanded.

I watched in horror through tear-filled eyes as the gas stopped and two figures draped in hazmat suits stalked into the room carrying a case of tools. The one wasted no time as he pulled out a metal bar and struck Vala in her left knee. Then the right. Her accompanying screams broke my soul.

"Enough!" I ground out the words, fighting the ones that he had called forth. "They're in the sea...on an island, only accessible by boat or flight." Each lie only intensified my pain. I was panting the words as my mind ached.

President Dale smiled at me. "If that were true, your discomfort would end. Hit her again."

"No!" I screamed at the same moment metal hit bone.

As Vala screamed, I crumbled. "The Embassy," I said.

Instantly, my breaths filled with fresh air, and the pain was gone. I could see and think again. Vala was bent over, agony across her face as one figure lifted her head by her hair and waited for their next command.

"I answered you, let her go." I reached inward again, searching for my magic, my power. The pool was still opaque, but I could see sparks on the other side. It was coming back. I just needed time.

Aether... I whispered down the bond. But I knew it was falling on deaf ears, on a silenced connection.

"The Embassy." President Dale's eyes went distant. "That bitch," he snarled. "What do you know of Arithi?"

This was a line of questioning I could answer. "She is a bitch," I agreed earning an alarmed look. "She leads the Embassy and can shift into a red dragon. She's working with the Fern," I chose partial truths. If I could be truthful but not tell everything, perhaps I could still protect the Embassy...my people.

"There are different color dragons?"

"Yes. Green, black, and red." I left out some of the colors, but he didn't seem to notice.

"Are they all as powerful as the dark one at the warehouse?"

"I don't know. It varies from beast to beast. Magic is unpredictable."

He seemed pleased by my response. I looked past him, as he was deep in thought, to Vala, locking eyes with her chocolate ones. My heart broke at the way she nodded to me, a sign of trust and reverence. How had I earned that? I hadn't. I swallowed back the guilt as I mouthed, *I love you.* She smiled sadly in response, even from broken lips that bled. I didn't miss their quivering or the silent cries shaking her body.

Broken, they'd broken her.

They would pay.

A knock on the door came. President Dale growled as he strode to the door and opened it. "What?" he demanded.

"Sir, you're needed immediately to the control room. There's been a development." The guaraman looked at me nervously.

President Dale cursed under his breath before leaving me alone in the room, without another word or final glance. I looked across to Vala, but the window was once again transitioning into a mirror.

"Vala!" I shouted. "I'm right here! I will come for you!"

But before she could respond, I was once again looking at myself. Staring into the eyes of someone who sold out her people—the eyes of the unworthy.

CHAPTER 79

CHANCE

I dropped the delicious vessel's wrist to the pillow and savored the way her eyes dilated from the venom I'd just given her. Her body lay there sensually, as her face inclined toward me and her hands gripped my cheeks. She pulled me closer and pressed her lips to mine, moaning at the contact.

My cock hardened, ready. And yet...she wasn't Holland.

I shoved her back and allowed her to drop to the silken sheets before I stalked for the shower and savored the ice-cold water. Exactly what I needed. After cleansing all of her perfumed scent from my body, I cleaned my hair and immediately wished I'd cut it already. Clumps of dirt and iron-colored water filled the gold tiled basin before washing down the drain. It took washing my hair three times before it was finally clean. I stepped out of the shower and opted to simply drip dry, ignoring the towel that was set out for me.

My new suite.

Pride flared. I was no longer in the primary barracks. I had been moved to the *presidential* wing. I looked around—everything was either gold or silver. The golden floor echoed the gold-plated walls, the gold chandelier with tiny drops of golden orbs hanging delicately from it. The female I'd fed from was fast asleep in the bed, a place she did not belong. But aside from her, this place was perfect.

Foreign.

Expensive.

It reeked of forceful competency. And I liked it.

Growing up in my father's wing, which was far more luxurious than this, I should feel at home here, but instead, I felt uneasy—like an imposter.

I wanted this, I'd fought for this, I'd *earned this.*

I could sense the Tarragon roar in my mind, their wild desire to claim was becoming contagious. Strutting out of the bathroom, I entered my chamber and froze as I faced the floor-length mirror. The male in it was no longer a new adult, he was purely hardened by war and experience—he was a male in every sense that counted. I smiled as I admired my muscled legs, coiled back muscles, and large cock. There wasn't another like it.

Turning, I sauntered to the wardrobe and opened it.

"Dale," Holland's voice startled me.

I whipped around, my bolts flying with me and lighting my vision in red.

"Holland," her name came out a breath on my lips. "I-I'm so sorry."

What the fuck could I say to make it right? I glanced behind me and noted the way her eyes followed mine to the bed with the unconscious vessel draped across the sheets. "Nothing happened, just a feed. I would never, Holland, I—"

"Don't." She put her hands up, closing her eyes and visibly exhaling. "I just wanted to make sure *you* were all right. You weren't in your right mind the last time I saw you."

I swallowed, allowing the guilt to fester. She was worried about me? After what I'd almost done? I didn't deserve her. Static danced across my skin and made the gold stone glint red.

"You came to check on me?" The words were a whisper. I took a step forward and froze when her back straightened.

I could sense her reaching out to my mind, her emotions seeking to soothe my own. Her presence was a balm to my soul, an oasis in a desert, a beacon to my lost ship. I allowed her in, hell I ushered her presence in and savored the feel of her. Even my magic sparked, making room for her—willing her to blend with my power.

"I'm so sorry, Holland, I don't know what came over me. It will *never* happen again, I swear." I meant every word I spoke.

"I know it won't," she replied quietly, withdrawing her presence from my mind, leaving me to the coldness of my own thoughts.

"What can I do to make it right?" I asked, taking a small step closer. She held her ground and tipped her chin up, locking eyes with mine. Distrust showed there, but what was worse was the *pity* that filled her honey-brown eyes.

"You can stop using dark magic. Stop siphoning. You're strong enough without it. It's not right, it's not who you are." Her pleading sparked something inside, something ugly. I tried to shove it down, to see her point.

"Holland, I understand if you don't want to be with me, but what I've done and become is the only way to keep the Glenn safe, to keep you safe."

"No, it's not," she snapped. "You were strong before you siphoned. A leader before the explosion. This," she gestured to my red lightning covering the floor and walls in a web, "is not you. We were all impacted by the blast, but you can *choose* how to express it."

"Express it?" I shouted, the ire rising in my chest grew as my temper flared. "Holland, I didn't choose this! I never chose to have this power, this magic...it was *forced* upon me!"

"Like you almost forced yourself on me!" Her chest heaved. "No, don't play the victim, Dale. You had choices, we all did. They're what make us *who* we are."

"Damn the choices!" I snarled, noting the temperature rising in the room as the static grew in my vision, coating everything in electrifying red. "If I have to be the villain in your story, to *save* your life, to *save* Shae's life and countless others, I will! You saw those ghouls! You saw the dragon! We've been attacked, betrayed, we're at war. It's times like these that require hard choices, dark ones."

She growled at me and took a daring step forward, into the pool of static—static that climbed up her limbs but didn't harm her.

Taste. Make her see. Claim.

My magic coursed within me, thumping, willing me to take what it wanted.

No! I shouted to the pool of liquid anger inside of me.

"Dale." Holland's hand on my arm caused me to jump. "I can help you. Let me help?"

I felt her presence again, a gentle reassurance trying to calm my internal storm. Suddenly, I was aware of every nerve ending. Of every place her touch was and *wasn't*. The sensual high from my feeding still coated my senses and I wanted her. I needed her.

I became acutely aware that while Holland was dressed in the standard issue blue and black, I was starkly nude. Gloriously naked. In my birth suit with no shame. I smiled at her.

"Dale," she warned, tilting her head.

"Holland," I said as I cupped her waist in both hands and pulled her closer to me, crushing her body against mine. "Be mine?" I growled in her ear.

She whimpered against me but didn't resist. "Let me help you, let me save you from yourself?"

I laughed darkly. "There is no saving me."

"Yes," she protested. "There is. Remember who you were? Remember the male I met at Donavan's that first night? The one with a strong moral compass, the one with compassion for his past lover's family, the one—"

"What did you say?" I snapped. Her mention of Tate had my temper spiking, my ears blaring. The call for blood was strong. My fingers sank deeper into her waist.

"Tate." She challenged me with her eyes. "Dale, *you* sacrificed yourself for her. You broke the chain of command to find that base to see what was really going on. You valued life, and above all, rules. Let me help you," she said, wincing as my grip tightened.

"Never mention that name again, Holland. That female?" I laughed bitterly. "I just handed her over to my father, to the government, to answer for her crimes. To answer for turning me into this!"

A faint purple outline glowed on her forehead as she began to visibly shake. "She did this, Holland." I ran my fingers over her forehead. "She made me what I am."

"Show her mercy, save her, and in doing so, save yourself." Her eyes filled with unshed tears.

"You're an incredible female," I whispered. She had a good heart... she deserved to keep it. I shoved my magic and rage down. "If I must become the sin eater for you, then I'll happily bear that burden." I inhaled her scent, knowing it may be the last time.

My magic pulsed, crying for me to consume—if she wouldn't willingly give, I *could* steal what I needed. I had fed from several seethings upon return, even a guard or two, but I still felt *empty*. Perhaps I'd siphon from the vessel and see if she could *fill* me in other ways— maybe I'd even fuck her, fill her for a change.

I was insatiable.

"No." She pulled back and I forced my muscles to relax. Control, I was in control of myself and this magic. Not the other way around. "If you do this, if you continue to kill innocents in the name of war, your soul will be too far gone. I beg you, if you care for me at all, if you care for Shae at all, please don't do this. Please be done."

I looked into her eyes and I saw the hope there. The promise of forgiveness, acceptance. Only, I didn't want it. I didn't want to stop. The remaining shreds of my morals cried for me to follow Holland's suggestion, to end this madness. To spare lives. Only, the larger part of me longed for more power, more energy, more fuel...

"I'm sorry," I said and took a step back. "You better go, Holland. I release you from whatever...connection we shared. You needn't bear it anymore. This is on me and no one else."

"Dale, don't say that. I can sense the good in you still! It's there, hidden beneath pain and anger—being suffocated by a parasite that's trying to claim you as its own! Resist it. Stop feeding it. Come with me. Let Shae and I help you." She reached out for me, and I allowed her to grip my forearm, closing my eyes as I physically restrained myself from taking her right there.

"Go," I ground out.

"No, I can help. Let me—"

"I said GO, Holland!" I yanked my arm back and looked into her eyes, pain shown there. "It's the only way," I said trying to soften it.

Devour. Take. Eat. Mine.

I ignored the calls within to taste her energy, to siphon her power. But my control was slipping. I could sense my static beginning to carefully coat her skin and search for any way to sneak just a little.

"I said leave me! If you continue to speak treason, I'll turn you in, just like I did Tate," I snarled at her as I stepped backwards, allowing the air to separate us.

The desire to snuff out her internal flame became a steady drum, urging me to move and dominating every thought. I could see it, burning brightly and in a hue I couldn't identify. It was wild. It was pure temptation. It took all my strength to withhold.

"I—"

"GO! I don't want you here!" I snapped before stalking back to the table and pouring a heavy glass of bloodwine. "I need allies, not weak females who don't understand war and the sacrifice it demands. I don't want someone who can't handle me. I need someone who is strong enough to accept me as I am. Someone who can see the sacrifices *I'm* making."

Each word I hurled at her hit its mark. Her face fell and then she turned and rushed from the room, pausing only at the door. "Goodbye, Dale. I'll always be here if you need help finding your way back."

And then she was gone.

I hurled the glass of bloodwine at the wall and took pleasure in the way it shattered. I needed food, now. Without thinking, I stalked from the room out onto the balcony that overlooked much of HQ. From here I could feel the different pulses beating within every individual.

Human. Vampire. Seething.

All of their magic called to me. I surveyed the city and could see tiny dots everywhere, people milling about, guaramen beginning to rise for the day, others just going to bed in the late morning after a long night shift. So many people...so much *untapped* magic.

A sense of *wrongness* wafted toward me, and I searched desperately for it. A rise of shouts sprang from the camp below as the movement tripled. I lifted my eyes to the distance and spotted hundreds of thousands of figures rushing toward the battlelines we'd only drawn the day before.

So, this is what the Fern wanted? This was how it was?

I threw my head back and roared loudly, commanding red bolts that reached into the sky to strike the ground below. I felt the sense of evil watching, observing—close by. I squinted below, feeling for what was calling me.

And then I saw it. Blurry white streaks stalked the perimeter of our tents, and then as one, they raised their fists and poured red flames upon innocent guaramen. My anger sparked as I hurled bolts their way, but I was too far and my aim was insufficient.

Leader! the Tarragon shouted.

Coming. Stand firm, let none pass.

I needed my reserves filled. I surveyed the people rushing below, guaramen and seethings alike, and I couldn't hold back anymore. Frankly, I didn't want to. Restraint was not who I was, not anymore. I removed the lid on my inner magic and let the beast take over. I no longer saw with my own eyes, instead, I saw through a lens of power. The figures below weren't people anymore but individual flames— potential energy. I could see tiny little orbs dotting the ground, different colored bursts of fire, ripe for the picking.

I didn't hesitate as I reached out and *feasted.*

CHAPTER 80

AETHER

*A**ether...*

It was the faintest whisper down the bond, a silent cry. I'd heard it before, long into the night, and again this morning. Each time I tried to grab hold of it, to bring it to life, it simply slipped through my fingers.

I reached out again to Tate, her side of the bond was present—a little stronger, but still quiet. I growled in frustration as I overlooked the HQ tower. Red lightning bolts struck the ground haphazardly coming from a starkly nude figure standing on one of the balconies of the building.

A figure I recognized: Chance.

I growled as the need for revenge grew, demanding I act. I wanted nothing more than to skin him alive, burn him from the inside out, gut him, and leave his entrails dotting the ground, but mahogany eyes wouldn't allow it, she needed me. She was the priority. This was a rescue mission, I reminded myself.

All around were blurs of motion, seethings fighting as ghouls attacked with streams of flames. Most of the bloodshed was still in the field, but our message had clearly hit its mark. With James blinking in a dozen ghouls just outside city limits, chaos had erupted. Even from here, I could hear the screams and cries marked by death.

"Remind me again why you can't just blink in and grab her?" I growled.

"Because of wards. I'd be frozen in space. This is the closest I'd dare go, and even then, having us blink into the woods was still the safest. It gives us the best chance of continuing undetected," James replied, giving me an answer to the question I'd asked half a dozen times this morning already.

James had blinked us to the outskirts of the forest hours ago and we waited, hidden in the hills right above HQ city, for our signal. The horns blared and we knew our gamble had paid off. The battlefield twenty miles back became a blur of milky white and red-clad figures who began to charge the Glenn.

It was nearly time to attack.

I surveyed the city below. It had transformed into a war zone. Buildings were destroyed, the ground was scarred, corpses and black goo littered the ground along with disturbing *ash* and *bones*. Fire bloomed in the sky, red—the ghouls. It was disturbing what a dozen of those creatures could accomplish.

From what we could see, the Glenn was scrambling. Trying to understand *how* so many had snuck in while trying to keep the rest back, it was sheer chaos. The *perfect* distraction.

Since we don't have a battalion of our own, why not use the one sitting just outside the city? Camella's suggestion had been a gift from Mother Blood herself. And she'd been right, we snuck down the grassy hills until we nearly reached the pavement of the first city road. It wouldn't be long now.

I looked to the sky, searching but saw nothing but morning clouds.

Nerves began to dance along my hands and arms. This had to work.

"Aether, calm down. We still have time before we act. We're in position, now is the hard part. Now we wait," Camella said from beside me.

I knew she was right. It was literally just the three of us and no more. Tate deserved to have the entire Embassy here to save her, not this skeleton crew. Hate grew in me for Arithi, but at the very least she could *potentially* finally be of use to us.

I exhaled slowly. "You're sure they received the messages?"

"Absolutely, my contact delivered the letters before dawn."

I nodded in response.

"There are good people there, Aether. They'll come. Juda will have to act after the accusation that was levied. After what you revealed," Camella said moving to stand beside me.

It was a gamble, writing to the six chairs. One I'd never have taken if Tate wasn't already being held hostage and her identity known—revealing her heritage to a bunch of vipers could put her at further risk, past royals were hunted.

But my plan for her *origin* to remain hidden had failed.

And Tate was taken hostage by the Glenn.

I'd let her down in so many ways; I didn't protect her as I should've.

Now, I'd move heaven and earth to get her back—now was the time for risks. Five of the letters we'd sent explained *who* Tate was to the other chairs, and one was sent to Arithi, threatening her if she didn't aid in ending the seethings and ghouls. We'd also revealed that she was scheming with the Fern to attack the Glenn and evidenced by the presence of the ghouls during the trials as well as the ambush that occurred at the cabin—all of it was supporting proof. Still incredibly weak, but if we were lucky, it would spur action. We only needed a small host, a few dragons for our plan to work...

"I know, I just—"

Words failed me as the entire realm jolted, the light from the sun became blacked out, and the ground shook from the sound of a thousand thunderbolts. The sky lit up with a blush-golden-pink hue and a stream of pink fire formed a living pillar, hovering thousands of feet in the air.

"Aether," Camella said, eyes wide.

James placed his hand on my shoulder, resolve in his gaze. "He's dead, the king has passed."

The ground shook again as I willed my pounding heart to calm. Things had just become infinitely more complicated.

"We move the timetable up, we go now," I commanded.

"That's reckless."

"Not a good idea, we need to wait."

James and Camella's protests fell on deaf ears. It wasn't until James bound me with his magic that I paused.

"Aether, we have time. We need to wait until the battle is fully underway. Until backup arrives."

I flexed and unflexed my hands, willing my erratic heart to calm. James was right. We'd wait, but not for long. Fifteen minutes passed, and the battle ensued with the seethings and ghouls devouring one another, with strikes of lightning ending beasts and the Tarragon ravishing, and still we stood. I scanned the sky, one more time... searching.

Another boom sounded, and this time, the pink flames came pouring down from the sky in a cyclone, enveloping the HQ building.

Tate.

It was calling to her—the only royal in this realm.

"We move now," I bit out.

James looked sick but nodded. Together, the three of us began jogging down the bluff. Tate's time just got cut in half, and I would be damned if I wasn't there for her when she needed me.

Hang on, babe. I'm coming.

And even though she didn't respond, I could have sworn I felt the faintest flicker in response and hope flared in my chest.

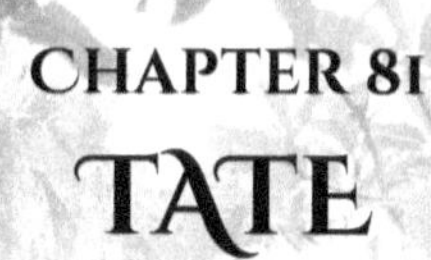

CHAPTER 81
TATE

I stared numbly at my reflection. My blonde hair with black tips was matted to my face as sweat surged from every pore. My skin was puffy from the tears I'd shed, and my voice was hoarse from shouting Vala's name.

I'd been left alone for blood knew how long. Aside from the two medics who administered the two doses of medication I'd received that numbed everything, mind included, I hadn't seen anyone. Restlessness gnawed at me, begging me to move, to *fight*. But every time I tried, it was futile. Recently, I'd been able to move my arms and legs, but still nothing nearly strong enough to break through the manacles digging into my wrists and ankles.

I ground my teeth as I pulled again in vain and cried out in frustration. My inner power was just below the surface, I could feel it humming and building, but was unable to access it.

A prickling attacked my skin, and an outside force swirled around me, filling the air with a strangely *sweet* scent. Odd.

I yanked harder on the chains and threw myself back into the chair as the door cracked open. Perhaps, if I feigned sleep, they'd get sloppy. I let my head hang limply along with my limbs. Feet shuffled in; louder than before but maybe it was merely the medication wearing off. Whispered tones sounded and then the distinct popping of knees.

What the—

Cold hands gripped my forearm and I sprung, I threw my head forward and crashed into a wall of ice. Pain exploded and I blinked in succession, trying to understand what I'd just encountered. A hallucination?

"Shit, Tate, sorry I didn't mean to hurt you. I'm still learning about this..."

I lifted my head, willing my heart to return to its normal rhythm. It couldn't be, could it? A wall of ice stood erect mere inches from my face, but behind it were steel blue eyes and a grown-out blue bob.

I whimpered as new tears sprung from my eyes. "Shae!"

"Tate," she said as she awkwardly side-stepped the ice and pulled me into a hug. "It's okay, we're getting you out of here."

"We?" I asked numbly, noting for the first time the short female standing behind Shae. Her light brown hair was bluntly cut and fell just past her shoulders. Her golden-brown eyes were keen and the aura floating from her felt strangely *ancient*. She stepped forward, visibly unalarmed by Shae's magic, or my restraints, or Shae's declaration to free me, or—

"Yes, we're here to help, but with one condition," the female began. I squinted, finally the dots connected.

"Holland," I said.

Her eyes flared and then she smiled, cold and threatening. "Tate, it's nice to finally meet you."

Shae shuffled forward awkwardly before extending her hand to Holland, waiting.

"In a minute," Holland said looking pointedly at Shae's hand. "But first, Tate I need you to answer me this: did you participate in the spread of dark magic?"

"What?" I gaped at her. "No, never."

She nodded and then looked deeply at me—*into* me. "If I freed you, what would you do?"

I paused, unsure of how to answer. A gentle pressure urged my mouth open, and words began to pour out, "I'm not sure how to answer. I want justice. President Dale needs to answer for his crimes. The seethings need to be destroyed. I-I need to get out of here and Vala needs to be saved and—" the pressure ceased and with it my mouth shut. What the hell?

I glared at Holland who merely smiled and shrugged. "Some skills can still be used for good."

I looked to Shae who simply winked at me. "Oh, come on, she only loosened your tongue to ease her conscience. You are technically a traitor to the Glenn, and we are at war. This is a big step for her." Shae nodded to Holland, pride swelling in her eyes.

Holland swallowed and then placed the key in Shae's hand, holding it for a beat longer than necessary, before retracting her delicate fingers. From this close, I could see the soft features of her face as her honeysuckle scent blanketed me.

Soft. Feminine. Pretty.

Her eyes snapped to mine and narrowed.

Fierce.

I smiled. I liked this Holland.

"One last thing," Holland said. "I need you to save Dale. Promise me, you'll do everything in your power to rescue him from what he's becoming." She swallowed, tears pooling in her amber eyes.

"Save?" I asked, trying not to laugh dryly. He was beyond saving. "I think it's too late for that. And if anyone could, it sure as hell isn't me."

"Tate." It was the softness in Shae's voice that tore me from my anger. "He's hurting. You know this isn't who he is. He's been corrupted, we can't reach him, but maybe you could..."

Her grey eyes begged, pleaded, and willed me to try. I exhaled and bit my lip. "Fine, I'll try."

Holland smiled sadly and Shae mirrored the action. What horrors had they seen? Shae shoved the key into the lock and opened the manacles, one at a time. When the last one sprang open, I lurched from the chair only to nearly fall into the wall of ice. Shae steadied me and helped me move around it, before I stood, facing the small female who was unafraid of me even with all the rumors flying about.

"Thank you." She nodded at me sadly as she spoke. Then, to my surprise, she pulled me into a tight hug. I stood there, arms at my side in shock.

Shae cleared her voice.

Right.

I pulled Holland into a hug and felt her trembling. Arms wrapped around from behind me as Shae joined in the hug. We stood there for a moment, huddled and holding one another in the most bizarre group hug.

I stiffened as Holland pulled back and finally, Shae released me. "We need to go," I said.

I reached down my bond and felt...a light stirring, the opaque pull was turning within and shining brightly. Any moment the magical restraints would be gone, and I'd be freed.

The air caressed my skin again, so similar to what Aether would do, but this was different. Where his was kind and soothing, this was curious—searching me, and probing slightly harder, awakening my magic—calling me to action.

"All right, so we're going to sneak you onto the battlefield, and you'll address Dale. You'll take back your power, and he'll finally be free from its hold," Holland spoke, striding for the door.

I followed after her on wobbly legs that slowly regained their strength. "Absolutely not," I growled.

Holland abruptly stilled, turned, and pointed a finger at my chest. "You gave your word. You did this to him, and you're going to fix it."

"I will try, but the last time we saw one another, he tried to kill me. I'm not having another face-off while I'm weak. I will try to save him, I'll do all that I can...but it needs to be in a safer environment, for *all* of us." I tried to sound confident as I strode unsteadily toward Holland, steps finally firm. I had absolutely no idea how to *take* magic back, but I wasn't about to tell her that. I continued until her finger was digging into my chest. "First, you're going to help me save one more female."

She stared at me, conflict warring in her eyes.

"She's right, Holland. We just need to get her safely out for now, away from all the citizens and from HQ," Shae said.

"And how long until she's back? How long until she *tries?* He could be GONE by then!" Holland shouted.

"Better him than all of us, now take me to Vala," I said slowly.

Her eyes flared and I swore the pressure in my mind built as small veins began to crawl across her face. A diamond appeared in her temple and her body became blurry with rapid motion.

"I—"

"Holland—"

The whole room erupted in clattering noises as the ground itself shook. I fell into Shae's arms and nearly buckled to the ground as my legs gave out. The mirrors and windows shattered, and even the tile cracked. On the other side of the jagged window, I could see Vala, her form hung limply in the chair. Blood covered her body, and her legs were still at unnatural angles.

Thunder clapped from above, the sound more like a bomb than actual thunder, and the room began to crumble. The wind gusted and began swirling as fire—*pink fire*—poured down and claimed everything in its path.

Hello, it seemed to say, beckoning me forward. *We've been searching for you.*

With renewed strength, I took a step forward.

The building creaked and screamed as floor after floor was ripped into the cyclone of flames directly above. Shae threw her hands up, and a dome of ice formed, blocking the loose debris from hitting us. It melted almost instantly as the heat from the flames intensified, and she reinforced it with layer after layer of ice.

Come...

I paused and looked up into the eye of the storm. Nothing but pink sky, pink flames, and the odd call of *home* met my senses. Energy pulsed around me, strengthening weakened limbs, and restoring my broken energy stores. The chains on my magic snapped, and the well inside began to bubble forth in waves of undiluted power.

"Daughter, welcome home. It is she who survived from annihilation. The blood of forgotten royalty, the one bonded with darkness, and whose reign will bring peace. Come." An ethereal voice spoke through the flames.

"What the hell!" Holland shrieked, looking at me like I'd done this.

"It's some Untish prophecy," I called back, not taking my eyes from the living flames.

"About you?" Holland's face turned a slight shade of green.

"Well, if it is, you'd be happy because presumably I'll vanquish evil and restore the scales of balance," I murmured.

The wind intensified, as the building was consumed by the tornado of fire. An inferno, that somehow didn't kill us.

"I don't know if I believe it, but either way you're saving Dale!" Holland shouted, her voice fading in the rush of wind hitting my ears.

"Tate, can you stop it?" Shae asked, standing close by.

"You really think *I* did this?" I shouted. "I don't know what's happening!"

"Not strong enough my ass, you're going to Dale. Now!" Holland demanded, stepping bravely toward me. Even with the wind blowing ruthlessly around the three of us, we were not pulled up into the storm. Shae reached out to stop Holland, but I didn't need her to fight for me.

I stepped forward and lifted my head into the storm. The pink flames called to me, the symphony of a lullaby I'd long ago forgotten. The magic of it all swelled and slowly surrounded me, filled me. I opened my arms to embrace its power. I could hear voices calling to me, Shae and Holland screaming for me to stop. I was vaguely aware of being lifted up, of my strength not only returning but doubling and then doubling again. I called the flames to me and instantly felt them *restore* me, and I roared.

I looked at my magic, at my inner fire burning brightly. Inside, I saw the eyes of a dragon, she'd finally awakened. I laughed hysterically as I called more and more power into myself. Savoring the way my nerves finally fired freely without the sluggish effect of the drugs.

Freed. Whole. Right.

More voices called to me along with one that I knew in my heart, one I'd recognize anywhere. Aether.

Hold on, babe. I'm coming.

I smiled as tears of joy fell down my cheeks. I couldn't just hear him; I could *see* him. He was trudging down the hill with James and Camella, carefully avoiding the battle taking place, and headed directly for the cyclone swallowing the HQ tower whole. He was coming for me.

I can't wait to see you come.

His head whipped up, searching for me.

Tate?

Yours truly.

I smirked in his mind, and awe flooded the bond as I saw his face fill with wonder.

I've got to get Vala, but I'll see you soon. Stay safe.

Not a chance, I'm coming to you.

I could sense his determination, nothing I said would change that. And maybe it was selfish, but I wanted him by my side. I wanted to be in his arms. I *needed* him.

"Tate!" Shae's shrill cry jerked me from my euphoria.

My eyes adjusted and I could see that it was no longer a small hole above my head, but a gaping expanse—at least thirty feet wide. There were only ten floors above us now.

"Stop this madness!" Holland shouted.

"It's not my doing," I responded slowly. Truth was, even if it were, I'm not sure I would stop it. This building needed to come down; it was a long time coming.

"Who are you?" Holland demanded with eyes full of terror as she beheld my haloed head.

"A survivor," I responded as I lowered and then stepped over shards of glass and crumbled mortar into the cell holding Vala. A cry tore free as I beheld her broken state, her legs snapped at angles that screamed *wrong!* I pulled at the manacles and they resisted. Anger rose in me and following nothing but impulse, I willed my power to flood into the metal—to heat it and break it.

A moment later, they dropped to the floor in a molten pile of liquid iron—leaving Vala's flesh unharmed. I ignored the gasps coming from behind me and worked my way through the other three restraints.

"Mother Blood," Holland whispered.

I picked Vala up, wincing as she cried out, even in her unconscious state, and turned to face the other two females.

"Tate, I didn't know…" Shae said, tears spilling down her face. "How could they?"

"I'm so sorry, I had no idea. I—" Holland put her hand to her mouth, her face reflecting the horror I felt.

"She needs help, we need to move. Now."

They both nodded and then froze. "I'm not sure where or how…" Shae began.

"Can you keep the building up?" Holland asked, suddenly unsure. I looked around and realized only five floors remained above us and that the cyclone of pink fire had doubled in size.

"Follow me," I spoke. I pulled inward at my pool of power and felt the threads of magic in the soil far, far beneath my feet; I felt the energy coursing around me in the wind and I simply willed it into a shield. A faint glimmer formed, light pink with golden swirls, protecting the four of us.

Shae's eyes bulged and Holland's jaw fell open. "A shield," I said simply and began to walk.

I didn't wait for them to respond as I pushed through the now-open door and made my way into the hallway. The building shook as more mortar was ripped free, revealing metal rods that twisted from the power of the wind before melting and then ripping free, being pulled into the cyclone. I could hear faint steps behind me.

Vala will need medical attention immediately.

Roger. We need to get you out of here ASAP. The king has died. It's time to go home.

The impact of the last word rippled through my mind.

Home.

Home.

Home.

My heartbeat followed the repetition of the word I knew would likely alter my life.

My blood began to buzz with a hope I didn't understand. But one thing was sure, if I was with Aether, I would be home. I continued to march through the building, noting the debris falling on my shield and then burning away.

"Perhaps she could just talk to Dale," I heard Holland whisper.

"No," I said simply. "Not now."

"But—"

"I said no." I looked at her and could see her visibly shaking and *felt* something primordial rolling from her. The diamond on her forehead pulsed a bright purple and then seemed to hum.

Odd.

The ground shook beneath me, but I pressed forward. At last, the hallway ended, and we emerged into the daylight. Into a war zone and unimaginable bloodshed.

CHAPTER 82

CHANCE

I danced between the tents, holding my own as I attacked yet another ghoul. I sucked its magic from it and savored the way it dropped to its knees, shrieking. Its power fueled my tank with a wild flavor. And still, it was not enough.

I drained more—vampires and seethings and ghouls—and still, it was not enough.

Not even close.

All around me, corpses dotted the ground. Most were burnt from the ghouls, and others were mere husks after my *feeding*. I fought back the pang of guilt from having ended their lives, but I needed my strength if I were to kill the ghouls—it would save more innocents in the end. My means were justified.

The beast in front of me released a final wail and then its power was gone. It fell face forward into the muddied earth. I looked around, my Tarragon were with me—beside me, above me, behind me. We moved as one choreographed unit. Roars came from above the hill as more ghouls crested, the first full wave was at our city. I screamed as I stalked toward the enemy line.

With me! I ordered the Tarragon.

I sent them mental images of what I wanted to happen, of the destruction that we would cause. Their excitement bounced back, triple that of my own.

My steps faltered as a clap sounded and the entire camp shuddered. The mud itself quaked as the sky screamed with angry whisps of wind and energy. The orange-pink sun turned wholly *pink*, the sky became nothing but blush, and a pillar of *pink flames* hovered in the air.

A foreign attack? A new weapon?

Leader! The ghouls!

My focus returned to the throng of white beasts flooding over the hill, red flames flowing freely from their taloned hands.

Attack! I commanded my Tarragon.

All around me, guaramen in various ranks ran. Duxes, who nodded at me in stern recognition, blades at the ready. Arches, who looked at me warily and with fear. Dokimoses, who refused eye contact and instead, shook in their boots—pathetic. It was one of the latter that I pulled from and took the little power he had to offer. Better for me to possess and wield it than for him to disgrace his country by cowering. I claimed his energy as my own and with half a thought, I snuffed out his internal light and inhaled it—he dropped to the ground dead.

I ignored the sound of his bones snapping as my Tarragon trampled over his corpse.

The enemy was just ahead.

Guaramen ran toward the line of fire carrying pitiful shields. Streaks of black scales swarmed, all running toward the ghouls.

My Tarragon howled in my mind a moment before their cries consumed the battlefield. We may have lost five, but the remaining six were strong. We would survive this, and we'd have fun. I smiled as I continued to stalk, noting the way the mud squished between my toes. Funny, I didn't notice the blood gushing from my feet until now. In fact, I'd forgotten clothing altogether. I pulled at the red static and sheathed my feet before wrapping my body in living, red lightning.

This would make for a memorable appearance.

I increased my pace and we ran into the fray of beasts and vampires alike. The moment the first ghoul was within reach, I released targeted missiles of power. They struck its chest, and it screamed as a dozen other ghouls locked their eyes on me. Together, they attacked with talons and flames. My Tarragon jumped in front of me and blocked the flames, and I called down lightning to strike the hearts of each ghoul.

The power was euphoric. One moment, they were attacking, and the next, I could feel each beating heart in my grasp—with a brush of my will, their hearts stopped, and I devoured.

Roaring filled my ears as the battlefield became blurry. My motions, my Tarragon's actions, became meaningless. Nothing mattered but the song of power. I danced to its melody, allowing bolts to fly—distantly aware that my own men were being struck down, that I was claiming their essences.

What does it matter? They'd be dead in moments anyway; this is a necessary sacrifice...

My magic purred within as it reassured me of my motives. This was, after all, for the greater good. So, I silenced my inner conscience, and instead, surrendered completely to the song of magic. My beasts beheaded vampires all around, most wearing the enemy red, but a few in the guara's black and blue. They slaughtered ghouls, gutted them, and tore their wings from them. They devoured their kills—my kills.

My power siphoned, filled, spilled, savored.

I left some hearts beating, even as I struck true, allowing them to be crippled—food for my beasts. A necessary sacrifice.

My movements became a blur, dancing on the waves of red static and might. I threw my head back, laughing like I was mad—perhaps, I was—and then I simply reveled in the consuming pleasure of obliter ating the enemy.

A vampire, draped in red, was flung back by an attacking seething —blood seeped from her chest. She looked to me, her enemy, for help, clutching her abdomen. I silenced the heart of the seething, lunging midair, before dropping next to the injured female. For a moment, relief filled her eyes. But then, as she noted the way my nostrils flared, terror claimed her features. I yanked her upwards and sank my fangs into the base of her neck. Red hot iron met my tongue and satisfied a different need. A different urge.

I pulled further, deeper, and savored the way she tasted until she too was empty. But not before I also snuffed out her inner flame.

The high from feeding from fresh blood and magic was alluring, much too tempting to not repeat. And so, I did.

Again.

And again, and again, and again.

I dropped the next corpse to the ground: a guaraman whose pathetic swordsmanship cost the life of one of our own. I swiped his blood from my mouth as a new wave of ghouls breached the hill, charging into the fray.

I threw a volley of lightning their way before rushing to meet them. Lightning writhed across my arms and became a living spear. Fuck yeah. As the nearest one reached me, I stabbed its gut with my sword of power—fucking Sire Fire, that's what I'd call the blade of lightning.

Sire Fire singed the inside of the ghoul, and I pivoted before digging it into the next. The ghouls sent flames my way, but my Tarragon blocked, allowing me to attack one at a time. This was far more exciting than killing from afar. I continued to dance between ghouls and seethings alike, my Tarragon with me, and stabbed then pulled their power and snuffed out their inner flame. Occasionally, I'd take a bite—draw some blood, and was immediately jolted with the first sip of ghoul blood. It tasted rotten, soiled, and yet... fermented? I pulled again, savoring its unique flavor before I dropped its corpse to the muddied earth on a pile of severed limbs and blood knew what.

My magic flared and with it, my vision heightened further allowing me a clearer view of the battle. We were winning. Fucking demolishing those beasts. A laugh shook my body as I called down a host of lightning. Except instead of it raining down, it rose up from *me* and hit the sky in a show of majesty. I lowered my gaze, prepared for the next attack, Sire Fire at the ready, and then...everything changed. The ground shook. Thunder three times that of the quake earlier boomed, and everything trembled. I fell forward, onto my face and into bloodied mud.

My power blinked out, momentarily stunned. All around me, time stopped. I swatted at the mud coating my face and froze. Death. Hundreds, no thousands, of guaramen covered the ground—nothing but husks. Some were burnt corpses, clearly the work of the ghouls, but others had been drained—siphoned. Limbs scattered the hills.

An alarming amount looked vampirical.

My stomach soured as my mind came back, pounding into my skull with sickening memories.

You did this.

Vile.

Wrong.

Holland was right.

Not too late.

I shook my head. I was helpless. My heart raced as I realized what I'd done, what I'd become. Holland, she'd been right. She'd been trying to help, and I'd been too full of bloodlust to understand. I needed—

The tearing of metal and the shattering of glass screamed from HQ as the main tower began to fall. It became swallowed by a massive cyclone of pink flames. I forced myself up as I watched in horror. The roof was ripped from the building, glass shards hurled through the air and impaled our own guaramen who were still in the camp. The mortar crumbled as the building began to become entirely demolished.

I stood, frozen and helpless as the windows continued to burst, and floor after floor shook before being torn from its purchase. The flames pulsed, and even from here, I could feel the lethal heat.

Holland.

I didn't think before I took off in a sprint toward the building, vaguely aware of the ghouls charging behind.

Stay and fight! I ordered the Tarragon. *Except you, you come with me.*

The largest Tarragon flew ahead of me. The carnage was everywhere. The tents that had dotted the city streets and field near the HQ tower were all burnt, they were nothing but flames and ash and destruction.

"Holland!" I screamed even as my feet pushed me forward. It couldn't be too late. It wasn't too late.

The building shuddered in front of me as the top half of it was sucked into the cyclone—feeding the flames. I swallowed back the pure fear that fueled me. I was strong, and so was Holland. We would be all right. We had to be.

And so, I ran, harder and faster until, at last, my body breached the flames.

CHAPTER 83
TATE

We exited the building just as it imploded. Where it once stood, there was now nothing but a gigantic hole in the ground with a pillar of fire engulfing it. The cyclone pulsed and then expanded even further, increasing the burned empty space. The shield held firm, and to my surprise, Shae was cooling the air around us. I arched a brow and she merely shrugged.

"Metamorphosis," she muttered.

I wasn't so convinced. We continued forward even as the smoke became thick.

Aether, where are you?

Coming, he grunted. *We're working our way through some soldiers and beasts on the perimeter of the cyclone, about to come in—*

No! We're coming out.

The last thing I needed was for him to get hurt. We'd be free of the storm soon. I stepped over debris and glass crunched beneath my boots as we continued to press forward. Sweat dripped into my eyes and Vala slipped in my arms before I recovered quickly. One glance at Holland and Shae confirmed what I suspected; they were baking. We needed to get a lot of space from these flames and quickly.

The gravitational pull increased, and it became harder and harder to move forward as I was being drawn to the storm's center. I grunted in frustration as I tried to step again. Holland and Shae surpassed me, looking confused.

I tried again and this time, I made no progress. It was as if my feet didn't know how to move.

"Tate, maybe I could carry Vala?" Shae offered.

"Maybe," I grumbled as I tried again and failed to move forward. "Fine, take her." I blew at the hair sticking to my face.

Shae took Vala's mangled body in her arms, careful not to add any pressure to her many, many wounds. Shae winced and then blew at Vala's head. To my surprise, snowflakes formed and began fluttering across her brow. A moment later, the entire dome was filled with white flurries, melting the moment they got close to the shield or my skin.

"Amazing," I said. "Shae, we definitely need to talk about this."

"Only after we talk about *you*." She gave me a pointed look. "Oh, heir of the prophecy."

"I'm not so sure about that," I muttered with a scrunched nose. No matter that I was beginning to accept the prophecy with each passing moment.

"We need to keep moving, Your Royal Peace-Keeping Highness," Holland said as she rolled her eyes.

I opened my mouth to respond when I spotted the diamond on her forehead. I squinted my eyes, focusing on it, and Shae shook her head at me in silent command: *don't* mention it.

"Yes, let's go," Shae said as she stepped forward.

I went to move with them and made it only a few inches. What the hell?

I grunted and released more magic, momentarily breaking the pull on me which sent me fumbling forwards only to be yanked back with a hefty ferocity. I landed on my ass.

"Tate!" Shae shouted. I looked to them and realized I'd been thrown out of my own shield.

"No! Keep going," I said as I nodded to Vala. "Get her to safety!"

Shae didn't move, only looked at me helplessly. I willed the dome to stay, to protect them.

Come home...

The call echoed around me as the flames pulsed and the magic tickling my skin sank its claws in deeper, eliciting a roar from my inner dragon—responding flames burst from my palms.

I willed the magic around me to release me and let me go. But... nothing. I swatted at it with my flames, but it still didn't relent—the pressure merely increased as I continued to be pulled backwards. A frustrated cry fell from my lips.

I'm coming in.

NO! I can't move, I don't want you stuck.

Aether's laugh filled my mind, dark and sensual. *If you're stuck, then so am I*—he paused a moment, and an image of him filled my mind: he was engaged in battle with Camella and James at his side, fighting wild seethings—*Don't you know we're a package deal?*

I smiled in spite of the absurdity. There was no reason for him to get caught in this also, but he would because that's who he was. A wave of love for the male washed over me and I allowed it to calm me.

To settle me. To ground me. To reinforce the knowledge of who I was, and with it, increase my confidence.

This time, when I stepped, I moved. Not much, but enough. Encouraged, I continued forward. This would work. Shae smiled and waved me on. She only hesitated a moment, before she turned and began approaching the wall of flames. The shield became covered in ice and I shook my head—metamorphosis indeed.

I kept moving, slow but steady. I'd be out soon, I'd be—

"Where do you think you're going?" the voice of evil shouted from behind. I didn't need to turn to know *who* stood behind me, to know he carried his cane, and that his ice blue eyes were boring into my back.

I smiled, viciously. I'd sworn vengeance, and now I'd get it.

He was responsible for Fletch. For Irene. For the seethings covering the hills, taking thousands of innocent lives.

Vala's broken limbs hung from Shae's arms as they moved, swaying unnaturally. He did that to her.

President Collin Dale would pay.

I growled as I turned to face the monster who'd destroyed so much of my life, who was the very essence of evil. I looked at him and saw only darkness. He stood not thirty feet away, cane hooked over his arm as his suit was pristine—even given the wreckage all around. His eyes were no longer blue, but they were *purple* and his skin a sickly grey.

I looked closer and noted the sweat drenching every part of his body, his suit wasn't clean—it was soaking wet.

"We didn't finish our conversation," he tsked at me. "Didn't your *mother* teach you it's rude to leave without saying goodbye."

A moment later, his power flung out in angry purple waves—it reached for my power, my energy, and began pulling. Just like with Chance, only this was different. This was *entirely* rotten and dark. I grunted from the impact as his power hit mine. Everything faded, even Shae's screams in the near distance became muted.

I snarled as I closed my eyes. Focus.

My magic bubbled at my skin and filled my veins, it was ready. I called it closer to the surface, even as I fought off the constant attack. A bit of my magic flared and was quickly sucked into the void *and* pulled into the beast in front of me.

Enough. This had all been enough.

In agreement, *she* arched her neck and roared—molten sparks flew from my hands and lips.

I pushed deeper into my well and yanked upward, full of power. I threw my arms to the side releasing the wave of magic. It slammed into Collin Dale; his jaw went slack as he struggled to regain his footing.

He attacked again, trying to siphon, but I snapped it off and then shoved it back down into his vile inner pit. I stalked forward, and with each step, the resistance I'd felt before not only stopped, but it made my movements lighter—easier. My body began glowing with energy radiating from deep within.

She snapped at the tether, but instead of begging me to free her, she fueled my stores by breathing her power into them. My aura doubled in size and the air crackled and sizzled, sparks flying.

More, stronger, now... My magic swelled, ready to flood every inch of my being.

"This is for Fletch."

I sent a volley of flames at the reprehensible male, and he screamed when they brushed his skin.

"This is for Irene!"

I released another wave of energy, and his aura became vacuum-sealed to himself.

"And for Shae!"

I hit him again with more flames that caused his clothes to burn and his face to turn bright purple, but he *still* tried to fight me.

"And this—" I poured more of myself into the flames, and they licked his flesh, scalding and burning. "—this is for ME."

And then I unleashed.

I called the torrent of barely restrained power to my fingertips, willing it to surround me and freeze the monstrous male mid-step. I broke through the shield he had pathetically erected around himself—having gone on the defensive—and I squeezed the very air from his lungs.

She danced and the call to home I felt doubled.

In emphasis, my magic rallied, and pink flames rushed from my hands. I sent them arching toward him, every bit liquid lava as much as gaseous flame, and ordered them to encase him. His screams filled the cyclone as he dropped to his knees.

Just before it became fatal, I pulled the fire back, allowing it to burn his surface without completely destroying his organs. He didn't deserve a quick death—my vengeance wouldn't allow it.

"Not so strong when someone can fight back, are you!" I shouted as angry tears poured down my face and my limbs shook with fury.

Images of Fletch's remains came to mind. He murdered Fletch. I sent another round of flames at him, allowing some to pierce his skin, the pain echoed in his screams.

I recalled the way the guaramen showed up at my door to tell me my mother was dead, killed for treason at *his* command. Enthrawment, just like Lucas. He'd stolen their magic, their essence.

I snarled as I threw more and more power into the inferno I was unleashing—savoring the way I could smell his flesh burning and see it beginning to fall from his face in charred chunks.

Even then, I didn't relent.

SHE ROARED.

Liquid flames spewed from my lips and then, as if having a mind of its own, it formed three dragons of pink fire that flew toward Collin before landing on his skin, scalding as the lava dragons sunk their teeth into him and *screeched*—echoing my inner beast's cries.

Vala's screams still echoed in my ears. He'd tortured her. He'd killed so many. He caused so much pain, and it was time he *endured* some.

Nearly all his skin was burnt, charcoaled, or had fallen from his face—revealing, not red flesh, but grey poisoned tissue. His body a reflection of his soul.

I stalked toward him, flames streaming from my hands as I moved.

"You killed them, you took their lives. You destroyed. You murdered," I spoke slowly, allowing my words to sink in as my feet took me closer to the male responsible for so much suffering. So much death. So much evil.

The cyclone flared as my temper rose and with it, I could feel *her* fully awakened, stretching the tether taut—nearly breaking. I raised my head and roared, fire flying from my lips, the flames becoming one with the cyclone. A cyclone in which I stood in the very center.

Any resistance or fuel of my motions stilled—my movements were my own, no outside force was tugging or pushing. As if I'd answered its call, *it* left me alone, even as the call to *home* reverberated through my very bones.

I was only ten feet away from Collin. He shuddered and tried to pull at my magic, tried to form a shield, still trying to breathe. I allowed him to inhale once and then squeezed his lungs.

He cowered, clawing at the air.

"Tate!" Shae's voice was a distant cry. I didn't need to turn to know she was close.

"Tate," another voice cried. "Have mercy!"

I gritted my teeth in irritation. Holland knew nothing of the agony this male championed.

Tate.

It was Aether's voice that broke through my bloodlust. I staggered back a step, releasing some of my control over the monstrous waste of life, allowing him to draw a breath, but nothing more. The flames shot from my hands, mere feet from his face, begging to devour—to finish him.

If his death will bring you peace, then do it. But do it with a clear mind, my love.

I sniffled and more tears fell as I saw the faces of all those he'd killed. Irene. Her green eyes, full of life. Fletch, his eyes full of humor. Myself as a child, mahogany eyes full of pain.

He needs to be stopped.

My resolve strengthened. I glanced to the left and saw Aether, striding toward me, every step promising death—my dark knight.

His is your life to claim, but should you wish it, I can do it.

His offer touched my heart and warmed my fractured soul.

No, this is something I have to do alone.

In agreement, *she* screeched within—shaking my soul and illuminating my skin with swells of magic.

I reached out, sending flames hurling toward Collin, and released the pent-up power.

"Tate!" Shae screamed, but this time it was full of panic, a warning.

Tate!

Aether's words reached me a moment before a red bolt streaked across the sky and hit the ground just in front of me, blocking my flames while simultaneously siphoning their energy. A nude figure wrapped in nothing but red light entered the storm, eyes wild and full of something far too natural for his crazed state—fear. Above him flew one of his beasts, one I knew far too well.

"This has to be done, Chance. You know it!" I shouted as he approached.

He moved slowly, still far away. "Tate, he's my father. He may have committed heinous crimes, but he deserves to live. We've sacrificed enough life." His voice was calmer than the last time I spoke to him, even his beast stayed stationary in the air above him—eyes boring holes into my soul as it snarled, revealing four black fangs.

I felt a spark of power flare at my back, burning through my shield, accompanied by a whimpered cry. From my peripheral, I saw Holland darting toward Chance. But she was getting too close to the flames pouring from my hands and too close to the cyclone snapping angrily, begging to devour all flesh.

"Holland!" I screamed in unison with Shae.

But she didn't stop. I grabbed the air around her and froze her mid-step. The wind became violent, and our clothes whipped about our bodies.

"Let her go," Chance snarled.

I could see Aether approaching from the other side, he'd have Chance in his grasp soon.

I swallowed, maintaining my resolve.

The flames pulsed with warning, and at the same time a dragon's cry filled the sky. My eyes landed on Aether's, worry shown there. A moment later, my fears materialized as a red dragon entered the eye of the storm.

CHAPTER 84

AETHER

James and Camella cleared the path for me, and with one final glance back, confirming they held the enemy at bay, I pierced through the cyclone. The moment I broke through the pillar of fire, my breath caught. She was even more magnificent than I recalled. She stood there, the avenging goddess. Her body was laced in pink light, pouring from every fiber of her being. She stalked toward a lone figure who was on his knees gasping for breath as skin fell from his body.

She released wave after wave of her power, flames swallowing him whole. She would end him. I continued to walk toward her and then her face turned to mine.

Tate...

Her eyes were on fire, wholly consumed by pink flames with a tiny black center. Her face glowed and nothing of her normal features and smirk could be found. She'd given herself fully over to her magic.

If his death will bring you peace, then do it. But do it with a clear mind, my love.

She looked at me and blinked. Slowly, her mahogany eyes

returned, and a torrent of tears poured from injured eyes, even as they evaporated almost instantly.

He needs to be stopped.

I understood that, far too well. She'd lost so much because of the male kneeling in front of her. He deserved death and not a kind one. But if she did it this way, would her soul be forever tainted?

She was an executioner of justice, and this was her life to take. Still, I offered to take this burden from her.

I watched as her eyes filled with flames once more and she stalked toward the cowering president, releasing more flames. A figure emerged from the other side of the cyclone, nude skin wrapped in red lightning, and he leveled his hands at Tate.

Tate!

I screamed her name as streaks of red lightning arched across the sky and hit the ground just in front of her. She stood unwavering, unrelenting, even as she engaged in conversation with the very person who'd betrayed her not once, not twice, but three times.

I began running toward Chance, prepared to end him—keenly aware of the beast watching Tate like she was its next meal.

My black flames gathered and with them my connection to every essence surrounded by air. I could feel the energy around Chance, and I reached for it—stilling it and stopping him in his tracks. His eyes locked on mine and flared.

I smiled as I hurled a wave of my power at him.

The ground pulsed and flames flared as a dragon breached the cyclone. She flew above, circling until she lowered herself and inhaled deeply. I knew what would come next.

"Shield!" I shouted.

One glance at Tate told me she had already shielded—the air held pink crystals, floating around her in a halo. I threw up my own shield and then sent it over Tate along with Shae who was holding an injured Vala.

I looked to Holland; she was frozen and encased in one of Tate's shields as well. Shift. I needed to shift. Red flames poured down, hitting our shields as the dragon roared. I pulled at my own inner thread and black hazy flames engulfed me, along with the ground. I urged my power forward and the air snapped, the pain was brief, and like an itch that'd been scratched, I flexed. Transformed, I let my beast take free rein.

I felt Tate's adoration down the bond and sent her a wink as I flapped my wings and raced toward Arithi. She'd flown high, impossibly high, and was spiraling down. I rose to meet her, prepared to attack.

Her large form got bigger and bigger and then a plume of red fire sprang from her throat. I hurled my own black flames to meet hers and cried into the sky. Even the flames flickered with the force of my roar. I released my talons and opened my mouth, Arithi did the same, and then we were a tangle of claws and teeth, tearing and ripping. She cried in pain as my teeth sank into her hide before striking me with her barbed tail. I prepared to strike again when I was hit on the side by a blurry, black beast. The Tarragon.

I ignored the pain, and sunk my fangs in deeper, piercing thoroughly through Arithi's scales. The ground was becoming precariously close, and I released my wings while shaking her and the beast free a moment before I would've hit. To my chagrin, they both recovered in time and were once again pursuing me.

There's my dark high general. There's my beast.

I roared and my confidence was bolstered by Tate's words; I flew with newfound aggression. Arithi's flames licked my feet, and her teeth grazed my tail, she was close. Too close. Red lightning struck the ground, streaking throughout the sky. It landed precariously close to Tate. Fear gripped my heart as she stalked toward President Dale who seemed to be rallying his power.

Tate! Watch out—

Arithi sank her talons into my side before her teeth clamped down over my throat. I roared as blood streaked down my scales. Arithi twisted and struck again with her tail before sending us into another downward spiral. I clawed into her side with my talons, striking true, but she would not relent.

The Tarragon attacked Arithi, sinking its fangs into her wing as it tore with its claws. Confusion clouded my mind for a moment before I recovered and spewed fire from my throat, covering her back. She flinched and loosened her grip slightly, but it was just enough. I twisted at the same time the Tarragon sunk its teeth in her shoulder.

She cried and released me to fight the Tarragon that was now biting and swiping without any apparent method. I plummeted toward the ground as my blood gushed out of my open wounds.

Aether! Tate's panic flooded the bond. I could feel her rallying her power, getting ready to feed me.

Don't you dare, I growled.

Arithi may be fast, but I was bigger. One good, rightsized bite and she'd be dead. I flared out my wings and began to climb. I searched the sky but couldn't see her or the Tarragon. Where had they gone? Red lightning cracked and then the pink flames started funneling from the pillar and toward the center, toward Tate.

I looked down to where Tate was engaged in a battle with both Chance and his father. Chance sent bolt after bolt at Tate, and in that moment, I knew what true undiluted terror was. President Dale regained his footing and, even as a walking corpse, he was pulling from Tate *and* the cyclone—he was siphoning. She resisted but then Chance's power hit her, and she lost control.

But she was not alone. We were in this together.

I began to lower when a dragon's roar shook me—Arithi was approaching, the Tarragon nowhere in sight, but she was low and close to the ground—her focus solely on Tate. I tucked my wings and dove, and with all my strength I reached out and slowed the air around Arithi's wings. Even as it drained my energy, I pushed all of my magic into slowing her and into falling. She was in the inner dome of the cyclone, but I was fast. My talons opened and just as she was about to release flames, I collided into her side and sent us both hurling into the dirt.

CHAPTER 85
TATE

The blow from Chance had been unexpected, I lost my focus and with it, my control over my magic. It fluttered around me wildly, unrestrained and unguided. Collin pulled at my power, siphoning it into himself—a snarl on his skinless face as he strengthened his broken, burnt body. More than that, he was *feeding* from the tower of flames itself. Twin waves flowed from me through the cyclone, one being pulled into Collin, and one being drawn *from* me into the storm itself.

I gritted my teeth as I shook out my tired limbs. I pulled back at my magic and willed it to obey me. In an instant, the floodgate stopped, and Collin growled as his power had been silenced along with that of the storms.

My magic was *mine*, and mine alone.

I wrapped the air around him tighter while maintaining my shield and the ones protecting Shae and Holland—the latter of whom was shaking violently and even from a distance, I could see grey marring her face and the diamond actually fluttering.

Dragons screeched from above and came hurling toward the

ground, closer and closer until they hit the blackened dirt with a sickening smack.

Aether!

I screamed his name aloud at the same moment.

Fine.

He rose and snarled, breathing fire at Collin—burning his newly healed skin from his head and filling the air with the scent of more burnt flesh. But Arithi rose, ready to battle. Aether winked at me, oddly both alarming and sexy in his dragon form, before he turned to face Arithi.

I could feel *her* smoldering with desire—both for him and to finally be freed. Even though the tether was now lit in bright pink light, it still refused to budge.

Red lightning rained down on my shield and then was directed toward Aether. I growled as I threw up a shield to cover Aether's back, but all this magic, all this holding...it was wearing me down, fast. Worse still, the cyclone had recovered and was once again pulling my energy into itself—willing me to follow.

The lightning struck the ground with forcefulness, and I braced myself against the onslaught Chance sent.

Holland stood in her shield, screaming at me to let her go. She kicked it and then took her pistol out and began firing shots into the shield—they bounced back and almost hit her.

I cursed under my breath as I removed the shield from Holland, Chance had been careful to avoid her, and I knew Aether would be too. At this point, she was a bigger threat to herself than anything else. Shae stood behind me, in her snow globe, holding Vala's body as she sunk to her knees, her face slack.

Collin stood again and snarled at me, and then he *smiled*—revealing black fangs. His bare flesh was completely purple-grey with black veins dancing throughout. Unnatural. He threw out his hands and pulled the energy from the flames into himself.

Chance's bolts continued to strike my shields—attacking Aether and myself, again, and again, and again.

Dragons roared and the ground shook as they engaged in battle. Aether dodged a swing of Arithi's tail and swiped at her wings—hitting his mark. She roared in pain before bellowing a gust of fire that heated the air around me, even from within the shield.

A thick bolt of lightning struck the shield protecting Aether and hit its mark repeatedly until the shield fractured and broke, releasing Arithi's flames.

Collin cried as the flames licked his skin before he managed to erect a shield of his own—willing the magic around him to do his bidding. The moment the flames stopped, he dropped his shield and then reached toward the beasts locked in battle. He began to pull. Black and red streams began to buzz in the air and then were swept in a current leading straight to Collin.

Need to stop him! I shouted to Aether.

Can't in this form, and—

Arithi clamped her mouth around his neck, positioning him so the majority of his magic was being stolen, not hers. Panic flooded my heart, part of it I knew was Aether's, though I couldn't say how much.

I pulled at the air surrounding Chance and threw a shield around *him*, containing his power—if only for a moment. His hands were raised, but only his dome was filled with lightning, and he began screaming at me as Holland made a desperate run to him.

I stared at Collin in front of me, the male who'd ruthlessly taken so many lives.

Enough. This had all been more than enough. It was time to end things, to end *him*.

I harnessed my remaining power, but my stores were running low. On instinct, I pulled the remnants of strength from my shields and dropped all but the one surrounding Shae. My hands began to glow, a soft pink, as the magic thrummed through my veins. I called every ounce inside me to the surface, my inner dragon roared with the sudden rush of power. My eyes haloed and everything became tinted in pink.

I screamed as I recalled my mother's death and the torture Vala had endured. I cried as I thought of how Fletch had died in front of me. I cursed the seethings he'd created. I roared as I thrust my hands forward and opened my mouth, unleashing the remnants of my magic, the torrents of pent-up energy, in a blaze of fire.

Bright pink energy burst from my hands and then turned white-hot as the air itself cracked, the ground shuddered and then caved—cleaved in half, leaving a gouge in the ground directly under the stream of power. Power that reached out, ready to strike true. To end evil.

A flash occurred and a shield formed over Collin—one of red lightning, unlike anything I'd ever seen. Thick red vines of power pulsing, reflecting, absorbing...

My power hit Chance's defensive wave, and I was thrown to my knees from the impact. Some of it passed through his shield, as evidenced by the male screams of agony, but some of it bounced off. It reflected and the stream of energy continued until...

No!

Time stilled.

The air itself seemed to freeze as my eyes locked with Holland's, and Chance's screams of warning filled the air.

Even as red lightning arched to block her, to stop the stream of power...even as I willed it back and tried to redirect it, Holland fell. Her scream of betrayal filled the cyclone as white-hot energy, pink flames, and red bolts struck the spot where she stood.

My power sputtered out and the lightning disappeared. Smoke rose from the ground, a crater the size of a mansion had formed where she once stood.

My heartbeat nearly stopped; I blinked as it sunk in. Holland was gone. Chance was running to the crater, and at the same moment, I could feel Shae attempting to be freed from my shield.

I didn't think, I moved.

Tate! Aether roared through the bond in warning.

But it didn't matter. Nothing did, not Collin's charred remains—burnt from my flames to the point where he was nothing but ash and broken bones that steamed in the air. He was gone. But that didn't hold my focus, no joy filled my soul as I rushed past his corpse and trampled his rotten bones.

No, I didn't stop until I reached the edge of the crater and peered in. Chance was on his knees, nude, clutching the emblem that once graced Holland's uniform, and was wailing. Nothing else was in the hole. No corpse, no ashes, no clothing, no bones...nothing.

I took a step into the hole and froze when his eyes looked up and locked on mine. Hate, blame, betrayal, loss, fear...

"I'm so sorry," I said through a choked sob, through a chest that was so tight I could barely breathe. She'd been special to him, of that I was certain.

"Sorry," he snarled. "You're sorry?" his voice raised to a shout.

Tate, we need to leave.

"I didn't...I tried to stop it, it just..." Words failed me as Chance crumbled before me. He was no longer a threat, but a boy. A scared boy who'd just lost his love—his family.

Chance lifted his head and screamed. Red bolts of lightning arched across the sky in emphasis of his agony. I took another step in, and then another. I ignored Aether's cries in my head, ignored his commands to stop. I ignored the sound of steps behind me and the dragons' roaring, the ground shuddering from their attacks.

My hand rested on top of Chance's shoulders, offering the only comfort I could as he shook. "Shhh," I murmured.

He sobbed and sobbed and sobbed.

The sky clapped with thunder, echoed by dragon fire. My skin began to prickle as wind whipped across my face, carrying with it the scent of war and destruction. The ground shuddered as the gusts increased, forcing me back a step.

My fingers left Chance's shoulders and he slowly looked up. "You did this," he spat.

His eyes were no longer empty and full of sorrow. No, they were lit with rage. He dropped the emblem to the ground and stood. "You will pay."

He called down a throng of lightning from the sky, directed at me, bolts to the heart, meant to kill. I slowly watched as the lightning streaked across the air, zigzagging in its path toward me. I reached within to form a shield, but my stores were gone. This was it.

Goodbye, Aether. You were always my forever, I sent down the bond.

A shield flickered to life in front of me, but it was weak. Pathetic. Nothing compared to the power about to breach its barrier.

She cried, an agonizing goodbye, even as *she* gave her last bits of power to bolster my pitiful shield.

"Tate!" Aether screamed and I was vaguely aware of the flash of black light that illuminated my back.

The lightning broke through the shield and continued toward me. Slowly, I exhaled, prepared for the instant, heart-stalling pain.

I surrendered to the moment and closed my eyes as the energy brushed my skin and...stopped. A gleam of bright white and pink light flashed, even from behind my closed eyelids I shuddered from its brightness. Only, no torment came.

Instead, every nerve tingled as something *new* awakened in me. My inner pool was no longer empty, but it was full and overwhelming. I was vaguely aware of the world falling away, of my grip on reality shifting. Wind snapped at me, and I was being lifted high into the eye of the storm. At an alarming rate, I was rising higher and higher and higher...

A twin presence, so close to my own, sifted around me searching and seeking.

I reached out to Aether, willing him to be with me—holding onto the bond with all my might. I could feel his darkness, his energy, and his magic responding to me. His aura filled my senses and soothed me even as this *other* presence dissected me.

It felt like my very being was being ripped apart, sifted through, and I leaned deeper into the comfort of Aether's presence. Something prodded, deep within my soul, and I gasped, eyes flying open at its pressure.

Chance loomed below me, screaming as he sent lightning after me, but it all was blocked by some invisible force. Shae was screaming at me, and I was vaguely aware of her cries for me to return. My chest stung with the sudden influx of energy, I reached out for Aether and then the entire world went blindingly white.

CHAPTER 86

CHANCE

Try as I might, my bolts never landed; each one just vaporized as it got near her. I continued to unleash my fury until she was gone.

Vanished.

Energy pulsed as the fiery cyclone dissipated until it was gone and the wind too, stilled. The sky returned to its normal evening hue, revealing the destruction. Everything had been leveled within the surrounding skyline. Buildings destroyed. Limbs scattered. Fighting still ensued in the distance, my Tarragon were winning—or at least, holding their own.

The space where I stood was marred, the ground black from the bursts of energy. All across the nearest expanse, there was nothing.

No one.

No father.

No Holland.

Even Shae appeared to have vanished.

I looked across the ground and realized *he* was also gone. I moved and my foot kicked the emblem, the only thing I had left of the female who was my everything. Who was killed and taken from me, just like my father.

Retribution.

My magic turned within, and I snarled as I called the Tarragon to me. I bent over and picked up Holland's emblem and squeezed. Its searing presence, an eternal reminder.

There would be sweet vengeance.

There would be blood.

I opened the floodgates to my magic and the whole world went red as my lightning streamed from the sky and my entire being became nothing but static and power—I became no more.

CHAPTER 87
TATE

White, and white, and more white. Energy, pure and undiluted, danced across my skin, tickling my nerves.

I was smiling, laughing, dancing.

Joy burst from my chest from the contact with this power. Every atom screamed in delight. I could feel *him* with me, his curiosity and wonder flooding our bond. My mate, Aether—with me even in death.

I laughed some more as I tried to spy my hands and couldn't, there was nothing but light. Nothing but peace.

"Daughter, well done," a voice boomed around me.

I looked for it but couldn't spot it. I searched for Aether, but only saw a dark flame flickering nearby.

"It is time for you to come home, to claim your birthright," the voice spoke.

Before I could respond, the world filled with pink of every hue: blush, bright pink, neon, fuchsia, pale pink...

And then my feet touched solid ground and my environment solidified. Gasps of shock surrounded me.

Slowly I rose, eyes wide and blinking as they adjusted to the lighting.

Strange-looking people, some with pointed ears, gaped at me. They all wore black and stood around a bed draped with black curtains. The sound of metal on metal filled the air as several guards removed their swords from their sheaths.

All eyes were trained on me, even as they advanced.

I flinched and lifted my hands in defense. A pink dome enveloped me, and the room pulsed in bright pink. They froze, eyes locked on my shield and power, and then they began madly whispering to one another.

"It couldn't be, could it?"

"Where have they been keeping her?"

"She's strong, look at her aura."

"Is she really a royal? *Thee* royal?"

"The lost heir?"

I shook my head and stepped back, legs hitting a large footboard, as large arms reached around me. Panic spiked a moment before his spicy bergamot scent filled my nostrils; salt and ash; rich and old.

Aether.

I sighed and I leaned further into his chest, savoring the way his power rumbled from him as black flames danced around our bodies— a threat to the crowded room.

The people, all tall and elegantly dressed, stared—their eyes, mahogany eyes, locked on a spot above my head. A spot that felt very much *alive*—burning with power. I stood there, dumbfounded. They looked at me in reverence, enough to set my already jumbled nerves further on edge.

"Aether," I spoke slowly.

"I know," he said, sending out another rumble of his power.

I swallowed, the impossibility of this was too much. Every person in the room, all these Fae and Untishee, not only had mahogany eyes but they also had pink hair—just like mine.

I turned to the bed and my worst fear was made true. There, beneath black silk, lay the king of Mydant—dead.

THE UNTISH SERIES CONTINUES

Thank you for reading *Daughter of Destiny*. Tate's story continues in the third installment of the Untish Series, ***coming soon!***

READ THE UNTISH SERIES NOW!

For further updates and to stay current on all Untish Series news, please join my newsletter! I look forward to sharing the rest of this story with you and delving into the deep intricacy of the Untish culture and magic system that we've just dipped our toes into.

How can there be light without darkness...?

ALSO BY REBECCA PARCHA

New to the series? Be sure to read *FANGS OF FATE*, book one in the *Untish Series*!

I am vengeance. *Tate Aaralyn*, a lone vampire vigilante who strikes fear into the hearts of monsters. My fangs puncture, and the flavor of iron-infused retribution drips down my throat when I exact justice.

Don't be like them. Don't succumb to bloodlust. Make the b^stards pay.

These rules have been my guide, leading me through life in the Glenn. And all had been flowing nicely until I met *him*...The male cloaked in secrets, wrapped in darkness, and holding the keys to my past and future: Aether.

Complex. Messy. Unexpected.

My whole world slipped into a tailspin of lies, betrayal, and secrets. As I'm forced into the guara with a male I loathe, yet somehow crave, I must not only untangle the truth of *who* I am, but also *what* I am.

I am the enforcer. *Chance Dale*, the vampire president's son with a prestigious position as Dux in the guara. I command respect and provide results. I will not let the Glenn down.

Not as I hunt the traitor living among us. Not as dark magic's inky ways begin to seep into our villages. Not as vile beasts fill them.

Nothing will stop me from this path, not even *her*. Even if one thing is clear: the very enemy I hunt, may be the one I love.

Fangs of Fate **is an epic first-person dual-POV romantasy that will leave you breathless! Buckle up, grab a glass of bloodwine, and clear your calendar for this morally-grey, intrigue-infused, and action-packed romance that stars vampires, dragon shifters, corruption, and deception — and secrets that can break even the strongest...**

READ NOW!

Acknowledgments

Thank *you* for embarking on this journey with me. *Daughter of Destiny* is the sequel to *Fangs of Fate* and is a story that needs to be told. I cannot begin to express my gratitude to you for taking a chance on me, a new author. I truly hope you've fallen in love with this world and these characters, who are very dear to my heart—even as they get darker and seem bleaker. How can there be light without darkness?

Thank you also to my amazing team, and to every single person who has helped make this dream a reality. Thank you to my husband, John, who has been unconditionally supportive. To all my friends and family who supported me, thank you for everything.

The story isn't finished! This is only the beginning for Tate, Chance, Aether, and Shae—along with all the other delicious morally grey characters.